How soft her throat was! Michelene's lily-of-the-valley fragrance filled his senses as he touched all five fingertips to the swell of her breast. Instinctively, she pressed nearer, and he felt the tautness of her nipple through the velvet bodice. Her breast was lush and firm against his palm.

"Your heart's beating madly," he whispered.

Michelene couldn't speak. She stared up at him with huge blue eyes, cheeks flushed, lips rosy. . . .

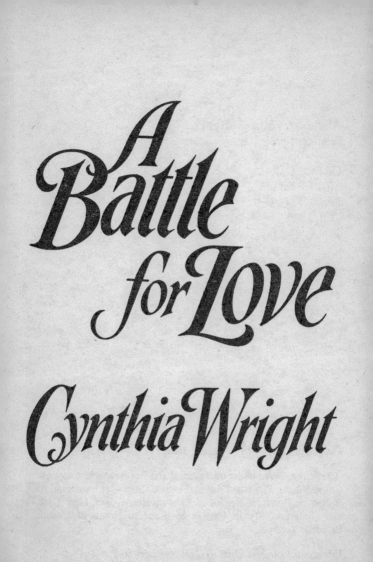

A Battle for Love

Cynthia Wright

BALLANTINE BOOKS • NEW YORK

All rights reserved under International and Pan-American Copyright
Conventions. Published in the United States of America by
Ballantine Books, a division of Random House, Inc., New York,
and simultaneously in Canada by Random House of Canada
Limited, Toronto.

Library of Congress Catalog Card Number: 86-90848

ISBN 0-345-33270-9

Manufactured in the United States of America

First Edition: July 1986

For Jenna,

*my enchanting, whimsical
daughter, who is wise
beyond her years*

ACKNOWLEDGMENTS

NINETEEN EIGHTY-FIVE WAS A TUMULTUOUS YEAR FOR ME—MORE action than could ever fit into one of my books! It's also marked a new beginning, and this seems a fitting time to say thank you to the people who have helped me, not only with this book, but always.

At the top of the list are my readers. Dozens of you wrote to me after the publication of *You and No Other*, and due to the chaos of 1985, I was late answering your mail. I want to emphasize how much I appreciated all your kind words. Now that things have calmed down for me, I promise to write back promptly.

I want to thank, particularly, the people who have seen me through good times and bad. My parents, Gene and Priscilla Challed, and my brother, Bill, head the list. Next come Cheryl Woodruff, my talented editor; Charles Schlessiger; and my dear friends and critics Kay Duley, Tom Huff, Catherine Coulter, and Kathy D'Huy. Thanks, too, to Jay Acton, Ruth and Curt Vera, Ed Remitz, Linda Schopflin, Richard Randall, Mark Cesa, Bertrice Small, Sophie Wright, Barbara Keenan, Joan Lichterman, and the rest of you who have lightened my life while I toiled over this book!

Special thanks to Richard Wright and to our daughter, Jenna, the light of both our lives.

Last but not least, I send heartfelt gratitude to Tim Underwood, who knows the reasons why, and to my real-life muse in Wimbledon, England.

Cynthia Challed Wright

And wilt thou leave me thus,
*   And have no more pity*
*   Of her that loveth thee?* •
Helas! thy cruelty!
*   And wilt thou leave me thus?*
*   Say nay! say nay!*

—Sir Thomas Wyatt (1503–1542)

PROLOGUE

Amboise, France
September 10, 1532

"BERNARD TEVOULÈRE PITTED AGAINST ARNAUD GUERRE IN the tournament!" exclaimed Aimée de St. Briac to her husband. "Ever since we arrived last night I have been deluged with tales of Bernard's affair with Élise Guerre. It's madness for him to joust against her husband!"

Thomas Mardouet, seigneur de St. Briac, drew off his helmet and took a chair beside his wife in the gallery of the king's château at Amboise. Below them was spread the courtyard, where a day-long tournament was in progress. St. Briac had just finished his own joust, teamed with King François against two of their other childhood friends. This was all harmless fun and exercise as far as Thomas was concerned, as all four men were nearing forty years of age, but Aimée did have a point about Bernard Tevoulère and Arnaud Guerre.

As they waited for the two men to take their places on the field, St. Briac's penetrating turquoise eyes gazed southward over the dreamy Loire River that lay far below King François's magnificent château. As boys, he and the king had played at jousting here, and some things never changed. Now they were men, with wives, children, and kingdoms, but their friendship endured, along with the games. The other games—the inevitable feuds and intrigues that permeated a court as large as François's—hadn't changed either. Often the king's court consisted of more than five hundred people, and far too many of them were at odds. Thomas and his wife, Aimée, spent most of their time at their château by the village of St. Briac, happiest in that world fashioned around their children, home, and vineyards. However, these visits to court were necessary. King François missed his old friend, and it did Aimée good to socialize, but there were drawbacks. The most current example was the joust they would soon witness be-

tween the feckless Bernard Tevoulère and his enraged rival,
Arnaud Guerre.

"I saw Bernard while preparing for my own match," St.
Briac told Aimée softly, running a hand through his damp
chestnut hair. "He's deteriorated sharply since our last visit
to court. This new life of his as chevalier to the king hasn't
done him any good; just the opposite, in fact. He was boasting about the fact that he's to fight Arnaud Guerre, laughing
over the chance to further humiliate his mistress's husband.
He'd had too much to drink. It was a sad sight indeed."

The king had come into the gallery, looking magnificent
in his black and gold armor, and silence reigned until he had
taken his place to oversee the remainder of the tournament.
Aimée accepted a goblet of wine from a servant and pondered
Thomas's words, her winsome countenance etched with worry.

Bernard Tevoulère was married to her dearest friend,
Micheline. Although Aimée, at twenty-five, was five years
older than Micheline, the two women were like sisters. They
had discovered each other when Aimée had traveled south,
babies in tow, to visit her parents near Angoulême. During
the few short years of their friendship, Aimée had returned to
Angoulême to see Micheline as much as to reunite her children with their grandparents. Micheline had remained behind
in Angoulême when her husband had become increasingly
bored with country life and began to spend more and more
time at court.

"Poor Micheline!" Aimée whispered to Thomas. "It infu-
riates me to think of her, living alone so much of the time
while he cavorts at court! If he hadn't managed to deceive me
so well all this time, I'd have told her the truth! What a fool
he is! Married to the finest woman in France, and yet he leads
a double life. I'd almost sympathize with Arnaud Guerre in
this joust, if I didn't know how much Bernard means to
Micheline—"

"Micheline's led such a sheltered life," St. Briac replied
quietly. "She's known him since they were children. Bernard
has changed, *miette*."

"Tragically!"

Thomas reached out to caress his wife's glossy black curls.
"Bernard must have been flawed from the beginning; these
circumstances have merely exposed his weaknesses. If the
man had any honor, he'd realize what's truly important in life
and bind himself to the lady he's blessed to call his wife."

A series of trumpet blasts announced the next contest. Bernard Tevoulère and Arnaud Guerre rode onto the field, pausing before the gallery to salute the king. Bernard, who was neither as tall nor as powerfully built as his opponent, lifted his visor and grinned confidently. While Élise Guerre stood to extend her hand to her husband, Bernard chuckled audibly and received a sharp glance from the king.

Moments later the two men on horseback were in position at opposite ends of the lists. Another clarion call signaled the first charge, which proved to be routine as lances struck shields and the horses reared back in reaction to the blows.

Aimée told herself that there was nothing to worry about. This was only a game, after all, not a fight to the death. Still, she couldn't help remembering another joust on this very field when an enemy of Thomas's had tried to kill him . . . and there was something about Guerre's bearing that sent a cold chill down her spine. Silently Aimée closed her eyes and began to pray.

She heard the trumpet, the charge of the horses, a loud crash, and then surprised gasps and cries of alarm from the assembled throng.

"Sangdieu!" hissed St. Briac. "Guerre struck at Tevoulère's helm!"

Filled with dread, Aimée opened her eyes to discover Bernard lying on the field, his head bent at an unnatural angle, while Arnaud Guerre remained on his horse, staring dispassionately at the body of his vanquished rival.

PART I

Well, fools must strike on the rebound,
While ladies volley in the air;
Collecting dues Love roams around;
All Faith is violated there,
Be hugs and kisses ne'er so rare.
Join hounds, arms, hawks and lovers' gains,
For all, at last, make mortals swear:
"For one short joy a thousand pains!"

—FRANÇOIS VILLON 1431–?

CHAPTER 1

Angoulême, France
September 10, 1532

Soft late-afternoon sunlight filtered through the abundant green woods east of Angoulême as Micheline Tevoulère cantered home astride her huge white stallion, Gustave. She was the picture of beauty in a pale yellow gown that set off her luminous eyes, which were the color of the spring's first French irises. Lifting her face, she tasted the wind, curling brandy-hued tresses flying free in her wake.

Approaching the modest stone manor house where she had lived since her marriage four years earlier, Micheline felt a familiar shadow steal over her heart. She loved this place, but it hardly seemed a home with Bernard away so much at court. Dismounting outside the stables, she handed Gustave's reins over to the groom and then noticed the other horses in stalls that were usually empty.

"The seigneur and madame de St. Briac arrived this past hour, madame," the boy explained.

A radiant smile lit Micheline's countenance. "What a wonderful surprise!" Gathering the books she'd brought back from her father's house, she raced toward the manor's rear entrance.

Aimée was there to greet her. They embraced warmly, then continued into the spacious flower-filled kitchen, where Micheline set her books on a long oak table and turned to beam at her friend.

"I cannot believe my eyes! It's as if you dropped from heaven, *chérie*! I'm so sorry I wasn't here when you arrived. I went to take a pie to Papa, then stayed to search his library for something I hadn't read more than twice before. With Bernard away so much, I'd be lost without books." She paused, shaking her head in renewed disbelief. "It's abso-

7

lutely marvelous to see you! You're just what I've needed,
Aimée.''

The older woman heard the hint of melancholy in her
friend's voice, and her heart ached in response. "I've missed
you, too, Micheline. Thomas has gone to see my parents, so
we have plenty of time for a long talk. Have you any wine?''

"What a question!''

Aimée took a chair and watched as Micheline poured Burgundy into pewter goblets. She was so lovely and unspoiled,
so filled with keen intelligence and heart-melting warmth.
Aimée thought not for the first time that all these gifts were
wasted in the seclusion of the Angoulême woods. When
Bernard and Micheline first married, it seemed a promising
union. Micheline's mother was dead, her father bluff and
distant, her brother moved to Paris; only Bernard appeared to
nourish the lonely young girl's heart. As an adolescent he had
been her best friend, teaching her to ride, to climb trees, to
swim, and, eventually, to kiss. Micheline had never had
much time for other girls, for they seemed shallow and
witless in comparison to her dearest comrade. By the time
they wed, at sixteen, Micheline felt as certain of Bernard as
she was of the sunrise. Who could have foreseen that Bernard
would turn faithless as he grew into true manhood?

Micheline set the goblets on the table and took the hand
that Aimée stretched out to her.

"Do you remember when we first met?'' Aimée asked
softly.

"Yes—of course! It was just before Bernard pledged himself as a knight to King François and went off with the army
to Italy. You'd come south with Juliette soon after her birth,
and stayed for a month. I don't know how I should have
endured Bernard's departure without you. You are my most
cherished friend, Aimée! You came into my life just as I was
learning that I couldn't rely on Bernard alone to fill my
days.''

"And you know how dearly I love you in return,'' Aimée
replied softly, tears stinging her eyes. "I could never confide
in my own mother, and though my sister and I have made
peace, we will never be intimates. It's important to have
friends outside of one's marriage—and to nurture other interests, as you have done.''

"*Alors,*'' Micheline murmured, dropping her eyes. "I have
always had solitary passions, like these books. I thought

when I married Bernard that I had found someone who would share these things with me. Something . . . happened to Bernard, though. . . . I have never spoken of these things to anyone, but I must tell someone! When he first went away, I told myself that he was helping France. I told myself that his wanderlust would fade. But when he came home, and we conceived a child, he rushed back to court!''

"I remember, *chérie*," Aimée whispered. "I was here when you lost the baby."

"How many times have you been here with me when Bernard has been away? I needed him so desperately then, but I learned in spite of my misery. I learned that I am capable of living without him. When Bernard finally did return home, he seemed almost relieved about the baby. I don't think he was ready to become a father."

"Perhaps that was the case."- Aimée nodded. "And how do you feel now?"

"I *miss* him! Desperately!" A starry tear clung to her thick lashes. "I'm confused. Sometimes, when he comes home, I feel that we are almost strangers, but when he's away, it's the Bernard of years past that I continue to yearn for. I gave him my heart when I was a child! I truly believed that God created him as my perfect mate! It's that Bernard that I wait for. Do you think he will ever come back to me?"

"I think that the Bernard you married still lives, and always will, in your heart, Micheline. And I think that he would have returned to you, in time . . . but that's no longer possible." Aimée rose, then crouched beside her friend's chair and gathered her into her arms. "Bernard won't be coming home, Micheline. He was killed, accidentally, in a tournament at Amboise."

Micheline's exquisite face went white with shock and disbelief. "No! *No! Mère de Dieu!* It cannot be!"

Holding her near, Aimée stroked her gleaming cognac hair, soothingly. "I'm here, dearest, and Thomas is here. You won't be alone. Thomas has to accompany the king to meetings with Henry VIII at Calais and Boulogne. You must come home to Château du Soleil with me and keep me company until he returns. We'll take care of each other, *chérie*."

CHAPTER 2

St. Briac-sur-Loire, France
November 12, 1532

IT WAS A CHILLY BUT SPARKLING AFTERNOON WHEN ST. BRIAC
returned home from the month-long meetings between King
François I and Henry VIII in Calais and Boulogne. As he
rode up the long, curving road to his ancestral château, a
smile played over his mouth at his anticipation of the reunion
with his family.

Château du Soleil shone in the sunlight, a marvel of soar-
ing, delicate towers, dramatically white against the backdrop
of the dark forest of Chinon. It was a castle of fairy-tale
proportions, and though Thomas had lived there since birth, it
hadn't seemed enchanted to him until the day he brought
Aimée there as his bride. Now, accompanied by a groom and
his faithful though insolent valet, the wizened Gaspard Lefait,
he dismounted before a courtyard that commanded a stunning
view of the wide, meandering Loire River. St. Briac's mind
was hardly on the scenery, however. Dusting off the buttery
suede doublet that accentuated his tanned, rakishly handsome
face and chestnut hair, he headed for the arched stone doorway to the east wing. All his senses ached for Aimée.

"Thomas! You're home!"

He tried not to betray his disappointment when his aunt,
Fanchette, hurried from the gallery to welcome him. "It's
good to see you, *ma tante*." He hugged her well-cushioned
body against his tall, hard frame. "It feels as if I've been
away forever."

"Nonsense. The leaves were turning when you went and
they're not yet gone completely from the trees."

Thomas smiled down at the woman who had run his household since the death of his mother more than twenty years
ago. She had raised his brother, Christophe, from infancy,
and earned an unimpeachable place in both their hearts over
the years. Even after Aimée became mistress of Château du

Soleil, Fanchette remained, and it was to the credit of both women that they had found a way not only to coexist, but love and help each other as well.

"I'm missing my wife," St. Briac said frankly. "Where is she?"

"She and Micheline went for a walk in the woods, but I expect they'll be back soon. Don't fidget, Thomas! It's time you learned patience!"

"You needn't talk to me as if I were Christophe, old woman," he teased. "Even he is grown and married now, with a child of his own—and his own house! When will you realize that we are *men*?"

"Probably never," Fanchette responded dryly.

St. Briac walked into the gallery and began to pace, marking off the squares of black and white marble on the floor, two by two. Gradually the sound of a commotion upstairs intruded on his thoughts of Aimée. Fanchette stood off to one side, tucking back a wayward wisp of white hair, and tried not to chuckle as she watched Thomas pause, incline his head, listening curiously, before awareness dawned.

"Has your lust for your wife caused you to forget your daughters, monseigneur?" she wondered. " 'Twould seem that they have arisen from their naps. . . ."

"Forget them?" he scoffed elaborately. "You insult me, *ma tante*!" Striding to the foot of the curving staircase, St. Briac called, *"Mes anges!* Come down and give kisses to your poor papa!"

His shouts were met with distant squeals of excitement followed by the patter of little feet, and then the sight of two sweet faces on the top step.

"Papa! Papa!!"

St. Briac ascended and caught them up in his strong arms before they managed to clamber down three steps. Amid much hugging, giggling, and kissing, he gloried in the scent of their sleepy toddlers' skin, the fine silky texture of their curly hair, the sight of cheeks still rosy from morning slumber, and eyes that sparkled with excitement and love for their adored papa.

Though Juliette was more than three years old and Ninon nearly two, they still seemed to be babies to St. Briac. They expressed their thoughts clearly these days and at times seemed more clever than their parents. Yet their little hands, elbows, and knees were dimpled, their faces round and sweet-smelling, and he could still easily fit a daughter in the crook of each arm.

Sometimes Thomas thought about the first child born to him and Aimée. Justin would have been deep into his sixth year now. There were moments, at night after Aimée slept, when Thomas imagined how his son might look and act had he lived. He'd have a pony by now, and be getting taller. His hair, black like his mother's, would have lost the baby curls. St. Briac could picture him laughing, running in the sunlight with a puppy, and then he'd force the thoughts away . . . yearning to sleep instead. Justin's death, after a year of life, had been a tragedy, but it had brought Thomas and Aimée closer together than ever. And time had brought these two rosy-cheeked little fairy princesses. The pain of Justin's loss made Thomas appreciate his daughters all the more. Aimée still longed ardently for another son, but Thomas felt no void. His heart was full.

"Papa," Juliette implored, "promise not to leave us ever again! We missed you frightfully!"

Ninon nodded solemn agreement, her dimpled chin quivering as if she might cry. "Promise, Papa!"

"We'll be together for a long time, *mes anges*," he said, smiling. "And if I do have to go away again, for a bit, you know I will always come home to you and your *maman*."

This seemed to satisfy them, and he kissed each brow in turn and hugged them closer. How lovely they would be when grown, St. Briac thought with a mixture of pride and consternation. Juliette had his chestnut hair paired with Aimée's leaf-green eyes, while Ninon had acquired the reverse combination—her mother's raven curls and Thomas's turquoise eyes. He'd have to refill the moat to keep the suitors at bay in years to come. . . .

"Where *is Maman*?" Juliette demanded.

St. Briac turned his head to gaze out the tall gallery windows. "I wish I *knew*," he murmured in response.

Out in the woods, Micheline and Aimée tramped over a carpet of rusty leaves, each lost in thought.

"Thomas is due to return soon, isn't he?" Micheline queried, reading her friend's mind. "You must be missing him terribly."

"Well, yes, of course. . . ." Aimée experienced a familiar pang of guilt, one that struck whenever they talked of her happy family life. She was conscious at all times of the grief Micheline continued to suffer, and although she had missed Thomas desperately these past weeks, part of her had been glad to devote all her attention to her friend. It seemed to Aimée that the sight of Thomas, who could not conceal his love for his wife, would have daily sprinkled salt over Micheline's wound. Even though two months had passed since Micheline had learned of Bernard's death, she continued to grieve, albeit silently. It often seemed to Aimée as if her friend were in a daze, merely going through the motions of life without feeling. Only lately had Aimée seen Micheline smile, and even laugh, with any sign of true pleasure . . . and now Thomas was coming home. What effect would that have on Micheline's progress?

"My dear friend," Micheline said, stopping to take Aimée's hand, "please do not hide your feelings on my account. I am well aware of the extraordinary love that exists between you and Thomas, and I delight in it for your sake. I would be a truly horrid person if I wished all the people I know to suffer as I have . . . to lose a loved one. . . ."

A beam of sunlight slanted through the nearly naked branches overhead, shooting golden sparks through Micheline's mane of cognac-hued curls. Her beautiful iris-blue eyes were luminous as they met and held Aimée's.

"*Chérie*, it is so unfair that you should have to bear such terrible grief!" Aimée exclaimed, hugging her near, tears pooling in her own eyes. "I would do anything to avoid worsening your darkness—"

"Why should your joy cause me sadness? I love you and your family, Aimée. I want the best for you, just as you wish the same for me."

Drawing back, Aimée gave her an anguished look. "It's my helplessness that torments me."

"I know." Micheline smiled.

"I want to *fix* things for you!"

"No doubt, if our positions were reversed, I would be as frustrated as you are. However, I fear that only time, and God, can 'fix' me. I know you understand my meaning after losing your little Justin. And you *have* helped, Aimée, by bringing me here to be with you. I'll be forever indebted to you and your family for extending hands and hearts to me when I needed them most." She paused, then continued gently. "But

your husband is coming home. You must return your attention to him and your children . . . and I should go back to
Angoulême before winter.''

''*No!*'' Aimee exclaimed, green eyes flashing. ''You
must not even think of that yet!'' Seeing that Micheline
would not be so easily dissuaded, she grinned engagingly and
took her friend's arm. ''Let us talk of this another time.
Juliette and Ninon will be finishing their naps, and you
promised to teach the cook your recipe for braised wild boar
with red wine. Tante Fanchette has been anticipating it so—she'll
scold us terribly if we're late!''

Micheline smiled and yielded. Emerging from the forest,
the two friends paused to appreciate the beauty that lay below
them. It was a splendid autumn afternoon. The sun danced
brilliantly over the vine-covered hillocks, down to the airy,
peaked towers of Château du Soleil and the luminous Loire
River that swirled lazily below them in the distance.

For a moment Micheline forgot her heartache. The beauty
of the day and the love of her friend warmed her heart. Life
seemed sweet.

As they approached the château, passing between rows of
orange trees, Aimée seemed to grow more alert, and her step
quickened. ''This may sound silly, but I've learned to trust
my instincts. I think Thomas may be home!''

Micheline felt a queer mixture of emotions when she and
Aimée entered the château's great hall and discovered St.
Briac sitting in a carved chair near the window, a daughter on
each knee. The three of them were engaged in private conversation, heads bent. Juliette held fast to her father's hand and
kissed it several times in as many seconds.

Aimée watched in silence, glowing, then spoke up at last.
''Poor *Maman*! No kisses for *her*! No one even cares that
she's here!''

''Oh, *Maman*!'' cried Ninon, instantly sympathetic. She
tried to squirm out of St. Briac's arms and go to Aimée's
rescue, but he held her fast. Laughing, he crossed the room
carrying his daughters, and Aimée met them halfway. Kisses
were exchanged in unison.

All four of them were laughing and hugging, lost in their
magical family love, while Micheline stood in the doorway,
her own heart swelling with bittersweet emotions as she
watched the happy scene. At length she called, ''Ninon!

Juliette! I'm going to cook a wild boar. Won't you come and help me?''

Thomas answered for them, setting the toddlers down on the floor. As they hurried across the floor, he grinned at Micheline and gave her a fleeting wink.

''Greetings, madame.'' His arms stole around Aimée's waist. ''And many thanks.''

CHAPTER 3

November 12–13, 1532

MICHELINE RETIRED EARLY THAT NIGHT WITH A BOOK OF POETRY by François Villon. Her chamber, located in the tower, was cozy and cheerful, with windows on three sides to keep it sun-filled during the daylight. Aimée had chosen the room for her guest for that very reason, hoping that it would alleviate Micheline's melancholy.

Now, propped against pillows, Micheline gazed out at the full moon that poured its light across the bed. A candle burned on the table next to her, but she had no heart for reading. It would be so much more convenient, she thought, if cheery surroundings and loving friends were enough to make one happy, but these past months had shown that her moods could not be shaped quite so easily. No matter how many distractions she had, her mind went around and around of its own accord, taking the past apart and putting it together again in an effort to make sense of it, then fretting over the future. That was the worst; it was almost better when she'd been numb and couldn't conceive of a future, for the one she imagined now seemed hopeless.

Putting aside her book, Micheline blew out the candle and stared into the silver-blue moonlight. Sleep, she told herself. However, when her eyes closed, she saw images of Thomas, Aimée, and their two cherubs. How fortunate they were! Micheline was convinced that any chance of her own for such contentment had died with Bernard.

If only her baby had lived, she would not be alone now! At eighteen, upon learning that she was with child, Micheline had felt certain that God was sending the baby to her to fill the void created by Bernard's increasing absences. Still, it had been an uneasy pregnancy from the start, and when she miscarried in the fourth month, Micheline had been devastated but not despairing. She told herself that she was young. Bernard loved her; he would grow up and come home for good and then the time would be right for other babies, conceived and raised in a proper, loving home. Now her dream had been destroyed, senselessly ended in a foolish tournament!

For most of these past two months Micheline had been numb in spite of Aimée's lively companionship. At first she couldn't bring herself to face the truth. *Bernard could not be dead; it was impossible!* At night she dreamed that he came home, whole and well, telling her that it had all been a mistake. Slowly the truth sank in, and with it came unremitting pain. Only during the past fortnight had that torment begun to ease, replaced by occasional moments of pleasure, even laughter, here at Château du Soleil, but Micheline still could not bring herself to consider the future. It stretched ahead endlessly, a dismal black abyss.

Burrowing into the pillows, Micheline envied people who had the ability to make their minds blank! Alone in the darkness, when the one thing she craved was escape, she could hear the pounding of her own heart as memories tumbled over one another, crowding her consciousness. Tonight, as always, hours seemed to pass before she drifted off, hoping for oblivion but unable to control the dreams that haunted her.

Aimée was leading her into the forest, where the sun and moon shone simultaneously. Micheline was uncertain of her bearings, but then Thomas called to his wife from afar and Aimée disappeared. Panicked, Micheline whirled around, only to be confronted with what seemed to be the ghost of Bernard. He was smiling at her from a clearing, just as he'd looked in the days before their marriage. Uncertainly she went forward and touched his outstretched hand. He was warm! Alive! A sunbeam washed his brown hair with golden lights, and he was slim and clean, his eyes agleam with love. Micheline didn't question it; Bernard's presence made perfect sense. He held her close against his white shirt. Somehow, time fell away and they were young again. There were no problems, no pain, no distance between them, only the innocent pleasure of young love. Micheline wasn't conscious of anything except Bernard's touch, his voice, the almost tangible sensation of being loved by him again. They walked together into a sprawling meadow and sat down in the lush grass. Micheline picked wild violets as they talked. Bernard teased her about the freckles that dusted her nose and cheeks, but she couldn't tease him in return, for she knew that he was sensitive about his less than muscular body and boyish features. Only with Micheline did the young Bernard feel secure. She never would have guessed that he might one day need to prove his masculinity in the world at large.

Soon Bernard reached for her hand again and, staring intently, drew her into his embrace. Her heart raced and she blushed just as she had the first time he kissed her when they were fourteen. This time he didn't stop after a few urgent kisses, though. Heedless of the sunlit open meadow, he opened her gown and caressed her almost roughly. Micheline had always wished that he would be gentler . . . slower. Sometimes she would feel an instant's pleasure, but those moments too often slipped away, lost in Bernard's haste for gratification. Now she could feel his hardness rubbing against her through her clothing. He pulled at her skirts and positioned himself between her legs. . . .

Micheline's eyes flew open and she sat up in the moonlight, her heart beating with the force of a hundred conflicting emotions. Hot tears stung her eyes and spilled onto her cheeks; there was a familiar ache of unsatisfied arousal between her legs that added shame to her grief and desperate loneliness.

Her bed had become a prison, sleep a form of torture. Blindly Micheline threw off the covers and fumbled in the darkness for her robe, then ran into the corridor. The château was quiet now. She fled barefoot down to the long moonsilvered gallery, tears streaming down her face as she realized that there was no escape from the agony that had attached itself seemingly to her very soul. . . .

The château was not as quiet as it appeared. Upstairs, Thomas and Aimée had just indulged in a favorite pastime: a long, shared bath. She was now sitting up in bed, naked under the covers, while Thomas combed out her long raven curls.

"I'm too tired to listen to the serious side of the king's meetings with Henry the Eighth," Aimée murmured with a yawn. "Save the details of the treaties and subterfuge for tomorrow . . . but do tell me about Anne Boleyn! Is she very beautiful? Do you suppose Henry will actually *marry* her?"

"Beautiful? No. But there is a . . . quality about the lady that some men might find attractive. She has incredible eyes. François certainly seemed taken with her—he gave her a diamond worth fifteen thousand écus. As for Mademoiselle Boleyn's chances to become queen of England, Henry recently made her Marquess of Pembroke, so I would wager in her favor. He's besot; there's no doubt."

"Do you think the French court life impressed them? Were the entertainments fine?"

St. Briac shrugged, laid the comb aside, and began to caress his wife's satiny arms and shoulders. "Fine enough," he replied absently. "Bear-baiting, and a rather bizarre wrestling contest between Englishmen and French priests . . . and, of course, there were balls and masques. François left Queen Eleanor at Fontainebleau, so he was free to partner Anne Boleyn in the dances."

Although Aimée was frankly aroused by her husband's increasingly intimate caresses, she could not resist the opening he'd provided for another avenue of conversation she was determined to pursue.

"So . . . the court is in residence at Fontainebleau these days? How I have longed to be there myself lately!"

St. Briac blinked in surprise, but did not waver in his own course of action. Drawing Aimée into his arms, he kissed her throat with warm lips. "I thought that you desired only to spend weeks on end here with me! Before I left for Calais, you could talk of nothing else except the son you intended to conceive before Christmas."

His fingertips were drawing fiery feathery patterns on her taut breasts. It took every ounce of control Aimée possessed to continue the conversation. "I do still want to conceive a son, but right now there is a more urgent matter that demands my immediate attention."

"What *can* you mean, *miette*?"

"You've been so busy stealing kisses from me and playing

with the babies that you've scarcely had time to notice. I'm talking about darling Micheline!''

"*Ma chère,* I have the utmost sympathy for Micheline's plight, and I hope that she will stay with us until she feels better, but I fail to see what this has to do with the two of us making a baby!''

Aimée tried to ignore the way his thick arched brows drew together, signaling St. Briac's waning patience with the conversation. "I am trying to tell you that I haven't time for such selfish indulgence right now! Your good wishes for Micheline are admirable, but I have spent these past two months with her and I realize that we, as her friends, must play a more *active* role in her recovery.''

Thomas lay back on his pillow and covered his eyes with a long, bronzed forearm. "I hate to say it, but if I don't, you will,'' he muttered. "All the signs point to one of your notorious *plans.*''

"How well you know me, *mon ange*!'' Aimée teased.

"And I suppose that instead of making love, you are going to force me to listen to it.'' Although he continued to take refuge behind his arm, and his tone was pained, Aimée recognized the loving surrender in St. Briac's attitude. He'd pretended to resist her reckless schemes since the day they met, but she knew that secretly he was quite charmed by this aspect of her personality.

"We must think of Micheline, Thomas. You and I have everything that she does not, and a whole lifetime ahead of us in which to enjoy our blessings.''

"And how do you propose to obtain our sort of blessings for Micheline?''

"Fontainebleau is the remedy!''

At this St. Briac removed his arm and stared at Aimée with his incredulous blue-green eyes. "*Fontainebleau?!* Surely you jest! Micheline is a lovely, unspoiled young lady. A few months at court are more apt to corrupt than bless her!''

Aimée leaned toward him excitedly, her silky black hair swirling about her breasts. "Not if we are there to watch over her! Don't you see, Thomas, it is her only chance to experience life so potently that it will force her to feel again, and . . . perhaps, to leave the past behind and discover that the future holds promise rather than pain.''

"Promise?'' St. Briac repeated sarcastically. "Are you speaking of a new husband? You know as well as I that the

court does not abound with the kind of men a lady like
Micheline deserves.''

''I found you at court, didn't I? Besides, where else do you
suggest I look? Here in the village?'' Aimée's temper flared.
''In any case, Micheline is not ready to think of marriage yet.
All I really want for her is to *live* again! She needs new
experiences and new friends! There is so much activity at
Fontainebleau that she is *bound* to feel a spark of interest.
You don't understand, Thomas, how desperately melancholy
she has been since Bernard's death. She thinks her life is
over!''

''Nonsense.''

''Yes! It's nonsense to us, but not to her! And if she stays
here in this insulated world, or returns to the countryside near
Angoulême, who knows how long it will take before something or someone comes along to make her take an interest in
life again?''

St. Briac gazed at his wife's animated face and sparkling
green eyes, then smiled. Aimée would never change. If life
didn't please her, she grasped it with both hands and tried
with all her might to reshape it. It was that very quality of
hers that had brought them together in the first place, and part
of the reason he loved her so ardently. He couldn't recall
having spent one dull moment in her company.

''You're determined about this, aren't you?''

Aimée recognized the warmth in his eyes and the surrender
in his voice. A familiar tide of love swept over her. ''I long to
see Micheline happy.'' Wrapping her arms around her husband, she buried her face in his strong chest. ''Part of the
reason I feel so strongly about this is that I'm certain Micheline
has never been truly fulfilled in life or love before.''

''That's a safe assumption,'' Thomas agreed dryly, ''considering the character of her husband. I've never been one to
speak ill of the dead, but frankly Micheline is well rid of
Tevoulère.''

''But *she* doesn't know that! We must be very careful to
keep the truth about Bernard from her. It would destroy her!
She cherishes her memories of him in his youth. Micheline
nurtures an illusion that he was meant to be her mate for life.''

St. Briac made a noise that succinctly expressed his opinion
on that subject.

''And yet,'' Aimée continued, ''I have a *feeling* that even
Micheline realizes, deep inside, that her marriage was not all

it could have been. Bernard was the only man she's ever known. She loved him, yes—but my instincts tell me that he did not fulfill her needs. Micheline simply doesn't know what she's been missing."

"I doubt that she'll make that discovery at court, *miette*."

"Perhaps not, but it would be a start. At least she'll see more of the world than she's been exposed to so far. She's like a wounded fawn, Thomas. First she has to heal and learn to enjoy the simplest pleasures; it may be quite some time before she's ready to think of love."

"I yield, madame." Thomas smiled, kissing his wife's fragrant hair. "We shall go to Fontainebleau for the winter, at least. Do you suppose, though, that in the meantime—"

Aimée turned her face up to joyously receive his kiss. St. Briac tasted the sweet secrets of her mouth and cupped her buttocks in his firm hands to press her softness against his hardness. "How I missed you, *miette*," he whispered.

She gloried in the hot swirling spiral of passion, giving herself to it as St. Briac's mouth burned her throat and then found her eager breasts. Now that the matter of Micheline was resolved for the moment, Aimée could concentrate on her husband. Arching against him, in ecstasy, Aimée decided that she was married to the most splendid man in France.

It was long past midnight when Thomas fell asleep. Aimée listened to his heartbeat, wide awake, dozens of plans circling busily in her mind. Gradually her sixth sense told her that Micheline might be awake as well. Reason differed; after all, the girl had gone to be bed hours ago, but it couldn't hurt to investigate.

St. Briac's long, elegant fingers were curved around her waist, keeping her near even in sleep. His fatigue from the arduous journey home was such, however, that he didn't stir when Aimée lifted his hand and crept out of bed. Donning a velvet robe, she lifted the latch and tiptoed out into the dark corridor.

Micheline sat near the bottom of the curving white marble stairway, leaning against a baluster fashioned of black wrought-iron flowers. The moonlight was brighter than ever, flooding the gallery through the floor-to-ceiling windows that opened onto the courtyard. Aimée approached Micheline carefully. She was so still that she seemed unaware of her friend's presence, but then, as Aimée drew near, she whispered gently, "Has the moon kept you awake as well, Aimée?"

"In part . . . the moon and thoughts of you." Aimée perched beside her and stared at Micheline's profile. It surpassed classical beauty. Her nose was a bit too short, her lower lip too full to be perfect, but the sweep of lashes above her deep blue eyes and the shadow of her cheekbone were extraordinary. Moonbeams silvered Micheline's shining hair, which fell back over her shoulders to expose the elegant line of her throat. Aimée was well schooled in the ways of passion, and she saw a great potential in Micheline. She may have been a bride, but there was an innocence about her that suggested Micheline had not even begun to plumb her depths as a woman.

"I'm sorry," Micheline was saying. "Don't worry about me. You should be giving your attention to your family."

"I have love enough for all of you," she replied warmly. "Will you tell me why you are still awake?"

"I . . . tried to sleep, but I dreamed of Bernard. He was alive, with me, and when I awoke and remembered the truth, I just could not stay there in that dark bed."

"I understand. I still have dreams like yours—about my baby Justin. I know it may be hard to believe now, but the time will come when you'll cherish your dreams of Bernard. He'll live again for you, and by then his occasional presence in your dreams will be a source of pleasure."

Micheline tried to smile. She wanted to believe Aimée, but what her friend said was now outside the realm of her imagination.

"I have some news that might take your mind off your dream," Aimée said suddenly.

"If you truly could, I would be so grateful!" replied Micheline earnestly. "I long for escape from this pit of melancholy. I yearn to find the way out, but it is like being lost in the woods, endlessly . . ."

"Well, perhaps my news may help you to find the way out. Thomas and I have decided to join the court at Fontainebleau for the winter—and we insist that you accompany us. You've never been to court, have you?"

"No." Micheline had always thought that she wouldn't enjoy court life, but deep inside her she realized that had only been her way of hiding her disappointment when Bernard did not invite her to accompany him.

"It's all quite gay!" Aimée declared brightly. "There is so much to do. You'll have new gowns and new friends. . . . There will be little time for melancholy. I know it will be good for you."

Micheline stared out to the moon-drenched courtyard. "Perhaps you're right. Perhaps it would be the best thing for me." She paused, then turned to search her friend's face with eloquent iris-blue eyes. "Do you really think Fontainebleau might show me the way out of the darkness?"

Aimée reached out to touch Micheline's cheek, her own eyes swimming with tears. "The way might be there . . . but it will be up to you to search for it. No one else can do that for you. And if you find it, you and you alone must travel the path that will lead you into the sunshine. It won't be easy, but if you have courage, you'll discover pleasure in living again."

"Aimée . . . do you truly believe it is possible?"

"Absolutely! I can't promise that you'll find your proper path at Fontainebleau, but I am *convinced* that it exists—and at its end lies happiness and fulfillment that you have yet to even imagine."

CHAPTER 4

Château de Fontainebleau
December 16, 1532

LATE-AFTERNOON SUN GILDED THE GREAT TREES OF THE FOREST. Oak, hornbeam, wide-girthed chestnut, and birch had shed their autumn finery to begin the long rest through winter. Naked gray branches arched toward the sky, impervious even to the thundering hooves of horses, packs of tired hounds, and fine-looking gentlemen riders returning from yet another successful hunt.

Bursting from the forest, the hunting party made for the palace gates, above which shone imposing high-roofed sandstone pavilions set in rhythmic order, their ornaments, pilasters, and capitals decorated with François I's bold *F*.

The king's horse galloped first through the gateway, hooves

clattering over the cobbles of the magnificent Oval Courtyard. As grooms rushed forward to relieve the men of their horses, the king stole a private word with his old friend Thomas Mardouet, seigneur de St. Briac.

"That was a fine hunt, *mon ami,* but I am dusty and drenched in sweat. Let us have a cold plunge before we sup."

St. Briac had been craving the restful company of his wife, but one look at the bold, determined profile of the king made him sigh inwardly and reply, "I am at your service, sire." To guard their thirty-year friendship, Thomas had always taken care never to complicate matters by accepting favors or rank from François, yet the fact remained that one did not refuse the king when he made requests in a certain tone of voice.

They walked leisurely across the cobbled courtyard toward the arched doorway that would lead them into the new *appartements des bains.* The Château de Fontainebleau was in the midst of a series of elaborate transformations. Ever since the king had decided, several years earlier, to spend more time near Paris, this once-modest hunting lodge had been the focus of dramatic changes. Much of the time Fontainebleau was noisy and dirty, filled with scaffolding and workmen, but as time passed, the king and his court had become used to the disorder. It was offset by the gradual emergence of new splendor for their enjoyment.

A new wing had been added to the keep, and so far housed the king's dreamed-of baths and sweating rooms. Upstairs a long splendid gallery was being constructed, and François had already begun to recruit the finest artists from Italy to ensure its perfection. He was extolling the virtues of Rosso and Primaticcio to Thomas when a familiar figure appeared on the stairway next to the entrance to the *appartements des bains.*

"You go on, Thomas," the king murmured. "I'd like a word with Madame Tevoulère."

St. Briac arched an eyebrow, but left his friend alone to greet Micheline.

When she reached the bottom step, François exclaimed, as if surprised, "Well, well! If it isn't the loveliest lady in all France! How do you fare this afternoon, madame?"

"Very well, sire." Micheline flushed slightly under the obvious scrutiny of her monarch and dropped her eyes. Clad in a simple gown of dark blue silk which was properly modest for a widow, she nonetheless felt his hazel eyes sweep the curves of her body. Eager for distraction, she produced a book from the folds of the cloak she carried. "I hope you won't mind, sire. I took you at your word and borrowed this from your splendid library. I thought I might read in the garden."

"Mind? *Pas du tout!* Have I not told you that all I have is yours for the taking?" François grinned at his own subtle wit, then leaned forward to read the title of the volume Micheline had chosen. "*Roman de la Rose!* An inspired choice, my dear. 'Twill do you good to read of romance. I've worried that you might have forgotten such pleasures!"

Micheline hardly knew how to reply. When the king reached for her hand and kissed it, the uneasy flush in her cheeks intensified. "I mustn't keep you from your bath, sire. *Au revoir.*"

François watched as Micheline walked under the archway leading to one of Fontainebleau's elaborate gardens. The sight of her hair, gleaming in the sunlight, and the gentle sway of her hips made him sigh. Finally he turned and went to join Thomas inside the bathing room. Quickly the two men shed their sweaty garments and walked down the flight of wooden steps that led to the great square pool. It was five feet deep, with two spouts that provided hot and cold water. A wooden balustrade painted to imitate bronze surrounded the bath, and the vault and lunettes were decorated with paintings and sculpture.

"Ah!" sighed the king. "Could heaven itself be sweeter?"

St. Briac ducked his head under the water and emerged to shake the cool droplets from his chestnut hair. Smiling, he gazed about at the treasured paintings that François had displayed on the walls. More than once he had wondered if the damp air would be kind to such masterpieces, but for the moment it was difficult to worry about anything at all.

"I must agree, sire, that God Himself would doubtless be content here. . . ."

Several minutes passed, during which the two men scrubbed away the afternoon's grime and enjoyed the solitude. Finally the king said, "Thomas, do you remember the day I first told you about these baths? When Gilles le Bréton was here to plan them?"

"Of course!" St. Briac smiled at the memory, rubbing the water from his beard. "It was the first time I brought Aimée here after we were married."

"Immediately after Georges Teverant escaped his execu-

tion in Paris . . ." the king added ironically. Teverant's
last-minute escape from the Concièrgerie had been effected
by Thomas, Aimée, and assorted others. François knew it,
but could not say so aloud. The young man had been condemned to die as a scapegoat for the Baron de Semblançay,
an old friend of the king's who had also mishandled the royal
finances. François had been pressured by his mother, Louise
de Savoy, to punish *someone*, but he hadn't liked it and thus
was relieved when Teverant "escaped" execution.

"That was barely six years ago," murmured St. Briac.

"And so much has changed in the meantime," finished the
king. "Semblançay himself was executed, though I hardly
liked that better. For all his darker dealings, he was like a
father to me. . . ."

"Chauvergé died in prison," Thomas continued, turning
pensive at the thought of his longtime enemy, "and I can't
say that I miss him."

"But how I miss my dear mother," sighed François. "To
this day I can hardly believe that she is gone."

At that, he plunged into the water and swam across the
pool, while St. Briac pondered the other important events that
had marked the six years since he'd first brought Aimée to
Fontainebleau. The two young princes, who had become
hostages to Charles V in place of their father after the battle
of Pavia in Italy, had finally been ransomed in 1529 for two
million crowns. The negotiations for the release of the French
princes François and Henri had been effected by women—
Louise de Savoy and Margaret of Austria, the aunt of emperor Charles V. "The Ladies' Peace" followed years of
intermittent war between François and Charles, and it settled several matters that the men could not resolve without
constantly threatening to fight one another.

In return for the safe, ransomed return of his sons, François
had had to give up his claims to Flemish and Italian territory,
and had to reconfirm his marriage by proxy to Charles V's
sister Eleanor. In return, the emperor renounced his own
claims to Burgundy.

Still, St. Briac reflected, little had changed in King François's
own life, unless it was for the better. His châteaus were
grander and more numerous than ever. His sons were restored
to him. He might not care for Queen Eleanor, or for her
company in bed, but he still had the lovely and faithful Anne
d'Heilly, now twenty-four, who had become governess to the

king's daughters, Marguerite and Madeleine, this past year. When Thomas had first brought Aimée to Fontainebleau, those little girls had barely been older than his own daughters were now, so it was hard to believe that they were now nine and eleven. Meanwhile, the two princes who had gone to Spain to take their father's place as Charles V's hostages were growing up as well. François, the dauphin, was now fourteen, and this past August had been made Duke François III in conjunction with France's annexation of Brittany.

The king had ceased his swimming and paused to rest and reflect beside his friend. The two men leaned against the gilded edge of the pool and smiled at each other in silent communication.

"You are right, sire," Thomas said softly. "Much has changed in the last half-dozen years, and though not all has transpired as we might have wished, I think that on balance we must be grateful."

"I agree, *mon ami*," nodded the king. He laid a finger against his large, distinctive nose and grinned, hazel eyes a-twinkle. "And I give special thanks for the happy circumstances which have *not* changed . . . good times shared joyously with loyal friends—"

"And the faithful red deer, ever willing to lead us a merry chase through the forest of Fontainebleau!" St. Briac interjected, laughing.

Servants appeared with jeweled goblets of strong red wine and plates that were covered with bread, slices of venison and chunks of pork, oysters from Cancale, strawberries from the king's greenhouses, and tempting little wedges of Auvergne cheese. Supper would not be served for four hours, so the men, hungry after their exercise, ate contentedly.

At length, François paused to remark, "I find myself intrigued with this subject of change. How boring life would be if nothing ever changed. Take women, for instance. . . ."

Arching an eyebrow, St. Briac waited, trying not to smile. He sensed already what was coming. His friend had been circling Micheline Tevoulère this past fortnight like an eager bee confronted with a new and irresistible flower. Aimée, however, guarded her friend carefully, determined that she not be sacrificed for the king's pleasure. Micheline herself was unfailingly pleasant and courteous to François, while never offering him even the slightest romantic encouragement.

"Here at court," the king was saying between bites of

strawberry and cheese, "the women change like the seasons and most are forgotten. A few, however, stand out like . . . roses in a field of daisies."

With an effort Thomas swallowed his laughter and managed a nod of respectful agreement.

"Your wife's sister, for example. The beautiful Honorine. She graced our court for more than a year, a most enchanting ornament, but when she left to become the wife of Georges Teverant, I must admit that the loss was not deeply felt. This newest addition, on the other hand—"

"Micheline?" St. Briac wondered innocently.

"*Absolument!*" François cleared his throat, averted his eyes, and took a long drink of wine before continuing. "Micheline has made an utterly entrancing change in the court. I realize that you seem to lust after your wife alone, Thomas, but even you must admit that Madame Tevoulère is a female of exceptional depth. I . . . uh, I find that I could gaze upon her endlessly. Though she is not the most beautiful woman I have ever beheld . . . there is such vibrance in her movements, intelligence in her violet-blue eyes, and even shy humor in that incredibly sensuous mouth. . . ." He sighed, smiling. "Most astonishing, however, is Madame's *mind*! I don't think I've ever met a woman more widely read. You know how fond I am of Roman history, and I have discovered that this lady is nearly as well versed as I! Why, just yesterday we enjoyed a lively discussion by the carp pond about the works of Justinus and Siculus! My own complaint is that she continues to maintain a certain level of reserve when in my company. I have actually wondered if Madame Tevoulère could be immune to my charms!" François laughed at such a ludicrous notion, but then his tone took on a low urgency. "Thomas, couldn't you speak to her? Assure her that I won't bite her?"

St. Briac's amusement waned as he watched the king's face become transformed with longing. "Sire, I appreciate what you are saying, but if you imagine that I can bring Micheline closer to you, I must dispel that notion. She is Aimée's friend, and you know Aimée well enough to realize that her morals are not those of the court. She is trying to help Micheline recover from the shock of her husband's death, to learn to enjoy life again. She would not want her heart broken, even by her king."

"How can you suggest that I could break the heart of so

glorious a creature as Madame Tevoulère?'' François protested in outrage.

"It might be a matter of circumstances more than intention, sire," Thomas explained as gently as possible. Suddenly the water felt cold and tiresome and he longed to be elsewhere. "You know as well as I that you are married. For my Aimée, that would be enough, but there is also the matter of Anne d'Heilly. It would not be an easy matter to displace her, even if you wanted to, and I cannot help but wonder if you truly could want that."

King François frowned, displeased with the words and attitude of his friend. If St. Briac had been a courtier, if they had not shared their lives and affections as people, he would not have tolerated such a conversation. Besides, he was not at all certain at that moment that he would not have given Micheline Anne's place at court and in his heart. Micheline seemed unobtainable, and for the king of France, such a challenge was virtually irresistible.

François was not the only person at Fontainebleau who contemplated his future with Micheline Tevoulère. Even as he and St. Briac were talking, Anne d'Heilly sat at her writing table in her private chambers, worrying and planning. She was frankly scared. For years she had been secure in her position at court. The king might take other women, but they meant nothing; even this new queen, Eleanor, meant nothing to him. Why, François could scarcely bear to sleep with his own wife! Night after night he came to Anne instead. She was proud, too, that he trusted her judgment. Since the death of Louise de Savoy, Anne had gradually taken over for the king's mother, giving him advice in her place. Anne d'Heilly had more power than any other woman in France. That very autumn François had taken her to Calais and Boulogne for the meetings with Henry VIII—while Queen Eleanor had remained behind.

Putting down her quill, Anne glanced distractedly at the pages she had just written, then rose to stare at herself in the mirror. Everyone said that each year increased her beauty, and she believed them. Blond curls brushed her brow and rose-pink cheeks, while her wide eyes seemed bluer than ever. Her figure remained diminutive, its curves sweeter and more feminine than they had been when she first met King François, at age seventeen.

"Micheline Tevoulère is no lovelier than I!" she whispered aloud.

That was the crux of her dilemma. Anne had instantly sensed the king's attraction to the newest member of his court, but after a fortnight's scheming and panic she was no closer to finding a solution that she could effect on her own. She couldn't fight the girl; Micheline did not appear to covet Anne's place as mistress to the king—in truth, she seem to have no interest in François at all beyond that of respectful subject. At last Anne had realized that this was the basis of Micheline's appeal. She did not bat her long eyelashes in François's direction or hang on his every word. Micheline Tevoulère was the first woman in years who was not his for the taking, and that was the very reason he wanted her.

Anne knew now that there was only one solution to her problem. Micheline Tevoulère must be removed from the king's sight, from the court itself. Returning to her writing table, she thanked providence for allowing her to become friends with the king of England so recently. She dipped her quill into the ink and finished her letter by subtly reminding Henry VIII that she would repay any favor he might grant her. The English monarch was eager for François I to intercede with the pope regarding his divorce and impending marriage to Anne Boleyn.

"I am a romantic," she wrote Henry in closing, "and it warmed my heart to see the love between you and *your* Anne. I hope that the two of you can be married . . . and I shall do everything in my power to persuade my king to share my view if that happy event comes to pass."

As Anne d'Heilly was signing her name to the letter to Henry VIII, Micheline Tevoulère had been joined by Aimée in the gardens below, and they strolled aimlessly, unaware that others who wielded control were contemplating Micheline's future.

Even in December Fontainebleau was a place of unrivaled beauty. In winter the garden's hedges were clipped to form artful green tunnels that led into dormant flowerbeds punctuated with urns and sculpture. Micheline did not regret coming here. The constant activity was a welcome change from the period of darkness following Bernard's death. During the day she rode or walked with Aimée or one of the other ladies of the court. Meals were events, attended by hundreds of people, and nearly every night there was a ball or a masque or entertainment of some sort. Lovely new gowns had been made for Micheline, and she enjoyed the warm admiration of nearly everyone she met—especially the men. However, in spite of the invitation in their eyes, which was sometimes voiced aloud, she could not bring herself to respond. The thought of even being kissed by anyone but Bernard remained forbidden.

"I saw you talking to that handsome Chevalier d'Honfleur last night," Aimée ventured after a few minutes of companionable silence.

Micheline smiled and shrugged slightly, reading her friend's mind. "Guillaume is very nice," she allowed. "I agreed to go riding with him tomorrow."

"Good!" Aimée knew she should choose her words carefully, but, as usual, impulse overruled reason. "I would like to see you encourage *someone*, if only to *discourage* the king!"

"What do you mean?" cried Micheline. "I cannot feel the slightest stirring of affection for any man I have met here, beyond that of simple friendship—*including* the king! Surely he is perceptive enough to realize that!"

"I would guess that it is that challenge that intrigues him, *ma chère*. Don't fret, though. François is a gentleman at heart, though used to having his own way. You simply must continue to show respect for him and nothing more. Any encouragement at all would only heighten his desire . . . and determination."

Micheline paused to pick a sprig of mistletoe and gazed at it pensively. "I should feel fortunate, I suppose, to have found favor with so many important men. There are moments, when I talk to someone who is handsome, charming, and accomplished, and I marvel at the total absence of feeling in my heart. I've begun to think that Bernard's death killed something within me." She met Aimée's concerned gaze with wet iris-blue eyes. "I doubt I'll ever be attracted to a man again."

Aimée opened her mouth, then closed it, aching for her friend. Normally she was never at a loss for words, but at this moment she was speechless. She yearned to fix everything for Micheline, but lately Aimée had come to believe that only God could perform such a miracle. She could only wait and pray.

CHAPTER 5

London, England
February 5, 1533

DAWN HAD SCARCELY COLORED THE EASTERN SKY WHEN THE NOISE of the River Thames coming awake disturbed the slumber of Iris, Lady Dangerfield. She frowned slightly, still half-asleep, forgetting for the moment that she lay in the Earl of Sandhurst's bed. His town house, situated on the Strand and overlooking the river, was handsome and fashionable, but this daily commotion on the water could become tiresome.

Obviously, Iris reflected, opening one eye to find her bed partner still sleeping contentedly a few inches away, Sandhurst was used to the clamor. She forgot her own irritation as she gazed at him, lost in the spell he cast so effortlessly, even in his sleep.

Andrew Weston, Earl of Sandhurst, would become one of the wealthiest men in Britain upon the death of his ailing elderly father. Not only would the coveted title of Duke of Aylesbury belong to Andrew, but also vast estates in Gloucestershire, and Aylesbury Castle in Yorkshire. The mere thought of such riches and prestige made Iris ache inside, for she had married Timothy, Lord Dangerfield at sixteen, barely two months before meeting Sandhurst at Hampton Court. She'd been satisfied with Timothy until then, but the instant she glimpsed that golden head across the garden and felt the heat of his caramel-colored eyes even from a distance, Iris's heart melted helplessly. Then the Earl of Sandhurst had slowly, casually, made his way to her side. When he smiled and reached out with strong, agile fingers to lift her hand to his mouth, she'd burned for him, nearly fainting.

That had been four years ago, and the fire raged brighter than ever within Iris. She could not disguise it, and the force of her ardor seemed almost to amuse Andrew. He was fond of her, she knew, and sometimes she could almost pretend that he might marry her were she free. But, of course, it was impossible, and in her heart Iris was aware that even if Timothy should die, Andrew would not make her his wife. He did not seem to want to be bound to anyone except himself. That was the basis of Iris's appeal; she was familiar, beautiful, passionate . . . and blessedly unavailable. Since she couldn't have him herself, Iris rationalized that Andrew's independent nature was good. Naturally he would *have* to marry one day, years from now, to produce an heir. But Iris tried not to think about that. The idea of another woman having what she burned to possess was torture. The mere possibility that Andrew might love his future wife even a little made Iris physically ill.

Longing to touch him now, she stared instead. Her gaze lingered on his tousled hair, which curled slightly against his brow and along the nape of his neck. As a child Sandhurst had been very blond, but now he was thirty-two, and his hair darkened to light brown in winter. The strands were burnished, though, as if brushed with gold dust, and each spring the gold lightened and spread while his skin bronzed under the sun.

Iris thought him the most beautiful, masculine creature alive, and there were few women who would disagree with her. His face could have been sculpted, particularly the elegant cheekbones. Although his eyes were closed now, she could easily remember their magic—one moment agleam with intelligence and humor, the next staring into her soul, rousing her passions without a word or a touch. Sandhurst's nose was straight and aristocratic, but not perfect. None of his features was exactly perfect in the classical sense, but each seemed to redefine perfection because it was part of him. His mouth might be considered a trifle wide, but it was so wonderfully chiseled and endlessly inviting that Iris felt dizzy just looking at it. Just above Andrew's upper lip, on the left side, was a small scar that cut down into the firmness of his mouth—this obvious flaw in his beauty made it doubly captivating. Thank God, Iris thought, that Sandhurst wore no beard to conceal that arousing scar, or the strong, graceful line of his jaw, or—

"My dear Iris," he murmured suddenly in a voice husky with sleep and edged with irony, "you are a woman of breeding. Were you never taught that it is rude to stare, especially at *me*, at this uncivilized hour, and at such length?"

There had not been even the flicker of an eyelash to betray

his consciousness. Iris blushed, but whispered, "Forgive me, my lord. I only was staring because I could not touch. . . ."

"Why not?" One side of Sandhurst's mouth quirked slightly, brown eyes opened lazily, and he was turning on his side to reach for her.

Even in winter his skin was golden brown against Iris's milky-white flesh. Leisurely he traced her full breasts with one fingertip, smiling into her green eyes as he gathered her closer and breathed the scent of roses in her coppery hair.

"But . . . what about this uncivilized hour?" Iris somehow managed to tease, her breath already coming in little gasps. He was so warm and sleek and strong, she couldn't stop touching him.

"Perfectly fitting—for us," Sandhurst was replying succinctly. He kissed her then, before she could ponder his words, and moved over her, letting Iris feel the hard length of his manhood. Damn, but she was a hot little bitch, hotter each time he touched her, it seemed, even after four years.

A loud, irritating tapping began on Sandhurst's bedchamber door. Impossible, he thought dimly. No servant could be so foolish. Must be coming from somewhere else . . .

The racket continued until Andrew finally lifted his head and shouted, "For God's sake, *stop that!*"

"Sandhurst? Are you awake? It's Rupert! I must speak to you!"

Rupert! What the hell was his illegitimate twit of a half brother doing in London—at *his* town house—at *dawn*?

"God's bones, Rupert, do you know what time it is? Go downstairs and have the cook bring you an egg or something. I'll join you after I've bathed and dressed." If Andrew had been more awake and less aroused, he'd have wondered why he bothered to carry on a conversation with so unwelcome a guest.

"No, no, *no!*" Rupert's tone grew shrill. "I must speak to you *now!* I'm coming in!"

Furious by now, Sandhurst threw off the covers, bare feet meeting the utterly chilly, rush-strewn floor. He yanked on his hose before throwing open the door.

"Be grateful I'm sparing your life, crackbrain!"

Across the chamber Iris clutched the thick covers against her chin and stared in shock. It was the first time she had ever seen her lover lose his temper. Normally, when angry, his voice and eyes grew cold and a muscle twitched in his jaw.

No one had been foolish enough to incite him past that point, at least in her presence. Now Sandhurst was pulling Rupert into the room, shutting the door, and leading the slight, spindly younger man to his dressing room. Rupert gaped openly in Iris's direction until he suddenly found himself closed in the dressing chamber with his ominous-looking half brother.

"Please, Sandhurst, don't be mad at me!" he whined. "I've come to help you!"

Lord Sandhurst took a deep breath, his nostrils flaring, before replying evenly, "Pray explain. *Quickly*."

"The duke is here. Our father!"

"I appreciate the clarification," Andrew said sarcastically. "Now, be a good fellow and tell me what the devil is going on!"

"Well, *well*, we were all settled in at Aylesbury Castle for the winter. Patience, my dear wife, and Father, who had a chill, and our younger sister, Cicely—"

"Rupert, I *know* who lives at Aylesbury Castle! I am still a member of the family." It galled Sandhurst to be instructed by this stammering fool. If only his own mother, the duchess, were still alive, Rupert Topping would never have managed to infiltrate the family. Five years ago Andrew's mother had died after an accidental fall, and the duke, ill and lonely in his castle, had allowed his old lover, Jane Topping, to return with the son she insisted was the duke's, and keep him company. Sandhurst, already estranged from his father, lived far to the south in London, and Cicely, at eight years of age, was not a fit companion for a crotchety old man. So Jane Topping made herself at home, while Rupert, then nineteen, treated his father as if he were God. The duke basked in the boy's admiration. After Jane, too, died, Rupert had stayed on, playing the dutiful son in the Earl of Sandhurst's absence. Even the horse-faced Patience Topping, recruited as Rupert's wife last year from the village of Bubwith, had wormed her way into the family's bosom.

Lord Sandhurst's scorn and disapproval of the entire situation that the duke had allowed to develop were almost surpassed by the repulsion he felt for his "brother." Each time they met, Rupert all but kissed Sandhurst's boots and crawled in his wake. As a consequence, Andrew stayed far away from his family, and the already cool relationship with his father virtually disappeared.

"Oh, I *know* that you are one of the family, my lord!" Rupert was blubbering. "You'll never know how grateful I am—How *honored*!—to know that I am your relative! I must confess to nearly worshiping you, Sandhurst. I would do anything to help you, to bridge the gap between you and our father, to heal the wounds, to—"

Andrew closed his eyes. "I perceive your meaning."

"Well, the thing is, I had a suspicion that Lady Dangerfield might be here, and I was afraid that our father's valet might come to inform you of our visit. Kettlewell tells Father *everything*—he's almost like a spy!" Something in Sandhurst's eyes caused Rupert to attempt to get a grip on himself. "Well, that's getting ahead of the story. You see, this is what's happened. We were all settled in for the winter, as I told you, when King Henry sent word that he wanted to meet with Father at Whitehall. We had no idea what it was about, but the duke graciously allowed all of us to accompany him. Cicely was especially eager for the chance to visit *you*, you won't be surprised to hear!" He paused to nod cheerfully several times. "We arrived in London two days ago and went immediately to Whitehall. Exciting times, I don't mind telling you! Father met several times with the king, then last night he suddenly announced that we must come to your house at once. It was past midnight when we arrived—you were, umm, asleep—and the servants saw us to our beds."

Now that the gist of the story was revealed, Sandhurst hated to prolong the interview, but curiosity got the better of him. "You are not exactly privy to the intimate details of my life, Rupert, so I wonder what led to your suspicion that Kettlewell might find Lady Dangerfield in my bed."

Rupert blushed and dropped his eyes. "Lord Dangerfield arrived back from a journey to Cornwall yesterday. As I understood the story, he went to his home, but his wife was absent. Then he—uh—visited the court at Whitehall, where he imbibed a rather injudicious amount of ale and told anyone who would listen that Lady Dangerfield was embroiled in an open affair with *you*, that she was doubtless in your bed as he spoke, that—"

"Am I to assume that you were one of those people who 'would listen'?"

"Only for your sake, Sandhurst!" Rupert assured him eagerly. "Only to help you!"

"I'm a grown man. I don't want your help." He turned

away before reason fled entirely and he said something brutal. "Leave me now to bathe and dress. You may tell my father when he awakens that I will join him in his chambers."

Sandhurst returned to his own bedchamber to discover that Iris had gone back to sleep. Drawing back the covers, he lightly spanked her shapely bottom and perched on the edge of the feather tick.

Iris sat up, rubbing her eyes and pretending to be offended.

"Don't play the coquette with me, sweeting; we haven't time." Andrew spoke distractedly, staring out the leaded-glass windows. Snow swirled against the panes. "Didn't you tell me that your husband returns from Cornwall today?"

"Yes, but not until the afternoon." Iris ran her fingertips down the long, tapering line of his back. He appeared slim, lithe, and graceful in his clothing, and only those who had seen Sandhurst naked knew how hard and muscular his body actually was. "Come back to bed, my lord," she purred. "I'm still hungry."

"Save your appetite for Dangerfield. He's back, and he knows you weren't in *his* bed last night. I'd suggest that you dress and hurry home to appease him, if you still can. . . ."

Joshua Finchley, faithful valet to the Earl of Sandhurst, prepared a hot bath for his lordship, then laid out fresh clothing and took his leave. Unlike most noblemen, his master preferred to shave, bathe, and dress himself.

It was past eight when Sandhurst stepped into the corridor, clad all in rich, soft gray velvet. Puffs of white silk showed through the slashings of his doublet, which was sewn tight at his narrow waist. More white silk made ruffles at his wrists and the fraise that stood up against his golden-brown neck.

"Andrew!" cried a familiar female voice. He turned to find his sister, Cecily, running toward him, her face alight with love and excitement.

"Child," he murmured, and caught her up in his arms. "How you've grown."

"I'm almost a lady. I'm thirteen. A boy in Yorkshire has already asked for my hand!"

Sandhurst blinked, then smiled. "He was refused, I trust!"

"Of course, silly!" Cecily stood on tiptoe, beaming up at him. Gleaming black curls framed her heart-shaped face, which was dominated by beautiful sable-brown eyes. She was petite and slender, with gentle curves that he hadn't remembered . . . no longer a baby sister. "I've missed you tremendously, Andrew! How can you leave me up there with . . . *them* like this." Cecily's voice had dropped to a whisper. She glanced down the hall toward Rupert and Patience, who appeared to be standing guard outside the duke's bedchamber.

"I'm not a fit guardian for a young lady," Sandhurst replied with more than a twinge of guilt. If only their mother hadn't died, none of these problems would exist!

"That's silly, and you know it! Do you think it right that I'm being raised by—"

"My lord?" Rupert and Patience called in unison. "Your father is waiting."

"I'm coming." He looked down at Cecily's earnest little face and told her, "We'll talk about this later, all right?" Then, walking down the corridor toward the duke's bedchamber, Sandhurst could only feel a familiar rush of hostility. This was *his* house, after all, and he was thirty-two years old, yet despite his unwavering efforts for more than a dozen years, other people continued to attempt to manipulate *his* life! They arrived without an invitation, ordering him about—

"Andrew? Andrew, where are you?" cried the querulous voice of his father.

Lord Sandhurst paused for a moment and closed his eyes. Old instincts rose to the surface, but he pushed them back. He'd learned, years ago, that fighting with his father gained him nothing but frustration, though it had taken him many more years to perfect the more subtle approach that he now used in his everyday life. Opening his eyes, he gave Rupert and Patience his most charming smile and went through the doorway.

"Father, how good it is to see you." Approaching the bed, Sandhurst extended his hand.

The Duke of Aylesbury wore an old nightgown faced with fox. He sat up in bed, propped against a mountain of pillows, his white hair combed back from his craggy face. In his youth the duke had looked not unlike his handsome son, but now his excellent bone structure served only to accentuate sunken cheeks and a sharp chin. His life had been bitter, made bitterer still by this rebellious son and heir who had the effrontery to smile at him and extend his hand in pretended affection.

"I'm too old for your games, Andrew. Sit down."

A muscle twitched in Sandhurst's jaw, but he obeyed silently, thinking, He dares to give me orders in my own house!

"I see no point in wasting time on aimless chatter," the duke continued. "I've come to tell you that you're going to be married. King Henry has found a wife for you, and I've agreed."

CHAPTER 6

London, England
February 5–6, 1532

LORD SANDHURST'S BROWN EYES WERE STARTLED. "I MUST BE hearing things. I could have sworn I heard you say that you and King Henry had chosen a *wife* for me!" A half-repressed laugh escaped his lips.

Unable to resist the impulse to toy with his prey for a moment, the duke smiled. "I did not say that *I* had chosen a wife for you. You have only the king to thank on that score. All I have done is set the seal on his plans." Aylesbury's smile widened maliciously.

"Have I no say in this? No voice in my own destiny?" Somehow, he managed to sound reasonable, though white knuckles showed on his left hand that gripped the carved chair rail.

The duke's smile faded. "You can say whatever you like, my golden son, but I don't think you'll fight the will of the king the way you've always fought me. It's time you learned that there are more important things than *your* wishes! You have never done the smallest thing to please me, your father, but you'll please me now whether you want to or not!" He let out a hoarse bark of laughter. "For years I've begged you to take an interest in my estates, to live with me and learn from me. I've longed to see you married, with sons of your own, before I die. I've encouraged you to cultivate the king, to make a place for yourself at court, but it seems that the most you could bother to do has been to waste your charm on

Henry's favorite ladies. Even the future queen becomes dreamy at the mention of your name! You're a *fool*, Andrew, and now you're going to pay for it!''

The old man was leaning forward, his face crimson as he railed at his son. For his own part, Sandhurst thought that he must be having a nightmare. Dimly he heard himself say, ''Perhaps I've turned away from you because I sensed that your interest was not in me but in the family title. As the future duke it seemed that I was to be molded like a piece of clay, not a person. You've always been more interested in controlling me than in loving or understanding me.''

''Bah! You needed a firm hand! You still do! If you wanted love and understanding, you should have listened to me and taken a wife years ago. That's what a good woman is for.'' The duke smiled again, thinly. ''You see, I'm doing you a favor! After your French bride begins warming your bed, you'll thank me! The chit probably won't even speak English, which'd be a blessing. If she can't talk to you, there will be just one thing for her to do—spread her legs!''

The sound of his father's cackle made Andrew want to cover his ears. ''This is insane,'' he muttered.

''Tell it to King Henry,'' the old man shot back.

''What if I were to do just that? I'm not some twelve-year-old who needs a marriage arranged for him.''

''You don't seem to be able to arrange one on your own!''

''But why does the king care?''

The duke shrugged. ''As I understand it, someone with power in the French court wants this girl disposed of—tidily, of course. A proper English husband who would take her to live across the Channel seemed the solution. Henry was glad to give his aid, because he needs François the First's assistance in winning over the pope, more than ever now, I'd say, since there are rumors that he and the Marquess of Pembroke were secretly married last month.''

''But why was *I* chosen to be sacrificed?''

''Perhaps it was the will of God,'' the old man suggested with another malevolent smile. ''Besides, you're an ideal candidate. You're an eligible, wealthy aristocrat. Henry has known me all his life, and he doubtless did this partly as a favor to me as well as for himself. He would seem to have reasons of his own for wanting to see your wings clipped.''

Andrew raked a hand savagely through his gleaming hair.

"And if I refuse to be a party to this madness? Will the king send me to the Tower and deprive me of my head?"

"Oh, no, we decided that the punishment should fit the crime. If you choose to rebel again, not only against me but the king of England, you'll lose your inheritance. Obviously no one can take your title away from you . . . or mine, when I die. But you would receive nothing else. Henry has agreed to make Rupert a baron this year, and upon my death all my wealth and estates would pass to him."

Sandhurst couldn't bear to look at his father any longer. Dazedly he walked to the window, every muscle in his body clenched. Yet through his rage he had to repress an urge to laugh wildly at the sheer lunacy of the situation.

"Your bride arrives in April. Her name is Micheline Tevoulère," the duke continued, his tone triumphant now. "You'll be married at Aylesbury Castle, of course, and King Henry has assured me that he intends to be present to join in the festive celebrations!"

A fire blazed in the winter parlor of Lord Sandhurst's town house, casting shadows that leaped and danced up the walls. On one side of the chamber his lordship presided over a table covered with the remains of supper. He was alone except for his friend Sir Jeremy Culpepper, who nibbled leftover bits of cheese, meat pie, and a fig someone had discarded after one bite.

"I still can't believe it," Sandhurst murmured dazedly. He'd lost count of the tankards of ale he'd consumed that day. Raising the latest, he took a long drink and sighed loudly.

"You've said that already," Jeremy complained. "Dozens of times. What's that little carcass on your dish? Quail? Did you pick it clean?"

Glancing heavenward, Andrew pushed the plate across the table. "How can you eat at a time like this?"

"*I'm* not the one getting married to a stranger . . . from *France*," Culpepper replied cheerfully. "D'you suppose the chit speaks English at all? What'll you do if she can't *learn*?"

Leveling a deadly stare at his friend, Lord Sandhurst said, "If you find this amusing, you can go upstairs and have a few laughs with my father." He drank again, then added, "Besides, now that the shock's wearing off and I've had the day to think about it, I doubt seriously that I could participate in this farce."

Sir Jeremy Culpepper was a rather stout young man with curly orange hair, an unguarded tongue, and a tendency to flush when overcome by emotion. His cheeks were quite red now as he cried, "Be reasonable, Sandhurst! You'll be ruined if you refuse to go along with this plan of the king's! Not only will you be penniless, but you'll be shunned at court. Come to think of it, you'll be shunned by *everyone* in Britain!"

"Oh, please, say no more! You're scaring me!"

"But how would you live?"

Andrew felt himself relaxing, muscles untensing as a smile played about his attractive mouth. "I believe that I could make my own way rather well. You know, this house is mine. I bought it with profits from the horses I've been breeding in Gloucestershire. I could sell it and buy another place in the country, then support myself with the horses." He paused, running a forefinger over his lower lip in a characteristic gesture. "The prospect of being out from under my father's thumb is rather appealing, actually."

"Now, look, Sandhurst, you've got to consider this matter carefully! You're talking about a decision that would affect the rest of your life—and the lives of your descendants, for generations to come. Just because you chafe under your father's admittedly overbearing efforts to dominate you, that's no reason to cut off your nose to spite your face! He's an old man; he'll be dead soon. How will you feel then if you're breeding horses at some manor house while *Rupert* is lord of Aylesbury Castle and the *Sandhurst* estates in Gloucestershire?! What will you tell your children? Don't raise that eyebrow at me! I'm quite certain that once there's no one commanding you to take a wife, you'll want to do just that. How will your children feel about what you've done when they grow up and *Rupert's* offspring own what's rightfully theirs?" Jeremy paused, breathing hard, then leaned forward to play his ace. "And what do you think your mother would say if she were here?"

Sandhurst wasn't smiling anymore. He closed his eyes and drained the tankard of ale. "I can't just go like a lamb to the slaughter, Jeremy." He sighed. "My father would have a collar and a leash fitted for me, and I'd be angry for the rest of my life."

"I know, I know. And you'd doubtless take it out on your

poor little French wife, and then on your children,'' Culpepper fretted. He drank from his own tankard, brows knit in thought.

His lordship was thinking, too, turning the various aspects of the situation over and over in his mind, yearning to discover a ray of light in the darkness.

''It's possible,'' Jeremy murmured doubtfully, ''that the girl in France might be a beauty. Perhaps she's clever and charming, even a bit of a rebel, like you—maybe that's why they want to exile her!'' Warming to his imaginings, he reached for a half-eaten sweetmeat on a distant plate and nibbled on it happily while continuing, ''just think, Sandhurst, perhaps all this really *is* the will of God! What if that French girl turns out to be your perfect mate? You might take one look at her and fall desperately in love!''

''Hmmm.'' Sandhurst's tone was wryly amused, but his friend's ravings planted the seed of an idea in his mind. ''It's more probable that Mademoiselle Tevoulère is a plain, shy fourteen-year-old with spots . . . or a fat widow that the French king cannot bear to look upon any longer.'' He rubbed his fingertip along his mouth again, staring into space. ''How*ever* . . . it might be prudent to investigate further before I make a decision.''

Sir Jeremy Culpepper swallowed the sweetmeat and leaned across the table to grip Sandhurst's forearm. ''Yes! Yes! You're brilliant! That's the answer!'' Then a shadow crossed his face as he dropped back into his chair. ''But how can you *do* it?''

Raising his eyebrows, he answered, ''I'm not certain. I suppose I shall have to go to France. The girl's supposed to remain with the French court until the 'wedding' in April, so that would give me nearly two months.''

''Do you propose to just present yourself to François Premier First and announce that you've come to inspect Micheline Tevoulère before agreeing to the marriage?''

Andrew laughed softly. ''Obviously not. No, I'll have to pretend to be someone else.''

''And why would a made-up person be welcome at court?''

''Ah, now there's the rub—hmm? Obviously I can't use my title to gain entrance, so I'll have to think of something else to offer.'' He smiled. ''My canvases and brushes may be of use at last, Jeremy.''

Culpepper had nearly forgotten that Sandhurst could paint. He'd shown talent as a child and the duchess had sent him off to Florence to study for a year under the Italian masters. That had been a dozen years ago, at a time when she was as eager to separate him from his father as to nurture his artistic abilities.

"Are you any good at it?" Jeremy demanded bluntly, which elicited more low laughter from his friend.

"Actually I am. Hard to believe? You'll be even more surprised to learn that I still paint from time to time when I'm at Sandhurst Manor. Remember the portrait of Cicely in the hall?"

Jeremy stared in consternation. He'd always assumed that Holbein or one of the other artists favored at court had done the exquisite painting of Lord Sandhurst's sister which dominated the town house's great hall. "You're ribbing me," he muttered, then took a candlestick from the table and went out to investigate. In the lower righthand corner of the canvas he discovered a familiar *S,* barely a shade darker than the rose of Cicely's skirt.

A kitchen maid had come in to clear the table at last before retiring for the night, so Sandhurst didn't notice at first when his friend reentered the parlor. Jeremy stood clutching the candlestick, its flame accentuating the stunned expression on his face.

His mouth gaped open before he managed to exclaim hoarsely, "It's unbelievable—incredible!"

"Come and sit down before you faint," Andrew said, laughing. Turning to the little maid, he said, "Bring us fresh tankards of ale, please, Mary, and then be off to bed. It's late."

Jeremy staggered back to his chair. "Why didn't you say anything? I never imagined . . ."

Accepting the two cold tankards, Sandhurst waited until Mary had disappeared into the kitchen before handing one to Jeremy and replying, "There was never a reason to talk about it. It amused Cicely to have her painter's identity our secret, and the entire pastime has been just that for me: an amusement to pass the long hours in the country. Now, however, my adequate talents may prove highly useful."

"If *I* could paint like that, I'd be boasting to anyone who'd listen! God's bones, Sandhurst, there's absolutely no question that you could pass yourself off as an artist at the French court! You've got charm and wit and extraordinary good looks to go with your talent. How could you fail?"

"You flatter me, Jeremy, but I do agree that the masquerade ought to succeed if I keep my wits about me." He laughed aloud as the plan fell into place. "How amusing it would be to become acquainted with Micheline Tevoulère under such circumstances! This should prove to be a highly enlightening escapade."

Beaming and nodding, Jeremy exclaimed, "By God, I wish I could be there too!"

"But you *will* be there!" Sandhurst informed him smoothly. "You're coming with me. I'll need an extra pair of eyes and ears, not to mention a valet—you know, for appearance's sake. Joshua's perfectly capable of looking after my clothes, but I doubt that he'd be up to subterfuge. Besides, I don't want to involve him in all this. The less he knows about what we're up to, the better."

Jeremy's mouth hung open again, forgotten by its owner. "But—but—that is—I don't see how—" He fell silent, digesting his friend's speech, then narrowed his eyes suddenly. "Wait just a moment! You're saying that you expect me to be your *valet* while we're in France?!"

"Don't get into a huff, old man. I didn't mean to imply that you are my inferior in any way."

"Next door to it!"

"Look, you won't exactly *be* my valet; we'll just pretend that you are. It will be a role, like my role as a painter of portraits." Andrew gave him his most engaging smile. "We'll both be commoners for a few weeks. It'll be a lark!"

Sir Jeremy Culpepper shook his head. "This is all more your style than mine, Sandhurst. What if we're found out? God's teeth, imagine the humiliation!"

A bold, feminine voice called out from the doorway, "I'll go, Andrew! Let *me* be your valet!"

"Cicely! What the devil have you been up to?" demanded her brother.

Lady Cicely Weston stepped into the light, clad in a long white nightgown, her black curls tumbling down her back. "I couldn't sleep, so I came downstairs, but when I heard the two of you talking, I decided to stay hidden and listen," she replied frankly.

She was so like him that Sandhurst could not be angry. He tried to stare at her sternly, but then amusement caused his mouth to quirk and Cicely came scampering across the parlor to throw her arms about him.

"Child, you're incorrigible," Andrew murmured, actually charmed by the openness of her affection and the sweet warmth of her cheek against his. "I ought to have you beaten."

Cicely giggled and curled up on the chair next to his. "You're being silly again, darling brother. And you probably think *I* was being silly when I volunteered to be your valet, but I was *not*! I was deadly serious. Jeremy doesn't want to go, and I do, so why not take me? I can dress as a boy and sneak about unnoticed, because I'm so small, and I'll listen to every word I hear, and—"

Sandhurst held up his hand to silence her. "No," he said gently.

Realizing what he must say, Jeremy cleared his throat. "Actually, Lady Cicely, I intended to do this thing all along. It's—uh—sort of an old game between your brother and me . . . arguing in cases like this." He knew this explanation sounded as lame as it was, but it was the best he could do at a moment's notice.

"What a lot of nonsense!" the girl cried.

"In any case, I would not take you, child," Andrew told her softly. "There would be too many risks involved. As I'm your brother, it's my place to protect you, not allow you to be subjected to unknown dangers."

"Are you saying, then, that I have to go back to that horrid, damp castle with that horrid family of mine?"

"Present company excluded, I trust!" Sandhurst teased her gently, his eyes warm with love. "And yes, I'm afraid that you'll have to go home with them, at least for now. I promise to give some serious thought to your situation when I return from France. Does that sound like a fair bargain?"

Cicely made a moue, but relented. "I suppose."

"Now, don't pout." He lifted her onto his lap and kissed her shining hair. "Gad! You're almost a woman!"

She smiled in spite of herself. "I've been telling you that forever."

"Well, then, you'd better go back to bed. Growing girls need their sleep. And, Cicely, you won't say anything about my plans to go to France to anyone, will you?"

"Of course not!" she exclaimed, offended, but gave him a kiss good night. "Can we have breakfast together in the morning? Father wants to leave early, I think."

"You and I can have a private breakfast in my chambers,"

he promised, raising agile fingers to stroke her curls. "Good night, Cicely."

Jeremy watched them, thinking that this was a side of Sandhurst that he'd rarely seen: affectingly warm, tender, and gentle. Cicely paused beside his own chair to smile and bestow a kiss on his cheek, then walked to the door, where she paused and looked back at the two men.

"I hope that Mademoiselle Tevoulère is a toad!"

Before Lord Sandhurst could blink, she was gone. Raising his eyebrows, he chuckled in wonder, then returned his attention to Jeremy Culpepper.

"A toast, my friend!" They raised their tankards as Andrew proclaimed, "To our adventure!"

"And its safe conclusion," muttered Jeremy. He drank deeply, Sandhurst's laughter echoing in his ears.

CHAPTER 7

Château de Fontainebleau
February 22–27, 1533

ANNE D'HEILLY STOOD IN THE KING'S MAGNIFICENT OVAL BED-chamber, waiting for him to return from the morning council meeting. She held the letter that had arrived from King Henry VIII the previous day, silently rehearsing her speech to François. If he guessed that she was behind this suddenly arranged marriage for Micheline Tevoulère, God only knew what would happen. Now that events had been set in motion in England, Anne was realizing just how great a risk she had taken. All that she had worked for years to attain might be lost if her king discovered her scheme.

Fretfully she went to the window and looked for François in the Oval Courtyard below. The sight that met Anne's blue eyes replaced her doubts with a familiar rush of consuming jealousy. Micheline had just strolled from the gardens through the Port Dorée, while the king was entering the courtyard from his council chambers on the other side. Though surrounded by courtiers, he left them instantly and went to meet

Micheline, who was looking particularly lovely in the winter sunlight. Clad in a cloak of forest-green velvet trimmed with fox, she wore her warm auburn curls loose, spilling over her shoulders and down her back.

Anne burned at the sight of her rival's beautiful smile; it lit her face as the king drew near and bent to kiss her hand. The girl had become François's *friend*, gently rebuffing his advances over the weeks until he retreated and settled for what Micheline was able to give. Anne knew, however, that he had not given up. On the contrary, the king was probably more determined than ever. The slow seduction of Micheline was a constant test for his patience and ingenuity.

Unable to watch a moment longer, Anne d'Heilly turned from the window and paced back and forth, from one end of the long oval chamber to the other, until at last the outer door opened and the king appeared. Richly garbed in his usual black velvet cap, wide-necked shirt, slashed doublet, and fur-trimmed cape, all set with numerous precious jewels, his vital presence seemed to fill the room.

"Why, Anne!" François exclaimed in surprise. "What are you doing here? I thought my daughters were to have their first Latin lesson this morning!"

"They are copying some phrases, *mon cher*, so I stole away to have a word with you in private." She went to him, smiling, her demure fraise looking like white rose petals beneath her cream and pink face. "Why don't you sit down and I'll bring you some wine?"

"Exactly what I had in mind. I've some dispatches to look at before mass, so I hope that your business is brief."

"I'll be as brief as possible," Anne promised. She placed a jeweled goblet of wine beside him on a table, then bent to stroke his neat beard and bestow a few kisses, hoping to sweeten his mood. François grinned at her. Heartened, Anne took the chair opposite his and summoned her courage. "I received a letter from King Henry that has given me much cause for thought, sire."

François had leaned back in his carved walnut chair, sipping his wine contentedly, but now he looked up in surprise. "Why would Henry write to *you*?"

She shrugged ingenuously. "I wondered the same thing, until I discovered that the letter had to do with a marriage he hopes to arrange. I suppose he thought that I might be the person to consult on . . . affairs of the heart."

"What's this all about?"

"Do you know the Duke of Aylesbury? Or his son, the Earl of Sandhurst?"

"I met the father some years back . . . at the Field of the Cloth of Gold, as I recall. I'm not acquainted with the son, but I've heard that he's a dashing sort. Unconventional and independent."

"Yes, and a constant source of concern to his father," Anne supplied, elated by her king's response. "Apparently the duke is dying, and he wants to see his son married, so he sought Henry's help and authority to bring that about."

"*Mon Dieu!* What can that possibly have to do with *you*?"

"Well, it seems that Lord Sandhurst has a fondness for Frenchwomen, so his father thought that he would be more agreeable to the marriage if the bride were French . . . and beautiful and intelligent, of course!"

"Next you'll tell me that Henry suggested *your* name!" François's hazel eyes twinkled, but there was a wary glint in them as well.

"Don't tease me!" Anne scolded with a giggle. "Personally I think the entire idea is marvelous. Think of it, *mon cher,* a Frenchwoman in the English court . . . and soon an English duchess. Henry himself wrote that he believes such a marriage would help to strengthen the bonds of friendship between our two countries, and I must agree with him."

François pondered this for a moment, and his expression told Anne that he found merit in her argument. "It could be a good thing, certainly, from the standpoint of diplomacy, even though we have the upper hand in that area these days."

"But it is always wise to plan for the future, sire," Anne said, her blue eyes wide with sincerity.

"That's true." The king nodded. "Does Henry want you to find a bride for the Earl of Sandhurst?"

"Not exactly. He already has one in mind." She took a deep breath, praying that she wouldn't make a fatal mistake in the series of lies she was about to tell. "It seems that one of those English visitors to Fontainebleau early last month returned home singing the praises of Madame Tevoulère."

"Micheline?" cried François, instantly suspicious of the man who had dared to become enamored of his own flower of virtue.

"Yes, that's right." It took every ounce of Anne's control to keep her tone sweet and concerned when she longed to grab the goblet of wine and pour it over his head. "Apparently Henry is convinced that only Madame Tevoulère would be a proper candidate for Duchess of Aylesbury—and, sire, I have to agree with him."

"*Why?*" wailed François. Then, remembering that his mistress had no inkling of the regard he felt for Madame Tevoulère, he struggled to appear more calm and disinterested. "That is, she is still grieving for her husband. There must be someone else who would suit better."

"Don't you see that this would be the perfect solution for Micheline's problem? Here in France she cannot forget her dead husband. Even six months after his death she continues to languish. You must believe that I mean this kindly, sire: She may never begin to live again on her own. She may require a loving push. New surroundings, a handsome new husband, wealth and position—all of these would mean a fresh start in life for Micheline. If we are her friends, we will do what is best for her."

Listening to Anne, the king flushed with guilt. "I suppose it would be selfish for us to deprive Micheline of such an opportunity," he murmured. "Very well. You may speak to her, and if she agrees, so shall I."

All through mass Anne d'Heilly pondered her next move. Her interview with the king had been a success, and though he had bade her speak to Micheline Tevoulère, Anne knew she must lay careful groundwork before that conversation could take place. She knew enough of the personality and character of her rival to realize that Micheline would never agree to an arranged marriage with a stranger, no matter how advantageous it might be. She was a romantic, or she wouldn't still be grieving for Bernard Tevoulère and rejecting the attentions of nearly every man at court, including the king himself.

The priest was speaking. In front of Anne, who sat with the two young princesses, François knelt beside Queen Eleanor. It was often the only time he spent with his wife in the course of an entire day and night. To the king's left was the seigneur of St. Briac, his wife, and their two utterly adorable children. At the end of the row sat Micheline Tevoulère. Anne surreptitiously studied the face of the praying girl. She looked past her loveliness to the sensitivity and intelligence that were so apparent as Micheline communicated silently with God.

She's thinking of her dead husband, thought Anne. She still feels bound to him spiritually, and that's why she's unable to think of any other man.

Anne d'Heilly had known Bernard fairly well during his increasingly frequent stays with the court. As time had passed, his earnest shyness had seemed to melt away. He had gained confidence in himself in proportion to his growing prowess as a knight, and then, one day, he'd begun an affair with one of the younger girls at court. Soon he was drinking too much and becoming increasingly boastful. Still, there were always ladies at court willing to be entertained by Bernard, and gradually Anne had nearly forgotten that Bernard had a wife at all . . . until the day Thomas and Aimée arrived at Fontainebleau with the exquisite, grieving Micheline Tevoulère in tow. The girl knew nothing of her dead husband's debauched behavior at court and nothing of his ignominious death at the hands of a jealous husband. Everyone seemed to think that this virtuous widow needed protecting from the cruel realities of life.

Pondering all this, Anne began to realize what it might take to cause the idealistic Micheline to turn her back on the past and accept marriage to a stranger from England. . . .

Dawn broke frosty and clear. Rising early, Micheline shared crusty bread, fruit, and milk with Aimée and her daughters. Then, shortly after eight o'clock, she donned her cloak, bade the others good-bye, and set off for what had become her habitual morning walk in the woods of Fontainebleau. Micheline loved the contrast between the pristine gray forest, all stark branches and carpeted with dead leaves that warmed and nourished the plant life through the winter, and the opulent artifice of the king's château—where few people or things were ever quite what they seemed.

Tramping now through the damp brown leaves, Micheline spied a great roebuck, gray now to blend with the trees. His head was bent as he munched on some late breakfast, but he raised it instantly at the first sound of Micheline's approach. She stopped, smiling at him, and was gratified to realize that he knew her now and trusted her. Instead of running away, he returned to the bit of green nourishment he'd discovered.

Once again, Micheline mused that she almost felt more at home here in the forest than in the "civilized" court. Thomas and Aimée were wonderful and unaffected, and she'd come to like the king, but there seemed to be an invisible barrier between herself and nearly everyone else. Micheline couldn't decide if her alienation was of her own making or theirs, and yet she didn't care enough to try to dispel it. Her heart was still with Bernard; more here, perhaps, than at Château du Soleil, for he had lived here without her. Micheline constantly imagined him doing the things that she did now, speaking to the same people, inhabiting the same chambers.

Aimée had tried to persuade Micheline almost daily to begin to let go of the past and look ahead to a new life, but Micheline had come to realize that she felt safer with her memories. Her instincts told her that it would be a mistake to seek her future in the court of Fontainebleau. So far, except for her few friends, Micheline had sensed no depth or warmth or felt any rapport with the people who had tried to win her favor at court. Their values were different from hers. Some suggested that her problem lay in her sheltered past: They advised her to broaden her horizons and become more worldly, but Micheline had learned to trust her heart, and it told her, over and over again, to be herself. Any changes would evolve naturally, inside her. She didn't like to think about it now, but the memory of Bernard's seemingly forced transformation haunted her. He had tried to be someone he wasn't and had lost his life in the process.

Rosy-cheeked and refreshed, Micheline emerged from the forest after more than an hour. She had brought a bit of crust from breakfast and stopped now at the pond to feed the crumbs to the carp that darted about in the water. Having walked the length of the pond, she stopped and held her breath at the sound of voices on the other side of a tall sculpted hedge.

"I am thoroughly fed up with the holier-than-thou behavior of Micheline Tevoulère!" a girl was complaining.

Micheline, though embarrassed, was about to show herself rather than go on eavesdropping, but an answering female voice brought her up short.

"Isn't *everyone*? We're all itching to tell her what her sainted Bernard was *really* like! Why, if she only knew . . ."

"That he'd made love to me?" giggled the first girl. "Why, it was months before I even knew he *had* a wife! The man was shameless!"

"And it wasn't only you, Felice, in case you've forgotten.

From what I've heard, it sounds as if Bernard Tevoulère slept with half the women in the court!"

"Someone said he even bedded St. Briac's wife!"

"Well, I don't know if I believe *that,* but I've heard enough stories about the naughty little games he liked to play."

"And I can assure you, those stories *are* true! I'm a witness! The longer he was at court, the more outrageous Bernard became."

"Certainly no one was surprised when Arnaud Guerre dispatched him in that jousting match. Arnaud had murder in his eyes for weeks beforehand, but Bernard seemed to delight in tormenting him—reminding him of the fact that Élise Guerre preferred Bernard's talents in bed to those of her husband. Bernard had become so cocky, he seemed to be daring Arnaud to do his worst!"

"Poor little Bernard," sighed Felice. "I confess I rather miss him! I'll never forget the time he brought a bowl of grapes into bed. I wonder what his prim little widow would say if she heard what he *did* with those grapes!"

The two women shared peals of wicked laughter.

Feeling as if she might retch right there, Micheline turned and bolted. Her skirts became tangled and she tripped, but picked herself up and ran on, back to the Château de Fontainebleau, which now loomed ahead of her like a hell on earth.

Unable to speak or even think, Micheline managed to repress the urge to be ill as she rushed across the courtyard, her head bowed, past everyone who greeted her. The seigneur de St. Briac was one of these, and he stared after her, perplexed, before returning to his chamber to seek out his wife.

Micheline's rooms were modest but afforded a splendid view of the gardens behind the Oval Courtyard. In any case, she had felt more at home in this plainer chamber than if she'd been favored with more luxurious quarters. Now she threw herself on the testered bed and tried not to think. When she did think, she attempted to block out what she had heard, and when that failed, she dismissed the overheard conversation as idle gossip and lies. Still . . . the girl called Felice had spoken so casually of having slept with Bernard herself that Micheline instinctively sensed the truth. Memories like heart-piercing arrows attacked her: Bernard's coolness, which alternated with uneasiness, during his visits home, the lame excuses he made to return sooner than planned to the court, the emotional distance she had felt between them when they made love . . . all of it made sense now.

Bernard's death had left a wound that had barely begun to heal. Now Micheline felt as though it had been ripped open wider than ever. She was unable to cry. Curled like a baby on the bed, she stared at the wall and wondered if she was dying. *Could* one die of a hopelessly broken heart?

"Micheline?" a voice called softly from the corridor. "It's Aimée. May I come in?"

She couldn't reply, and a moment later the door opened hesitantly. Through a fog Micheline saw Aimée approaching the bed, her expression concerned.

"What is it, *chérie*? Are you ill?" She sat down on the bed and stroked Micheline's hair. "Did someone say something to upset you?" Somehow, Aimée sensed that her friend's pain was emotional rather than physical.

Not wanting to disturb Aimée, Micheline managed to say, "I'll be fine. It's . . . nothing, really."

"You can tell me, you know," Aimée said gently. A suspicion spread within her like a dark stain. She knew about Bernard's increasingly blatant infidelities when he had been at court; in fact, Thomas had taken to reminding her lately when voicing his own frustration over Micheline's seeming inability to stop mourning. Her devotion to her undeserving dead husband stymied them both, but they could find no solution short of telling Micheline the cruel truth, and that was out of the question.

Now Aimée wondered if someone else had done just that. What else could have devastated her friend this way?

"There's nothing to tell," Micheline was whispering. She struggled to sit up, then pasted on a wan smile. "I just felt a bit faint. Too much exercise, perhaps." Although Micheline was dry-eyed, Aimée heard the tears in her voice, and her own eyes stung in sympathy.

The chamber door had been left ajar and now it swung open. "Madame Tevoulère, may I have a few words with you?"

Aimée looked up in surprise to find Anne d'Heilly entering the room. Before she could protest, Micheline said numbly, "Oh, yes . . . of course. Please sit down."

"Merci!" Smiling brightly, Anne took the chair next to the bed. She wore a charming gown of sweet-briar pink, but her eyes were sharp as she scrutinized Micheline under thick lowered lashes. She was pleased with what she saw, wondering if François would be quite so enamored of this pale, pinched-looking girl.

For her part, Micheline was glad for the distraction—from her own consuming pain and Aimée's questions. She couldn't tell anyone what she'd learned, ever.

"I have something of great importance to discuss with you," Anne was saying kindly, "though it is rather *personal*."

Aimée made no move to leave them alone, and Micheline merely murmured, "You may speak freely in front of Madame de St. Briac."

"Well, if you're sure." Anne straightened her skirts in annoyance. Why did Aimée have to be such a busybody? "The king himself has asked me to raise this matter with you, madame." She proceeded then to unfold the same tale that she had told François, dwelling on the Earl of Sandhurst's attractive reputation, the beauty of England, and of the estates that would one day belong to the new Duke and Duchess of Aylesbury and the fresh, bright future being offered to Micheline. "Of course, it's an honor, as well, to have been chosen as the prospective bride to Lord Sandhurst. Just think, madame, you will soon be a countess! It's a chance to begin a whole new life, away from the . . . memories of the past." Anne paused to give her words time to sink in, then added brightly, "And, as I've doubtless mentioned, the earl is said to be exceedingly handsome and charming. Every eligible girl in England has been angling to become his wife. How fortuitous for *you* that he has a weakness for Frenchwomen!"

Aimée was thunderstruck. She would have spoken her mind immediately, but she was so certain that Micheline would veto these ridiculous marriage plans on her own that she kept silent.

"Can you tell me when and where the wedding would take place, mademoiselle?" Micheline queried instead. She looked rather dazed.

"Mais, oui!" exclaimed Anne. "You would go to England in April, and, as I understand it, King Henry himself intends to attend the ceremony, which will be held in the church at Aylesbury Castle, in Yorkshire. Of course, King François will see to it that you have everything you could possibly

need before you leave France. We'll have such fun planning your wardrobe!''

Micheline sighed, and Aimée stared at her sharply, a sudden feeling of panic swelling with her. Before she could speak, though, Micheline said softly, ''As you wish, then . . . I'll accept the earl's invitation to become his wife.''

CHAPTER 8

February 27, 1533

DUSK WAS APPROACHING, HERALDED BY A COLD, PENETRATING wind. The forest of Fontainebleau seemed to close in on the two men on horseback.

''I don't like it, Sandhurst,'' complained Sir Jeremy Culpepper. ''Not one bit. The whole place gives me chills.''

Laugh lines crinkled the corners of Andrew's brown eyes. ''Too late, my friend! Can't turn back *now*! Besides, you'll feel different when you're sitting before a blazing fire with a cup of wine and a dish of hot supper.''

''In the servants' kitchen!''

''Now, now,'' Sandhurst soothed, trying to smother his laughter. ''You never know; they may send *me* there as well! I'm not at all certain where unknown painters rank in the hierarchy of a king's court.''

Jeremy was too disgruntled to reply. He glanced over at his friend, who rode slightly ahead, and thought that it was highly unlikely that Sandhurst could ever be banished to the servants' quarters, even if he actually *were* a servant! His presence was too splendid to waste. Even now, at the end of a long day, he sat gracefully erect on his horse, his attractively wind-ruffled hair gilded by the late-afternoon sun, his profile half-amused and unmistakably aristocratic, and his body so lithe in the fawn doublet, breeches, and boots that he wore that Jeremy felt sick with envy.

''I've just got one thing to say!'' Jeremy heard himself shout.

Sandhurst turned his head slowly and tried to look serious. "Well, don't keep me in suspense!" he begged.

"Now that you've got me into this—this *incredible* scheme—against my better judgment, I might add—it had better be worth it! If I'm going to *lower* myself and pretend to be your lackey for the next few weeks, you'd damned well better accomplish something to make it worthwhile! Don't open your eyes at me like that! I'm talking about the girl, and well you know it! If you don't fancy her, I'd appreciate it if you'd decide that right away so that we can be done with this foolishness and go *home*! And if we stay on and on, you'd better plan on marrying the chit, because *my time* is valuable, whether you appreciate that fact or not!" Jeremy's face was red long before he finished his tirade.

"Egad!" exclaimed Andrew, the barest quirk of his mouth betraying his amusement. "You're hungrier than I thought! As for that speech, it was most impressive, but I can't promise to obey all those commands just yet." Gently he nudged his horse with his knees and, as it eased into a canter, glanced back in Jeremy's direction and added, "I must admit that I don't hold out much hope regarding the outcome of our undertaking."

"What!" Culpepper yelled in disbelief.

"I mean, what kind of woman would agree to marry a man she's never even seen? Not *my* sort, I fear."

As it turned out, a hot meal and several mugs of wine did go a long way toward improving Sir Jeremy Culpepper's outlook. He sat alone at the long scrubbed table in the kitchen, nearly oblivious to the pandemonium that surrounded him. Supper was being prepared for the king and his court, but the head cook had been sympathetic and hadn't made Jeremy wait for his. He found the *pain moullet,* a soft bread made with milk and butter, extremely soothing to his voracious appetite. The bread was teamed with a steaming dish of rabbit stew flavored with green peas and carrots, and sprinkled with pomegranate seeds and fresh herbs. Jeremy had never eaten anything quite so flavorful in all his life.

In a different part of the château, the earl of Sandhurst, now known as Andrew Selkirk, was standing in the long expanse of King François's unfinished gallery. The shell of it was complete, but the planned frescoes and carved paneling would take years. The king himself stood off to one side, reading a letter that had been sealed with the Earl of Sandhurst's crest.

> *To His Majesty, the King of France:*
> *The bearer of this letter is Andrew Selkirk, a very accomplished painter who has created masterful portraits of members of my family. He brings you an example of his fine work, a likeness of my sister, Lady Cicely Weston.*
> *It is my hope that you will give Selkirk a place at your court during his sojourn in France. Your Majesty's fine reputation as a patron of the arts leads me to believe that you will find Selkirk's visit an enriching one.*
>
> > *Most Respectfully,*
> > *Andrew Weston, Earl of Sandhurst*

François looked up from the sheet of parchment, scrutinizing the handsome man who waited nearby.

"How do you like my new gallery, m'sieur?"

"I've just been admiring the portions of paneling that are completed, sire. Very impressive."

François found himself warming to the Englishman's easy charm. "I understand that your king Henry uses much gilding in his houses, whereas I use little or none. I prefer timber finely wrought with divers colors of natural wood, such as ebony and brazil."

"I admire your taste, sire. I agree that these woods are richer than gilding, and doubtless more durable as well."

"My sentiments exactly." The king beamed. "I bid you welcome to my court, M'sieur Selkirk. I think that we shall deal well together."

"Your Majesty is both kind and generous."

As they walked together through the gallery, François inquired casually, "The Earl of Sandhurst is your patron?"

"I have made some paintings for him."

"Are you well acquainted?"

Andrew assumed a thoughtful mien. "Only slightly, sire."

"May I ask your opinion of the man?"

"I am not really qualified to judge," he said. Somehow, his inner amusement with the conversation allowed him to remain outwardly serious.

"Please, I urge you to be frank. You see, Lord Sandhurst is betrothed to one of the ladies of my court, and I would see her happy."

"Betrothed, you say? How interesting! Well, that's a surprise. In answer to your question, I can only say that it would be difficult for this lady not to be happy in a marriage with Lord Sandhurst. He has a great deal to offer! Perhaps it would be more to the point to wonder if this lady will make *him* happy."

François stared in consternation. "M'sieur, I can assure you that Micheline Tevoulère could make *any* man happy! She is a particular favorite of mine, and I confess that I am loath to relinquish her to your countryman." His hazel eyes were distant. "In fact, perhaps you should start your efforts here by painting her. I would like to be able to gaze at her likeness after she leaves France behind." The king stopped and met Andrew's neutral gaze. "There's no reason to tell her that you know the Earl of Sandhurst. In fact, the less said about him the better. I still entertain the hope that she may yet change her mind. . . ."

"I shall be pleased to paint this lady's portrait, sire, and you can rely upon my discretion where Lord Sandhurst is concerned," Andrew replied solemnly. Inwardly an urge to laugh aloud warred with consternation at François I's revelations. Was he to assume that Micheline Tevoulère was the king's mistress?

For days Aimée had appealed to Micheline to change her mind. The king would understand, she said. How could Micheline consider marriage to a stranger? she implored. It was a mistake! One day Micheline's heart would heal and she would rediscover love, Aimée insisted. All her entreaties met with Micheline's numb resolve.

"I am simply at my wit's end, Thomas!" Aimée was exclaiming as she stepped out of her bath and reached for the linen towels that had been warming in front of the fire.

"I've noticed," her husband remarked from the adjoining bedchamber. "Why don't you come in here and let me distract you?"

Laughing helplessly, Aimée did go in and sit naked on St. Briac's lap, kissing him deeply. He was half dressed for supper, and the sensation of her soft damp breasts against his bare chest made him forget all else.

"Thomas . . . please, we can't—"

"*Vraiment?*" he murmured, holding her near as he blazed a trail with his mouth across one of Aimée's shoulders and down her tender inner arm. "According to whom?"

She shivered, frankly aroused as he tasted the sensitive bend of her arm. "According to me. For now, at least. After supper we'll have—" She paused, gasping. St. Briac's lips had found her wrist, and Aimée knew that next he would lift her hand and savor each finger. She knew, too, that he was well aware of the moist heat between her legs. One more moment and there would be no turning back. Clinging to the thought of Micheline, alone and vulnerable to the cattiness of the court ladies, Aimée wrenched free. "It's not that I don't *want* to, Thomas! I'm thinking of Micheline! You and I have the whole night ahead to romp in bed."

St. Briac let her go, reaching for his shirt instead. He was aware that there was a part of him that was jealous of all the attention his wife paid to Micheline Tevoulère, and it made him ashamed. Although he was fond of the girl himself, that same selfish part of him was secretly pleased that she was going away to England. Nothing that he and Aimée had tried to do for her seemed to have had much effect, and he wanted his wife back. Still, guilt made St. Briac sigh and say, "It's all right. I understand. It's rather like being pushed aside at the crucial moment in bed because one of the babies is crying. I'm used to it." Aimée smiled warmly at him from the bureau, where she was removing undergarments, and that smile made him even more magnanimous. "I know your side of all this, *miette*, but what does Micheline have to say about it?"

"Oh, she says the same thing over and over again until I could scream!" Sparks seemed to flash from Aimée's green eyes. Tightening the delicate laces of her chemise, she reached almost angrily for her petticoats. " 'There's nothing for me here,' " Aimée mimicked. " 'I can't forget the past! At least in England I can attempt to begin a new life!' *That's* what she says!"

"Has it occurred to you that perhaps this *would* be the best thing for Micheline? I'm surprised that you aren't more sympathetic to her plight, *miette*, since you were once so desperate to escape your own lot that you ran away with the king's court train."

"That was different!" Aimée shot back hotly. "I was

younger. I didn't have the opportunities and advantages that
Micheline has—and I was being sold off in marriage to that
horrible Armand Rovicette! *That's* a reason for me to sympathize with Micheline, Thomas! What if this Lord Sandhurst is
grotesque? Why, Micheline's life could be a nightmare! There
is simply no reason for her to do something this foolhardy."

St. Briac watched his wife slip a gown of emerald-green
satin over her head and went up behind her to lace the back.
"My darling, I understand your feelings, but you must allow
Micheline to make her own decisions. You of all people must
understand how it would make her feel to be pressured, even
by a loving friend like you."

The soft tenderness of his voice brought tears to Aimée's
eyes. Turning, she buried her face in his fresh shirtfront and
wept silently for a moment. St. Briac's arms held her near as
he stroked the tense length of her spine. "Don't you see,
Thomas," she choked at last, holding fast to her husband,
"*this* is the most important reason why I don't want Micheline
to go through with this plan! She has no idea what she's
missed so far . . . and what she may forgo for a lifetime if
she marries the Earl of Sandhurst!" Lifting her face, she
gazed into her husband's eyes and said, "Love, real love,
between a man and a woman is a miracle. Micheline must
search for that miracle, not run from the challenge by escap-
ing to England!"

Micheline was living in a daze, which kept her numb most
of the time. It spared her the pain of introspective thought and
protected her from memories. She still didn't sleep well, and
her dreams could not be kept at bay, but somehow she sensed
that it could be worse.

Activity, though distracting, was often fraught with risks.
Tonight, as she dressed for supper, Micheline wished fervently that she didn't have to go downstairs and mingle with
the entire court. She lived in fear of hearing the voices from
the carp pond, which would mean facing one of the women
her husband had made love to. Sometimes, when the court
gathered before meals to socialize, Micheline imagined that
people were whispering about her, pointing at her, laughing
at her. They all knew about Bernard, she realized now, and
they must all think her a fool.

But it would be worse to stay in her chamber. Then they
would think they had won. They would chatter openly about

her, and call her a coward. So she bathed and dressed each
evening and pinned up her curls in the current fashion, then
went to supper with Thomas and Aimée, her head held high.

In her anguish, Micheline gave little thought to what lay
ahead for her in England. However, aside from a wild urge to
escape France and all its painful memories, she did occasionally take solace in the knowledge that there were few ladies at
François I's court who would not trade places with her if they
could. To be asked by King Henry himself to become the
wife of the future Duke of Aylesbury was honor enough, but
the further thought of the position and riches that awaited
Micheline must have been enough to make Felice, and every
other woman who had committed adultery with Bernard,
writhe with envy.

"Micheline, are you ready?"

It was the seigneur de St. Briac, calling gently at her door
as he did every evening. Micheline paused to glance in the
mirror, appraising the curls that framed her slightly pale yet
lovely face, and the elegant gown of golden velvet that she
wore. Sprinkled with tiny emeralds and topaz, it nipped in
perfectly at her waist, while its deep square neckline flattered
her bosom. She wore only one necklace, a band of emeralds
at the base of her neck, plus earrings of topaz and emeralds
that set off her cognac-hued hair to perfection.

"Yes, I'm ready," Micheline said, and opened the door
with a convincing smile.

Andrew longed to lean against the elaborately carved chimney piece, but the juniper-scented fire kept him at bay. He
was fully aware that Anne d'Heilly had been the king's
favorite for years, but here she was, chatting and smiling at
him coquettishly from a distance that made him nervous.
Another inch and the lady would be kissing him!

Glancing toward the sumptuously garbed men and women
that were filling the hall, Andrew said, "I begin to regret the
fact that I had no time to bathe and put on more appropriate
clothing. I fear I shall be rudely conspicuous at supper."

"*Pas du tout.*" Anne laughed. Her eyes swept the fawn
doublet and breeches that skimmed his lithe, masculine body
more appealingly than any amount of velvets, jewels, and
furs ever could. "You have just arrived, m'sieur; everyone
will understand. Aside from that, you are an *artist*. Such
people may dress as they please." If she'd had a bit more

wine, Anne might have added that Andrew Selkirk was more attractive, no matter what he wore, than any other man in the room . . . at least until St. Briac arrived. The painter said that he hadn't bathed that night, yet his hair shone like newly minted gold in the firelight, and she was close enough to know that he smelled quite irresistible.

"You are very kind, mademoiselle." Andrew smiled.

"Call me Anne. . . ."

His attention had wandered, however, to the stairway at the far end of the hall. A handsome couple was descending, but it was the young lady behind them who caught his eye. Even from this distance he recognized the intelligence and sensitivity in her face, and the glow of her eyes. The lady's hair seemed, in the torchlight, to be a mixture of gold and fire, and though her gown was fine, Andrew found himself staring at the elegant curves hugged by the velvet.

"M'sieur!" Anne exclaimed, pretending to pout. "Have you forgotten me?"

"Hmm? Oh, no, no, of course not." He gave her a distracted, though devastating smile, and inquired, "Can you tell me the name of the unaccompanied young lady who is at the bottom of the staircase?"

Anne narrowed her eyes at Micheline and demanded, "Why do you ask?"

A master at devising charming replies at a moment's notice, Andrew said, "The lady has an interesting face. It's not as beautiful as yours, mademoiselle, but it might be a challenge to paint."

"Oh." Anne tried to decide if she'd been complimented. "Well, that is Micheline Tevoulère. She's betrothed to a countryman of yours—the Earl of Sandhurst."

"Really!" Andrew exhaled slowly and rubbed one forefinger against his mouth. "That's very interesting. . . ."

PART II

The knight knocked at the castle gate;
The lady marvelled who was thereat.

To call the porter he would not bin;
The lady said he should not come in.

She asked him what was his name;
He said, "Desire, your man, Madame."

She said, "Desire, what do ye here?"
He said, "Madame, as your prisoner."

—WILLIAM CORNISH 14?–1523

CHAPTER 9

February 27–28, 1533

BEFORE SANDHURST COULD CONTRIVE SOME MEANS OF MEETING Micheline Tevoulère, the king came up to them and put a possessive arm around Anne's waist.

"I'm pleased to see that my Anne has been entertaining you." He smiled. Clad in cloth of silver, black velvet, diamonds, and ermine, François cut a splendidly royal figure. "Supper will be served momentarily, but first . . ." He scanned the crowd distractedly. "First I would like to introduce you to your first subject."

"Ah!" cried Andrew, feigning surprise. "Very thoughtful of you, sire."

As if the king had sent a silent message, Micheline became visible among the chattering assemblage just a few feet away from them.

"Madame Tevoulère!" François called. The sound of his raised voice caused others to fall silent, and Micheline looked around immediately. "Will you join us?"

When she came smiling out of the crowd, Sandhurst thought that she was even more radiantly beautiful close up than she'd appeared to be on the distant stairway.

"How may I serve Your Majesty?" she inquired respectfully.

The king was satisfied that Micheline truly wanted to go to England and marry the Earl of Sandhurst, but he hadn't liked the shadows that had appeared under her eyes and in her manner these past few days. Anne assured him that it was probably just a case of nerves, so François hoped now that the fresh new presence and charming personality of this artist might lighten her mood.

"I would like you to meet a guest at our court, *ma chère*," he told her kindly. "Allow me to present Andrew Selkirk, a gifted painter from England who has agreed to make some

portraits while he is with us.'' Turning to Sandhurst, the king
smiled. ''M'sieur, you have the honor to meet Micheline
Tevoulère, a true gem among the ladies of my court.''

''It is a pleasure, m'sieur,'' Micheline murmured. For the
first time in days she was conscious of something penetrating
the fog that surrounded her: Andrew Selkirk's warm, brown
gaze.

''The pleasure, I can assure you,'' he said smiling, ''is all
mine.'' Lifting her slim hand, Andrew pressed a kiss to her
fingers, wondering at the sudden flutter of her pulse.

''Perhaps you would sit with M'sieur Selkirk when we
sup,'' François was saying to Micheline. ''Since he's just
arrived, he knows no one else.''

''Certainly, sire,'' she replied obediently. For some reason
her cheeks felt flushed, and she glanced downward so that the
stranger from England would not misunderstand.

The boards had been laid and the court wandered over to be
seated. The sight was impressive. The huge hall was paneled
in walnut and hung with panoramic tapestries depicting King
François during various triumphant moments throughout his
reign. Servants were lined up beneath the tapestries, holding
flaming torches, wine vessels, and golden dishes. The sound
of musical French voices filled the air as the splendidly
garbed lords and ladies found their places.

Sandhurst took it all in with his usual casual curiosity.
He'd supped with King Henry at various castles in England,
so his sense of awe had melted away long ago. A servant
poured wine into his silver goblet from a pewter vessel with a
long spout. Andrew sipped it and turned to look at the girl
everyone meant him to marry. She had placed her fingers on
the stem of her goblet but did not lift it. Instead, she stared
into the distance, seemingly at a torch on the far wall, her
utterly beautiful blue-violet eyes filled with secrets and
melancholy.

''Will you raise your glass with me, mademoiselle?'' he
queried softly.

''Oh! Of course, m'sieur!'' Hastily Micheline turned to
meet his smile. ''You will pardon me if I seemed rude, I
hope. I . . . haven't felt quite myself lately.''

''Then let us drink to the rebirth of your high spirits.''

Micheline nodded and they lifted their goblets and sipped

together. High spirits, she thought ironically. How long had it been since she had been acquainted with such pleasure?

"And now," Sandhurst continued, "I would like to make a more selfish toast—for luck."

This time she didn't have to remember to smile. "By all means, m'sieur."

"Will you drink with me to France?" Micheline had already raised her goblet, but he held up his hand. "Wait, there's more!"

"I didn't think that sounded particularly selfish," she heard a voice that appeared to be her own remark lightly.

"That was just the preface!" Andrew laughed. "We must drink to a happy sojourn for *me* in France."

"Excellent," Micheline approved.

She almost had the goblet to her lips when he added, "And to many valuable new friendships . . . for both of us."

She watched him drink then, raising his eyebrows at her over the silvery rim of his goblet. Unaccountably her cheeks were warm again, but somehow she managed to sip her own wine.

Before Micheline could wonder if she was ill, distraction appeared, in the form of a peacock that was arriving at the table in full plumage. It was set down amid a flourish of trumpets and the applause of all present. The bird's beak was gilt, its tailfeathers spread brilliantly, and it rested on a mass of brown pastry painted green to represent a field. Eight banners of silk were arranged around the peacock, which towered above the other appointments of the table.

"Very impressive," Sandhurst murmured.

Detecting a note of satire in his voice, Micheline glanced over in surprise. A funny, unfamiliar bubble of delight rose inside her, then she blushed again, and Andrew gave her a fleeting wink. Truly flustered now, Micheline turned her attention to the food. Suddenly she felt as if she'd been dropped into some foreign place and filled with completely unknown sensations. Was she ill? It couldn't be Andrew Selkirk's fault; he'd done nothing except smile at her, converse in a friendly manner—and look at her in a way that made her suspect he could see into her very soul. The latter was a product of her imagination, Micheline decided now as she tasted the peacock. The man simply had rather magical eyes. Probably the old woman he bought his eggs from blushed when he looked, smiling, at *her*. Charm could be a dangerous gift, especially for its recipients.

There was much more to eat besides the peacock. Micheline nibbled at sturgeon that had been cooked in parsley and vinegar then covered with powdered ginger, boar that had been grilled and larded with *foie gras*, tiny ortolans, and juicy breast of heron. The next course was a salad that consisted of raw greens mixed with cooked vegetables and red poultry crests.

Conscious of the silence between her and Andrew Selkirk, Micheline tried to dispel the signs of her earlier disconcertion by turning to him and inquiring politely, "Does our food compare favorably with that in England, m'sieur?"

For a moment it seemed he might laugh at her, but then he drew his brows together in what she perceived to be mock seriousness and replied, "Oh, yes, mademoiselle. Most favorably. Particularly since I do not dine habitually with King Henry!" Andrew leaned toward her conspiratorially. "Can you keep a secret?"

Micheline nodded nervously. Her heart was pounding, and she was certain he had noticed the rapid rise and fall of her breasts. Why should this man's proximity affect her so? She took a deep breath, which worsened her plight, because it caused her to inhale his appealingly masculine scent.

Apparently oblivious to Micheline's inner turmoil, Andrew whispered, "I don't have *peacock* for supper as a rule. You'll think me a peasant, I daresay, but the truth is that I normally dine on only three courses." Golden sparks danced in his brown eyes as he asked her, "Are you shocked?"

Micheline heard helpless feminine laughter. Was it hers? "No, m'sieur, I am not shocked! In fact, I will tell you a secret in return." The way he inclined his head in anticipation was so captivating that her heart seemed to skip a beat before she continued. "I am not accustomed to peacock either. I grew up near Angoulême, and though my father is seigneur of our village, we lived simply. After I married, my life was simpler still, and to be honest, I prefer it that way. I am only here at all because my dearest friend, Madame de St. Briac, thought that the excitement of court life would help to dispel . . ."

Sandhurst sensed that she'd never meant to reveal so much, but he wasn't about to let her stop there. "Yes?"

Though her eyes had clouded, she finished softly, "My

husband died this past summer, m'sieur, and I have been in pain of one sort or another ever since, it seems."

He blinked and raised a finger, running it back and forth over one side of his mouth. Micheline Tevoulère was a *widow*? The fabric of this arranged marriage was taking on some unforeseen wrinkles. . . .

"I am sorry, mademoiselle—or, I should say, madame—to hear of your loss, and for the carelessness of my first toast this evening." Without thinking, Andrew took his hand from his mouth and laid it over her own hand. "Take heart, though. You are young, with your whole life before you. One never knows what lies ahead."

Micheline, gripped by sadness a moment earlier, now felt giddy as she looked at the hand that covered hers. Andrew Selkirk's skin was golden, even in winter. His hand was well-shaped, square, and strong, yet the fingers were long, and she had already noticed the particular grace that marked their movements. More important, Micheline felt a warmth and energy that seemed to flow from his hand to hers. It sent a pleasurable tingling up her arm, to her face, across her back, and to her breasts.

A servant set a dish of Loire salmon sliced with eggs before her, and she freed her hand even as her heart beat madly in her chest.

"I—I appreciate your sentiments, m'sieur. *Merci*." She stabbed a morsel of salmon with her fork, a utensil that had been unknown to her before Fontainebleau, and gave him a weak smile.

Sandhurst ignored the dish placed before him and lifted his goblet instead. He wondered, sipping the fine Grenache wine, whether Micheline Tevoulère was in earnest, or if she might be so skilled in artifice that she could deceive him. Yet what was there for her to gain? She had no idea of his true identity, and as far as Andrew knew, she did not even know that he was to paint her. His mind went around and around. If Micheline was as ingenuous and heartbroken as she seemed, *why* would she agree to marry a stranger from a strange country? Could it be that she didn't *know* of the proposed betrothal?

"Madame . . ." he ventured at length, "you'll pardon me, I hope, if my curiosity has caused me to dare too much, but I have to ask."

Micheline had abandoned her salmon after three bites and

now was drinking liberal quantities of wine in an effort to return herself to the safer, hazy existence she'd become accustomed to. "Ask away, m'sieur," she said recklessly.

"It may have been only a rumor that I heard, completely untrue, but I was under the impression that you were betrothed to the Earl of Sandhurst."

"Oh." She hardly knew what to say to him concerning that unwelcome piece of strange reality.

"I understood that you were going to England in April to be married to Lord Sandhurst," Andrew pressed. "Am I mistaken?"

"No . . . no, you are not mistaken." Micheline held out her goblet to a passing wine squire, then drank of it. She couldn't bring herself to meet Andrew Selkirk's compelling gaze. "However, I do not wish to discuss this matter with you, m'sieur."

"Hmm." Lifting his eyebrows, he gazed at his dish of salmon and eggs and sighed. "Well, I will respect your wishes, madame, but—" Now Sandhurst raised his eyes to Micheline's slightly averted profile. In the torch and candlelight her hair seemed to sparkle, and her features were exquisite. "I like you, and we may truly become friends. You see, the king has asked me to make my first painting in France one of you."

Micheline swiveled to stare at him, her mouth an O. "I don't understand!" she finally exclaimed.

"His Majesty holds you in high esteem. It seems that if he cannot have you present in the flesh, he would at least keep your portrait as a reminder."

Hot blood suffused her cheeks again, and she looked away, only to discover not just François I but her friend Aimée staring at her from across the table. What was happening?

"Look," Andrew said gently, "we'll make a pact. Since we must spend a great deal of time together until the portrait is finished, I promise not to speak of your late husband or your betrothed unless you raise the subject first. How's that?"

Dishes of figs, dates, walnuts, red sugar plums, and pear pastry were being presented, along with a sweet dessert wine. Micheline selected a sugar plum and took a tiny bite, wondering how it could be that she felt a deeper intimacy with this stranger than she felt with Aimée or the king.

Micheline sensed that Andrew Selkirk had some kind of *affinity* with her mind and soul, although she doubted that he

could actually know much specifically. It was as though the
bond between them had been forged the instant they met . . .
or long before, somehow. He knew her already. How long
could she keep *anything* from such a man?

"*Eh bien*, m'sieur," Micheline told him, thinking that she
hardly had a choice, "I agree to your pact. And I would like
very much to be your friend, if you will have me."

It was long past midnight when Sandhurst returned to the
modest chamber he would share with his "valet," the erstwhile Sir Jeremy Culpepper. There had been entertainments
after supper, mainly jugglers and tumblers who cavorted among
the rushes and fresh herbs strewn over the tiled floor, but
Andrew had not been greatly entertained. Anne d'Heilly had
claimed him as soon as they left the table, holding his arm a
bit too tightly as she led him around to meet other members of
the court. Occasionally Sandhurst had caught a glimpse of
Micheline through the crowd. She stood off to one side with a
pretty, dark-haired girl, smiling absently as her friend acted
very gay. When at last he was free, Andrew went to the place
where Micheline had been. He made the acquaintance of the
enchanting wife of the seigneur de St. Briac, who told him
that Micheline had pleaded fatigue and gone to bed. They had
talked for a bit, but in his disappointment Sandhurst was too
distracted to notice the appraising, thoughtful way that Aimée
stared at him. At length, as the revelry continued unabated,
Andrew also excused himself.

Sighing now, he opened the door, half hoping that Jeremy
would be asleep so that he could think.

"At *last*!" an annoyed voice exclaimed. "Where have you
been?"

"I've been playing my part with the king and his court,"
Sandhurst replied shortly.

"Oh, *yes*! A real hardship, I'll warrant! You were forced to
eat all that food I watched the cooks preparing . . . and drink
all those fine wines! How was the *peacock*?"

Andrew had to smile at that. "Adequate," he pronounced
dryly. "Why are you in such a state?"

Jeremy sat up in his narrow bed, his cheeks crimson now.
"Perhaps I can't sleep on this frightful straw mattress! *Your*
bed doesn't have one, by the way. *You've* got goose down!"

Unlacing his shirt and doublet, Andrew couldn't resist

lifting an eyebrow and saying reasonably, "That's good. I *deserve* it, don't you think?"

"Are you itching for a fight, Sandhurst? I'd be glad to oblige you, solely on the basis of the *name* you christened me with when you presented me to the head chamberlain! Why didn't you let me devise my *own* masquerade?"

His lips twitched as he sat down to pull off his boots. "You don't care for 'Jeremy Playfair'? I thought it had a rather honorable ring to it."

"Do you have any idea how many times I've been called 'Playfair' tonight?" shouted Culpepper. "It's driving me *mad*!"

"Have a care, Jeremy. You'll give yourself an attack." Tugging off the second boot, Sandhurst sighed. "I do miss Finchley at times like this. A man likes to be looked after at the end of a hard day."

"You push me too far, you know," Jeremy growled, looking about for a weapon. "Next you'll suggest that I play your valet in private as well as in public . . . and they'll find you smashed on the courtyard below our window!"

Laughing softly, Sandhurst bent to remove his fawn breeches and hose. Too tired to look for water to wash with, he drew back the covers on his bed and lay down with a contented sigh. "I'm only teasing you, Jeremy. You *do* know that, don't you?"

Sandhurst's moments of sincerity were utterly disarming. The color softened in Culpepper's cheeks as he muttered, "Yes. I suppose I do."

"I couldn't get through this masquerade without you."

The two men exchanged affectionate smiles. "I'm glad to be here . . . in a way," Jeremy allowed. "It'll be another adventure for us to laugh about later—and if it actually does any good, well, then . . ."

"I met her tonight. Micheline Tevoulère, I mean." Staring up at the plain green velvet tester, Sandhurst found that her name tasted sweet upon his tongue.

Suddenly ashamed of the time he'd wasted with his ridiculous outburst, Jeremy rose on an elbow to stare at his friend. "*And?*"

"It's a long story and I am exhausted. I'll tell you all of it tomorrow, but for now let's just say that the situation holds possibilities."

CHAPTER 10

March 1, 1533

"I CAN'T GO FOR MY WALK THIS MORNING," MICHELINE TOLD Aimée as they finished a light *petit déjeuner*. Ninon had gone to sit in a corner, where she now rolled a tennis ball for their rambunctious new puppy. Her little rosebud mouth was smeared with honey and bread crumbs, so Aimée moistened a serviette and gave it to Juliette, who proudly went off to play mother.

"Why not?" Aimée returned a trifle absently. If Juliette rubbed Ninon's face too hard, the two-year-old would start to cry, so half her attention was with her daughters.

"That Englishman is going to begin work on my portrait at eight-thirty." Micheline's tone was as neutral as she could manage, for the truth was she didn't know how she felt about the large amount of time she'd be spending with Andrew Selkirk. Part of her was impatient that her days would no longer be her own, but at the same time she was rather excited. The latter feeling was decidedly disquieting. The man both tantalized and alarmed her. Most confusing was the realization that she wasn't alarmed because of anything *he* had said or done but because of her reaction to him. All the previous day Micheline had avoided the Englishman, until, last evening, his redheaded valet had brought her a message from his master. In his flawless French Andrew Selkirk had written to politely request that they meet this morning in the king's second antechamber to begin work on the portrait.

Micheline stood now to keep that appointment, brimming with a mixture of emotions, not the least of which was a pleasant sense of anticipation.

"Well!" Aimée exclaimed, trying to decide what approach to take. "This should be an exciting experience for you!"

"Sitting still while someone paints me?"

"It's a *change* certainly." Unable to help herself, Aimée added, "And the company of M'sieur Selkirk should prove

75

highly diverting! I own that I find just *looking* at the man an 'exciting experience'!''

The sound of her friend's mischievous laughter made Micheline blush. "Aimée, you should be ashamed of yourself. You're married to the handsomest man at court! As for me, I have no interest in Andrew Selkirk or any other man, and well you know it.''

"Don't forget the Earl of Sandhurst," Aimée said recklessly, then immediately regretted the jab. If Micheline became angry, it would only make her more stubborn.

The younger girl turned away to hide her flaming cheeks. "I'll be late. *Au revoir.*"

The king's second antechamber, located in the old keep, had recently been decorated with frescoes and stuccoes by the Italian artist Primaticcio, who was currently at work on the magnificent François I gallery.

At this hour the king was downstairs at his council meeting, so the huge square room was quiet. Micheline entered hesitantly, her eyes immediately finding Andrew Selkirk. He sat at a table that was covered with sheets of heavy paper, an inkhorn, and several white swan's quills. Sunlight poured through the massive windows, gilding the Englishman's ruffled hair as he bent over one of the papers, appearing to write.

"*Bonjour*, m'sieur," Micheline said softly.

He looked up in surprise, then gave her a smile so white and charming that her heart began to thud immediately. "It's good to see you, madame! You look lovely."

For a moment Micheline forgot to speak. She stood rooted to the spot, watching as he rose and came toward her. Andrew wore a doublet and breeches of unembellished sage-green velvet slashed to reveal hints of white linen, and fine leather boots. His movements were the epitome of masculine grace, reminding her of the particular elegant agility with which he'd used his hands the night they supped together. At some point Micheline realized that she should walk forward to meet him, but then it was too late. When Andrew Selkirk lifted her hand and kissed it with warm, firm lips, she had to resist the impulse to flee. In the name of God, why did *this* man, who was little more than a stranger, have such a devastating effect on her mind and body? Never in her life, even with Bernard, had she felt this way.

"You are well?" he was asking gently.

"Oh—yes! Of course!"

"Good." He smiled again, which made Micheline dizzy, and continued to hold her hand lightly. "You look a trifle pale . . . and I thought I felt you tremble, but it must have been my imagination."

Her face was suddenly hot. Did he *know*? Could he be enjoying a joke at her expense? "I am fine, m'sieur."

"Ah, yes, I see the color in your cheeks now. I hope you didn't think me rude, but I asked only because sitting for a portrait can be surprisingly tiring. My last subject complained so loudly that I had to learn to paint while she talked, since she found it impossible to remain still after approximately ten minutes." Andrew gestured with one hand for her to precede him across the chamber. "I hope you'll be comfortable in this chair. If you are not, kindly make a fuss and we'll find a better one."

Micheline found her nerves melting under the spell of his easy charm just as they had the night she met him. The chair he indicated was positioned so that the sun was at her back, warm and soothing.

"This will be fine, m'sieur," she assured him.

Sandhurst walked over to his table and stared at her for a moment, then returned to adjust the angle of the chair. "The light is very important to me," he explained, still narrowing his eyes thoughtfully at Micheline. "It must be just right, so we can work only in the early morning and late afternoon."

"Oh." Suddenly Micheline realized that she had uttered nothing but inanities since entering the room. Casting about for a topic she might raise, she heard herself ask, "Who was the lady you painted who was unable to remain both still and silent?"

Sandhurst blinked. All this was much easier, he'd found, when *he* held the reins of the conversation. "She was only twelve years old at the time, but still qualifies as a lady, if only by title. My subject was Lady Cecily Weston. . . ." He paused, biting the inside of his lip, then added, "Sister to the Earl of Sandhurst."

"Oh!" Micheline said again. She took a deep breath, but no more words came out. Andrew Selkirk must know the Earl of Sandhurst! Part of her wanted to ask a dozen questions and realized that indeed she *ought* to, but stronger still was her apprehension about the possible answers. In truth, she simply didn't want to think about her future husband yet.

Andrew sat down behind his table, trying not to smile. He'd seen the surprise and curiosity in Micheline's wide eyes, and had recognized the panic too. She didn't *want* to know about the man she was to marry. Why not? And again he wondered how and why the marriage had been sought in the first place.

"Where is your canvas, m'sieur?" Micheline queried, happy to change the subject. "And your paints, and—"

He held up his hand, chuckling. "Not so fast! If we're to create a proper portrait, a few preparatory exercises must be performed!"

"They must?" she echoed. What was he talking about?

"Yes!" The girl's mixture of guilelessness, nervousness, and intelligence was simply enchanting. Her manner was open yet laced with mystery, and surrounding all these qualities was a beauty more luminous than Sandhurst had ever known. "I like to do a series of sketches first. Pen drawings. I'll work on those today, and if the results are satisfactory, we *may* be able to begin the actual portrait tomorrow."

"What are the drawings for?"

"They help me become accustomed to your face, and body, and spirit." Micheline's sudden blush made him glance away out of kindness. Andrew picked up one of the swan's quills, dipped it into the inkhorn, and began to sketch her. "To create a portrait of any depth, it's important, I think, to develop a sense of what the subject is like. Understanding, if you like. Also, the drawings help me decide what the best design would be for the finished painting." As he became more involved in what he was doing, Sandhurst's sentences took on a disjointed quality. "The position of your body, the tilt of your head, the expression on your face, the most flattering style for your hair and gown—they're very important. Critical, in fact." He met her eyes and smiled briefly. "We'll look at the sketches together, if you'd like, and you can tell me what you prefer, or if you have any thoughts about the way you want to look. It won't be just *any* portrait, after all—"

"I know," Micheline broke in. "And I would be pleased to see the drawings when you finish, m'sieur. It's kind of you to offer."

"Not kind at all. At least half the credit for any painting

must go to the subject, I believe. That's why I like to paint people. They can talk back and share more actively in the artistic process."

Aside from her heightened sensations in the presence of Andrew Selkirk, Micheline was now disconcerted by having to carry on a conversation with someone who rarely made eye contact with her. He'd be scrutinizing her hair or her neck or her nose while she spoke, so that she wasn't certain if he was listening, or else he was actively sketching, which made her feel as if she shouldn't speak at all.

After a long minute of silence Andrew laughed softly and met Micheline's eyes. "Don't be so stiff, madame! Relax. We are not in church, and I can assure you that there is nothing sacred about my work." The sight of her nervous, obedient smile only increased his amusement. "Why don't you talk to me. As I recall, you said that you grew up in Angoulême. Tell me about it."

It seemed that Micheline had little choice. Uneasily she said, "It's not a very exciting story, m'sieur. We lived some distance east of the town of Angoulême, in the country, near Nieuil. When I was a child, King François had a hunting lodge very near my family's château, but he wasn't there very often. I couldn't have been more than ten when he went off with the army to fight in Italy, and then, of course, he was held captive for over a year. He did visit after his return, and my parents attended a celebration at the hunting lodge, but soon after it became the property of a man named Grunn. Apparently he owned some land in the forest near Château de Chambord that the king coveted, so they made an exchange."

Sandhurst had given no indication that he heard her at all, but now he glanced up to remark dryly, "Very interesting. What about *you*?"

"Well . . ." She faltered, blushing. "There's not a lot to *tell*. Because we lived in the country, I had a quiet childhood. My brother, Paul, was many years older and not very much company. I spent a great deal of time outdoors. I liked the woods—I still do. I love animals. My mother saw to it that I learned to read. We had a wonderful library. I think that my father likes books better than people, but at least the books became my friends as well." Micheline was relaxing now, gazing at a fresco rather than at Andrew as she continued. "As far back as I can remember, Bernard Tevoulère was my best *human* friend. He was a year older than I, and he taught

me to ride and swim and climb trees. He taught me everything. When I was twelve, he gave me one of his own horses
as a birthday gift." She smiled softly, remembering the eu-
phoria she'd felt that day as they raced across the meadows.

"You're fond of horses?" Sandhurst couldn't resist asking.

"Oh, much more than that!" she declared. "I can't tell
you how I've missed my Gustave these past months. He's
getting old, but somehow that makes me love him more than
ever. Sometimes I think that horses are more human than
people."

Andrew's brows went up as he digested this. "I'm inclined
to agree with you, madame. But please—pardon my interruption. I like this story about you much better than the first one,
about King François's hunting lodge!"

His voice warmed her from a distance, encouraging her to
continue. Micheline hesitated for a moment, then told herself
that after this month she would probably never see Andrew
Selkirk again. Her confidences seemed safe with him.

"Well, let's see . . ." She sighed, remembering what must
come next. "That twelfth birthday marked the end of my
childhood. The next year my mother died, and Paul went
away to Paris, leaving me alone with Papa. I don't know
what I would have done then without Bernard. I had to take
care of my father, and he barely took the time to talk to me
unless it was to ask for something. So Bernard and I became
closer than ever, and we were growing up. I stayed with Papa
as long as I could bear it, then married Bernard when I was
sixteen. We had four years together."

A hand touched Micheline's wrist, then covered her fingers. Tears sparkled in her iris-blue eyes as she looked over,
to find Andrew Selkirk sitting back on his heels next to the
chair.

"I'm sorry, Michelle." He spoke her name in this shortened
form without thinking. "I never meant to cause you pain
when I encouraged you to tell me about your past."

"Don't apologize! I feel better somehow. Sometimes here
at Fontainebleu my old life seems like a dream. Talking to
you about those years helped to make them real again."

He reached up with a forefinger and caught a tear that
spilled onto Micheline's cheek. Staring into his deep brown
eyes, she felt a inexplicable tremor that jolted her very
core.

"The light's going," Andrew said gently. "Why don't we borrow two of the king's best horses and have a good long ride."

To Micheline the cold wind on her face and the strong, rhythmic movements of the horse provided the perfect tonic for her spirits. She and Andrew rode full out across the fields that skirted the dark forest, a bright midday sun beaming down on them to soften the chill in the air.

From time to time Sandhurst glanced over at Micheline, admiring with an expert eye her skill. It was clear that she rode well, and with great enthusiasm, but she also rode properly. There was an undeniable elegance in the motion of her body; she and the horse were one. The combination of abandon, feminine grace, and rapport between Micheline and her steed struck a chord within Andrew. Horses were one of the great passions of his life. In the past he'd known women who had enjoyed riding, but they'd always pretended to *adore* it, hoping to win his favor. Unfortunately Sandhurst had an instinct for spotting artifice. He'd long ago given up hoping that a woman might simply be herself, for better or worse, and have faith in her own worth, without resorting to a lot of elaborate games designed to fool him.

"M'sieur!" Micheline called gaily over her shoulder. "Are you holding back to make me feel better?"

"I think you took the faster horse!" He laughed. Leaning forward so that his knees pressed hard against the stallion's sides, Sandhurst drew alongside Micheline, then slightly ahead. She was laughing, too, as they raced, and he felt a wave of pleasure at the sight of her curling auburn-gold hair, which waved behind her like a banner. Micheline was clad all in rust-colored velvet. A soft velvet cap set with emeralds puffed sideways in the wind, while her gown was covered by a matching cloak trimmed in sable.

"Stop showing off!" she cried as he gradually passed her. Never one to lose without a fight, Micheline urged her steed forward faster, but it was not enough, and even in her frustration she had to admire Andrew's skill and his masculine beauty as he rode.

Sandhurst brought his horse slowly to a walk and waited for Micheline to reach them. "Let's have something to eat," he suggested, swinging down from the stallion's back.

Seeing a pond nearby where the horses could drink,

Micheline nodded breathlessly. Andrew had walked over to help her down, and though she certainly didn't need his aid, she capitulated and slid down into his waiting arms. The sensation of his strong hands encircling her waist was pleasurably unsettling.

"I apologize," he said with a smile. "If I were a gentleman, I'd have let you win."

"Don't be ridiculous!" Micheline declared. "I don't like people who do that. *I* certainly wouldn't have let *you* win if I could have helped it!"

"I know." He appeared pleased by this knowledge.

Together they took the bundles of food down from behind his horse's saddle, then the two steeds wandered off to rest and drink at the pond.

Sandhurst, with Jeremy's expert help, had raided the château's kitchen while Micheline changed clothes for their ride. Her eyes widened now as he spread a cloth over the long grass and produced a slender, fragrant loaf of bread, apricots and strawberries grown in the king's greenhouses near Paris, slices of young chicken and ham, a little rush basket of curdled Vincennes cheese, and a generous stoppered flask of wine. There were even cups, serviettes, knives, and butter.

"Oh, m'sieur, it is a feast!" Micheline exclaimed. Suddenly she was ravenous.

"Wait." Sandhurst held up a hand. "Before we eat, I want to settle something."

She paused in the act of tearing off a piece of bread and waited.

"Are we friends?"

"Why, yes . . . I think we are, m'sieur."

"Then kindly do me the favor of calling me Andrew."

"*D'accord* . . . Andrew. Will you call me Michelle?" She blushed under his warm regard and admitted, "I liked it when you said it earlier."

"I liked it too." Sandhurst smiled. "And I would be honored."

They took a more direct route back to the château, through the forest of Fontainebleau. In another hour the light would be favorably soft, and Andrew was eager to return to his sketches.

"I'm glad that one of us knows the way," he remarked to Micheline as she rode ahead of him.

"I always use this path when I get so far from the château. It would be easy to become lost in these woods. It's wider, too, than the rest, so we can go faster."

A companionable silence reigned between them then. Andrew watched the path unfold ahead of them, but he was frequently distracted by Micheline's graceful form. His gaze wandered over the line of her back, admiring the fire of her tumbled curls and occasional glimpses of her lovely profile. Thus, he barely noticed a sharp turn in the path ahead. Micheline took it with barely a pause. An instant later there was a loud crashing sound that mingled with a woman's scream.

Sandhurst reined in his stallion in the midst of the turn in the path. The horse came to a standstill just feet away from an enormous pile of cut birch trees. Swinging down, Andrew found that the path's obstruction was waist-high. Micheline's gelding was on the other side, its saddle empty, prancing fitfully about while its rider lay crumpled on a bed of brown leaves.

He was at her side immediately. Micheline was trying to sit up, and Andrew knelt to cradle her against him.

"Are you hurt? What happened?"

She blinked in confusion. "Oh, I feel so foolish! The horse—he's all right, isn't he? He made the jump—more alert than I—but it all happened so fast that I had no time to prepare. Suddenly I was falling . . ."

"Do you have any pain?"

Gingerly she flexed her arms and legs and moved her torso from side to side. "No, nothing's broken, I'm sure." Micheline looked up to give Andrew a reassuring smile, only to find him staring at her in a way that made her forget all else. *Bon Dieu!* she thought, never before have I encountered such compelling eyes! Suddenly she was keenly aware of his hard thighs pressing against her, the strong fingers laced through her hair, the velvet-clad masculine chest that cast its shadow over her more delicate form.

"Michelle." Andrew's voice was husky. Now that she was in his arms, reason was forgotten. Her eyes were opened wide, her soft lips slightly parted, and color slowly stained her cheeks. The yearnings Sandhurst had repressed since the first moment he saw her rose up and took control.

Micheline's heart was pounding as he turned her deftly in his arms. The instant her breasts met his steely chest they

tingled and sent a current of warmth through her body. Even
during the most intimate moments of her marriage she had not
experienced such intense sensations. Without thinking she
reached up and touched Andrew's sculpted face . . . and then
he was kissing her.

Often Micheline had stared at the mouth that now touched
hers. His lips were warm, firm, practiced—gentle at first,
tasting and savoring, then opening more forcefully as passions stirred and swelled. Micheline lost herself in the bliss of
Andrew's utterly masculine embrace. He was harder, warmer,
and more agile than Bernard had been, Micheline's senses
confirmed. Andrew even smelled better—his clean male scent
was intoxicating, and he tasted wonderful! He kissed her now,
long and hungrily, his thumb rubbing softly along her cheekbone and his lean fingers splayed within her glossy hair.
Micheline was hungry too. She strained against him, longing
to be closer still, and then her horse stamped beside them,
whinnying, and she broke free.

"It's only the horse," Sandhurst murmured in amusement.
"He won't tell anyone."

Feeling his warm mouth on her throat, and the accompany-
ing shiver that traveled down through her body, Micheline
stiffened.

"Let me go!"

He drew back in surprise, his brows raised.

"You always mock me with your eyes!" she accused him
irrationally. "Loose me!"

Staring as if he feared she'd lost her reason, Andrew sat
back on his heels and held up his hands in surrender, achingly
conscious of the proof of his desire that was outlined against
his breeches. "The last thing I was trying to do was 'mock
you with my eyes,' " he protested. "What's amiss?"

She suddenly felt vulnerable and humiliated, lying there in
the leaves. Struggling to her feet, Micheline cried, "You
attempted to *use* me, m'sieur, like some kitchen wench, out
here in the woods in broad daylight."

"I intended no such thing!"

"You think that I am a loose woman because I have been
married before, that I must now burn for the touch of a man,
but I can assure you that I haven't missed it at all!"

Sandhurst rose lithely, brushing leaves from his velvet
doublet. In response to Micheline's outburst he glanced up
and murmured satirically, "Indeed? Well, perhaps that's the

problem. Perhaps you have been missing a man's touch all
your life . . . unaware until a few moments ago—''

"You flatter yourself!" she interrupted, outraged. "In any
case, I'd say that's a matter for my *husband* to consider,
m'sieur. I *am* betrothed to another man, you know.''

Andrew swung easily onto his horse, then coolly lifted both
brows, his mouth quirking in a way that made her face burn.
"How quickly we forget. . . .''

CHAPTER 11

March 1–2, 1533

ARRIVING BACK AT THE CHÂTEAU, SANDHURST TURNED TO MICHEL-
ine in the courtyard and told her flatly that he wouldn't be
making any more sketches that afternoon. Then he went to
the *appartements des bains* in an attempt to scrub and sweat
away the edginess and desire that lingered from their encounter in the forest. Jeremy, summoned to bring fresh clothing,
waited for his friend to dress, and the two of them walked
back to their chamber together.

Andrew, his damp hair brushed back from his face, wore a
brooding look that few people ever saw. Jeremy knew it well.
He didn't like the signs: a muscle moved in Sandhurst's jaw
as he clenched and unclenched it, and the scar above his
mouth was almost white.

Hoping that a bit of humor might help, Jeremy ventured,
"Is something wrong, master? Have I been lax in the perfor-
mance of my duties?"

Without slowing his pace or looking over, Andrew did
smile slightly. "You're a twit."

Jeremy was unable to think of an appropriate response.
Upon reaching their chamber, Sandhurst went to the table that
sat before a window overlooking the courtyard.

"Make yourself useful, Jeremy, and take a look at these."

He walked over to find that his friend had spread fresh pen
drawings across the table. "Is this—"

"Micheline. Yes."

"God's teeth, Sandhurst, did you really do these?" he demanded in astonishment.

The sketches, though simple enough, were remarkably life-like. The artist had conveyed a sense of depth, of rounded grace emerging from the flat page, with a rain of parallel hatchings slanting from left to right across the paper in the shadowed areas. Culpepper could almost feel the delicate curves of Micheline's face: her high cheekbones, rather abbreviated nose, the tiny cleft in her chin, the sensual fullness of her lower lip, and the sweep of long lashes over eyes that were beautiful, intelligent, and somehow sad all at once. In contrast, her hair and shoulders were only suggested compared to the telling detail of her face.

"What do you think?" Andrew queried, not bothering with his friend's question.

"I think you're a genius!" Jeremy exclaimed, orange curls bobbing with the force of his nods. "I had no idea!"

"That's not what I mean," Sandhurst said slowly, his own gaze fixed on the series of drawings. "What do you think about the girl?"

"Oh! Well, she's beautiful! I've caught glimpses of her here and there, and I'd say that you've captured her looks with extraordinary accuracy." He paused, remembering their conversation in London, and chuckled. "She's certainly a far sight from what we imagined in England! No fourteen-year-old with spots, or a fat widow that the king longs to banish! In fact, I heard last night that François rather fancies her himself. I was talking to one of Anne d'Heilly's maids, and she thinks the king's mistress might be responsible for finding an English husband for Madame Tevoulère. She was worried that the girl might eventually come out of mourning and respond to François's advances. . . ."

Sighing shortly, Sandhurst arched an eyebrow. "Indeed? If that's the case, Anne may have complicated all our lives for nothing. It's doubtful that Micheline is capable of responding to *anyone's* advances."

"Oh!" Dumbfounded, Jeremy wondered if it was possible that the Earl of Sandhurst could have just suffered his first rejection . . . at the hands of his betrothed. What irony! "Am I to assume that your outing in the woods—uh—took an unfavorable turn?"

Andrew shot him a menacing look. "Oh, the meal was

fine! I was beginning to rather *like* the chit! It was later, after she took a spill from her horse, and I, ah—comforted her.''

"I see!''

"No, you don't. She liked it all well enough for a while. Perhaps too much! At that point she began reminding me that she's betrothed to another man.''

"But that's *you*! I should think you'd be *pleased*!''

"Well, I'm not!'' Sandhurst tossed down the drawing he'd been staring at and began pacing. "How would you like to be put off in favor of a *stranger*?''

Jeremy was becoming confused. "But that's you!'' he repeated.

"Micheline doesn't know that!''

"Why don't you just tell her and put an end to this insanity? We can take her home to England with us and everyone will live happily ever after.''

"Absolutely *not*!''

Shaking his head, Jeremy sat down on his meager bed. It all seemed perfectly simple to him, but as usual Sandhurst couldn't settle for the easy route.

"Have you decided, then, that you don't want to marry her?'' he queried rather weakly.

"I'm certainly not in love with her, if that's what you mean.''

"When did love become a prerequisite for marriage?''

"Perhaps it needn't be, but if I'm going to spend the rest of my life with one woman, it would be much more agreeable if we cared for each other. The thought of leaving my wife in the country while I enjoy a separate life in London is distasteful to me.'' As he talked, Andrew unconsciously rubbed his right thumb and forefinger together. "In any event, it's doubtful that Micheline Tevoulère would tolerate such an arrangement.''

"I don't mean to pry, but since I *am* personally involved to some degree, would you mind telling me what you're going to do? You won't tell the girl who you are, you're not in love with her, she's being loyal to a stranger that she doesn't know is you. . . .'' Jeremy's voice trailed off as he began to sense what was ahead.

"I'm not quite certain yet,'' Sandhurst was saying thoughtfully. "Perhaps I'll just wait and see what develops.''

Jeremy nodded dolefully. He should have known before they left Britain that it couldn't be a simple yes or no for his

friend. Sandhurst's nature had always led him to fight against
the current rather than surrender to its flow. Jeremy's instincts
suggested that Sandhurst might risk everything to discover if
Micheline Tevoulère would fall in love with a penniless artist
and choose him over an English nobleman. He sighed misera-
bly, wondering how long it would take for this situation to
resolve itself one way or another.

"You needn't moan and carry on, because it won't do any
good," Sandhurst said edgily. "After all, this is a matter of
principle."

Jeremy managed a rather sickly nod. "I was afraid of
that. . . ."

Wisps of steam drifted upward as Micheline reclined in her
bath. Extending a slender, shapely leg, she soaped it leisurely,
enjoying the lily-of-the-valley fragrance that enveloped her.
The water was very hot; in fact, the serving girls who had
filled the tub had warned her against getting in too soon, but
she welcomed the heat. Her breasts, gleaming at the water
line, were rosy, and she felt warm all over. How comforting
it would be, she reflected drowsily, to be able to wash
Andrew Selkirk's touch and kisses from her body. What was
more difficult was erasing them from her mind.

"Bonsoir!" Aimée called from the corridor. "May I come
in?"

"Yes, of course!" Micheline smiled, thinking that Aimée,
always full of energy and conversation, would be a perfect
distraction.

Aimée was already dressed for supper. Her glossy ebony
hair was swept up and studded with amethysts, and she wore
a beautiful gown of lavender silk. Pausing at the dresser to
pour herself a goblet of red wine, she inquired, "How was
your day? Did you enjoy posing for the portrait?"

"Well enough, I suppose."

Aimée sat down in a *caquetoire,* a chair with a trapezoid-
shaped seat and arms that bowed out to accommodate a lady's
voluminous skirts. Micheline's tone had suggested that she
didn't wish to discuss the matter further, and now she appeared totally engrossed in washing her left arm.

Never one to be put off easily, Aimée persisted. "Were
you posing for M'sieur Selkirk all day? I didn't see you once
after breakfast!"

"He did sketches of me until the sun made the light too

harsh," Micheline said carefully. "Then, we, umm—went riding for a while."

Aimée leaned forward in an effort to get a look at her friend's face. "That explains why you both were absent during the midday meal! Did you take a *dejeuner*?"

Micheline only nodded.

"What fun! You and M'sieur Selkirk would seem to be cultivating a friendship!"

"It grows cold in this bath. Would you hand me the towels?"

"Of course!" Aimée spread two on the floor for Micheline to stand on, then delivered the rest. "Why don't you put on a nice warm robe and join me in some wine, *chérie*? I've a feeling it might do you good."

Micheline obeyed silently, taking a plainer chair that Aimée had moved opposite her own. For a long minute she didn't move, sipping the strong wine and gazing into the fire.

At length Aimée leaned toward her and touched her hand. "Why won't you look at me? I wish that you would tell me what is bothering you. Did that Englishman do something to offend you?" She had a sudden frightening vision of Selkirk forcing himself on Micheline in the woods. Please, God, not that!

Setting down her wine, Micheline began combing out her damp hair. "Andrew is not dishonorable, if that's what you mean," she said tentatively. "At least I don't *think* he is." This last statement was accompanied by an involuntary smile.

Aimée blinked when she heard her use Selkirk's Christian name. "*Something* happened. I *know* it! I'm not asking only out of curiosity, Micheline. You should talk to someone. You've been through so much this past year, and have kept too many feelings inside. It will help you sort them out if you talk to a friend." Aimée was thinking, too, that they really knew very little about this English painter. Devastating good looks and charm were well enough, but could the man be trusted? The better informed Aimée was about Selkirk's behavior, the better able she would be to intercede if problems threatened.

"You needn't be suspicious of Andrew," Micheline said softly. "He has actually been very kind to me. He seems to genuinely like me. We had quite a nice day." She reached for her wine and sipped reflectively. "There's something about him that makes one relax and speak quite freely. He puts people at ease. He's charming, yes, but it's not an empty charm. He's warm, and witty in a dry sort of way, and I felt that he was honestly interested in everything I said. He encouraged me to talk while he drew me this morning, which made that much less monotonous, and I found myself telling him all about my past. It felt quite natural.''

An odd shiver prickled Aimée's scalp and traveled down her spine. She'd never heard Micheline talk this way before. All the signs were there. Whether Micheline realized it or not, she was infatuated with Andrew Selkirk, and Aimée only prayed that it wasn't love. With an effort she spoke in an even tone.

"Was your ride in the forest as nice as the morning had been?"

"Yes, for the most part. As it turns out, Andrew shares my love for horses, and we had a marvelous time racing across the meadows. He won, of course, but he wasn't smug about it in that way men often are. We had a lovely meal—he'd stolen all sorts of wonderful things from the kitchens! I can't remember the last time I had so much fun.''

Seeing the dreamy look in Micheline's blue eyes, Aimée felt slightly sick. How could this have happened and *what* could be done about it? "You must tell me the rest, *chérie*. Something must have gone wrong; I could see it in your face earlier.''

"It wasn't Andrew's fault. We were riding back to the château through the forest. I went ahead since I knew the way, and I suppose I wasn't paying attention. We came around a turn and there was an enormous pile of trees. My horse made the jump, but it was all so sudden that I flew off—''

"Mon Dieu!" Aimée exclaimed. "Are you hurt?"

"No, no. I must have fallen correctly, and the leaves were a cushion. But Andrew rushed to my aid, and he held me against him . . . and he kissed me.''

"I knew it!"

"That's all, though. It was just a kiss. When I asked him to stop, he did.''

Aimée nodded thoughtfully and sipped her wine, then caught Micheline's gaze and held it. "And why did you ask him to stop?"

"Well, because it was wrong! I—I'm betrothed to another man!'' Her cheeks were flushed with emotion.

"Are you certain there wasn't another reason?" Aimée asked gently.

Micheline closed her eyes and put her hands up to cool the heat in her face. "It's so difficult for me to even think this, let alone say it!" When she opened her eyes, they were brimming with tears. "Oh, Aimée, do you remember the day I told you I didn't think I would ever be attracted to another man again?"

"Andrew Selkirk has changed your mind, hasn't he? But, Micheline, this man is a painter! He's not the marrying sort, or he would be married by now. It's quite obvious that M'sieur Selkirk loves women and they love him. He may break hearts without intending to. Is he aware of your betrothal?"

Micheline nodded mutely, swallowing tears.

"And even if this did prove to be true love for him, what kind of life would you have? Selkirk must travel to paint—he may not even *have* a home!"

"It's all beside the point, Aimée. I've agreed to marry the Earl of Sandhurst, and I intend to keep my word." Micheline spoke with careful control, determined not to cry. "What I am feeling about Andrew is just a temporary flight of fancy. From now on I will keep my emotions in check. It will be a test of my maturity."

Wincing slightly at her friend's speech, Aimée wondered, "But what if it's not a 'flight of fancy'? What if it's *love*?"

Micheline averted her eyes. "I don't want to fall in love. That's part of the reason I agreed to marry Lord Sandhurst. There's more pain than pleasure in love."

The court was sitting down to supper when Micheline Tevoulère entered the hall. The crowd was so large that no one remarked upon her tardiness. The seigneur de St. Briac made a place for her to his left and she gave him a bright smile.

Across the table Sandhurst watched Micheline while attempting to converse with Queen Eleanor, who sat next to him. He felt sorry for the naturally vivacious queen, who had entered into marriage with François with high hopes that had been immediately dashed by Anne d'Heilly. Since her arrival in France three years ago, Eleanor had felt awkwardly out of place. Queen Claude had died in 1524, and Anne had been establishing her position at court since the king's return from captivity in Spain seven years ago. Eleanor had been used as a bargaining chip between her brother, Emperor Charles V, and François, and though she was now both queen and wife, her husband generally pretended she didn't exist. François did not even want children, since Claude had given him seven, five of whom still lived. A woman of great passion, Eleanor nearly always slept alone; and most of the power she should have had as queen had long ago been claimed by Anne d'Heilly.

"Are you married, M'sieur Selkirk?" the queen was inquiring in Spanish-accented French.

"No." He forced himself to stop glancing at Micheline and turned to smile at Eleanor. "My friends tell me that I'm growing old and should take a wife, however."

"How sad for the rest of us," she murmured, then put a bite of roasted lark into her mouth, regarding him as she chewed. The Englishman's looks were so arresting that his intelligent, charming personality seemed almost incidental. Tonight he wore a doublet of slate-gray velvet that fit close to his tapering chest. Snowy-white linen showed through the slashings and made a pleated fraise against his tanned neck. The torch and candlelight accentuated not only the numerous golden strands among Andrew's light brown hair but also the sculpted contours of his face and the scar above his mouth. Unlike every other man present, he wore no jewels on his clothing or on chains about his neck. Many of the courtiers had rings on every finger; Andrew Selkirk wore only a sapphire set in gold on the last finger of his left hand.

Now his handsome face was in profile, for he was looking at Micheline Tevoulère. The queen, desperate to keep his attention, queried, "How did you come by your scar, m'sieur?"

His brows flicked upward in mild surprise. "I took a spill from a very large horse when I was very small, Your Majesty. I'm told I fell right on my face, and a sharp stone inflicted this injury."

"And yet you wear no beard," she mused. "You know, my husband first grew a beard to cover some scars on his face, and now it seems that every man has followed suit."

"Shall I?" Andrew wondered, amused.

"Oh, no!" she cried. "It would be a crime to hide *your* face, m'sieur. And that scar is . . . dangerously appealing."

Hardly knowing how to react, he replied carefully, "You flatter me, Your Majesty!" then turned his attention to the lark on his own dish. Sandhurst was all too familiar with the queen's expression. Her dark almond-shaped eyes had gone dreamy and her frankly sensuous lips were slightly parted when she gazed at him, as if she found him more appetizing than she did the food. Andrew sighed inwardly. The last thing he needed right now was the queen of France lusting after him!

Micheline, meanwhile, appeared not to notice Sandhurst or his plight. She was conversing with Robert de la Marck, seigneur de Florange, who sat to her left. Florange was as old a friend of the king's as St. Briac. Though over forty now, he was still known as "the young adventurer," and he still loved women as much as ever. Tonight he basked in Micheline Tevoulère's beauty. Clad in a gown of rich blue velvet sprinkled with pearls and rubies, she wore more of the gems on thin gold chains about her neck and studded throughout her upswept brandy-hued curls.

"I shall miss you when you go to England, madame," Florange said frankly, sipping his wine.

"There will be another lady to take my place at court, monseigneur," she replied. Dessert was being served and Micheline took advantage of the slight interruption to glance down at Andrew as she reached for a cluster of grapes. The sight of Queen Eleanor's rapt expression while he spoke to her, gesturing with one hand, made Micheline's face burn.

"There are some ladies who cannot be replaced," Florange was saying wistfully. "A few years back, your friend Aimée was one of those special cases. She became betrothed to St. Briac before any of us had a chance, and now you have done the same!"

"You flatter me, monseigneur."

They chatted on until the last course, the *boute-hors*, consisting of wine and spices, had been served. Florange found himself fascinated as much by the contrast between Micheline and Aimée as by his companion's physical beauty. Aimée had always been effervescent and guilelessly outspoken. Micheline, on the other hand, was much more reserved, even careful. There was a mysterious luminance in her large blue eyes that hinted at not only sadness but passion. Her manner bespoke a confident intelligence and breeding; there was never any effort on Micheline's part to impress. Florange thought that Micheline Tevoulère was a tantalizing enigma, one that he wished he might solve himself.

People were rising from the table as jugglers and tumblers streamed into the hall. A dancing monkey capered about through the fresh herbs and rushes strewn across the floor, behaving outrageously for the amusement of the court. Micheline had begun to feel uneasy with the seigneur de Florange's scrutiny and now seized upon this disruption to gravitate toward Thomas and Aimée.

Before long a minstrel appeared, singing to the accompaniment of a harp. To Micheline's surprise, the king approached her and bade her dance with him. She seemed to have no choice and was happy that she was familiar with the *gaillarde,* a dance that consisted of advancing, bowing, and retiring in a pattern that conformed with the music.

"You are looking exceptionally beautiful tonight, *ma chère,*" François remarked with a wink.

It seemed to Micheline that a plague of insincerity must have spread among the Frenchmen. "How kind you are, sire."

"I speak only the truth." He reached up to touch her hand and struck an attitude. "How is your portrait coming along?"

The mere thought of Andrew Selkirk made her blush, but she hoped that the king would assume that the rosemary-scented firelight was to blame. "M'sieur Selkirk has made only pen drawings thus far, sire, but I was able to look at them, and he appears to be very talented."

"The drawings resembled you?"

"In a flattering way, yes."

"Bon!" François beamed. "I can't say I'm surprised, however. He brought a painting of the Earl of Sandhurst's sister to show as an example of his work, and it was absolutely splendid!"

Micheline was still digesting this information as the music ended. The king bowed; she curtsied and took his arm to return to the crowd. No sooner had they parted than Andrew Selkirk appeared before her and requested the next dance.

Micheline was about to refuse, but there was something in his deep brown eyes that gave her pause. "If you wish, m'sieur."

"I do wish."

The music began and at least two dozen couples milled into the middle of the hall. Sandhurst and Micheline came last and stood facing each other for rather a long time, their eyes locked. The music had begun and the other dancers had advanced, bowed, and retired once before Sandhurst made a move. When he did, he only stepped forward, touched her hand, and declared, "I want to talk to you. Alone."

Micheline blinked in surprise, then blushed. "That is not possible, m'sieur."

"What is amiss? Are you afraid I'll go mad and ravish you?" He almost asked if she wished it, but held his tongue. "I wish only a few moments of private conversation in the courtyard."

Caught in the spell of his eyes and the pressure of his hard male hand on hers, Micheline capitulated.

"*Alors*," she whispered. What harm could there be in a few moments alone with Andrew Selkirk?

CHAPTER 12

March 2–6, 1533

IT WAS PAST MIDNIGHT AND THE SKY WAS BLACK, COVERED BY A ruffled blanket of silvery-blue clouds. The exit Sandhurst had chosen at random led into gardens rather than the courtyard, so Micheline found herself alone with the Englishman in a green tunnel of clipped hedges.

"Everyone was watching us leave!" she whispered in distress. "I could feel their eyes on us!"

"What do you care? You're quitting France in a few weeks, aren't you?"

"*Oui*, m'sieur!" Micheline was confused over why she was so angry with him, except that it helped to distract her from his nearness. She could see his eyes, intent as always, in the moonlight, and if she took one step, their bodies would meet.

"Do you speak English?" Andrew asked suddenly.

"Of course!" Micheline replied in his native language. "And I am fluent in Spanish and German as well."

Her accent delighted him. She spoke with confident perfection, and each word was quite clear, but all the same there

was a French lilt in her English that was utterly appealing.
Sandhurst laughed softly, and the sound was low and masculine in the darkness. Micheline's heart stirred involuntarily.

"What was it you wanted to say to me, m'sieur?" she
inquired sternly. "I hope I have not made a spectacle of
myself before the entire court so that you could ask me if I
know English!"

He wanted to touch her, to press her soft body against his
hard one, to taste her mouth, to open her gown . . . but all of
these things were out of the question.

"I realize that I told you I would not speak of your betrothal to the Earl of Sandhurst unless you raised the subject
first, but the events of this afternoon compel me to break that
promise." The square bodice of Micheline's gown revealed
high curving breasts that shone in the moonlight. "I want to
know how you can justify marrying a man you've never
seen!"

"Why are you so concerned?"

"I do not care for games, Michelle. You and I are not
strangers. Indeed, we are friends . . . and more, I suspect. I
have begun to feel that I know you, even understand you to
some extent, and the more I know, the harder it is for me to
comprehend how this betrothal could have happened. You
simply don't seem the kind of woman who would commit to
wedding a total stranger, regardless of his title or wealth."

Micheline turned from his gaze, her face in profile as she
replied softly, "It does not matter if I know this man or not.
Nor do I care for his title or wealth, beyond the knowledge
that I shall live in comfort. Even if I were acquainted with the
Earl of Sandhurst, I know now that I could not judge him. I
have learned, lately, that believing you know a person as well
as yourself is the mark of a fool . . . or a person in love."
She glanced up to find him staring hard at her, and gave him
a sweet, rueful smile. "Perhaps people in love *are* fools, and
in the future, I intend to be neither. None of us really knows
anyone, as you have doubtless realized in your acquaintance
with me, m'sieur. Everyone wears a mask, portraying a
character that he thinks will be most acceptable to the
audience."

"You're quite disenchanted for so young a lady," Sandhurst
murmured.

"I've lived more than most my age, and I like to think of
myself as realistic now. I have lost my appetite for dreams."

"And for romance?"

"Yes." Micheline looked away again.

"Appetites have a way of returning," he remarked thoughtfully.

"I appreciate that bit of advice, m'sieur. I shall be on my guard."

Sandhurst reached out slowly and encircled her slim arm with his fingers. He felt her stiffen, her eyes still averted.

"Have you no *feelings*, Micheline?"

Stung, she turned to retort, and found herself in his arms. Like a butterfly in a net, she yielded to Andrew's strength, for she was caught up in a powerful current of sensation that made her weak yet exhilarated all at once. What had passed between them that afternoon had done nothing to abate Micheline's yearning for this man; in truth the taste had left her hungrier than ever. She had tried to keep such cravings at bay, yet now that he was touching her, her mind was effortlessly overpowered by her senses.

Andrew's hands were touching her. One was on her back, seeming to burn through the velvet as he pressed her against his hard chest, and the other was at the nape of her neck, where strong male fingers laced through her hair. She could feel the muscles in his arms flex against her softer flesh, and then there was the sensation of his mouth upon her own.

Quel splendeur, Micheline thought. They kissed gently, over and over, learning the texture of each other's lips. When he kissed her more purposefully, his mouth opening on hers so that she could taste him, Micheline thought that she could not stand if he were not holding her. Her bones seemed to melt, while an odd, exquisite heat began to radiate from the place between her legs. Bernard had *never* made her feel this way! Was Andrew Selkirk a sorcerer?

As she returned his kisses, her lips parting in a sweet, sensual way that made Sandhurst's blood pulse to his loins, he slid his hand caressingly down from her neck. How soft her throat was! Micheline's lily-of-the-valley fragrance filled his nostrils as he touched all five fingertips to the swell of her breast. Instinctively she pressed nearer, and he felt the tautness of her nipple through the velvet bodice. Her breast was lush and firm against his palm.

"Your heart is beating madly," Sandhurst whispered as he raised his head.

Micheline couldn't speak. She stared up at him with huge

blue eyes, her cheeks flushed, lips rosy. Finally, as his mouth
scorched the base of her neck once more, she gasped, "*Nom
de Dieu . . .* what am I doing?"

"You're feeling, Michelle," Andrew murmured, aware of
the effect his warm breath had on her. "Relax."

Somehow she found herself on a stone bench farther into
the garden. He was caressing her arms through the velvet of
her gown, kissing her temples, her eyelids, her throat, her
shoulders, and then the first curves of her breasts. They felt
swollen, aching in the same way as her woman's place.
Andrew was unlacing the front of her gown just a bit.

"You smell delicious," Micheline heard herself whisper as
she buried her face in his gleaming hair. She wanted to tell
him how much she loved his hands, but something stopped
her.

"So do you, fondling," he returned, looking up with an
engagingly boyish smile that totally melted her heart. "And
you taste even better."

"*Sangdieu!*" She uttered St. Briac's favorite epithet when
Sandhurst's mouth touched her suddenly bare breast. Liquid
fire seemed to course through her veins, leaving showers of
sparks in its wake. First he tenderly kissed the taut nipple,
then circled it with the warm, moist tip of his tongue. Micheline
felt faint. His hand moved to cup her other breast while he
kissed the first hard peak the way he had kissed her mouth.

Micheline had never dreamed of such arousal. She could
feel Andrew's heart beating against her midsection, and suddenly she realized that he, too, was aroused. The thought of
his manhood made her tremble with excitement.

"Selkirk!" It was the voice of St. Briac, calling from the
château. "Are you out there?"

Micheline plummeted back to reality as Andrew lifted his
head abruptly.

"Help me, m'sieur!" she cried frantically, fumbling with
the laces on her gown.

"We aren't obliged to answer, you know." he told her in a
low voice, his brown eyes searching her face.

"Yes! We must go back!" Her cheeks were flaming. "I
am so embarrassed! What shall we say?"

"We don't have to explain to anyone, Michelle. You and I
are adults." Her obvious humiliation bothered him, but he
brushed her hands aside nonetheless and laced her bodice
neatly.

"It's cold. We shouldn't have come outside at night!" Micheline exclaimed. Suddenly she was shivering all over.

Sandhurst blinked, but helped her up and put an arm around her. "I apologize, madame. It was thoughtless of me."

"No, no, I was foolish. I just didn't *think*!"

Glancing down at her, he saw the familiar distracted expression on her lovely face and knew that the barriers had gone up once again.

"You go on inside. I'll explain to St. Briac."

She obeyed gratefully as they approached the château. Thomas made a tall, broad-shouldered silhouette against the windows, and Micheline was relieved to see that his expression was one of concern rather than anger.

"We began to walk, chatting about the portrait," Andrew was saying casually, "and forgot the time. Micheline finds that she's a bit chilled, so she's going in."

"*Bonsoir*, gentlemen," she called over a shoulder, then the door closed behind her.

St. Briac stared after her. "You do know that the lady is betrothed."

"I'm reminded of that fact hourly, it seems. Was it concern over Madame Tevoulère's honor that sent you in search of us?"

"No. I'm Micheline's friend, not her keeper. The king was speculating about your absence and I merely hoped to avert a serious problem. If François thought that you had designs on Madame, he'd banish you from court in an instant."

"Why? Because his own designs on her have been thwarted by the lady herself?"

St. Briac rubbed his bearded jaw and smiled ironically. "Perhaps. Micheline is a fascinating woman, and all the more fascinating to the king because she was a challenge. He only agreed to this betrothal with the Earl of Sandhurst because he'd become resigned to the fact that Micheline wouldn't yield to him . . . or to any other man. He's quite fond of her, so when she insisted that this was what she wanted, he agreed to it. I've seen him watch you with her tonight, though, and I assure you the king isn't about to let someone else succeed where he's failed."

"Hmmm. For some reason I thought that this betrothal was the king's own idea."

Thomas shook his head. "My wife told me that the request came from King Henry—and that Micheline was mentioned specifically. It seems that Lord Sandhurst has a fetish for Frenchwomen.''

"Really!" Andrew exclaimed in surprise, smothering a wild urge to laugh. "And how did he happen to choose Madame Tevoulère?''

"There were some visitors from England at the court in January, and word has it that they returned home singing the praises of Micheline.''

"I see. That's very interesting.''

"Well, it's none of my affair, and though I'm not certain I approve of this marriage, Micheline's mind seems to be made up. I'd hate to see her . . . hurt in the meantime.''

"As you say, her mind is made up, and she strikes me as a singularly headstrong woman. It's highly unlikely that she'll be swept away by passion on my account, don't you think?'' Sandhurst made a sound that was part distress, part discomfiture. "In any event, I like Madame Tevoulère a great deal. I have no intention of harming her. I hope that she'll be happy as much as you do.''

St. Briac narrowed his eyes slightly in the moonlight, trying to read the Englishman's face. "Well, good. I'm relieved to hear it.''

"Now that we've settled all this, I'm ready to go back inside. I could use another cup of wine, followed by a long night's sleep.''

The next morning the king went on a hunt with a few of his courtiers, including St. Briac. Usually a band of privy ladies joined the men periodically during these excursions, but this time cold weather prevented that. Three days without female company seemed like torture to François. He found himself thinking excessively of Micheline Tevoulère and brooding about the scene between her and Andrew Selkirk. The sight of them dancing together had elicited comments all around about the attractive pair they made, but the court had positively buzzed when the Englishman led Micheline out into the garden. What had they been doing for so long? If Selkirk imagined that Micheline was within his grasp, it was up to the king to set him right. It was hard enough for François to restrain *himself*, but it was easier somehow to accept defeat knowing that she would marry a stranger. He was not about to let some common painter turn her head.

The hunting party arrived back at Fontainebleau in the

evening of the third day. The next morning, after his council meeting, François sent word to Andrew Selkirk that he would like to see him in the royal chamber immediately.

The message was carried two rooms away to the antechamber, where Sandhurst was at work on his portrait of Micheline. The light was perfect, soft and golden, and he was staring intently at his subject, brush in hand.

Since the night in the garden Micheline had been distant, and Sandhurst had accepted her unspoken rules. He sensed that she was afraid of the feelings he'd stirred up in her, and was honest enough to admit, if only to himself, that those feelings had been reciprocated. Still, Andrew wasn't prepared to face them. It was easier to step back, to be charming, witty, and casual, and to paint. These past three days they'd continued to converse, but not about personal matters. Micheline asked questions about his craft and watched the progress of her portrait, and they talked about horses and their separate countries, sometimes speaking in English, and occasionally they laughed together but broke off if the air grew too heavy with intimacy. That tension in the air was present all too often. At times all it took was an unexpected glance or smile and then Andrew and Micheline seemed to be touching across the room, both of them aching in silence because they were not.

When the page arrived with the note from King François, Sandhurst read it with a measure of surprise. He knew the king had just returned the previous night, and it was now barely nine in the morning. What was so important?

"It seems that your king wants to see me," he informed Micheline while wiping his hands on a rag. Turning to the page, he asked, "Shall I wash up first?"

"No, m'sieur. His Majesty bade me bring you immediately."

Sandhurst looked askance at Micheline and shrugged. "I've no idea what this is about, or how long it will take. If you want to do something else—"

"I'll wait." She smiled. "I can study my painting for flaws."

"Since there aren't any," Andrew parried with a laugh, "that should keep you occupied indefinitely!"

He followed the page to the royal bedchamber, pausing momentarily in the doorway to admire the great oval room, with its antique borders, rich ceiling, and magnificent chimney.

"Ah, M'sieur Selkirk! There you are!" François rose from a carved walnut chair, smiling in greeting.

"At your service, sire," Andrew replied with a touch of satire, "provided you'll tolerate my appearance."

The king narrowed his eyes for an instant. The Englishman looked quite dashing, with his tousled burnished hair, shirt-sleeves rolled up in the absence of a doublet, and the shirt itself unlaced to reveal a portion of his chest. There were smudges of paint in various colors on not only Andrew's hands and forearms, but also a few on his snowy shirt and tanned jaw.

"Think nothing of it. I'm glad to see that you are hard at work. Sit down, won't you?"

Sandhurst took a chair opposite the king's. A servant brought them jewel-encrusted goblets of wine, then departed after a nod from his monarch.

The two men chatted briefly about the weather and the just-completed hunt, then François inquired about the progress on the portrait of Micheline.

"It's going quite well," Sandhurst replied carefully, watching the Frenchman over the rim of his goblet. "Madame Tevoulère is an ideal subject. Her face is not only beautiful; her spirit is beautiful as well. It is a challenge for me to capture both the inner and outer woman on canvas."

"You seem quite taken with the lady." François spoke casually, but his hazel eyes were slightly narrowed as he stroked his trim beard and waited for a response.

"What normal man would not be?"

"That's all very well, m'sieur, but I must ask you to keep your admiration to yourself. As you are well aware, Micheline is betrothed to one of your noblest countrymen—"

"It's hardly a love match, sire," Andrew heard himself interrupt in an even, hard-edged voice.

"It is what Madame Tevoulère has chosen! Lord Sandhurst will one day be a duke! His reputation is unblemished; he is wealthy; he has everything to offer!"

Andrew regarded his wine for a moment before glancing up to reply. "In short, the Earl of Sandhurst is everything that I am not—including honorable, I take it."

"I do not wish to quarrel with you, M'sieur Selkirk. The truth is that I like you very much, and I am highly respectful of your considerable talent. However, you *are* a commoner . . . and you are an artist. I've never known a painter who was constant. You must travel because of your work; what could you offer a lady like Madame Tevoulère even if she were within your grasp?''

"Love, perhaps?" Sandhurst wondered ironically, touching a forefinger to his mouth.

"Now, now, m'sieur, let us be serious!" François exclaimed with a hearty laugh. "We are both men; you can be frank with me! It's not Micheline you love, but the challenge! You are blessed with good looks and considerable charm, and are no doubt used to winning the affections of any lady you choose. You're a free spirit. I'm certain that you have enjoyed the favors of highborn, beautiful, and frequently married females in your bed, but Micheline is not like them.''

"I am aware of that, sire.''

"If that is true, then you will keep your distance. This lady is vulnerable. Her heart is mending still after the death of her beloved husband. I am asking you to leave her in peace.''

Sandhurst rose, well aware that it was rude to do so before the king dismissed him. "I appreciate your advice, sire, and in response I can only repeat what I said to the seigneur de St. Briac in the garden the other night. I have no intention of causing Madame Tevoulère further distress. I admire the lady very much and value her happiness as much as you do.''

François stood up, narrowing his eyes at the Englishman. "In that case, you won't have a problem remembering your place. This is not a conversation I wish to repeat.''

Sketching a bow, Andrew replied, "Nor do I, sire. If you'll excuse me, I ought to return to work.''

"By all means. I hope that you will direct all your attention there. Good day, m'sieur.''

Alone again, the king slumped in his chair, sipping his wine. He sensed that he'd lost this battle of wits, but his opponent had prevailed so subtly that he couldn't really call him on it. He wanted the painting completed, but at length he decided that if Selkirk appeared to be courting Micheline's favor in the future, he would be asked to leave Fontainebleau.

Across the room, the door to the queen's second antechamber was slightly ajar. On the other side Anne d'Heilly drew back and knit her brows thoughtfully. She'd been strongly attracted to Andrew Selkirk herself since the first moment she saw him, but now it seemed to her that it might be advantageous to encourage whatever was brewing between him and Micheline. It galled her to think of her rival with so devastatingly attractive a man, but overall, this might be better for Anne than her original scheme of marrying Micheline off to an English nobleman.

If the girl ran off with a penniless artist, she would disgrace not only herself but her king as well, for *he* would have to explain to the jilted bridegroom. How *furious* François would be! Anne thought gleefully, rubbing her delicate hands together. It really would be perfect. Such outrageous behavior would make Micheline's permanent absence from the French court an absolute certainty.

CHAPTER 13

March 10–11, 1533

DRESSED ALL IN PINK AND LOOKING AS SWEET AS A RIPE STRAW-berry, Anne d'Heilly sat at her writing table and stared out at the bank of pale gray clouds that rose above the white horizon. It was going to snow. Everyone said so. A huge storm was predicted—an oddity in France, but not an impossibility. The temperature was right, just below freezing, and there was an eerie stillness in the air outside, broken periodically by sudden gusts of wind. People were pointing most often to that thick layer of clouds and the lack of color in the sky. Those two signs meant snow, and lots of it.

Anne twisted her long necklace of pearls around a finger, thinking. A snowstorm could be used to bring Micheline Tevoulère and Andrew Selkirk together. The question was where—and how?

Thomas had gone riding with the king, so Aimée, missing the company of her friend, decided to test the waters and visit the antechamber where Micheline's portrait was in progress.

"May I come in?" she inquired hesitantly from the doorway.

Sandhurst made a sweeping gesture of welcome with one hand, a paintbrush between his fingers. "Welcome, madame."

He smiled. "No doubt my subject is starved for the sight of any face but mine."

Clad in a gown of soft peach velvet parted in front to display a silken leaf-green petticoat, Micheline was looking especially lovely. There was not much sunlight this morning, yet her curls still gleamed softly, and she wore a contented smile that shone even in her eyes.

"How good it is to see you!" Micheline exclaimed, rising to embrace her friend. "I called on you day before yesterday, but Suzette told me that Ninon wasn't well and that you were with her. Do tell me that my little angel is recovered!"

"Little hellion is more like it, as well you know!" Aimée laughed, returning Micheline's hug. How good it was to see her dear friend glowing and laughing, whatever the reason! "Ninon complained of a sore throat, and she sniffled for an hour or two, but I think she's stronger than her father. After a nap she ate ravenously and now is jumping up and down in our chambers in anticipation of the snow!"

"I'm glad to hear it! And I'm so glad you've come. I have missed you terribly, Aimée."

"It's mutual, *chérie*. I decided that it was time to discover whether all these hours you've spent away from me have been worthwhile. May I see the portrait?"

Micheline glanced up. "Andrew?"

"Why not?" he replied lightly. "*I* have nothing to hide!"

Approaching the painter and his canvas, Aimée's eyes traveled lightly over Andrew Selkirk and she almost sighed aloud. Even in fawn breeches and a simple paint-smudged white shirt, he was the handsomest man she had ever seen— besides St. Briac, of course, who was in a category of his own. This Englishman might deserve his own category, too, Aimée mused, for he also seemed to possess that rare combination of splendid looks and charismatic personality. Both attributes were different from her husband's, but no less potent. Aimée decided all of this quite dispassionately, for she was in love with St. Briac, but she couldn't help wondering what effect Andrew Selkirk must have on Micheline, whose heart was like a budding flower that longed to open.

"What do you think?" her friend was asking.

"Just bear in mind that it's far from complete," Andrew interjected.

Aimée turned her attention from the two of them to the portrait. "*Parbleu!*" she whispered. "It's extraordinary!"

Although the painting was unfinished, it was unmistakably Micheline who looked at her from the canvas—or rather looked at Andrew Selkirk, for her exquisite iris-blue eyes were filled with longing and sadness. The rest of the face was perfectly Micheline, too, from the proud tilt of her chin with its tiny cleft to the sensuous curve of her lower lip to her abbreviated nose and elegant cheekbones. Aimée was transfixed.

"Capturing Micheline on canvas has been a tremendous challenge for me," Andrew murmured as he studied the painting himself for the thousandth time. "Of course, it's impossible—"

"Oh, no, m'sieur, you have had astonishing success!" cried Aimée.

"Isn't he talented?" Micheline chimed in. "Look at the background!" It consisted of muted trees that might have been those in the forest of Fontainebleau during springtime. A soft meadow receded from the figure of Micheline, leading to the trees, which were veiled in a thin mist. "Andrew used a technique called sfumato that he learned from a master who trained under Leonardo da Vinci. That haze over the trees is effected with oil glazes laid one over the other, which softens the background."

Sandhurst elaborated rather absently. "The purpose is to create a dreamlike atmosphere, only for the background. It's thought that this allows the inmost nature of the true subject to be sensed more deeply. In this instance, I like the contrast. It seems to work for Micheline . . . making her beauty and the radiance of her spirit that much more striking."

"I agree, m'sieur." Aimée nodded, staring up at him. He was so intent on the portrait that he appeared not to notice her scrutiny. Could Andrew Selkirk actually be in love with Micheline—permanently? This painting told her that the answer was yes. Even the most perfect technique couldn't allow one to reach inside Micheline's soul, could it? Aimée resolved to see the other portrait she'd heard that he had brought to Fontainebleau as a sample of his work, so that she might compare the two.

Meanwhile, Micheline had begun to blush, uncomfortable with all the emotion in the air. "How fortunate I am that Andrew was so well trained in Florence! He knows all manner of tricks to make me look more beautiful in this portrait than I could ever hope to be in life!"

Sandhurst merely turned his head and stared at her with

brown eyes so compelling that Micheline's cheeks fairly flamed. Standing between them, Aimée felt invisible.

"That's nonsense," he said softly in English. "No amount of training or talent could begin to do you justice, Michelle."

Aimée didn't speak English, but the tone of his voice was universal. The currents of yearning in the room made her wish she could disappear.

"I should be going," she murmured hoarsely. "My daughters will be looking for me."

Just then a page appeared with a message for Andrew. He broke the seal, noting that it was Queen Eleanor's, and scanned the words, his brow furrowing.

"The queen asks that Micheline and I meet her at her cottage in the woods. Apparently the king will be dining there as well, and they want to have a private meal with us to discuss our progress with the portrait." He looked up. "Rather odd, don't you think?"

"They may want you to paint the queen," ventured Micheline.

"*C'est possible . . .*" acknowledged Aimée with a puzzled frown.

"I don't like the look of the sky. What if a snowstorm descends while we're off at this cottage?" he said, worried.

"I've been to the queen's little retreat in the forest," Aimée reassured Sandhurst. "It's nicer than most houses in France. Very cozy, with plenty to eat and plenty of firewood. The king had it built deep in the woods, hoping that the queen would go there to meditate, leaving him alone with Anne, I suppose. At any rate, I can think of worse places to be snowbound, if it comes to that."

"If the king's there, I don't suppose we'd be snowbound long," added Micheline. "Besides, it sounds like a pleasant change to me. I'd enjoy the ride."

"Well, then, we'll go." Sandhurst paused, smiling ironically. "Not that we had any choice . . ."

By the time Andrew and Micheline set out for the queen's cottage, the snow had already begun to fall, swirling about them in gentle gusts that seemed quite harmless.

They rode the same horses as before, both riders bundled up against the elements. Micheline wore a hooded cloak of green velvet that was lined and trimmed with fox, while Andrew had changed into breeches, doublet, and a fur-lined

jerkin of toasty brown velvet. The latter two garments were
embroidered with fine golden thread. Micheline had never
seen him so richly garbed, and thought to herself as she rode
behind him through the lacy curtain of snow that Andrew
looked positively royal. He certainly had every other attribute
of a highborn gentleman. He sat gracefully erect in the saddle, exuding an easy confidence. Micheline had never glimpsed
a profile more aristocratic than Andrew's. Better still, he was
keenly intelligent, strong yet tender, and possessed a taut,
articulate sense of humor.

Why couldn't Andrew Selkirk *be* the Earl of Sandhurst,
instead of a common itinerant painter? It was impossible that
her betrothed, for all his titles and noble blood, could be a
better man. Micheline sighed softly, her breath making a puff
in the frigid air, and reminded herself that it was all just as
well. Love was a trap; no one knew that better than she. If
Bernard, whom she had trusted and loved since childhood,
could not be faithful to her, then no one could. It would be
even more dangerous to give one's heart to a man like
Andrew, who could have any woman he chose. It was ridiculous to imagine that he might be content and loyal to one
woman for a lifetime. It was probably better that he hadn't
married.

As for the Earl of Sandhurst, he must not want love any
more than she did. They would become friends, Micheline
hoped, and build a life together rooted in mutual respect. She
would have lots of children, many friends, estates filled with
books, and certainly there would be wonderful horses. It
would be a comfortable, secure life, which was just what she
longed for.

"Are you all right?" Andrew called, turning in his saddle
to look back at her. "Warm enough?"

"Oh—oh, yes!" Her heart skipped at the sight of his
gentle smile. Snowflakes glinted like diamonds on his ruffled
golden hair.

"Good. You were looking terribly serious."

"I was . . . just wondering what Queen Eleanor wants with
us."

"Well, we'll find out soon enough. According to her directions, we are halfway there."

A minute later Andrew chose a right fork in the path,
which led them deeper into the forest. After another half hour

Micheline caught sight of a stone building through the trees and thickening snowfall.

The cottage appeared charming, as Aimée had promised, and there was a small stable in back stocked with plenty of hay, but there was no smoke coming from the chimneys. Sandhurst saw to the horses first, his brow tensed with worry, then he joined Micheline where she waited in front of the cottage.

"I don't think the queen has arrived yet," she said, looking puzzled.

"I suggest we find out." He knocked, but there was no response. "I suppose we should go inside and wait. Would that be ill-mannered?"

"I don't think that Queen Eleanor would expect us to stand on ceremony in this weather. In any case, she's a nice person. Even if the sun were out, she would doubtless want us to make ourselves at home until her arrival."

"I'm surprised that servants weren't sent on ahead to start a fire and prepare things," Andrew remarked. He threw open the heavy wooden door and stood back to allow Micheline to enter first.

"*Mon Dieu!*" she exclaimed. "Isn't it pretty!"

"Quite," was his wry response.

What appeared from the outside to be little more than a well-tended peasant's cottage was a different matter inside. The walls were paneled in carved oak, and the floor, richly tiled in a pattern of red, blue, and ivory, was strewn with fresh herbs and dried rose petals. The furnishings were elegant pieces of oiled walnut, and included crimson-upholstered chairs, a dresser filled with dishes, a long table bracketed by benches, and, on the far side of the room, a luxurious carved bed hung with blue and gold velvet curtains. Its deep feather tick boasted a counterpane made of what appeared to be the pelts of white foxes.

There was plenty of dry wood stacked against the wall, and Sandhurst busied himself laying ample fires in both stone fireplaces. Micheline, meanwhile, was opening cupboard and dresser doors to discover all manner of fresh provisions. There were potatoes, apples, carrots, pomegranates, a large chunk of cured ham, eggs, a pitcher of sweet cream, a jar of sweetmeats and dried figs, several stoppered flasks of strong wine, and a dish of butter. In addition, Micheline found four newly killed pigeons hanging next to the back door.

"No one could starve to death here," she remarked, "but I don't see what the queen intends to serve us and the king for dinner."

"Perhaps her servants are bringing it from the château. It's obvious that they've been looking after this place. Those pigeons couldn't be more than a day old."

"Everything is quite fresh, owing partially to the temperature, I suppose. The cream looks like it's straight from the cow." Micheline went over to the fire, removed her kid gloves, and held her hands out to the leaping flames. The cottage was fairly small and warmed quickly now that both fireplaces were ablaze. Out of the corner of her eye Micheline saw Andrew pause at the window and stare pensively out at the dense flurry of snowflakes. "Are you thinking what I'm thinking?" she ventured after a long minute of silence. "That the queen may not be coming?"

"It *has* occurred to me," Sandhurst replied with a dark smile. "If she has any sense, she'll remain at the château, and I don't doubt that the king has returned there himself after his ride. The snow's so thick you can scarcely see the trees."

Micheline went to stand beside him. Staring out at the swirls of white flakes that had already completely covered the leafy ground, she found herself acutely conscious of Andrew's nearness and the fact that they were alone together in this cottage. There was no one else nearby, nor was there even another chamber to escape to. A shiver of panicky excitement washed over her.

"What shall we do?" she wondered in a small voice.

"I wouldn't subject even the horses to this storm, let alone *you*," Sandhurst said flatly. "We've no choice but to stay here and hope that the weather clears." He looked over at Micheline, with her wide blue eyes and flushed cheeks, and tried to remember that he was supposed to be a gentleman. "In the meantime, I'm hungry. Let's see if we can't prepare something hot to eat."

Two hours later, the snow was several inches deep, the queen had not arrived and seemingly never would, but the cottage was warm and fragrant. Andrew had plucked and cleaned the pigeons, then announced that *he* would cook them. Peeling potatoes, Micheline had watched dubiously as he shed his doublet and folded up his shirtsleeves. He'd proceeded to combine fresh herbs and bread crumbs, which he then mixed with egg and used to stuff the pigeons. These were placed in a pot with red wine, cloves, and ginger, and a few scoops of snow, which now simmered invitingly over the fire beside Micheline's pot of potatoes and carrots.

Andrew brought cups of wine for the two of them, and they sat side by side in the walnut chairs, their stocking feet sharing the same stool near the hearth.

"Where did you learn to cook?" she asked.

He gave her a mysterious smile. "My mother taught me." Unwilling to lie to her, he realized nonetheless that she would accept this explanation, thinking that his beginnings must be poor. In truth, the Duchess of Aylesbury had been proper in every sense except for her penchant for dismissing the cook and taking over herself. As a little boy Andrew had helped her chop and mix things on rainy afternoons in Gloucester-shire, and now those times were treasured memories. His mother had been happy and relaxed, enjoying the creation of a meal, and he had basked in her glow.

"You are very fortunate to have your mother. I can't tell you how much I miss mine."

"We are alike in that, Michelle. My mother died, too, five years ago."

"I'm sorry." Micheline gazed at him sadly and it seemed that she could see his soul in the depths of his eyes. She wanted to put out her hand and caress his arm, feel the warmth of his skin. All afternoon she had been beset by sudden waves of happiness. Never in her life had she known such pure pleasure as she felt in Andrew's company, especially now that they were isolated from the rest of the world. Sipping her wine, Micheline found it astonishingly easy to shut out all the warning voices in her mind.

For his part, Sandhurst was making an effort to listen to his own conscience. He wanted Micheline to choose him for himself, out of love, not out of guilt because he'd bedded her. This situation sorely tried his powers of resistance, however. She sat within touching distance, guileless yet sensual, sipping her wine as if they had lived together for a lifetime. Firelight played over her burnished-cognac hair, which she had let down to dry. It spilled in long, loose curls over her shoulders but did not obscure the creamy curves of her breasts, which swelled above the bodice of her gown. Farther down, peach velvet tapered in to accentuate Micheline's tiny waist, then flared out to obscure the lines of her hips and legs.

Sandhurst's eyes wandered to her trim ankles and slim feet
while he imagined the rest.

Micheline smiled dreamily. "This is nice, isn't it? I'm
rather glad the queen didn't come. This cottage is a welcome
change from the crowds and space of the château."

With an effort he forced himself to remember the issues at
hand. Sighing harshly, Andrew said, "Perhaps I'm slow, but
I still don't understand why you are so determined to marry
the Earl of Sandhurst. Is there a reason why you don't want to
love your husband?"

Micheline looked at him and blinked as if he'd offended
her. "I don't see why you had to bring that up *now*!"

"What better time?" he shot back, suddenly determined to
erect barriers between them.

"I don't believe there is *any* right time for questions such
as yours, m'sieur!" Eyes flashing, she sat up straight in her
chair. "Why should I tell you things that even my dearest
friends do not demand to know?"

His own gaze softened. "I think you know the answer to
that, Michelle."

She felt like sobbing. There was *something* between her
and Andrew Selkirk, but whatever it was, it had no future.
For this one day she would have liked to enjoy their relationship for its own sake. Why did he insist on asking questions
that she could not answer? It was impossible for her to tell
anyone about Bernard's infidelities; her heartache and humiliation were still too acute. Staring at the fire, Micheline felt an
abrupt surge of anger. This man had no right to demand that
she bare her soul to him, and she had no obligation to tell him
the truth.

"*D'accord,*" Micheline said heatedly. "If you must know,
the reason I cannot marry for love is because I cannot forget
my dear husband Bernard. I shall love him through eternity,
and thus it is impossible for me to give my heart to another
man."

Sandhurst's brows flew up. "Really! Are you certain?"

Somehow, she managed to meet his intent gaze. "Absolutely."

"Hmmm. That's very touching, Micheline, but I don't
believe it."

"That is *very* unfortunate, m'sieur!" Micheline exclaimed.
"And now it is my turn to ask *you* a question!"

"I can't wait," Sandhurst said dryly.

"You told me the other night that you painted the sister of the Earl of Sandhurst. Please tell me what you know about him."

"Surely you don't expect me to sing the praises of my competition!"

"You and I are supposed to be *friends*, aren't we? I wasn't aware that you were competing for my hand in marriage."

He had to admire her nerve. Smiling, Andrew murmured, "Now you know my secret."

"Do not tease me! I would appreciate it if you would simply be kind enough to answer my question!"

Color stained her cheeks and her eyes sparkled in a way that Sandhurst found frankly arousing. So much passion was hidden within Micheline that even she was not aware of.

"You ought to find out these things for yourself before you pledge your heart, fondling," he said gently, "but I can tell you that Lord Sandhurst is not an ogre. He's not old and fat and boring, if that's what's worrying you. As for his positive qualities . . . I'm not really qualified to list them."

Micheline watched in frustration as Andrew rose to check the pigeons. Helplessly her eyes wandered over his narrow waist and hips below the billowing white shirt that was tucked carelessly into his breeches.

"They're almost ready," Andrew announced, turning to find her gaze fastened on his body.

"Oh. I should fix the apples. Then we'll eat."

"Yes," he murmured, suddenly ravenous for Micheline. "I suppose we shall."

CHAPTER 14

March 11, 1533

DUSK WAS WRAPPING THE COTTAGE IN A MAUVE EMBRACE. MICHE-line looked out the leaded-glass windows as she put dishes and candles on the table and thought that the snowflakes looked like fluttering pink primroses against the twilit sky.

Andrew's pigeons were delicious and juicy in their sauce of red wine, complemented perfectly by potatoes with parsley and butter, baby carrots, and sautéed apples. Hungry as they were, both of them also craved this opportunity for relaxed conversation, and they spent most of the meal talking about books. Sandhurst was astonished to hear all that Micheline had read, and they discovered that they had many favorite books in common, since she was very familiar with English authors and poets.

"That was part of the reason I learned other languages," Micheline explained, her rich auburn hair agleam in the candlelight. "Papa speaks and reads everything from Latin to German, so our library was filled with books in every language. I loved to read so much that once I'd exhausted every printed word of French, I begged him to help me with the others."

"How old were you?" Andrew wondered.

"Oh, still a child. I remember speaking English quite competently even before *Maman* died. I must have been seven or eight when I began exploring other languages." She paused, sipping her wine with a smile. "I think it's easier when one is very young, don't you?"

"Yes, and easier still for the child who has the desire to learn. Languages were forced on me by tyrannical schoolmasters, so naturally I hated every minute."

"Typically male!" laughed Micheline. She wanted to ask him about his education, even about his childhood, but feared that he might be embarrassed to tell her. She had come to believe that Andrew's family had been part of the lower class, and that he had raised himself this far by dint of hard work, innate intelligence, and talent. It was a pleasant surprise to hear that he had gone to school at all.

"I brought my parents considerable grief in that respect, I'm afraid," he was saying reflectively. "I never wanted to do what I was told; I always had a better plan. Now, of course, I'm grateful that an education was pressed on me against my will. If I'd never learned to speak French, I probably wouldn't be here, would I?" He gave her a smile across the candles, but his thoughts were far away, remembering the years he'd spent at Corpus Christi College at Oxford. So much of the time Sandhurst had rebelled against being told what to read, write, and learn, for he often had interests in any subject except those being taught at the moment. The rift between him and his father had widened dangerously during that period, since the duke had insisted that he stay. They had been on such bad terms when he finished at Oxford that his mother had arranged the year of art study in Florence. Now, after talking to Micheline, Andrew felt an odd softening in his heart toward his father. He'd been fortunate to have received so fine and extensive an education, and fortunate to have a parent who was wise and strong enough not to bend under the unusual force of his son's will.

Unsure how to respond to Andrew's words, Micheline rose to prepare a dish they might share for the last course. She cut wedges of cylindrical Auvergne cheese, made from pure fresh cream, and set out sweetmeats, then split a pomegranate and placed it in the center. At the table Andrew was pouring more wine for both of them, but he glanced up as she approached, noting the gentle sway of her hips and the swell of her bosom above the square-cut bodice of her gown. He envied the emerald that nestled warmly between her breasts, its delicate gold chain glinting in the firelight.

Micheline's cheeks warmed under his regard, and suddenly she wondered how they would pass the hours that stretched before them.

"Do you play chess, Andrew?" she asked abruptly.

Sensing the reason for her question, Sandhurst warred unsuccessfully with an amused smile. "Naturally, madame."

"I saw a lovely carved board and ivory pieces in the chest!" she exclaimed. "Would you care for a game?"

He swallowed first an inappropriate reply, then laughed, but finally managed to nod. "Your whim is my command."

Micheline rushed to bring the board, ivory pieces wobbling on top, while Andrew casually selected a wedge of cheese. He'd never seen anyone look as relieved as she did as she placed the board between them and divided the white and black pieces. Smiling to himself, Sandhurst thought that he ought to be offended, but oddly enough her eagerness to seek a diversion from being alone with him only warmed his heart. How different Micheline was from the other women he'd known!

"I warn you," she was declaring, "I'm awfully good at this!"

"No doubt . . ." Andrew's eyes, filled with amused affection, captured hers and held them until she blushed.

Micheline thought that the game of chess would be her

salvation, but the opposite was true. Before her marriage she had played so often with her father that she often won, but this was much different. The silence combined with Andrew's nearness to unnerve her. She found herself more aware of his fingers on the chess pieces than she was of their destination. He snacked on cheese and pomegranate seeds while she tried to concentrate on her moves, and Micheline couldn't resist the urge to study him under her lashes. Watching him rub a drop of red juice from his mouth with his fingertip, she felt a frightening surge of desire. The sight of his burnished hair in the golden light made her ache to sink her fingers into it. She yearned to kiss the scar above Andrew's mouth, his sculpted cheekbones, the place in his jaw where a muscle clenched when he was angry.

Occasionally he would look up suddenly, catching her in a moment of lust, and Micheline would stare at the board, her cheeks on fire. She was shocked at herself, and shocked at her own body, which seemed to be suffused with longings her mind could not suppress. Still, these hours at the queen's cottage felt like an interlude out of time. With each passing minute Micheline found it increasingly difficult to remember past and future, promises and responsibilities. The barriers she had so carefully built against Andrew in her mind and heart were melting away.

"Check." Sandhurst lightly moved his black knight to capture her queen.

Micheline was aghast. How could this have happened? She saw the board clearly for the first time and burned with embarrassment as she remembered her boast at the beginning of the game. Without one superior word or glance Andrew had casually played so well that now she had no choice but to resort to a defensive strategy. Now all her attention was on the board. Sipping her wine agitatedly, Micheline surveyed the possibilities. She tried to protect her king with her rook, but Andrew was steps ahead of her.

"Bad luck, fondling," he murmured with a rueful smile. One move of his bishop allowed him to tell her softly, "Mate."

Breathing anxiously, Micheline glanced down to see that her breasts were moving in rhythm with her heart. She attempted a cheerful smile. "It must have been all the excitement of the day. I just couldn't concentrate!"

"Perfectly understandable."

When he spoke in that low, masculine voice, tiny shivers of pleasurable panic ran over Micheline's nerves. He really did have the most irresistible voice of any man she'd ever known. Crazily, hoping that the sight of his face would calm her, she looked up slowly. Andrew was staring at her in a way that took her breath away. Golden firelight played over his face, casting soft shadows and accentuating each chiseled feature. His eyes, though, were what rendered Micheline literally breathless. Chin down slightly, he looked at her with a warm, melting gaze that was utterly compelling and sensual all at once.

"We shall have a rematch," she managed to whisper.

"Certainly, but not tonight. It's getting cold in here, and that bed looks like the place to be."

"Why don't you put on your doublet? And your jerkin?"

"I can't sleep with clothes on," Sandhurst told her with a small, slightly wicked smile. "Besides, those furs on the bed look warm enough."

"I didn't mean in bed!"

"I know what you meant, Michelle." Lifting his cup of wine, he drained it. "Don't look so nervous. I have myself under control. Didn't I just prove it during our game of chess?"

What was going to happen? she wondered wildly. "Do you intend that we should sleep in the same bed, m'sieur?"

Sandhurst gave in to low, irrepressible laughter that Micheline found terribly appealing. "I don't see that we have a choice, madame." He arched a brow. "Shall we be formal? Would that make it easier for you?"

Feeling foolish, Micheline tried again. "You needn't mock me, *Andrew*. It's just that—"

"Don't say it!" He held up his hand. "I know; you are betrothed to the dreaded Earl of Sandhurst! Never fear, sweeting; your honor is safe with me. I won't trespass on your side of the bed unless you insist."

She straightened her back and replied primly, "In that case, we shall both sleep soundly."

Several irreverent replies danced on his tongue, but he managed to swallow them. "You're such a comfort," Andrew said at last, and pushed back his chair. When he began to gather up their soiled dishes, Micheline waved him off.

"No, no, you cooked the pigeons. It's my turn to clean up. You're tired and cold; go along to bed."

He laughed, his white teeth flashing in the firelight. "You shouldn't pretend to be selfless when we both know you're hoping I'll be fast asleep when it's time for *you* to slip under those furs!"

"Don't be rude!" she retorted hotly, clattering the dishes together.

Shaking his head and smiling, Sandhurst put a pot of melted snow over the fire so that she would have hot water to clean with, then crossed the room and began undressing. Micheline made a show of tidying up, but she couldn't resist sneaking a guilty sidelong glance in his direction.

Silhouetted in profile against the orange flames in the other fireplace, Andrew had removed his shirt and was now bending to shed his breeches. Micheline glimpsed broad shoulders and the play of muscles over his back and arms, but when a lean hip and the hard curve of a buttock became visible, she turned away in haste. A confusing whirlpool of feelings swirled within her—and at its vortex were acute excitement and shame.

Finally there was nothing left to do. The cottage was truly cold now. Every dish and pot had been scrubbed and put away. Across the room Andrew had closed the bed's velvet draperies and was presumably asleep within. Micheline put two more logs on the fire, then poured herself another cup of wine. She drank it standing up, hoping that it would slow the wild beating of her heart, but instead it seemed to intensify the unremitting warmth between her legs.

At last Micheline approached the bed. She unlaced her gown, removed it, and laid it over the back of a nearby chair. Next came her petticoat. Few people wore clothing to bed, including Micheline, but the idea of sleeping naked beside Andrew Selkirk was too incredible to entertain. Still wearing a thin chemise, she parted the curtains, lifted the fur spread and the covers under it, and slid into bed with the utmost care. The velvet draperies shut out all light and evidence of the outside world. Micheline lay motionless, feeling Andrew's warmth in the bed and hearing his soft, rhythmic breathing. She was afraid to breathe herself, or make the slightest movement that might disturb him. For what seemed like hours she remained thus, thinking her heartbeat would never slow and sleep would never come.

*   *   *

Deep into the night Sandhurst dreamed that ripe breasts were touching his chest and a soft, shapely leg was sliding over his own hard limbs. Meanwhile a hand had crept around his bare waist.

"Mmmm." The voice's owner pressed her face against Andrew's shoulder and made another contented sleep sound.

His eyes opened to total darkness. Iris? he wondered fuzzily, then gradually remembered that he was not in England but in France, not in his own bed but—

Silky hair scented with lily of the valley caressed Sandhurst's jaw. He held his breath. *Good Lord!* It was Micheline! Quickly he reminded himself that she was asleep. She had probably gotten cold and snuggled against him for warmth, totally unaware of what she was doing. Yes, that must be it. Completely innocent, he told himself sternly, clenching his teeth against his own involuntary arousal. Micheline chose that moment to sigh, her breasts swelling against him through the thin stuff of her chemise, while her hand slipped down to Sandhurst's hip and brushed his fully hardened manhood for one heart-stopping instant.

Smothering a hoarse moan, he turned slowly on his side to face her. Micheline nuzzled his chest. It began to occur to Andrew that whether she was asleep or not, her behavior was not all that innocent. Perhaps she was having a dream—about *him*—but on some level Micheline knew what she was doing.

Tentatively he brought his hand up under the covers, softly cupped her breast, and felt the nipple harden against his palm. Micheline was raising her face, searching in the darkness. Sandhurst needed no further encouragement. His open mouth closed over the delicious softness of her parted lips. After a moment she returned his kiss in earnest, matching his passion, and Andrew gathered her into an intimate embrace.

Awakening, Micheline could see nothing in the blackness, but she knew immediately that this was no dream, and that it was Andrew Selkirk who was kissing her with such ardent expertise. Resistance didn't occur to her. She cared for nothing except the ravenous hunger that seemed to consume both her body and soul. Now that she was in Andrew's strong arms, she didn't want to ever leave them.

Micheline wrapped her own arms tightly around him, glorying in the taut warmth of his skin and its intoxicatingly male scent. Desire mixed with violent emotion to make her shiver. When she put her tongue into his mouth, tasting and

exploring with unrestrained eagerness, Sandhurst could feel
her lips trembling. An elemental need much stronger than
simple physical passion radiated from her body, and his heart
swelled in response.

He found the ribbons of her chemise and deftly unlaced
them, then lost patience and tore the delicate garment open to
bare all of Micheline's enticingly curved body. Burying his
face in the valley between her breasts, Andrew felt the wild
beating of her heart and kissed the satiny flesh that covered it.

"How lovely you are," he murmured tenderly.

Micheline sank her fingers into his hair, arching against the
mouth that sought her aching nipple. A moan rose from the
deepest part of her when his tongue burned the sensitive peak
as he kissed her there, rhythmically, until a fire seemed to
spread downward to rage between her legs.

Although Andrew lingered hungrily at her breasts, his right
hand strayed lower, bestowing feather-light caresses over
Micheline's slim legs, flat belly, and the curves of her hips.
When, at length, his agile fingers touched her intimately, he
nearly groaned aloud. She was hot and wet, pressing upward
against his exploring hand. Sandhurst thought he might die
right there, when suddenly Micheline's own hand found his
throbbing manhood. Never before had he known such exquisitely torturous arousal, not even with women a thousand
times more experienced than Micheline.

Barely able to contain himself, Andrew kissed her shoulders, throat, ears, and eyelids before their mouths came together again and he turned her against the pillows.

Now her fingers were caressing the muscles of his back
while he cupped her buttocks. Sandhurst's hardness tantalized
Micheline's moist softness, and then he pushed gently inside
of her. Eagerly her hips arched upward in welcome, then met
each thrust so that their bodies joined, over and over again, in
fervent harmony. She was panting against his mouth, her slim
body tensing gradually in his embrace, and then she made an
incoherent sound. The incredible sensation of Micheline's
tautness contracting rhythmically around his manhood trig-
gered Andrew's own climax. Stunned by its force, he didn't
even feel her nails digging into his shoulders.

Pleasure washed up over Micheline's body like waves breaking on the sand. Never in her life had she imagined such an
experience. What had happened to her? How had Andrew
done it? His face was buried now in her tumbled curls, their

hearts thudding in unison. She loved the sensation of him still inside her, still pulsating in the afterglow.

"Oh, Michelle," he whispered, and let out a ragged sigh.

The hair that curled against his neck was damp when she touched it. Unable to speak, Micheline could answer only by turning her face to kiss Andrew's mouth. Even in the darkness she didn't have to search for it. He was part of her now.

CHAPTER 15

March 11, 1533

"HOW CAN YOU BE SO CALM DURING A CRISIS?" AIMÉE DEMANDED of her husband. "I'm worried sick!"

She was pacing to and fro in their bedchamber while little Ninon toddled determinedly in her wake.

"Watch that you don't trample the baby," St. Briac warned mildly. Seated by the window in a ray of soft dawn sunlight, he was braiding Juliette's chestnut hair. It was not yet seven o'clock, but they were all up and dressed, roused by Aimée, who had barely slept all night.

"What if they were lost in that blizzard?" she cried now. "Micheline might have frozen to death for all we know!"

Thomas arched a dubious brow. *"C'est impossible, miette.* She and Selkirk set out in the full light of day with a clear set of instructions to bring them to the queen's cottage. That man is more than capable of seeing to Micheline's safety, and in any case, I would say that she could have taken care of herself even without him."

"But it was all some sort of mistake! The queen told us herself last evening that she had never invited them to the cottage, nor was there any plan for François to go there!"

Gaspard Lefait, who had served impertinently and loyally as St. Briac's manservant for twenty years, entered at that moment, carrying a freshly laundered doublet. The sight of his master braiding Juliette's hair made him stop, wincing.

"Oh, monseigneur," he moaned. "What next?" With a

heavy sigh he thought back to the days when he had followed St. Briac into battle and witnessed the seductions of the most desirable women in France. Since Aimée's appearance in his master's life, nothing had been the same.

St. Briac was laughing. "You're just jealous, windbag, because you haven't a pretty girl like my Juliette to sit on *your* lap!" Tying the last bow on her braids, he bent to kiss his daughter's rosy cheek, then lifted her down. She promptly went to Gaspard and raised her arms, thinking to console him.

The old man's heart melted. He handed the doublet over to St. Briac, then lifted the little girl into his arms. When she kissed his cheek, Gaspard blushed and cleared his throat. "Perhaps the children would enjoy it if I bundled them up and took them out to play in the snow," he suggested gruffly.

"That's very kind of you, Gaspard!" Aimée approved, while Ninon and Juliette squealed with excitement.

St. Briac only smiled, his turquoise eyes agleam with fond amusement.

When they were alone, Aimée began to pace again.

"I wish you would stop that," he complained. "Micheline is a grown woman! How would you have felt if someone had hovered so protectively over *you*?"

"I'm only worried about her safety."

Thomas sighed. Setting down the doublet, he walked over and put his arms around his wife, then tipped up her chin and kissed her soundly. "You know what has happened as well as I. They've spent the night together in that cottage, which was the wisest thing the way the snow was coming down last night. There is always more than enough food there, and I'm sure they've been perfectly comfortable. The snow has stopped now. I've no doubts that they'll return this morning, but if they are not here by noon, I'll go to the cottage myself. Now do you feel better?"

Her green eyes were still worried. "Oh, I know that you're right. . . ."

"It's not Micheline's safety from the storm that concerns you so much, is it, *miette*?"

She shook her head, then rested it against his broad chest. "No, I suppose not. I saw them together yesterday. I saw the way she looks at him. Oh, Thomas, what if—"

"They are both adults, Aimée."

"But—"

"You can't live Micheline's life for her. I know it's hard to watch someone you love make mistakes, but you can't interfere. Besides, she's an intelligent girl—"

"Who knows nothing about her own heart! I admit that I felt this betrothal to the Earl of Sandhurst was a terrible mistake, but this—this romance, or whatever it is, with Andrew Selkirk may be even worse! What are the chances of him proposing marriage? And if he *did*, what could he offer her?"

"I'll agree that Micheline's life has become rather complicated of late, but you're going to have to let her resolve matters herself."

"I'm going to pay a visit to M'sieur Selkirk's manservant," Aimée said suddenly.

"What?"

"I want to see the portrait he brought from England. I told you how impressed I was by the way he had captured Micheline's spirit on canvas. If that quality is missing in this other painting, I'll feel better."

"Go, then, if it will set your mind at ease. I'll finish dressing and get something to eat." He cupped Aimée's little face in his hands and kissed her, wishing that she could spare him a fraction of the attention she lavished on Micheline.

Jeremy Culpepper chewed a bite of greengage plum and wondered what Sandhurst was up to now. He'd said the queen had invited him and Micheline to her cottage, but kitchen gossip had it that Queen Eleanor hadn't ever intended to leave Fontainebleau and was professing complete innocence about the note Andrew had received. No one really expected the couple to come back last night considering the snowstorm, but all the servants were buzzing about what the betrothed Madame Tevoulère might be doing alone in a secluded cottage with that dangerously attractive English painter. *Quel scandale!*

A knock sounded at the door and Jeremy jumped. Sandhurst would never knock, and the only other person who might visit him was the amorous little saucemaker who liked to purr that she found him adorable. It was *awfully* early in the day for that sort of social call. . . .

He opened the door to find the seigneur de St. Briac's pretty wife. God's toes! Jeremy thought. What if she's one of those married women who like a bit of diversion with the servants? Her husband's a giant!

"*Bonjour,* m'sieur," Aimée said charmingly. The sight of Selkirk's valet made her want to giggle. He was the picture of consternation, eyes popping while his curly, uncombed orange hair stuck out in several directions. "You are—"

"Jeremy—uh—Playfair." He choked on the name, cursing Sandhurst silently. "How may I help you, Madame Mardouet?" This really was *too* much. He had to not only claim that idiotic surname but also act the servant, as if he were no better than a dog she might deign to pat on the head.

"I know that this might sound odd, m'sieur, but I would appreciate it if you could show me the painting your master brought from England. I have admired the portrait he is making of Madame Tevoulère, and am curious to see more of his work."

Odd indeed, thought Jeremy, especially at seven in the morning!

"Come in, madame. I hope that you'll excuse the chamber's appearance—and my own. I didn't expect—"

"It is I who owe *you* an apology, M'sieur Playfair!" Aimée declared. "It is very early, and I came on a whim, hoping that you would pardon my rudeness."

Jeremy began to like the lady. She wasn't condescending in the least, and they chatted easily as he uncovered the portrait of Cicely Weston and propped it on the table by the window.

Aimée blinked. "*Parbleu!*"

"Quite beautiful, isn't it?" Culpepper said proudly. He wanted to give credit to Lord Sandhurst, then claim him as a friend and equal, but instead he had to continue, "Mr. Selkirk is extremely talented. I couldn't believe it myself when I first saw this. It's as if Lady Cicely Weston were here, alive in this chamber."

"Cicely . . . Weston?" Aimée was staring at the portrait, her spirits sinking. This manservant was right. If it had been love that brought Selkirk's painting of Micheline to life, then he must love this child as well. Her personality was revealed on the canvas, or so it seemed. Miss Weston appeared intelligent and willful in a charming way, and though she couldn't have been much more than ten years old, her eyes were also filled with adoration. Of course, they held none of the sensual overtones of Micheline's, but it was love all the same.

"Weston . . ." Aimée repeated absently. "That name sounds familiar."

"Lady Cicely is the sister of the Earl of Sandhurst."

Never one to use devious means to gain information. Aimée decided to be frank with Selkirk's manservant. "M'sieur Playfair, are you aware that Micheline Tevoulère is betrothed to Lord Sandhurst?"

He wanted to laugh, but swallowed instead and replied, "Yes, I have heard about that, madame."

"The lady is my dearest friend, and as you might imagine, I've been rather concerned about the fact that she and the earl have never met."

"Perfectly understandable." Jeremy nodded.

"I hope, then, that you'll understand my curiosity as well when I ask if you know Lord Sandhurst at all. I'm eager to discover what sort of man he is."

What would Andrew want him to say? Jeremy was naturally outspoken, and this lady inspired one's confidence. "The earl is a very fine man," he said finally, deciding that honesty was the safest course. "He's blessed with extraordinary good looks, intelligence, and charm. I doubt that there's a lady in Britain of marriageable age who wouldn't gladly take Madame Tevoulère's place. Don't waste time worrying that your friend has chosen ill. I don't think that there's the slightest chance that she'll be unhappy in this marriage—or that she won't love her husband."

Aimée thanked him, stole a last glance at the portrait of Lady Cicely Weston, and left Andrew Selkirk's chambers. Alone in the corridor, she leaned against a paneled wall and sighed in frustration. What in the *world* was the answer to this dilemma? Perhaps this situation wasn't fair to Micheline. How could she choose between a man she'd never seen and Andrew Selkirk? If Playfair's words were true, Lord Sandhurst might be even more appealing than this impoverished painter! Was that *possible*?

Sunlight bright as melted butter poured through a gap in the bedhangings. Micheline awoke reluctantly, sensing that the hours out of time were at an end. Andrew lay facing her on his side, still sleeping, while she rested on her back, nestled close in his embrace. She gazed over at his face, tears stinging her eyes. Everything about him was excruciatingly dear to her. She adored each brown hair as much as those that were gilded, the laugh lines that crinkled around his eyes, the unique shape of each of his brows, the slight flare of his nostrils, the scar that set him apart from every other handsome man, and the fresh stubble of beard that glinted in the sunlight as if his face had been brushed with gold dust.

Andrew's hard-muscled right arm curved over her slim body, his fingertips resting lightly on the swell of Micheline's breast. She studied his fingers, which, though sturdier than one might expect of those of an artist, were handsomely shaped. And his sensitive gift for painting carried over to the way he used his hands, mouth, and entire body, in the act of love.

A sharp pain spread through Micheline's breast. She was so afraid, now that daylight had invaded their private world. It did no good to lie here mooning over him, for her suffering would only be worse later. She had to leave the bed before Andrew woke. Even more frightening than the thought of his warm kisses and the splendor of his lovemaking was the prospect of gazing into Andrew's honey-colored eyes. Even in the darkness she'd felt the power of their spell. In daylight she might drown in them and never find her way out.

Slowly Micheline edged away. When his hand slid from her breast, Andrew made a sound and rolled onto his back, freeing her completely. Realizing that it was only a matter of time until he sensed her absence, Micheline slipped quickly but carefully to the edge of the bed. Her torn chemise was there. She took it with her as she emerged naked in the sunlit but chilly air of the cottage. The abrupt change from the scent of Andrew inside the bedhangings sent another sharp twinge through her heart.

D'accord! Micheline thought fiercely. From now on I must adjust to a life that does not include the dangerous pleasure of Andrew Selkirk's presence! The joys of this past night must last me a lifetime. It will be painful at first, but in the end the pain will be much less. I have already come perilously close to falling in love, but I have escaped! I must not look back!

Repeating this litany to herself, Micheline donned her petticoat, gown, and stockings. Without a chemise she felt doubly conscious of her tender breasts and womanhood. She washed with the melted snow left from last night, then stirred the embers in the hearth and added wood. Soon the cottage felt warmer. Micheline sat down before the fire to brush her hair.

Across the room the curtains stirred on Andrew's side of the bed.

"Michelle! Come back!" Sandhurst moaned in mock agony.

She tried to steel her heart, wishing that she didn't have to talk to him just now . . . or look at him. What if he touched her?

"You must get up, Andrew," she said in as neutral a tone as she could manage. Walking over to the bed, Micheline drew back the draperies to let in a flood of sunshine. Andrew still lay on his back, looking tanned and tempting against the white pillows. In defense against the harsh light, his strong forearm came up to cover his eyes.

"It's cold," he complained. "Come back to bed."

As hot blood rushed to her face, Micheline wished that her cheeks would not invariably betray her. "Morning is passing, and everyone at Fontainebleau will be worried about us. We should go back now."

Her voice gave Sandhurst pause. Suddenly he was fully awake, sitting up in bed and reaching for Micheline's hand.

"What's amiss?"

She perched on the edge of the bed, but averted her eyes from his penetrating gaze. "Nothing! The snow has stopped, the sun is out, and we must be on our way before they come to search for us."

Wondering if this was a dream, he ran his free hand through his ruffled hair and tried to think, but thought only confused the situation further. The truth was in his heart, what he felt and what he *knew* that Micheline felt. Shortly after dawn Andrew had awakened to discover her naked body curled trustingly against his own. The sight of her face, and the contented smile she wore even in sleep, had reassured him that all they had shared in the darkness had been very real. Micheline had looked as transformed as he felt, but now that she was awake, everything seemed changed.

"Look at me, Michelle."

She managed only a quick, painful glance. "You really must rise and dress now—"

"Why are you acting as if you're afraid of me?"

"Don't talk nonsense." Instinctively she tried to free her hand from his, but Andrew held fast.

"Was last night nonsense?" he demanded.

Micheline's blush deepened. "No, no—of course not. But . . . it was a mere interlude of pleasure. I am not ashamed of what I did, but you should understand that I do not care to dwell on it. Last night is gone, and I would like to put it behind me. What we did changed nothing.''

''Indeed!'' Muscles clenched in Sandhurst's jaw. ''*You* are not changed?''

''I am betrothed to another man. That is what I must remember from now on.''

He sighed harshly. ''You've evaded my question, but I'll let it go for the moment. I have something to say to you, Michelle, and I will say it only once. Last night was much more than 'a mere interlude of pleasure' for me, and in spite of your protests, we both know the truth.'' Reaching out with his free hand, Sandhurst lifted her chin and forced her to look at him.

Her heart thundering, Micheline stammered, ''No—I—''

''Be brave and allow me to finish.'' There was no charm in his voice, only determination and an edge of anger. ''I have slept with enough women to know the difference between a purely physical romp and an act of love. What we shared was unquestionably the latter. I've never experienced anything like it. Perhaps because I'm older and more jaded than you, I find myself quite stunned by the honest emotions that have grown within me since I first saw you on the staircase at Fontainebleau. Love's a precious commodity, Michelle. I'd come to doubt its existence, but now I know better.'' He paused for a moment, searching her eyes. ''I love you, Micheline, and I want you to be my wife.''

Andrew's words had a violent effect on her. Trembling, she pulled free and turned away. ''No! You must not say such things! It is impossible. We have to return to the château and pretend that none of this happened!''

He wanted to hold her and force her to tell him what was wrong, but sensed that it would do no good. ''I've stated my case, Michelle, and I won't change my mind. If you should see the light and decide to choose love over wealth and nobility, you can come to me at any time before I leave Fontainebleau for England.''

''You aren't leaving now?'' She was unable to keep the panic from her voice.

''Oh, no, I'll have to stay long enough to at least complete your portrait.'' Sarcasm dripped from his words. ''Don't say you'll miss me!''

Micheline hardly knew what to say. "I'd hate to think I'd driven you away."

"Don't worry, madame."

When Andrew ripped back the covers and emerged naked from the bed, Micheline fled to the other side of the cottage. Pain suffused her body as she listened to him dress. She longed to cry but couldn't, longed to speak the truth but wouldn't.

CHAPTER 16

March 11–22, 1533

SANDHURST BURST INTO HIS CHAMBERS AND SLAMMED THE HEAVY paneled door. Jeremy Culpepper, who had been napping peacefully on his friend's grander bed, jumped and let out a startled exclamation. To his even greater surprise, Andrew neither teased him nor pretended to dress him down for invading the testered bed in his absence. In fact, he didn't seem to even notice.

"Put on your boots and jerkin. We're going for a walk."

"Look here, Sandhurst, there's a foot of snow outside in case you haven't noticed!"

"That's why you'll need boots. Hurry up."

Jeremy blinked in consternation but did as he was told. Only when they were out in the courtyard did he dare speak again.

"Where were you all night? The court can talk of nothing else but you and that girl snowbound—"

"At the queen's cottage in the forest," Andrew finished shortly.

"Queen Eleanor says that she never sent you a note, and the king insists that he had no plan to go there either. It wasn't some sort of scheme on your part to get Micheline Tevoulère alone, was it?"

"Jeremy, I have no patience for this mindless chatter. I *did* receive that letter signed by the queen, and it hardly matters now *who* sent it!'' The long muscles in his legs were taut as he strode through the snow.

Culpepper could scarcely keep up.

"Well, as long as you were both safe—"

"Safe from what?" Andrew shouted, giving vent to his frustration now that they were away from the château. "The elements? I'd have had an easier time dealing with that cursed snowstorm!"

"Oh. I see." But he didn't see, and had no idea what to say next.

"She's a study in contradictions. First she tells me that people who love are fools, then turns around and says that the reason she's marrying a stranger is because she will love her dead husband through eternity!"

Assuming that "she" was Micheline Tevoulère, Jeremy trotted along beside his friend and chose what seemed a safe response. "The chit sounds confused!"

"Perhaps, but it's more than that. There's something she's not telling me!"

"Oh! What's that?"

"How do I know? She hasn't told me, you fool!" Sandhurst strode on into the forest, thinking while Culpepper raced to keep up. Eventually his pace slowed. "I suppose I may as well tell you—I have reason to be certain that Micheline is in love with me."

"Love!" cried Jeremy. It was not a word he was accustomed to hearing from Sandhurst. If this French minx was in love, Andrew must be eager to flee. . . .

"It gets worse," he continued with quiet amusement. "I'm in love with her as well."

Jeremy froze in his tracks. "I don't believe it!"

Turning to look at him, Sandhurst lifted tawny brows and smiled slightly. "It's the truth. It's as if fate caused my father and the two kings to bring us together."

"But—"

"You've chosen just the right word, my friend. *But* Micheline won't have me. She's determined to go through with this marriage to the Earl of Sandhurst."

Culpepper shook his head forcefully, hoping to jar his thoughts into a pattern that would make sense. "But that's *you!*" was all he could reply, seemingly for the dozenth time since they'd arrived in France.

"Don't you see? That doesn't *matter*! Micheline has no

idea that it's me—and she's choosing what amounts to a stranger over the man she loves. You'll think I've lost my mind, but I find myself quite resentful and jealous toward the Earl of Sandhurst.''

"You're right about one thing—I *do* think you've gone mad! For God's sake, Sandhurst, just tell the girl the truth!"

"Don't you see? I cannot. If I told her now, and we married, that would be ever between us. I would always wonder if she loved me or my title more, and worry that I hadn't been good enough to win her on my own." Andrew stared off into the distance. "No, I don't intend to tell her who I am. Either she will choose me for myself and for love, or there will be no marriage."

As March passed, Sandhurst's words to Jeremy in the forest seemed discouragingly prophetic. Work on the portrait of Micheline continued, but she was extremely reserved, avoiding his eyes, his touch, unnecessary conversation . . . in short, any form of personal contact with Andrew. There were moments when he glimpsed something in her eyes—pain, or fear perhaps—that made no sense to him. Why should Micheline fear him?

He could feel the strong currents of yearning that suffused the air whenever they were in the same room, and sensed that Micheline might capitulate if he were to hold her, kiss her, and demand that she admit the truth, but Sandhurst's pride was too great. Either she would come to him by choice, or not at all.

One sunny afternoon found Andrew seated on a stool in front of Micheline's portrait, studying her image pensively. He had dismissed her early, unable to concentrate in her presence. The painting was very good, too good, perhaps. On canvas Micheline gazed at him in a way she never allowed herself to do these days. Her beautiful face glowed with the love she could not admit, and yet there was a hint of that sadness that baffled him so. Staring at the portrait, Sandhurst tried to decide if it was sadness, regret, or fear . . . or a combination of all three. Of course, the greater mystery was what *caused* so poignant a shadow on the face of someone so fresh and young. Micheline would have him believe that the culprit was grief for her dead husband, but all his instincts told him otherwise.

"*Excusez-moi,* m'sieur. . . ."

Andrew turned his head to discover a young page standing in the doorway. "Yes, what is it?"

"His Majesty requests your presence in the royal bedchamber. If you'll follow me . . ."

Sighing heavily, Sandhurst rose. What could the king want this time? They'd already played cat-and-mouse after the night of the snowstorm, and Andrew had given nothing away. Since then, there certainly hadn't been anything between him and Micheline that would further arouse the monarch's suspicions!

"Ah, Selkirk!" François turned from the window to greet the Englishman. "You're looking rather worse for wear! Sit down and have some wine."

"Thank you. Now that you mention it, I am tired. If this is about Micheline Tevoulère—"

"No, no, absolutely not!" The king took a chair and Andrew followed suit, then they both sipped goblets of strong Hungarian wine for a moment. "Ah, that's good. Revives the spirit, hmm?"

"Quite." He nodded dryly, wishing *his* spirit could be revived so easily.

"As it happens, I am well pleased with your behavior regarding Madame these days. I know that you have been keeping your distance, and I appreciate how difficult that can be." François's brows went up over his hazel eyes for emphasis.

Sandhurst had supposed that the king had harbored feelings of his own for Micheline, but this near confession startled him. Instead of answering, he merely drank his wine and waited.

"I propose that we put Micheline out of our minds and turn our attention to more . . . receptive subjects. You may be aware that François Rabelais arrived at Fontainebleau today. He is our rather astonishing monk who left the monastery three years ago to pursue all manner of things. Last year, as a physician, he dissected a corpse at Lyons, and now students have begun following his example. He has also written a book, called *Pantagruel*, and has come here now to bring me the first copy. The story sounds interesting . . . about the king of Utopia, who is Pantagruel, and his friend Panurge."

"Having read Sir Thomas More's book, I am familiar with the theme of Utopia," remarked Andrew. "And I have heard of your Rabelais as well. Quite a colorful character, isn't he?"

"*Mais, oui!* I must say that court life has become rather boring of late, and Rabelais's appearance is a perfect curative. I never could bear March. We're all fed up with winter, itching to ride and hunt all day, and along comes Lent to make the month even more tedious. Forty days of *fish!*" The king rolled his eyes.

Sandhurst was beginning to wonder if the king had been into the wine with Rabelais before summoning him. "Yes, well . . ."

"We'll have another visitor soon that will cheer us all, including my children! When your king and I met this past autumn, we agreed that it would be a fine thing if his son were to come to the French court to be raised alongside my own boys. I received the happy news this morning that the Duke of Richmond will arrive in a week!"

Andrew went pale. The Duke of Richmond and Somerset was actually Henry Fitzroy, illegitimate son of Henry VIII and Bessie Blount. In the absence of other children, the king had bestowed two important titles on the boy when he was only six. Now fourteen, the young duke had been introduced to the Earl of Sandhurst on countless occasions, and Andrew knew that he would blurt out the truth immediately if they met at Fontainebleau.

"A week, you say?" he echoed.

"Yes. My own François is the same age as young Henry, so he especially is looking forward to his arrival. But enough about that. More wine?" A steward rushed to refill their goblets. "You are wondering why I wanted to see you, *n'est-ce pas?*"

Andrew nodded absently, his mind racing with the news about the Duke of Richmond.

"I understand that you are nearly finished with Madame Tevoulère's portrait. I had heard such wonderful things about it that I confess I went for a look myself last evening, and I found it breathtaking. Congratulations, m'sieur."

"Thank you, sire."

"My—uh—friend Mademoiselle d'Heilly has her heart set on being your next subject, but a different idea occurred to me today. How would you like to paint the incomparable Rabelais?"

"I realize, sire, that it is an honor to be asked, and I wish that I might oblige, but unfortunately I shall have to return to England shortly."

"Shortly?" The king's brow gathered. "How shortly?"
"Within the week . . ."

The next evening Micheline went down to the hall for
supper, clad in a sumptuous gown of powder blue and white
velvet, her flame-tinted hair cooled by a silvery crispinette.
These meals had become an ordeal for her, since she was
always aware of Andrew Selkirk's presence above all else.
Tonight was different. Boards were laid, as usual, on
trestles, to make three extensive tables that ran lengthwise
down the hall, while the king's table was placed horizontally
at the head of the huge room. Ever since Andrew's arrival at
court, he had been given a place among the privileged, but
tonight Micheline glimpsed him sitting far away at one of the
other three tables. Moreover, his place was filled by François
Rabelais, who had chosen a seat next to Micheline.
The eccentric, charismatic genius from Chinon proved a
perfect supper companion for Micheline. Although three years
out of the monastery, he still wore his monkish cowl, but his
attitude was anything but holy.
"Ah, my good September soup!" Rabelais cried gustily
when the first goblet of wine was poured. "Drink up, madame. I taste the essence of violets in this wine. It is obviously a product of Chinon grapes!"
Spellbound at first, Micheline did as she was bade, and
soon was completely distracted by the lively company of
Rabelais. He had an opinion on everything. While Micheline
enjoyed a dish of sturgeon eggs and olives, Rabelais held
forth on the subject of astrology. His tone was mocking, his
choice of words humorous, and yet his points made sense to
Micheline.
Soup followed, composed of trout, herring, salted freshwa-
ter eels, whiting, almonds, ginger, saffron, cinnamon powder, and sweetmeats. Grenache wine was poured, and Rabelais
pronounced it less wonderful than the Chinon vintage, but
wonderful all the same. Micheline smiled, thinking that this
man who was called "the Michelangelo of laughter" seemed
to enjoy *every* sort of food and drink.
Soon everyone at the table, including the king himself, was
listening to Rabelais. No one was safe from his sharp, ingenious
tongue. He gaily attacked the Sorbonne, various theologians
and pompous scholars, and let his humor stray dangerously
near the monarchy. His listeners laughed, albeit nervously

through course after course. They were served fish of every sort: sole, turbot, salmon, carp from the Marne River, and breams. Among the side dishes were orange-apples, rice with fried almonds, sorrel and watercress, and porpoise with sauce. The torchlight seemed brighter than usual to Micheline, and once, when laughter seemed to come at her from every direction, she found herself pushing back her plate and remembering the intimate evening she and Andrew had spent at the cottage in the woods.

"Are you meditating, madame?" Rabelais inquired.

Pastries shaped like swans and plums stewed in rosewater, and white and vermilion sugar plums were being served along with a sweet German wine. More wine was poured, and the rest of the company lapsed into quieter conversation. Micheline smiled at the erstwhile monk.

"In a way, I suppose I was. I often wonder why the things in life that give us the most pleasure are also the most complicated."

"Complicated by *whom*?"

"Other people, I suppose, and even by ourselves . . ."

"Madame, you are clearly an intelligent young woman. Let me tell you something that it has taken me most of my forty years to learn. There are all sorts of fools in this world: the metaphysical fool, the predestined fool, the fool elect, and the fool imperial." Rabelais cast a mischievous glance down the table toward the king. "Don't be a fool yourself because you've allowed other people to exert pressure on your life. I've come to believe in freedom. We only have one life . . . and when it ends, we can only hope to go to the great perhaps. With that in mind, I've adopted a new motto."

Dancing bears and monkeys wearing hats and playing miniature harps were entertaining the court, but Micheline noticed none of this.

"Pray tell me, m'sieur, what is your motto?"

"*Faye ce que vouldras.*" Rabelais grinned, finishing his wine. "Do as you please!"

By morning Micheline had taken ill. Aimée, who rushed to her bedside, watched in alarm as Micheline retched until she lay pale and exhausted. She could only pray that it was something her friend had eaten or a result of the strenuous festivities of the night before. There had been a great deal of toasting going on between Rabelais and Micheline.

Suzette, Aimée's maid, went to give Andrew the news, which he accepted skeptically. It seemed much more likely that Micheline merely wished to avoid him now that her presence was no longer necessary for the completion of the portrait.

Two more days passed. Sandhurst completed his painting and presented it to the king, who had been scarcely civil to him since he declined to remain at Fontainebleau at François's beck and call. The sight of the portrait did banish the king's ill temper, however, and he even called Anne d'Heilly in to view the masterpiece.

"Magnifique!" she exclaimed. "Why, Madame Tevoulère looks almost beautiful!"

"I should hope so, since she is more than that in life," said Andrew.

Sheathing her claws, Anne smiled at the Englishman. "M'sieur, have you been to visit our poor Micheline? She has been desperately ill."

"Has she? I heard that she was not well, but I wasn't certain if it was serious."

"Oh, *mais oui!* Madame de St. Briac has feared for her life!"

Sandhurst looked sharply toward the king. "And your physician? What has he to say?"

"It is a digestive malady. I hardly think that the lady is fit to receive male visitors."

Observing the way François glared at his mistress, Andrew felt suspicious again. It seemed highly likely that all of this was merely a ruse to keep him from Micheline—at her own request.

"I would not want to disrupt Madame's recovery," Sandhurst said evenly. "If she is better before I leave Fontainebleau, I will see her then."

"Leave?" cried Anne. "When are you leaving?"

"Before the week is out, my lady. I have pressing business in England this April."

Anne had hoped to have her own turn of solitary portrait sittings with the irresistible Englishman. Sighing, she murmured, "How sad for us. I do hope, though, that you won't be a stranger in the future."

Sandhurst glanced up, a smile playing over his mouth. "That remains to be seen, mademoiselle."

CHAPTER 17

March 30–31, 1533

MICHELINE WAS DREAMING ABOUT RABELAIS. HIS FACE, ALTERnately whimsical, serious, and laughing, advanced and retreated, telling her over and over again, "You've only one life, and then comes the great perhaps. Do as you please . . . do as *you* please . . ."

She awoke covered with a sheen of perspiration, her eyes wide and alert.

"Aimée, I must see M'sieur Rabelais!"

"*Chérie,* you cannot! He left Fontainebleau two days ago." Aimée pressed a cool cloth to Micheline's brow. "Why on earth do you want to see *him!*"

"I hoped to seek his advice—about love," she whispered.

"What knowledge could Rabelais have on such a topic? The man's a monk!"

"Yes," Micheline agreed as her stomach began to gurgle in a familiar way, "but he seemed to know about all of life. . . ."

Aimée watched as her friend turned her face away to stare out the window, her eyes filled with melancholy. It hurt Aimée to see her like this, but she told herself that it would be better in the long run. Andrew Selkirk was only an infatuation. Why, Selkirk's own manservant sang the praises of the Earl of Sandhurst! What better recommendation could there be?

Micheline drifted back to sleep throughout the day, waking only to take periodic nourishment. She had been very ill, and remained extremely weak. Remembering the horrors of the first day, Aimée could only thank God that her friend had lived.

In the evening Suzette came to relieve her mistress so that Aimée might sup with her family.

"You must call me if Madame Tevoulère becomes ill

again," Aimée told her softly. "And she must be left alone to rest. If anyone calls, tell them she cannot have visitors yet."

"*Oui*, madame." Suzette nodded.

It was past eight o'clock when a knock sounded at the door. Micheline was sleeping fitfully, tossing and making sounds, but she did not awake. Suzette went to answer the knock.

"I wish to see your mistress."

It was Andrew Selkirk, the Englishman who had kept every female servant on pins and needles since his arrival at Fontainebleau. Suzette had been married for over six years, but she was no exception. Blushing, she smiled dreamily up at Andrew.

"I wish I could oblige you, m'sieur, but I've orders that Madame must not have visitors."

Sandhurst was all too familiar with the maid's expression. Usually he was loath to take advantage of feminine weakness, but this case did seem to be special.

"You seem to be a girl of extraordinary beauty and understanding," he murmured, his brown eyes melting her defenses. "Couldn't you make an exception in my case? I'm certain that Madame Tevoulère would thank you for it. You see, I'm leaving Fontainebleau tomorrow, and this is my only opportunity to tell her good-bye."

"Oh . . . well . . . I suppose, in that case—" Suzette found that she could scarcely speak in his presence. "The thing is, she's asleep, and I don't know if it's wise—"

"I promise to be careful, mademoiselle. I won't disturb her. If she doesn't awake, I'll leave quietly."

"*D'accord*," Suzette replied weakly.

"I'll be only a moment." Sandhurst gave her a potent smile. "You'll trust me alone with Madame Tevoulère, won't you?"

Suzette was still nodding when the door closed and she found herself alone in the corridor.

On the other side of the door, Sandhurst turned to behold Micheline lying in a great testered bed, looking extremely pale and small against the pillows. He was ashamed for ever suspecting that her illness might have been a lie, but his guilt was quickly replaced by concern. He crossed to the bed, perched on the edge, and took her limp fingers between his two tanned, strong hands.

"Fondling, can you hear me?"

After a moment Micheline blinked and smiled weakly. The dreams improve, she thought. How real he seems!

"I have to talk to you, Micheline. It's very important. Do you understand?"

She beamed at him and nodded slightly.

"I have to leave Fontainebleau tomorrow, but I couldn't go without seeing you. Have you reconsidered? Is there anything you want to say to me?"

His face swam before her. So many thoughts were tangled in her mind that she couldn't sort them out. Rabelais. Yes, that was what she wanted to tell Andrew.

" 'Do as you please,' " Micheline whispered, smiling.

"I see." A muscle flexed in his jaw. "Well, then, good-bye."

Her eyes were closed. "The . . . great perhaps . . ." she seemed to murmur.

"Quite." Sandhurst stood, then stared down at Micheline's lovely face for a long moment. "*Adieu,* Michelle."

That same night Sandhurst sought out Aimée de St. Briac, who assured him that Micheline was in no danger any longer. She was only weak now from the two long days of profound upset to her digestion, and the king's physician had recommended these vast quantities of rest.

"Does he have any idea what caused this?" Andrew asked, his tawny brows knit with concern.

"The physician says it could only be something Micheline ate, but since everyone else at the table partook of the same foods, we are all quite mystified."

"Hmm." Thoughtfully he rested a forefinger against the edge of his mouth.

"Was there something else, m'sieur? My daughters are waiting to be kissed good night."

"I ought to tell you good-bye, madame. I return to England tomorrow."

Aimée felt a sharp pang of sadness. It was a shame that things couldn't have turned out differently. If only Andrew Selkirk were another sort of man . . .

"We shall miss you, m'sieur," she said sincerely. "It has been a pleasure to know you, and I wish you good fortune."

Lifting her hand, Sandhurst kissed it lightly and managed

to smile. "I return your sentiments. Good-bye, madame. Kindly make my farewells to your family."

"I shall. *Au revoir,* m'sieur."

Lying warm and naked in the great testered bed, Aimée watched her husband undress in front of the fire. In spite of her mixed feelings about Andrew Selkirk, now that he was leaving, a burden seemed lifted from Aimée's shoulders. At least there was no choice anymore. Micheline would *have* to marry the Earl of Sandhurst, and some sixth sense told Aimée that all would be well. She could return her attention to Thomas, and this seemed a perfect time to begin.

"Mmm," she purred, "I've missed you. . . ."

"Have you!" St. Briac glanced over at his wife, his mouth flickering with amused surprise. "Since when have you been able to spare the time for such selfish emotions?"

"If you are referring to my preoccupation with Micheline, I can happily report that matters seem to be resolving themselves without me. She is nearly good as new, and Andrew Selkirk leaves tomorrow for England. There's nothing left for me to worry about—at the moment at least!"

Thomas stopped in the act of unlacing his breeches. "Did you say that Selkirk is leaving?"

"That's right—in the morning. He asked me to tell you good-bye."

St. Briac reached for his shirt and put it back on. "I ought to speak to him before he goes."

"What! *Now?*" wailed Aimée.

He arched a brow, smiling. "Now you're getting a taste of what I've been enduring these past months! Rather unpleasant, *n'est-ce pas?*"

"You're being hateful," she accused him.

"Not at all. It's just that I happen to like M'sieur Selkirk. I'd like to remind him that he had at least one friend here at Fontainebleau." Pulling on his doublet, St. Briac leaned across the bed and dropped a kiss on Aimée's pouting lips. "It's time you learned patience, *miette.* You're much too spoiled."

In the doorway he glanced back and caught sight of a pillow flying from the bed. St. Briac dodged the missile just in time, and then the sound of his low laughter drifted back to Aimée from the other side of the door.

*   *   *

Thomas discovered Andrew Selkirk in his modest room, folding shirts and drinking wine.

"You ought to leave that to your manservant," St. Briac remarked.

The thought of Jeremy's reaction to such a statement made Sandhurst smile. "Oh, Playfair is off making a long farewell to a little saucemaker he's gotten to know rather well. In any case, I don't mind. The activity distracts me."

Thomas didn't need to ask what the Englishman needed to be distracted from. "Have you seen Micheline? Does she know you're leaving?"

"Yes on both counts." Andrew proffered a goblet of wine to St. Briac. "If you don't mind, I'd rather not discuss it."

When the shirts were folded and stacked, the two men took chairs in front of the fire. The flames leaped and danced, gilding Sandhurst's hair and handsome profile. They talked for a time about horses, England, and the wines made at Château du Soleil. At length, Thomas inquired, "Are you familiar with Paris? I can recommend excellent lodgings."

"I'd appreciate that. The auberge we picked at random on the way here left much to be desired." Ironically the Duke of Aylesbury owned a magnificent house in Paris, but Andrew had no intention of going there. He didn't want word to reach his father that he'd been in France at all. "We ate cold vegetables and hard bread on a greasy board and the wine was *piquette*. Playfair and I had to take turns sleeping during the night to ensure the safety of our belongings. Needless to say, I shall be grateful for your recommendation."

"My sister, Nicole, is married to an artist named Michel Joubert. They live quite comfortably on the Right Bank, and I can assure you that they would be more than happy to give you rooms for a night."

"But it would be too great an imposition! They've never met me."

"Trust me, my friend. My sister enjoys guests above all else. I will write a message for you to take to her. She will be delighted to welcome you—and equally delighted to hear all the news of my family."

"Well, if you are certain . . ."

St. Briac laughed. "Absolutely!"

"In that case, I am grateful."

The two men rose and shook hands. "It is late," said Thomas. "I'll say good-bye now and wish you godspeed."

"I've enjoyed knowing you, m'sieur," replied Andrew.

"I have to tell you that I am sorry your story with Micheline could not have had a happier ending. I only hope that my wife is right and that Micheline will not have cause to regret her choice."

"Madame is for Lord Sandhurst?" Andrew inquired, his brows flicking upward.

"She heard that he is everything wonderful in a man." Thomas shrugged. "And I'm sure that if you care for Micheline, you also must wish her happiness in her marriage."

Sandhurst watched as the other man went to the table and took up a quill to write a brief message to his sister. On another sheet of parchment he wrote her name, address, and directions to help Andrew find the house easily.

"Don't look so angry, Selkirk," Thomas admonished when he put down the quill. "After all, the lady had already given her word to marry the Earl of Sandhurst before she ever met you!"

When Andrew spoke, there was an unmistakable edge of steel in his voice. "You're right, and I do hope that Micheline will be happy, but it *won't* be with the Earl of Sandhurst. Of that much I'm certain."

"Why do you say that?" St. Briac demanded, utterly taken aback.

"Forget it. I was just raving."

Andrew laughed then, but Thomas felt uneasy. After they exchanged farewells again and he took his leave, he walked only a few paces down the corridor before stopping. Raking a hand through his crisp chestnut hair, he ran the Englishman's words through his mind over and over. *Sangdieu!* What could he have meant?

"Greetings, my lord!"

St. Briac looked up to see Jeremy Playfair, weaving slightly as he approached.

"Playfair!" he exclaimed softly, elated. The young man looked more than slightly intoxicated, which was fine with Thomas. Taking Jeremy by the arm, he drew him farther away from Andrew Selkirk's door. "I have something to ask you, and I must demand that you give me an honest answer."

This Frenchman had always appeared merry enough to Jeremy, but now he towered over him in a manner that seemed altogether menacing. "Certainly, my lord!" he babbled. "If I can!"

"A few minutes ago your master said that he wished that Micheline Tevoulère might be happy, but that it wouldn't be with the Earl of Sandhurst. He emphasized that he was certain about that. What did he mean?"

"Why—why—it's because he don't intend to go through with the wedding!"

St. Briac's confusion grew. "Who doesn't?"

"Lord Sandhurst!" As soon as this was out, Jeremy's eyes nearly crossed as he realized what he had said, but Thomas was still in the dark.

"How would Andrew Selkirk know that?" An absolutely wild notion occurred to him. "That is unless . . . you don't mean—"

"I can't say another word, monseigneur! If he finds out, he'll see me hanged! He'll have me drawn and quartered! I must go now."

St. Briac caught the young Englishman by the collar of his shirt. "Be easy, my friend. I give you my word that I will not betray your confidence."

"Do you swear? Swear that you won't tell a soul in all the world that it's been Sandhurst himself here at Fontainebleau!"

So there it was, a truth that left Thomas stunned. "I swear," he sighed.

"Sandhurst meant no harm! The marriage was being forced on him by the king and the Duke of Aylesbury. He considered refusing outright, but the stakes were high, and so we thought it might be prudent to at least have a look at the chit. You see, I'm not Playfair, either; I'm Sir Jeremy Culpepper, Sandhurst's friend."

"I think I can guess the rest. Your friend fell in love with Micheline, and his pride was stung when she continued to choose a stranger over him. I can imagine how he must feel."

"Sandhurst's always been cynical about love and marriage, but now I think he'll never take a wife. A shame, isn't it?"

"Yes, M'sieur Culpepper, it is a shame. I must be off now. Thank you for your time."

"You won't forget?"

"My oath? Rest easy, m'sieur; my word is good."

Before Château de Fontainebleau awoke at six o'clock, Andrew and Jeremy mounted their horses and clattered over the moonlit Oval Courtyard.

"God's toes!" exclaimed Culpepper. "I don't know about

you, but I shall be bloody glad to be back in England. France is well enough, I suppose, but there's no place like home.''

Sandhurst looked up at Micheline's darkened windows and expelled a harsh sigh. "Indeed . . .''

It was still dark when Micheline awoke. She had tossed fitfully all night, not because of illness but because she was feeling herself again and had had enough sleep to last a lifetime.

As soon as the first pink streaks stained the eastern sky, Micheline roused Suzette and told her she wanted a bath. This was soon accomplished, and as she scrubbed herself in the *cuve*, Micheline rehearsed every word that she would say to Andrew. All the time that she'd been sick, she had dreamt of him. Since her conversation with Rabelais, everything seemed to make sense. The monk's pronouncements had been unorthodox, yet perfectly suited to Micheline's problems. She had allowed silly fears and events from the past that had nothing to do with Andrew cloud her judgment. Rabelais was right. Micheline would only have one life, and now she was determined not to waste it. Andrew was everything Bernard couldn't be; his strength and tenderness emanated from a steel core, while Bernard had been innately weak. Now that Micheline's eyes were open, she knew that she would never compare Andrew with Bernard again.

Suzette fretted aloud as Micheline dressed, worrying that she should not have gotten up and that this sudden burst of energy might trigger a relapse. The younger girl placated her by nibbling on some bread and sliced orange, but she would not be persuaded to return to bed.

Finally, clad in a gown of buttery-yellow silk, her freshly washed cinnamon-hued curls spilling loose down her back, Micheline was ready. It was past seven now. Andrew would certainly be awake.

"There's someone I must see, Suzette. Don't worry—I'm not going outside!''

"But, madame, what if my mistress should come? What shall I say?''

"Aimée never leaves her own rooms until eight-thirty, but if she should appear before I return, simply tell her that you couldn't control me. Tell her I was incorrigible!'' Laughing gaily, Micheline opened the door and came face to face with St. Briac.

"*Bonjour*, monseigneur!" she greeted him. "I've recovered!"

"So I see." His smile was distracted. "Micheline, I need to talk to you."

"Can it wait? I was on my way to speak to Andrew Selkirk."

"Save your breath, *chérie*. I hate to tell you, but he's just left for England."

PART III

O Lord, what is this worldes bliss,
  That changeth as the moon?
My summer's day in lusty May
  Is darked before the noon.
I hear you say farewell. Nay, nay,
  We depart not so soon.
Why say ye so? Whither will ye go?
  Alas! what have ye done?
All my welfare to sorrow and care
  Should change, if ye were gone,
For in my mind of all mankind
  I love but you alone.

ANONYMOUS

CHAPTER 18

March 31, 1533

"LEFT? LEFT?! BUT HOW CAN THAT BE?" THE BLOOD DRAINED from Micheline's face as St. Briac led her over to a chair.

"He said that he told you good-bye, *ma petite*. Don't you remember? I had the feeling that he didn't want to think about whatever passed between you."

"I—I thought Andrew was here, but later it seemed that it must have been another dream. The physician gave me so many sleeping draughts that even when I appeared to be awake, I was scarcely conscious. What could I have said to Andrew?"

St. Briac held tight to Micheline's trembling hands in an effort to calm her. "I don't know. Perhaps he expected you to change your mind about marrying him when you heard that he was leaving."

"But I would have! I've thought and dreamed of nothing else for days!"

"Are you certain, Micheline? I want you to be honest with me. Why did you refuse him in the first place?"

Something in Thomas's face gave her hope. Perhaps, if she told all to him, he would find a way to help her. And so Suzette was sent from the chamber and Micheline spilled the tale of her marriage to Bernard. She told of her adoration for the young man, of her implicit trust in him, and of the confusion she had felt when he began spending more and more of his time with the court.

"Bernard had been the one ray of sunshine in my life ever since *Maman* died, and now, looking back, I see how naive I was . . . and how hungry I was for love. Bernard seemed the answer to all my prayers. When he began to change, I couldn't face it. I was certain I must be at fault, so I tried harder than ever to be a good wife, hoping that Bernard would want to stay with me in Angoulême.''

"And instead he did the opposite,'' St. Briac said grimly.

"I told myself that all would be well . . . next month, or next season. There didn't seem to be any meaning to my life without Bernard. When I lost the baby, I felt that I had failed him.''

Thomas reached out to wipe away the tear that spilled onto Micheline's cheek.

"You know how desolate I was when Bernard died. Our marriage was my life. Even after I came to court, I continued to grieve, but then . . .'' She sobbed.

"Trust me, Micheline. I'll help you if I can.''

She tried to smile through her tears. "I haven't been able to tell anyone, not even Aimée.'' Taking a deep breath, Micheline looked into St. Briac's sympathetic turquoise eyes and repeated the story of Bernard's infidelities that she had heard in the garden. How long ago that seemed! She had been a different person then.

"It broke my heart. I felt robbed of my last shred of pride and my last illusion about Bernard. I didn't think I could ever feel the slightest attraction to any man again, let alone—''

"Fall in love?''

"Yes! And even after my love for Andrew became almost overwhelming, I tried to deny it. I was so afraid that giving in to my feelings would bring me even more heartache than I'd suffered because of Bernard.''

"What changed your mind?''

"Many things . . . I suppose it was inevitable. I'd turned away from the truth in my marriage, but when it caught up with me, it had grown to drastic proportions. Deep inside, I probably knew from the first night I met Andrew that I would eventually have to surrender to my feelings. Love and fear have been struggling in my heart ever since . . . and, of course, the problem has been compounded by my betrothal to the Earl of Sandhurst. I hid behind that commitment as long as I could.'' Micheline gave him a shaky smile. "Too long, it seems. Then I met François Rabelais. The things he said to me stirred up my deepest emotions and made me see the truth!''

"But then you were taken ill,'' St. Briac sighed. He rose to pace before the fireplace. "Are you really prepared to cast aside caution now?''

"I don't see it quite that way, monseigneur. Andrew is not Bernard. That, of course, was apparent from the start, but what I had a harder time realizing was that he would not repeat Bernard's behavior just because he is a man. While I was ill, I had a great deal of time to think about Andrew. At last I know what it is to be a woman, in love with a *man*. None of us knows what the future will bring, but for now I am resolved not to waste another day because I'm afraid to live."

"And it doesn't matter that he can't offer you wealth or nobility?"

Micheline laughed softly. "Of course not! Andrew is better than any nobleman. All I ask is to share his life—if he'll still have me."

Her eyes widened in silent appeal. St. Briac rubbed his bearded jaw and made a low sound of frustration, then returned to sit across from Micheline.

"Please," she implored, tears springing once more to her eyes, "say that you know where Andrew has gone! If I could not find him . . ." That thought was too terrible to articulate.

"As it happens, I do know—"

Micheline leaped nearly into St. Briac's lap. "Oh, monseigneur, I love you!" she exclaimed, weeping and laughing at once. "Tell me, please, tell me!"

"I'll do better than that, *ma petite*. I'll take you to Andrew myself, though God knows what Aimée will have to say about it." Thomas spared a sigh at the prospect of trying to explain to his wife without breaking his oath to Jeremy Culpepper. Then he rose and grinned at Micheline.

"Make haste, madame! We leave for Paris by midday!"

As it turned out, St. Briac was able to persuade Aimée that Micheline should be reunited with her true love, once she was convinced that her friend truly did love Andrew, but when he told her of that day's journey to Paris, she took a stand.

"I hope you do not entertain thoughts of leaving me behind, Thomas!"

"As a matter of fact, I *do*!" He pretended to be busy selecting clean clothing to take along.

"I'm going," she declared.

"You must stay and look after the babies. Besides, I shouldn't be away more than two days."

"Suzette can care for the girls, especially for so short a

time. I will not be denied this adventure! What if something goes wrong? Micheline may need me! Besides, I want to visit Nicole. I miss her.''

St. Briac tried to repress a smile as he thought back to the last time he had ordered her to stay behind like a good wife. Aimée had followed him to Paris anyway—pregnant and dressed as a boy.

"I may be lord of a village and all the surrounding lands, but I cannot master my own wife," he sighed.

Aimée crossed the room and stood on tiptoe, wrapping her arms around his neck. "Don't be silly. I shall be happy to allow you to master me—as soon as we're alone in bed tonight." After kissing him sensual, she added, "In Paris."

Micheline's final task before leaving Fontainebleau was to meet with King François in the royal bedchamber so that she might make her farewells. Thomas was there to back her up, but Micheline needed little support. With newfound confidence she stated her case to the king, expressed her gratitude for his hospitality and friendship, and told him that she hoped he would wish her well.

François's hazel eyes clouded as he beheld Micheline's radiance. If only . . . he thought. It was bitterly ironic to him that a penniless English painter had managed to succeed where he had failed, but a part of him realized that Micheline could never have been happy as a mistress—even to the king of France. She was blessed with a richly spirited heart and rare intelligence, and a place in line behind Queen Eleanor and Anne d'Heilly wouldn't have suited her. Of course, François thought that Selkirk was totally unworthy, but to point that out would only alienate Micheline. She was clearly in the throes of romance—a condition that the king had learned was intense yet fleeting. He harbored a secret hope that she would come to her senses one day and return to the French court.

Summoning a regal smile, François murmured, "You deserve all the best in life, madame. My thanks to you for gracing my court." He pressed a lingering kiss to her hand. "I wish you joy."

Micheline was surprised to feel tears stinging her eyes. "I will never forget your kindness, sire, and I shall always remember my time here at Fontainebleau with great fondness."

She hurried off to the stables then, but St. Briac remained with his friend until she had disappeared from sight.

"I wouldn't worry about writing to Henry the Eighth just yet about this if I were you, sire," he advised. When François glanced over in surprise he added, "I mean . . . the outcome is still uncertain. Why not wait until I return from Paris and can make a full report."

Then Thomas took his leave and the king went to the window. Anne d'Heilly appeared, as if on cue, to console him, but as they watched the trio emerge from the stables and ride under the Porte Dorée toward the forest, a satisfied smile curved her pretty mouth.

The day-long journey to Paris seemed endless to Micheline. The travelers rode northward over the broad King's Highway, which was paved and lined with majestic plane trees. During a midday pause at an auberge, where they rested the horses and partook of food, Micheline found that she couldn't swallow a bite. She was completely focused, body and soul, on reaching Andrew.

When at last Thomas, Aimée, and Micheline approached the walls and ramparts of Paris, the sky was violet. Soft, lacy snowflakes had begun to swirl down, dusting their hair.

"I'm so excited!" Micheline exclaimed. She sat up straighter on her horse, already aware of the energy of the city that lay beyond these three-hundred-year-old walls. "I've never been to Paris before!"

Aimée beamed at her friend, remembering her own first visit to the city.

"At least the smell isn't quite so repulsive at this time of year," St. Briac allowed.

Of course, a large portion of Micheline's excitement was nervousness. She didn't really care that much about Paris; it was thrilling to be here because Andrew was somewhere within the city's walls. The road from Orleans, which passed Fontainebleau for the king's convenience, entered Paris through the Porte St. Jacques. As Micheline rode through the gates, she imagined Andrew doing the same a few hours earlier.

They made slow progress up the rue St. Jacques, which was crowded with carts, livestock, and students from the university. The latter occupied much of the Left Bank, a huge, confused agglomeration of colleges, spires, convents, and lecture halls, with the attending hostels, taverns, open-air book stalls, and shops of those engaged in the academic trades. Micheline had never imagined houses and buildings crowded so closely together, or such a maze of narrow lanes.

"There is the Sorbonne," Aimée told her, pointing. "It was Thomas's college."

Micheline stared through the dimming twilight and sprinkling snowflakes. She saw a massive Gothic structure, with towers flanking the high arch of the main door, and a steeple rising above. Beyond were the shapes of many more buildings, and the figures of students and officials rushing to and fro over snowy cobbled pathways.

"I have heard about the Sorbonne from my father," she told St. Briac. "He said it was the finest college in the university, and that there is a Latin library with over one thousand volumes!"

"That's true." He nodded. "The Sorbonne has always been an excellent college, with faculties of theology, canon law, medicine, and the arts, but I must give credit to King François for improving not only the Sorbonne but every college in the university. The curriculum has been expanded, the professors receive salaries—"

"And now François should decree that women may attend!" Aimée interjected.

Her husband smiled. "I agree in theory, *miette*, but I fear we won't live to see that happen . . . and unfortunately neither will our daughters."

Micheline had no heart for that argument or any other, for her thoughts were with Andrew. Had he seen all of this for the first time today? Probably not. Older than she by a dozen years, he must be well-traveled and likely as familiar with Paris as he was with London. What was he doing now? That thought gave her pause, for she had seen the way women flocked to be near him.

"Are we nearly there?" she queried.

"Patience, Micheline. It's not far." St. Briac heard the urgent note in her voice and prayed silently that nothing would go amiss.

They turned left on the Quai St. Michel, which bordered the Seine. All along the river booksellers were closing up their stalls for the night. The Pont St. Michel took the trio across the Seine to the Île de la Cité, the island that was the heart of Paris. Passing to the right of the dark pepper-pot towers of the Concièrgerie, Aimée and Thomas exchanged glances, remembering the day they had risked their lives to rescue Georges Teverant from his condemned-prisoner's cell.

They were caught in a crush of horses and carts on the Pont au Change, the bridge that connected the Cité to the Right Bank. Micheline paid little notice. She gazed out over the Seine, which shimmered in the moonlight while snowflakes danced downward through the night sky to melt when they touched the water. Four- and five-story houses huddled close along the riverbanks, their windows beginning to glow, one by one, with candlelight. After the sameness and solitude of Fontainebleau, Micheline felt happy to be in Paris. . . .

When they emerged on the Right Bank, the light had gone, and she was left to her mixed feelings of apprehension and elation.

"I am so grateful to both of you for coming with me," she said after a time. "I never realized that Paris was such a tangle of streets!"

"We're your friends, *ma petite*," St. Briac replied. "It's our pleasure to help you if we can." What he didn't say was that he had come not only to aid her in locating Andrew but also to bring her back to Fontainebleau if the Englishman had changed his mind, either about staying at Nicole's *or* wanting to marry Micheline.

He turned then into the narrow alleyway that led to the stables behind his sister's house. Even as they were dismounting, Michel Joubert came out of the rear door of the narrow four-story dwelling.

"Who is it?" he called.

"It's Thomas, Michel. I have Aimée with me—and a friend of ours."

They went to meet him in the light of the doorway. Michel was a dark-haired, slender man in his mid-thirties. Always an artist, he now taught painting at the university as well.

"How good it is to see you both!" he exclaimed, embracing them fondly. "Nicole will be ecstatic!"

"Michel, I'd like you to meet Micheline Tevoulère," St. Briac said, putting an arm around the girl.

Warm greetings were exchanged, and then they came into the kitchen. The first thing Micheline noticed was a tiny vase of crocuses on the long, bleached table. It prepared her for the charming beauty of Thomas's sister, who seemed not a bit surprised by this unexpected visit from her brother. Nicole Joubert looked very like St. Briac, in a feminine way. She was tall and graceful, with gleaming sable curls, bright blue eyes, and a merry air about her.

After introductions were made, they sat down at the table and accepted bowls of *galimfrée*, a fricassee of poultry sprinkled with verjuice, flavored with spices, and surrounded by a sauce composed of vinegar, bread crumbs, cinnamon, and ginger. Even though they had eaten heartily at Barbizon that afternoon, Micheline found that she was suddenly quite ravenous.

"How good it is to see you all enjoying my cooking!" laughed Nicole. "Your friend, M'sieur Selkirk, ate with equal enthusiasm before he went out this evening."

St. Briac, sensing Micheline's questions, held his hand up to silence her. "So, Andrew arrived?"

"*Mais, oui!* He came this afternoon!" Nicole paused to give her brother a puzzled glance. "Didn't you know, *chérie*? I thought you sent him here!"

"I did. I only wondered if Selkirk would take my advice."

"Oh, absolutely. What a charming man—and so handsome! He almost made me regret my marriage!" She laughed then in a way that caused Michel to bend down to kiss her.

"Incorrigible wench," murmured her husband.

Micheline was hoping that all this activity would distract the Jouberts from her flaming cheeks, but Nicole noticed everything.

"Ah, Micheline! I see that I am not the only woman whom M'sieur Selkirk has charmed!" she teased.

"*Ma soeur,* you have a busy mouth," St. Briac remarked.

"A family trait!" Nicole replied blithely.

"What woman could be oblivious to Andrew Selkirk?" cried Aimée. "Just because we are married, we are not dead! But tell me, Nicole, are we not in danger of being overheard?"

"Oh, no. M'sieur Selkirk and his manservant went out earlier—to a favorite tavern of theirs in years past. I had the feeling that he was longing to drown his sorrows. He'll doubtless be out late—and if a *fille de joie* gets her hands on him, he won't be back at all tonight!"

Aimée decided that it was time to take matters into her own hands.

"Thomas, don't you and Michel have some manly subject that you should discuss alone?"

"Yes! Now that you mention it, we do!" Having no idea at

all what this subject might be, St. Briac led his brother-in-law off to the next room and closed the door.

Since Andrew Selkirk might return at any moment, Aimée decided that there was no time to be lost. Even though she knew nothing of his true identity, she described the situation to Nicole in a way that brought tears to the eyes of all three women. Nicole knew what it meant to marry for love rather than wealth or position, since she had done just that herself. Michel's career as an artist had had its twists and turns, but she had never regretted her decision.

"How wonderful for M'sieur Selkirk!" she declared, smiling approvingly at Micheline. "Since the moment he walked through the door, I have thought that he looked like a man in need of love."

"I mean to give it to him!" Micheline vowed. "In that way, we need each other. I never knew what love truly meant until Andrew came into my life, but now that I've made this discovery, I realize that nothing else is really important unless one has someone to love, who gives love in return. All I want, for the rest of my days, is Andrew by my side. Everything else is incidental."

Nicole wiped a tear from her cheek. "You've learned the most important lesson of all, *chérie*—and it cannot be taught, only experienced." She paused, gathering her thoughts for the more practical details of the current situation. "How shall we effect this reunion? I gather that M'sieur Selkirk may need to be persuaded that Micheline is in earnest."

Mentally Aimée counted the bedchambers in the Joubert household. "Perhaps all they need is an opportunity to be alone," she suggested.

Nicole laughed. "That may be unavoidable unless you wish to share a bed with Micheline while Thomas sleeps with Andrew. I've made a small chamber for Playfair, the manservant, in one of the hanging rooms built out over the street, but that's the last spare bed."

"Good!" Aimée proclaimed. "It's a perfect solution!"

Both women looked to Micheline for approval, and she managed to smile and nod in spite of the tremors that shook the pit of her stomach.

CHAPTER 19

April 1, 1533

HAPPILY AIMÉE CRAWLED NAKED INTO BED BESIDE HER HUSBAND that night. The sensation of his arms drawing her near filled her with joy.

"Thomas . . . ?"

His mouth was blazing a trail from her mouth to her breasts, tasting the sweetness of her skin and enjoying each inch of the journey.

"Mmm?" he managed to answer, then raised his head to inquire, "Is this any time for a conversation?"

"I only wanted to tell you that I had another reason for wanting to accompany you to Paris . . . and return to your sister's house." Happiness swelled Aimée's heart as she continued. "Do you remember what I told you the first time we came here? When we had to hide in the attic from Chauverge?"

St. Briac laughed and kissed her nipple, teasing it with his tongue as it grew taut in response. "How could I forget? Never have I felt such a mixture of anger and exultation as I experienced that moment when you told me you were with child. Only *you* would dare to travel to Paris in that condition—"

"I haven't changed, *mon ange,*" she interjected, running her hands over the hard muscles of his back.

Suddenly St. Briac tensed, lifting himself up on steely arms to stare at Aimée in the darkness. "You *don't* mean—"

Nodding, she wrapped her arms around his neck and buried her face against his shoulder. "Yes. And it's a son this time. I can feel it." Aimée's mouth curved against his skin. "Not that I have anything against girls, but it would be nice—"

"I can't believe it!" he shouted, not caring who heard him. "You rode all this way to Paris, when you *knew*—"

"Shh!" Aimée put a finger over St. Briac's mouth and grinned when he bit it lightly. "Your son wouldn't want to be coddled. Besides, he'll need a head start to keep up with his sisters.''

"What am I to do with you, *miette*?"

"I have several suggestions, monseigneur."

In Andrew's bedchamber across the hall, Micheline barely heard St. Briac's raised voice. Her thoughts were occupied by Andrew Selkirk. Where was he? It was past midnight! When would he return? And when he did enter this chamber, what would happen?

She imagined all sorts of women, seemingly more beautiful than she, twined about Andrew in the corner of a tavern. One would not need to be a *fille de joie* to lust after Andrew Selkirk! Perhaps he had gone home with a willing lady and would not even return to the Joubert house tonight!

At that moment the door swung open, revealing a familiar male silhouette, then closed. Micheline held her breath, suddenly terrified, as she watched Andrew strip away his clothing before the meager fire.

He is here! she thought joyfully before another sudden wave of fear washed over her. It had been so very long since she had been fully conscious in his presence, and in all that time Micheline had dreamed of nothing else. Still, now that Andrew was truly present, walking naked and splendid across the room to bathe his face in a basin of cold water, Micheline wished that the floor would open and swallow her up.

She wished that she were the kind of woman who could throw herself across his body when he got into bed, but she wasn't. Instead, Andrew slid between the sheets and instantly sensed her presence. His first thought was that it must be the Jouberts' serving girl, Rosette, who had blushed, stammered, and finally tried to kiss him that afternoon.

Turning on his side, Sandhurst touched a cheek that felt hauntingly familiar. "You really cannot stay. I'm sorry," he said gently.

Micheline was totally undone by his nearness. The sensation of Andrew's fingers against her cheek sent her in search of his mouth. No sooner had their lips met, Micheline's opening helplessly, than Andrew drew back.

"I must be dreaming!" he said to himself.

"I'd be tempted to agree, m'sieur, except I have dreamed so long of this moment that I cannot be confused."

"*Micheline?* Is it really you?"

Tears sprang to her eyes. "Yes. Yes! Of course it is I!"

"Just a minute. Don't move." He scrambled off the bed, felt for a candle on the table, lit it in the fireplace, and returned to hold the flame before her face.

The light illuminated Andrew's expression, too, and Micheline smiled fondly at the sight of his caramel-colored eyes, so wide with shock, and his mouth open, closed, then open again as he tried to find words. A lock of dark gold hair fell engagingly over his brow.

"How *good* it is to see you," she whispered. Impulse prompted her to lay her hand on the hard-muscled expanse of his chest. "You're warm. It's so hard to realize that this is not another dream."

Micheline's touch released a long-suppressed flood of yearning inside of Andrew. He reached back to replace the candlestick on the table, then caught her up in his arms. His mouth slanted hungrily over hers, tasting and plundering, while Micheline matched his ardor. They were both naked, kneeling on the feather tick, their bodies pressed together. The soft curves of her breasts burned his hard chest, and farther down their hips met, Andrew's fully roused manhood hot against her belly and between her legs. Micheline's hands gloried in the rich texture of his hair and the breadth of his shoulders, while Sandhurst ran his fingers down the elegant curve of her back before molding her buttocks and drawing her closer still.

Micheline was moaning, her breath warm in his mouth. Every fiber of her being craved the union of their bodies. As one, they fell back on the pillows and she arched her hips against him, aching until with one hard thrust he filled her. They moved together with a rhythmic violence, breathing harshly, passion seeming to crackle in the air that surrounded their straining bodies.

Finally Micheline was jolted by a climax that swept out in wildly pulsating currents of delight, down her thighs, over her breasts, even to the tips of her fingers and toes. Moments later Sandhurst found his own release, and the two of them lay entwined in the aftermath, gasping for breath.

Slowly coherent thought seeped into Andrew's consciousness. He forced himself to withdraw from the addictive warmth of Micheline's body and lay on his back a few inches away from her.

"I cannot believe that I just did that! Damn!" he cursed.

"Andrew, what is it?" Micheline reached out to him in confusion.

"Don't touch me! For the past twenty-four hours I have steeled myself to live without you, told myself to forget you, tried to convince myself that I am strong enough to put all that was between us in the past and get on with my life. Tonight I went out with Jeremy and drank wine and saw a few old friends, and I actually enjoyed myself for a moment or two! I was beginning to feel quite proud of myself, thinking I was conquering the heartache I felt at Fontainebleau with the sheer force of my own will. Ha! Don't you find that amusing? I walked in here, found you, and the force of my will and all my resolutions went right out the bloody *window*!"

"If you'd just allow me to explain—"

"Yes, that's right, *explain*! Did you come here for one last good-bye, since you weren't in any condition to send me off properly last night?"

Stung, Micheline reached out and slapped him sharply, but Sandhurst caught her wrist in a punishing grip. "Spare me the dramatics, madame, and tell me what brings you to Paris . . . and to *my* bed."

Emotion boiled up within her and sent tears spilling down her cheeks. "I—I came here to tell you that I love you! *I love you*, Andrew! You must believe me!" She sobbed. "I don't even remember talking to you last night. The king's physician kept giving me sleeping draughts, and after a while everything seemed a dream. When I awoke today, feeling well, and learned that you had left Fontainebleau, I *had* to come after you. Andrew, I *love* you! I was wrong before, and I admit it. I want to marry you more than anything in the world . . . if you'll still have me."

Sandhurst rubbed both hands over his face, then folded them and pressed his mouth against the clenched knuckles. "Oh, God."

"Is that all you can say? Have you changed your mind?"

"Michelle, this is all well and good, but I can't just wipe out everything you've said in the past on the basis of your new, more welcome sentiments." He turned to stare at her through the shadows. "You were so adamant about choosing marriage to the Earl of Sandhurst over my simpler but heart-felt proposal. What happened to your resolution never to love again . . . and your lifelong devotion to your dead husband? It's certainly gratifying to hear you change course again and say that you love *me*, but how do I know that you won't reverse this position tomorrow, or next month?''

"Andrew, I swear to you that I am sincere. I simply couldn't face my true feelings before."

"Why not?" The softness of his voice was belied by a steely undercurrent. "Tell me, Michelle. I've seen that haunted look in your eyes. If you expect me to believe that you love me, you'll have to start by being honest."

"*Alors.* I will explain." She shivered in the darkness and Sandhurst relented and reached out to draw her into his embrace. Safe in the warm circle of his arms, Micheline rested her head against his chest and haltingly told her story.

She spared no detail, revealing all that St. Briac had heard that morning and more. Somehow, it was easier than she had expected. What had caused her such desperation in the past now seemed a fading memory.

"I see my marriage in a different light now," Micheline whispered at one point. "After I learned of Bernard's infidelities at court, and it dawned on me that I had been clinging to an illusion, I felt disgraced. Every time I thought of Bernard, and our marriage, a knife twisted in my heart. It wasn't until you came into my life that I saw the past clearly. Bernard brought me a great deal of happiness when we were young. In a way, he was the father I sought to love and protect me. I suppose I became too great a responsibility for him and so he ran away. I'm not bitter anymore about Bernard. I feel sad for his sake, but in my own case, I've grown up only these past few months, learning first of all to rely on myself, and then . . . what real love can mean."

Micheline went on to explain the stages she'd passed through before facing the truth about her love for Andrew, including the odd influence Rabelais had had on her. When her story was finished, ending with her journey to Paris with Thomas and Aimée, Micheline sighed with pleasure. "I feel so different, but I don't suppose I've really changed. Do you remember the day I told you that there were a lot of doors I'd kept shut inside of me?"

"I remember everything, fondling," Sandhurst replied, kissing her fragrant hair.

"I was just afraid to open those doors, because I couldn't be certain what lay on the other side. As my love for you developed, courage came with it, and I couldn't hide any longer."

"What did you find on the other side?"

"Freedom. Freedom from the past and all the fears that were suffocating me. I feel as if I've shed a tremendous weight. My heart is light now, perhaps for the first time."

Andrew was silent for long minutes, lost in thought, until Micheline turned her face up to gaze at him.

"You haven't changed your mind, have you?"

"About loving you? Marrying you?" He smiled and kissed her tenderly. "No. No, I haven't changed my mind. I'm just digesting all of this. Why don't we get some sleep, and hopefully I'll have sorted out a few things by morning."

That wasn't quite what Micheline had hoped to hear, but it was difficult to worry when they snuggled down under the covers and she lay in Andrew's warm masculine embrace. Sleep seemed impossible, yet moments later she was breathing evenly, one slim hand curled around his forearm.

Sandhurst, meanwhile, stared into the darkness, thinking.

Blinking against the sunlight that flooded the bedchamber, Micheline turned her face away and attempted once again to open her eyes.

"Good morrow, Michelle." Sandhurst sat in a carved chair near the bed. Washed, shaved, and dressed, he was eating an apple and looking exceedingly handsome.

"What time is it?" She pushed back her mane of auburn curls and rose on an elbow.

"Ten o'clock. Don't look so guilty! You must have needed the sleep." He, in turn, had needed the early morning to speak to St. Briac. Andrew had suspected that word of his true identity had slipped out, but the Frenchman had reassured him that he was the only person who knew. Most important, Micheline still thought Sandhurst was a painter named Selkirk. St. Briac swore that love alone had prompted her to travel to Paris in search of the man she meant to marry.

"What of you?" she was asking. "You claimed that you needed to sort things out. What have you decided, Andrew?"

He moved to sit on the edge of the bed, offering her the apple, which she nibbled at solely because it was in his hand.

"I've decided to take you back to England with me, fondling. How could I refuse?"

"Oh, Andrew, I love you!" She reached up to trace the sculpted line of his cheekbone, and felt that she would die of happiness when he caught her hand and brought it over to his mouth.

"And I love you, Michelle." He kissed her sensitive palm. "I've never said that to another woman, nor have I even considered marriage in the past. I'm deadly serious now, though, and for that reason I want to put off our wedding until we're in England."

She looked stricken. "But—!"

"We're both rather besot at the moment, but we have to keep in mind that there's more to marriage than love." He paused, smiling ironically. "In truth, until I met you I wasn't even sure that love was necessary! The point is, I want you to see what your life will be like while you still can change your mind. There's a great deal you don't know about me—"

"I know enough! I know what kind of man you are!"

"There's much more involved than that, Michelle. England is quite different from France, and my usual life is different from the one I led at Fontainebleau."

"Andrew, I could be happy with you if we lived in a *hovel*!"

He had to laugh. "I appreciate that . . . and I can reassure you that my circumstances aren't quite that desperate, but all the same, I want you to see for yourself. I have relatives that even *I* have trouble tolerating—"

"I shall love them all!" she vowed.

"I doubt that. I'm quite serious about this, Micheline, so you would do well to save your breath. We'll go to England, you will see for yourself what the rest of your life would be like if you marry me, and then, if you remain certain, we'll have the proper sort of wedding you deserve."

Micheline sighed, pretended to pout, then suddenly gave him a blinding smile unlike anything Sandhurst had seen before.

"I yield, my love," she said. "But can we leave for England this morning?"

CHAPTER 20

April 1–4, 1533

"IS THIS SOME SORT OF PERVERSE JEST ON YOUR PART, SANDHURST?"
Jeremy Culpepper demanded, his cheeks red with outrage and
stuffed with the freshly baked bread he had been chewing.

"Shh!" Andrew laid an agile finger over his mouth and
shook his head with mock severity. Drawing his friend into a
corner of the kitchen, he whispered, "It's only for a few
more days, old man! Just until we reach London."

"I don't believe it! The chit's followed you to Paris,
begged to marry you after all, and *still* you won't tell her who
you really are! Sometimes I think you continue this farce only
because it amuses you to watch me humiliate myself answering to 'Playfair' and acting the part of your manservant!"

"Jeremy, stop ranting." The spark of humor had gone
from his eyes. "I have my reasons for not telling Micheline
I'm the Earl of Sandhurst, and I can assure you that they
have nothing to do with *you*. Instead of complaining, why not
look on the bright side? It's April. Spring's in the air, and we
leave for England within the hour." He gave Culpepper a
distracted smile. "Cheer up."

Pretty Thérèse Joubert, at ten the oldest of Nicole's three
children, came in then and Andrew greeted her, glad for the
interruption. She offered them some sweet butter to spread on
the warm bread, which Jeremy accepted. It seemed that his
appetite only increased when he was upset.

Sandhurst excused himself to check on the horses. Outside,
he glanced up to the third-floor window that Micheline had
flung open earlier to let in the sunshine. Last night's snow
was only a memory; today was warm and fragrant with the
promise of spring. Micheline was making final preparations
for the journey to London while Aimée kept her company. It
would be their last opportunity to talk for a long time to
come.

Sighing, Andrew wondered once more if he was right not to divulge his true identity to Micheline yet. He told himself that he wanted her to have a chance to become accustomed to one thing at a time. So much had happened just in the last twenty-four hours. What if Micheline had second thoughts as they traveled to England? It seemed better that she be given the opportunity to ease into her new life . . . or even to change her mind.

Sandhurst had other reasons that he was less willing to examine. Part of him still worried that Micheline might have acted on a romantic whim. It was difficult to forget all the things she had said to him during their weeks at Fontainebleau, and difficult to believe that the shadows were gone from her eyes forever. They were both new at love, and there was still a part of Andrew that remained detached, watching in cynical disbelief. He, too, needed the next few days, to erase any lingering doubts that Micheline truly loved him, before she learned that she was marrying the Earl of Sandhurst after all, and not Selkirk the painter.

Besides, Andrew had grown used to his new identity. He was in no hurry to reclaim his wealth, title, relatives . . . or past.

"For a man in love, you look altogether too serious," St. Briac remarked, coming up behind the Englishman.

Sandhurst mustered a faint smile. "In this case, love is proving to be fraught with untold complications. My heart may be filled with joy, but my mind is overcrowded with worries."

"Will you take a piece of advice from an old married man?"

"Gratefully!"

"Listen to your heart if you begin to despair. You and Micheline have genuine love on your side. I've learned, during years spent with Aimée that have been anything but tranquil, that problems which may seem insurmountable when they arise really can be sorted out—and later forgotten—if two people love each other enough. Have faith, and for God's sake, don't give up!"

"It sounds as if you're sending me off to war," Andrew remarked sardonically.

"Believe me, war is far simpler than marriage . . . but nowhere near as much fun!"

St. Briac's wry laughter was irresistible. Sandhurst joined

in, clasping the Frenchman's hand. "I appreciate your sage advice . . . I think!"

A hearty midday meal was served in the Joubert kitchen, complete with several toasts to the future happiness of Andrew and Micheline and the health of the next St. Briac baby. Then, amid loud cries of *"Au revoir!"* and *"Bonne chance!"* Andrew, Jeremy, and Micheline rode out into the crowded street, bound for London.

They first had to reach Calais, which lay on the northernmost coast of France. Sandhurst's first thought had been to hire a coach, but Micheline would not hear of it. She loved nothing more than riding. On horseback they could reach Calais more quickly, and since the weather was fine, what was the point of a coach?

Once they were out of Paris, Andrew watched as she galloped ahead. She wore a ladylike habit of hyacinth-blue velvet, and her curls were protected from the wind by a pearl-studded gold crispinette, but Micheline's manner was that of a free-spirited young girl.

"What a wonderful day!" she exclaimed, laughing as she looked back over a shoulder. "Don't dawdle, you two! We've a long way to go!"

Even from a distance he could see the sparkle in her violet-blue eyes. "Dear God, I hope she won't feel obliged to change once she learns she's to be a countess," he murmured.

"What's that?" Culpepper asked, his own gaze riveted on Micheline.

"I said, hurry up! Have you no shame? Do you want to be left in the dust by a female?"

Sandhurst was laughing now himself, and urging his steed forward. The sun struck sparks on his ruffled gold hair as he drew alongside Micheline and reached out to briefly catch her hand.

"I am the happiest lady in France!" she proclaimed, beaming at the man she loved.

Andrew arched a brow. "I only hope you will express corresponding sentiments when you are in England."

Micheline laughed and raised her face to receive kisses from April's new sun and breeze.

"How could I not? I shall be 'Mistress Selkirk' then!"

Behind them Jeremy Culpepper rolled his eyes and wondered if he'd ever see this coil unsnarled. . . .

* * *

It had been dark for an hour when the three travelers stopped at a quiet auberge called the Levrette, near the village of Poix, east of Amiens. The place appeared clean, which was a change from most inns, and the food smelled appetizing.

First, they ate in the common room. There was a rich stew, or *potage,* served on pewter dishes covered with thick chunks of bread. Micheline ate as heartily as the men, enjoying the mixture of veal, beef, mutton, bacon, and vegetables. They drank strong but sour wine from pewter cups, then Sandhurst bade the innkeeper show them their rooms. By then Micheline was glad to escape, for the stares of the other male guests, including two ruddy-cheeked monks, were making her nervous.

"Your chambers are at the end of the corridor, on the right." The innkeeper, carrying tankards of wine and ale to other guests, motioned vaguely with his bald head. "They're the only two I have that adjoin."

Andrew glanced back at Jeremy. "Go and see to the horses, won't you, Playfair?"

"But—" Color flared in the younger man's cheeks. "As you wish, *master!*"

Upstairs, Micheline followed right behind Sandhurst into the first room and put down her bag of possessions on the grander of two beds. When the straw tick made a crunching sound, she tried not to wince.

"A far cry from Fontainebleau," she said, smiling bravely, "but it won't matter as long as you're next to me."

Sandhurst crossed the chamber and opened a connecting door. "I appreciate the thought, fondling, but you'll be sleeping in here." Picking up her belongings, he disappeared through the doorway.

Surprise then embarrassment washed over her. Slowly Micheline followed her betrothed into a smaller room with a clean and serviceable bed for one.

"I don't understand," she whispered.

The sight of Micheline's flushed cheeks was nearly too much for Andrew.

"Last night was a mistake that I don't intend to repeat until we're married," he explained evenly. "It would be best if we didn't bind ourselves together with words—or acts—of love until . . . you are absolutely certain that you have made the right choice."

Her iris-blue eyes were wide with confusion. "I have already made my choice! I want *you*!"

"You may have second thoughts after we arrive in London."

The sight of his sculpted profile, accentuated by the firelight, filled her with longing that was heightened by his cool demeanor.

"What's wrong with you? Are you afraid that I'll meet the Earl of Sandhurst and be led astray?" Micheline approached him and declared, "I don't want Lord Sandhurst! As far as I'm concerned, he can take his title and his wealth and go to the devil!"

Andrew flinched slightly. When her small hands clasped his own, their eyes met and he opened his mouth. Whether he'd meant to speak or to kiss her, Micheline wasn't sure, for a moment later he was turning away.

"Sleep well, fondling. We have a long day ahead of us if we're to reach Calais by nightfall."

Micheline enjoyed the next day's ride, over countryside that was different from what she was used to. They passed through valleys that were already beginning to turn green. Farms and villages were set amid willow-hung canals, while wooded hills curved gently in the distance. Micheline wished that Jeremy would disappear and that she and Andrew could pause for a leisurely meal under one of the romantic-looking willow trees.

Instead, they ate quickly at a village tavern, then continued the long ride to Calais. Dusk was upon them when their destination appeared on the horizon, its towers and battlements seeming to rise straight out of the sea. The walls were broken by Lanterngate, the broad archway that led into a town Micheline found quite charming. The crowded, winding streets were lined with wooden houses with crow-step gables and pleasant gardens. They passed Our Lady Church, with its tall, graceful spire, and the cobbled marketplace, which boasted wares brought in on the ships, then stopped before the swinging sign of the Cross Keys tavern. Andrew dismounted, then helped Micheline down from her horse. She savored the sensation of his hands about her waist.

"Well," he said, "the worst is over. We'll sail at first light, and you can relax the rest of the way to London."

Relaxing wasn't exactly what Micheline longed to do, but there seemed little to be gained by arguing. Later that night she looked out the window of her solitary chamber, observing the shadowy ships that crowded the wharves along the foreshore. Moonlight played over their various shapes as they swayed in the glittering blue-black ocean, their pennants streaming in the wind. Which one will carry me to England? she wondered. And what waits for me there?

Micheline slept alone again, dreaming fitfully of Andrew, until her door opened in what seemed to be darkness and his voice urged her gently, "Dawn is breaking, Michelle, and we must sail with the tide."

An hour later she found herself on a trim, tastefully appointed yacht called the *Day Dream*. The waves were rather choppy under the lavender-gray sky, but the wind was with them. Once the sails were set, Andrew joined Micheline on deck. His normal good temper was returning now that they'd left France behind and England lay just a few hours away.

"Wherever did you get this magnificent yacht?" queried Micheline.

Culpepper, in the act of tying off a line, shot a look at his friend.

"That's not important," Sandhurst said in a tone that was light and firm at once. "What is important is that we have a comfortable means of travel across the Channel. Do you know, I surprise myself, but I'll own that I'm happy to be returning to England!"

"Are you happy that I'm with you?" she asked, eager by now for some reassurance.

"Yes, of course I am." Seeing Micheline shiver in the sea air, Andrew put an arm around her and held her close, then sought what seemed to be a safer topic. "I nearly forgot to tell you—St. Briac is going to send all of your clothes and other possessions on to London."

Micheline was surprised. She'd nearly forgotten the abundance of gowns, jewels, and accessories she'd accumulated in anticipation of her marriage to the Earl of Sandhurst.

"That's nice, I suppose . . . though it's a relief to know I won't really need all of that once we're married. I truly will prefer a simpler life."

"I feel badly that I haven't even provided you with a maid!"

"Don't be silly! I don't miss that in the least! Playfair is acting as chaperon, isn't he? And after we're married, I'd much rather have you all to myself. Servants only get in the way.

Why would I want a maid when I'll have a *husband* to brush my hair and unfasten my gowns?'' Her expression was sensually radiant.

Sandhurst shut his eyes for a moment, wishing he didn't have to think at all. "Why don't you go below, fondling? There's food and wine in the cabin, and a few books as well.''

Although she would have preferred to stay with him, in spite of the cold, and had even hoped to learn a bit about sailing, something in Andrew's eyes made her obey. When he took on that remote look, it worried her. Most perplexing was the fact that she couldn't explain to herself why he was keeping himself so distant. The possibility existed that he didn't really want to marry her, that she'd forced his hand with her blatant words and actions in his bed at the Jouberts'. That thought was enough to make her grateful for the books waiting below. She prayed that they'd be so fascinating that she would be totally distracted from the worries of real life.

Rough seas lengthened the crossing, and it was dark when the yacht anchored at Dover. Sandhurst had decided that a hot supper at a small inn called the Hand-in-Hand would do them all good, but then he intended to sail the remainder of the way up the Thames to London. As much as a part of him dreaded returning to his real life and telling Micheline the truth, he was eager to end his charade.

Micheline had thought that they would complete their journey by land, but she didn't question Andrew. If he had hired the yacht, it seemed likely that he would have to leave it at Dover. The fact that he didn't filled her with curiosity, yet a sort of peacefulness had settled over her. She sensed that Andrew was keeping something from her, but she also felt certain that there would be no more secrets once they reached London.

After supper they cast off in the moonlight and charted a northeasterly course along the coastline toward the North Foreland, at which point they could turn west and sail directly for London. Micheline remained on deck for a time, wrapped in a heavy woolen cloak that she'd found in the cabin. It smelled tantalizingly of Andrew, and she wondered, not for the first time, if it was possible that he could own this yacht.

"You must be awfully cold,'' he remarked, glancing up from his charts.

"Only a bit.'' In truth, she felt better than she had since

they'd left the Jouberts'. Andrew seemed more relaxed, and though everything that lay ahead was unknown, Micheline felt as if she were being borne into the future on the hands of fate. It seemed that whatever happened would be for the best.

Andrew had crossed the deck and extended a masculine hand which traced the line of her cheek. "We won't be in London until daybreak, fondling. The bunk in the main cabin is quite comfortable. Why don't you get some sleep?"

The sight of his handsome, moon-silvered face squeezed her heart with emotion. "I'll go on one condition."

"Name it, my lady." Sandhurst's smile flashed in the dark.

"Will you come with me and kiss me good night? I've been so lonely at bedtime. . . ."

"All right, if you'll promise not to test my powers of endurance."

"I promise!"

Happily she led the way below. In the cabin Andrew leaned against the bulkhead and tried not to look as Micheline stripped off her clothing swiftly, then climbed into the snug bunk, still wearing her chemise.

"What a good girl you are!" he chuckled.

"Tuck me in." She smiled.

"It's time you learned the way we say things in England, fondling. Your grammar's well enough, but there are certain turns of phrase that are decidedly British."

"Pray instruct me, m'sieur." Micheline was fairly beaming, basking in the glow of their love that seemed to fill the cabin.

He bent over her, his eyes mesmerizingly warm as he tightened the covers around her slim body. "You see, I'm tucking you *up*."

"I'll remember that, though I can't think when I'll have the chance to put that particular turn of phrase to use with any of my new acquaintances in London!"

Sandhurst smiled in a way that melted her heart. He stroked her hair, which resembled dark cognac spilled over the pillow. "It won't matter what you say, Michelle. Everyone will love you . . . just as I do."

"Hopefully not *just* as you do!" She laughed softly. "Don't forget my good-night kiss, Andrew."

He cupped her face in his golden-brown hands and bent toward her. Micheline felt pleasantly dizzy when his parted

lips gently touched her own, slowly savoring each taste and
sensation for a long minute. She wanted to twine her arms
about his neck and longed to feel the length of his body
against her own, but remembered her promise.

Finally Sandhurst lifted his head and sighed. "I'd better go
above before Jeremy crashes the *Day Dream* into Ramsgate."

Nodding bravely, Micheline whispered, *"Bonsoir, mon cher."*

He rose and walked away, but paused near the bulkhead to
look back at her. "Good night, Michelle. Remember . . . I love
you."

The sky had barely begun to lighten when Micheline awoke,
filled with excitement. Having found a pitcher of fresh water,
a basin, and a cube of castile soap, she washed and then
donned clean undergarments and a gown of azure figured
velvet, its low square bodice trimmed with pearls and gold
lace. A pearl necklace and pearl earrings were added, plus a
delicate gold chain with a sapphire that rested near her breasts.
Finally Micheline combed her hair, parted it carefully, then
tucked the long deep-auburn curls into a golden crispinette.
Appraising her reflection in a small mirror, she smiled, thinking that she would disgrace neither herself nor Andrew when
she first set foot in London.

Micheline felt slightly less confident when she ventured
from her cabin. It was so quiet except for the sound of the
river, and she had no idea where Andrew was, or where and
whether he had slept during the night.

She found him on deck, looking rested, fresh, and clean-
shaven. He wore a handsome doublet of tawny camlet that
she had not seen before, and his ruffled hair shone in the
sunrise.

"Michelle! You're up early." Sandhurst's eyes were warm
with delighted surprise as he adjusted a line, then crossed the
deck to take her in his arms. "How beautiful you are!"

Her only response was an incandescent smile, like the one
that had blinded him the last morning in Paris. It seemed to
Andrew that Micheline's whole heart was revealed in that
smile and the radiance of her sparkling eyes. Andrew stared
down at her, amazed by the magical glow that spread from
her body to his, before bending to kiss her, wonderingly at
first, and then more passionately, until Micheline's slim arms
rounded his shoulders and her fingers tangled in his hair,
pressing him closer still.

"Ah-hem!" Jeremy had to clear his throat several times, in various noisy ways, before the couple seemed to notice him.

At length Sandhurst raised his head and arched a brow. "What is it—*Playfair*?"

The other man glared at him. "The Tower's in sight. I thought you might like to know!"

When Andrew released her, Micheline looked around curiously. A pale pink mist hovered over the Thames, but still she was able to make out the branching masts of vessels ahead on the river, and a forest of bare spires that rose above the endless maze of gabled rooftops. London! They had arrived!

The closer they came, the more boats Micheline saw. The Thames was crowded, even at this hour, with vessels of every description.

"The city has such narrow streets that people would rather travel by water," Andrew explained.

"Look!" she exclaimed in delight, pointing at a trio of swans that passed the *Day Dream* in single file.

"You'll get used to them," he said, smiling, "and don't touch. They're fond of biting."

They sailed past the Tower, where the river ran through the bars of the Traitor's Gate, and soon approached London Bridge, with its twenty piers and nineteen arches. They dropped anchor there, amid the larger trading ships, and before long Micheline found herself on a barge, being rowed through the rapids under the bridge in progress upriver.

Andrew sat quietly beside her, his eyes hooded as he exchanged occasional glances with Jeremy, who constantly raised his brows this way and that and made all sorts of contortions with his mouth. His friend pretended to ignore him, and Micheline began to wonder if the poor manservant might have some kind of nervous disorder.

The barge drew up alongside a water gate that led to a splendid mansion of rose brick. Micheline was too awestruck by all she had seen to be surprised. This was obviously not Andrew's home, but only a means of reaching it, she reasoned. He handed her over to the first dry step while Jeremy dutifully paid the waterman.

Sandhurst was intending to sit with Micheline in the garden and tell her all, but his plan was spoiled by the appearance of one of his servants, who rushed down the steps to greet them as they came through the gate.

"Welcome home, my lord!" the boy cried enthusiastically. "We weren't sure if you'd ever come back!"

"Hello, Bartholomew," Sandhurst muttered, wincing when he heard the lad shout "Sir Jeremy" behind them.

Micheline's expression was confused. "Why does he call you 'my lord' and Playfair 'Sir Jeremy'?" The sight of his averted face sent a chill down her spine. *"Andrew?"*

"As it happens, I was just about to explain all that to you, Michelle." He led her over to a stone bench on the far side of the well-tended garden. The green shoots of daffodils and hyacinths were already poking up amid white, pink, and violet crocuses.

"Please, *do!*" Micheline exclaimed. "I have never been so puzzled! Whose house is this, and why are we here?"

Andrew stared out at the river, yet barely saw the fast-moving boats or the borough of Southwark on the south bank of the Thames. He sighed heavily, then turned to meet Micheline's urgent gaze.

"This house belongs to me, fondling, as does the *Day Dream*. Will you still love me if I tell you that I am not poor, but rich?"

"You know full well that I would love you in any condition, but I do not understand! How—"

"Wait. There's more. It seems that I have many things to confess. My name is not Selkirk, either, though it was my mother's name before she married. I don't make my living as a painter."

Micheline's head was spinning, and for a moment all she could think of was her discovery in December that Bernard had been a stranger all through their marriage, smiling and professing his love even as he deceived her.

"Sweet Michelle, it's time you knew the truth. I am Andrew Weston, Earl of Sandhurst."

CHAPTER 21

London, England
April 4, 1533

"YOU'RE TEASING ME . . . AREN'T YOU?" MICHELINE WHISPERED after a long moment of silence.

"You know I would not jest about something like this." Sandhurst took both her hands in his and found them cold as ice. "I know it's a shock, but I think that once you adjust to the idea, you'll find it quite agreeable."

"Agreeable?" she repeated weakly. "Should I rejoice that you have lied to me since the moment we met? Did everyone know? Were you all laughing at me behind my back?"

Closing his eyes for an instant, he sighed. "No one has laughed at you, fondling, and no one at Fontainebleau knew my true identity except Jeremy. I gather that St. Briac found out toward the end, but—"

"This must be a bad dream!" Micheline exclaimed suddenly, pulling her hands free. "A few minutes ago I was so happy! I felt as if I were coming home, that London was embracing me, because I was with you and this was the place where we would make our life together. Now I learn that I don't know you at all! You're a stranger who has deceived me!"

"Of course you know me!" Sandhurst protested. "The only difference is my surname. Michelle, *I love you.* Isn't that what counts?"

Tears glistened in her beautiful eyes. "How can I believe you? How can I believe anything you say, ever again?"

He raked a hand through his hair in desperation. "This isn't the place to discuss all of this, and there's a great deal that must be said. Let's go inside. You can see your rooms and freshen up, then we'll sit down and I'll try to explain how all this came about." Andrew gave her an engagingly hopeful smile, but Micheline dropped her eyes.

"D'accord," she sighed. "I don't seem to have any choice, do I?"

They walked side by side up the neat gravel pathways that led from the garden to a handsome arched doorway. Sandhurst was alarmed by Micheline's demeanor, for she stayed far away from him and would not even look in his direction.

Inside the great hall, with its carved paneling and beamed ceiling, an old woman and man waited to greet their master. The affection that shone in their eyes bolstered Andrew's spirits.

"Michelle, I'd like you to meet Throgmorton, my head steward, and Mistress Goodwyn, who runs Weston House for me." Smiling at the two servants, he explained, "This is Madame Micheline Tevoulère. She will be staying with us." He wanted to introduce her as his future wife, but couldn't be certain himself if that was still the case.

Mistress Goodwyn, a small, white-haired, rosy-cheeked woman, came forward first to embrace Andrew. Since she had been lady's maid to the Duchess of Aylesbury in her youth and had watched this boy come into the world, it was impossible for her to keep a respectful distance.

"Welcome home, my lord!" She gave him a smacking kiss on his cheek. "I've been worried about you!"

"I appreciate that, Nan." He turned then to clasp Throgmorton's outstretched hand. The old man, who had been a page in the last duke's household, was stooped now and nearly bald, but his mind was as sharp as ever.

"We've missed you, my lord," he intoned, then allowed a warm smile to stretch over his wrinkled face. "It's good to see you home safe."

The two head servants exchanged greetings with their guest, who had been watching the previous scene with interest.

"Madame Tevoulère will need a lady's maid, Nan," Sandhurst remarked. "I was thinking of Mary. She seems a sweet girl."

"That's true, my lord, but she's had no training as a lady's maid—"

"I don't mind," Micheline interjected in her perfect, lightly accented English. "I'm not used to having my very own maid, either, so we can learn together."

Mistress Goodwyn pursed her lips. "I'll tell the girl, then. She'll be over the moon, I'll warrant!"

"Would you show Madame Tevoulère to the rose room?"

Then he looked to Throgmorton. "Bartholomew's outside. Why don't you ask him to take her belongings upstairs."

"Aye, my lord." They both nodded.

Micheline followed the old woman up a broad wooden staircase with splendidly carved newel posts, handrails, and balustrade. It was quite unlike anything she had ever seen before, since all the staircases she knew of in France were circular and made of stone.

"What a magnificent house!" Micheline said to fill the silence.

"Oh, Weston House isn't much compared to Sandhurst Manor, or Aylesbury Castle for that matter, but it's much cozier. Lord Sandhurst bought it himself, you know, with his own earnings from the horses he breeds in Gloucestershire. He could've had a much grander place, but he's never been one to put on airs." Reaching the top step, Mistress Goodwyn turned back to look at the young Frenchwoman. "I've served the aristocracy all my life, madame, and when Lord Sandhurst struck out on his own, Throgmorton and I, as well as many of the other servants, *chose* to come with him. He's the finest nobleman I've ever known, because he knows that in spite of his title he's still a mortal being just like the rest of us." She smiled fondly. "Lord Andrew's a love. Even as a child he was a love. And so handsome! He wore that golden hair just like a crown. If only the duke weren't so mean-spirited . . . and if the duchess hadn't died, Lord Sandhurst would be a happy man today, just as he was happy as a child." Mistress Goodwyn led Micheline down the corridor, still talking. "That's not to say that he's *unhappy*, but these troubles with his father have cast a shadow over his life. I've always said that all Lord Andrew needs is the true love of a good woman, but it's hard for him to trust." She opened a paneled door and stepped aside so that Micheline could enter first. "Well, you know how men are. I've tried not to worry about Lord Sandhurst. The way I figure it, he'll dally with this one and that, and then suddenly he'll wake up one day and realize that he's in love, and then it'll be too late to struggle!" The old woman laughed fondly. "I often imagine the handsome babies he would have. How I long to see them before I die!"

Micheline could find no response to the housekeeper's speech, so instead, she turned her attention to her spacious, charming room. The gardens and the river beyond could be viewed through tall sparkling windows, a few of their diamond panes stained blue and rose. There was an enormous bed with carved ionic posts, and the counterpane, curtains, and valance to the tester were all embroidered in rose and ivory. Pretty pale pink dried rosebuds were scattered among the fresh herbs on the floor, and each piece of furniture was attractive and serviceable.

"It's simply lovely," Micheline murmured.

"A lady's room," nodded Mistress Goodwyn. "It's usually used only when Lady Cicely comes to visit, which isn't often enough to suit me!" Shaking her head, she returned her attention to the visitor from France. "Are you here long?"

Micheline flushed. "I'm not certain, Mistress Goodwyn."

"Well, it's good to have a lady in the house!" she approved. "Would you like a bath?"

"*Oui*. I mean yes. That would be delightful."

"Is there anything else I can get you, madame?"

"I wouldn't mind a cold glass of wine . . . and it would please me if you would call me Micheline."

The housekeeper blinked in surprise, then nodded. "As you wish—Micheline." For the first time Mistress Goodwyn began to wonder exactly who this girl might be, and why she was here.

Downstairs Sandhurst was served a frosty tankard of ale and seated himself in the winter parlor to consider what to say to Micheline. Jeremy had gone home, so at least he wasn't there to remind him of the coil he'd managed to ensnarl himself in. The more Andrew thought about it, the more dismal he felt. Why *should* Micheline ever trust him again? Especially in light of what she'd told him about her philandering husband, he could certainly see her point.

Perhaps a half hour had passed, during which he'd observed serving girls carrying buckets of steaming water upstairs for Micheline's bath, when Throgmorton appeared in the doorway.

"Lady Dangerfield is here to see you, my lord."

Before Sandhurst could tell him to send her away, Iris brushed past the steward and ran to kneel at Andrew's side.

Lifting his brows helplessly, he murmured, "That will be all, Throgmorton."

"Yes, my lord."

Iris was burying her face in his lap, rejoicing in the sensation of the hard muscles of his thighs against her cheek. "Oh, my darling, you are home at last! I have come almost daily, praying that you would have returned, and now my prayers have been answered!''

"I wasn't aware that you were on such intimate terms with God," Sandhurst remarked flippantly.

She raised her head and regarded him through narrowed green eyes. "Andrew, are you not happy to see me? You left London without a word, which was exceedingly rude of you, but I have overlooked your bad manners. For nearly two months I haven't known if you were alive or dead. I've been frantic!''

"How is Timothy?" he wondered.

"What?"

"Timothy Dangerfield. Your husband." Sandhurst reached for his tankard of ale, purposely avoiding her eyes.

"Why do you speak of him at such a moment?" She flung herself upward, rubbing her face against his soft camlet doublet. "Have you not missed me, my lord? Have you not hungered for me as I hunger for you?''

"Iris . . . you are married to another man, and from what I heard in February, Timothy was growing weary of your infidelity. Perhaps it would be prudent for you to turn your attention to your marriage.''

"I don't want Timothy!" Now she was sitting in his lap, nuzzling his cheek and ear. "I want *you*!''

Sandhurst sighed. "There's no point in living in a fantasy world, Iris, which is exactly what you've been doing for the better part of four years. You are another man's wife.''

She drew back and stared him. "That never bothered you before! When did you acquire scruples, Andrew?''

He had to smile at that. "I don't know that I have, sweeting, but I have changed in some way. You see, I am in love for the first time in my life, and I hope to make that lady my wife.''

Shock struck a blow at Iris's heart, followed immediately by a barrier of disbelief. "What nonsense!" she cried. "*You?* In *love*? How ridiculous! Next you'll tell me it's that French whore people are saying the duke is forcing you to marry!''

Andrew's brows came together. "That's enough, Iris." He reached up to lift her off his lap. "You'd better leave.''

"No! You must listen to me! You are talking such foolishness only because you have been away so many weeks! After you're used to being home again, you'll want things the way they were! Please, Andrew, remember how it was between us—'' She snuggled against him, searching for his lips and finding them, her arms twined like thin bands of steel around his neck as she pressed her open mouth to his.

Sandhurst's eyes were open as he moved to separate their bodies, but the first thing he saw was Micheline stepping into the doorway. She wore an enchanting gown of yellow silk, her brandy-hued curls arranged over her shoulders. In the first instant she had been smiling tentatively, but then horror transformed her expression. Before Andrew could push Iris away and speak to her, she fled.

"Damn!"

Iris wondered at his curse. She, too, had seen the girl in the doorway and suddenly felt more curious than amorous. "Was that your ladylove?'' she inquired archly.

This time Sandhurst wasn't polite. He lifted her up roughly and set her away from him. "Don't you have somewhere to go?''

"I hope that the rumors I've been hearing aren't true, Andrew! Don't tell me that you've knuckled under to your father and mean to marry a *stranger*! I thought that you were a *man*!''

"Iris, I am asking you to leave." Muscles clenched on either side of his jaw as he stood up. "If you must badger someone, go home and badger your husband. He's earned that honor, and perhaps it will cause him to believe you really care.''

With that, Sandhurst strode out of the room, but his outrage ebbed halfway up the staircase. Now he would be dealing with Micheline rather than Iris, and this would be delicate work.

Arriving at her door, he knocked but there was no answer. "Michelle? Are you there?''

Her only response was a muffled sob. Sighing, Andrew opened the door and beheld the woman he loved sitting on the rose and ivory counterpane, weeping as if she might die.

"Please . . . leave me alone.''

He took a deep breath and crossed the room, sitting beside her on the bed. "I realize that what you saw downstairs just now looked rather incriminating, but I assure you that there is a logical explanation.''

Micheline raised her tear-stained face and stared at him

angrily. "Oh, yes, I know how adept you men are at explaining such things! I've been all through this before, but the only difference is that my eyes are open now! I won't be made a fool of a second time—and I won't smile docilely while you make a mockery of my honest emotions!"

"For God's sake, Micheline, I am *not* Bernard Tevoulère!"

"No, that's true. At least he told the truth about his *name* and his background, and he managed to refrain from engaging in passionate embraces with other women when he was in the same house with me!" Her voice was bitter.

"Christ!" Sandhurst didn't know where to even begin attempting to explain. It had been complicated enough before that scene with Iris, but *now* . . .

"Do you know, after talking to your Mistress Goodwyn a while ago, I was feeling quite prepared to listen to your story with an open mind," Micheline was reflecting. "That was what I went downstairs to tell you. Rather pathetic, isn't it? I suppose I must be one of those people who never learn! However, I don't need to be hit over the head to realize the truth. It's very clear now."

"What is?" he asked, sensing that he wouldn't like the answer.

"Well, I can't stay here. Obviously you have been playing some sort of game ever since the day you arrived in France. It wasn't enough to arrange a marriage with a stranger; you had to make me fall in love as well! I was right the first time, when I made up my mind to avoid love at all costs. I was right when I told Aimée that it brings more pain than pleasure. You've managed to make my worst nightmare a reality, Andrew!"

"Now, that's enough!" Sandhurst gripped her slim shoulders with strong hands. "You are wrong, Micheline! Why don't you give more credit to your instincts? You trusted me from the moment our eyes first met at Fontainebleau, and you were right!"

She turned her face away, tears dripping onto his fingers. "Let me go."

"Not until you've listened to what I have to say." He sighed harshly. "Won't you look at me, fondling?"

"No," she whispered. "You'll cast some sort of spell on me with your eyes."

Andrew almost laughed at that. "Have it your way." He

reached up to brush the back of his forefinger over her wet cheeks. "Please, do not cry."

The sensation of his tanned finger caressing her face filled Micheline with a bittersweet yearning. "I thought you had something to say, my lord."

"So I do, but I wish you wouldn't call me 'my lord.' " She did not answer, and kept her face averted, so Sandhurst plunged onward. "First of all, I should tell you about Iris. That is, Lady Dangerfield. She is part of my past, and that is where I want her—in the past. I never loved her, Michelle; she is nothing compared to you! It's true, I suppose, that she may not have taken our—uhm—friendship as lightly as I. That was what you saw today. I told her that I was in love for the first time in my life and that I intended to be married. When you walked in, Iris was—trying to change my mind, but I put her from me immediately!"

Micheline looked at him briefly and arched an eyebrow. "What a coincidence that I just *happened* to come in during the very instant her lips touched yours—before you pushed her away, of course."

Casting a beseeching gaze heavenward, Sandhurst tried again. "If I were lying, don't you think I could have hatched a better story than this? God's bones, it's so feeble, it *has* to be the truth!"

There was such desperate honesty in his voice that Micheline's heart was swayed. "Assuming, for the moment, that I did believe you, what about this lady? How long has this *friendship* between you endured?"

"Oh, four years or so, but—"

"How could you be such a beast!" she cried, her violet-blue eyes flashing. "That poor girl! How must she feel, if she has loved you for four long years and suddenly you turn up with a new choice for your wife!"

Sandhurst blinked. Was there no possible escape from this coil? "Iris couldn't have become my wife in any case, Michelle! She's married to another man!"

Her mouth dropped open. "Is there not a person of moral character alive in this world? You speak of your adultery as if it will excuse all your other sins!"

His patience, worn to shreds, tore at that moment. "Enough of this! Am I going to be held accountable for every mistake I ever made up to the night we met? Listen to me, Micheline. I do not claim to be without flaw, and my behavior in the past has been far from saintly. However, three nights ago in Paris you wept and begged me to understand why you said certain things and acted the way you did during our weeks at Fontainebleau. Because I love you, I listened to your story with not just an open mind but an open heart as well. I'm asking you now to put aside the pain Bernard caused you and judge me as an individual. I want to tell you what brought me to Fontainebleau, and I ask you to remember that if I had not come under another man's name, we would not have met at all, for I would never have married a stranger.''

Her sensuous lower lip trembled. "I suppose you will tell me next that your strict code of ethics would have prevented you from taking part in an arranged marriage.''

"You know, I ought to slap you! Curb that shrewish tongue for a few minutes and attend me.''

In spite of herself, Micheline felt a shiver of excitement, which was heightened by the sparkle of loving amusement she glimpsed fleetingly in his eyes. "As you command, my lord.''

Sandhurst rose to pace the sunlit room. "I'll not claim that my life had been tragic, but I have had reasons of my own for not believing in love. Unlike you, I never agonized over it. It simply never occurred to me that I could fall in love, and, frankly, I didn't care to. My mother died five years ago, but even when she was alive and I was young, there was no warmth between her and my father. As for the duke, one of the relatives I mentioned to you in Paris, few people could surpass his talent for appearing singularly *un*lovable. And . . . there are other members of my family who have helped to spur my desire for independence. I went away to Oxford at sixteen and have lived on my own ever since.''

"What about the sister you painted who couldn't sit still?'' Micheline wondered.

"Cicely?'' He looked back, his sculpted features softening. "She's my one regret in this estrangement from my father. I adore that child, and—well, this isn't the time for all the details of my family relations. First things first.'' Andrew wandered back across the room and paused next to the bed. "I never gave this much thought until lately, but I suppose that the walls I erected between myself and my father carried over into other areas. That's why my relationship with Iris Dangerfield was so convenient. It was entertaining, it met certain of my needs, and yet I never had to open my heart. . . .''

"What made you seek this arranged marriage with me?" Micheline asked softly, puzzled.

"I didn't! The duke—my father—arrived here one day in February and *announced* the bloody thing to me! He and the king had made all the plans, and if I didn't go through with it, all the family estates and wealth would pass to my illegitimate twit of a half brother, Rupert Topping."

"But I was told that you had a weakness for Frenchwomen!"

Sandhurst smiled dryly. "I know. St. Briac passed along that tale in France. Quite amusing. *I*, on the other hand, was told that someone in the French court wanted to get rid of you and had asked King Henry to find you an English husband. Since he is looking for French help with the pope regarding his divorce, he was happy to oblige. Enter my father, who had been nagging me to marry and provide him with an heir. I was caught like a rabbit in a trap."

"I don't understand! Why were we told different stories?"

"Who knows?" He shrugged. "My instincts tell me that Anne d'Heilly was behind the plan. François's unrequited lust for you was beginning to worry her. However, it hardly seems important now. Once the thing was agreed upon, it took on a life of its own."

Sandhurst paused, staring out the window. "Well, at that point I felt trapped, but, rebellious as ever, I was determined to wriggle free. I decided to tell my father to go to the devil and take King Henry with him. I didn't care if I lost the family wealth . . . until Jeremy reminded me that *Rupert* would have everything that rightfully should have gone to my children. He had a point. Odds were that I probably *would* marry one day, and I *did* want children. I couldn't agree to marry a stranger for that reason alone, though, so Jeremy and I hit on a compromise."

It all fell into place in Micheline's mind then. "You decided to go to France and have a look at me," she supplied.

Andrew laughed softly. "It seemed a great adventure at the time, and it was just what I needed to counteract that feeling of being cornered by my father." He dropped down beside her on the bed and lifted one of Micheline's delicate hands. "To be honest, I never expected anything to come of it. I half hoped I'd find you repulsive so that I would feel completely justified in spitting in the duke's face . . . and theoretically in the king's as well."

She felt the corners of her mouth turning up. "It didn't quite work out the way you planned, did it?"

"Oh, Michelle." Sandhurst closed his eyes for a moment as a warm rush of emotion swept over him. "I think I fell in love with you when I first saw you on the staircase at Fontainebleau. I didn't even know who you were! I was standing with Anne d'Heilly. I asked her your name, and when she replied, I was stunned. Of course, I wasn't thinking in terms of love then. What drove me mad for so long was your seeming indifference! Every time you pushed me away and declared that you were betrothed to the Earl of Sandhurst, I burned with jealousy."

"For yourself?" she murmured, swallowing irrepressible laughter.

"That's what Jeremy kept saying. He'd shout, 'But that's *you!*'" Andrew chuckled at the memory. "I didn't care. All I knew was that you were rejecting me for a stranger. It drove me mad, and I was determined that if I couldn't win you on my own merit, there would be no wedding."

All of Micheline's outraged anger seemed to be melting away, but enough doubt lingered to prompt her to wonder, "Andrew, how can you be certain that your feelings for me are rooted in love rather than in the challenge of winning me?"

"I'm not a boy, fondling; I'm a grown man. I may not have been well acquainted with love in the past, but I think I am wise enough to recognize it now." Leaning forward, his mouth grazed her cheek. "In any case, I could ask the same of you. You thought you loved Tevoulère, but in Paris you told me that you never knew the meaning of the word until you met me. How do I know that you are not merely infatuated?"

"Point taken." She smiled. "I suppose the time has come for both of us to abandon logic and listen to our hearts."

"Does that mean I'm forgiven?"

"Let us say that . . . I understand."

"Can we forget about the past"—Andrew kissed her parted lips gently—"and make a fresh beginning?"

"Yes, Lord Sandhurst, I think we can."

His arms encircled her body with tantalizing slowness, until they were embracing. Micheline moaned with a mixture of relief and desire as their mouths came together. The past few hours she had felt like a ship cut loose from its mooring, but now she was home again.

"Madame?" A knock sounded at the door.

Sighing in frustration, Sandhurst got up to answer it. "Yes, Throgmorton, what is it?"

"Oh, excuse me, my lord, I didn't know you were here!" The old man actually appeared to blush. "It's just that— dinner is served . . . and Master Topping has arrived. He's already taken a place at the table."

CHAPTER 22

April 4, 1533

"FIRST IRIS AND NOW *RUPERT*?" SANDHURST EXCLAIMED INCRED- ulously, throwing up his hands. "Why don't we just have a ball and invite the whole of London?"

Throgmorton coughed, uncertain whether a response was desired by the earl. "I—uh . . ."

"Never mind, Throgmorton. It's certainly not your fault. I appreciate the advance warning—and we shall be down presently."

"Yes, my lord. Thank you."

When the door was closed, Andrew rubbed tense fingers over his face. "Argh!"

Micheline couldn't help smiling. "Didn't you say that Rupert is a twit? Poor thing. He probably worships you."

Rolling his eyes, Sandhurst returned to the bed and threw himself across it. "You don't know the half of it."

"You ought to make an effort to be kind to him."

"Don't say things like that until you've spent an hour in Rupert's company. He's absolutely—" He searched in vain for a word to describe his half brother.

The sight of Andrew sprawled on his back across the sun-drenched bed was more temptation than Micheline could resist. Mischievously she hitched up her skirts and crawled over to rest her face against his neck, breathing in the clean scent of his pleated white fraise. His arm rounded her back, drawing her near until her breasts pressed his ribs.

"I don't want to go downstairs," Sandhurst stated flatly.

"We must." Micheline caressed the soft camlet doublet that covered his chest.

"I have all the sustenance I need right here." Turning on his side to face her, he slowly ran his right hand down Micheline's spine, then explored the curve of her derriere through the fabric of her gown and petticoats.

They shared a sweet, lingering kiss.

"You have a guest, my lord," she reminded him, even as arousal coursed through her veins.

"The devil take my guest. *I* certainly don't want him," Andrew muttered. He kissed her again, then a third time. "As for dinner, you are infinitely more delicious than mere food."

Micheline pushed weakly at his chest. "I thought you said that we would not make love again until we were married."

"I'm reconsidering my position on that matter."

His mouth seemed to scorch her throat, and her breasts were already tingling within her bodice, but Micheline summoned all her powers of resistance. "I would rather stay here with you, but, Andrew, this is my first day in your home, and the impression I make could be lasting. I really think that we ought to go downstairs before your staff—*and* your half brother—form a poor opinion of me."

Sandhurst sighed heavily and released her, sitting up. "You're right, of course." He shook his head dazedly. "I must be going mad."

Crossing to the mirror, Micheline laughed and surveyed her radiant reflection. A quick application of her brush tamed the few wayward curls that flowed loose down her back. Andrew was waiting in the doorway.

"After *you*," he said with an ironic flourish, following Micheline into the corridor.

Downstairs Andrew tucked her hand around the crook of his arm and led her into the parlor, where Rupert Topping sat alone at a table set for three.

Micheline smiled with an effort, for she was more inclined to gape. Was it possible that this thin, pasty, ferret-faced person could be a blood relation of Andrew's? The young man who approached them, smiling madly, was barely taller than she, with lank brown hair, small nervous eyes, long teeth, a receding chin, and narrow shoulders. He wore an ill-fitting doublet of apple-green satin, a cloth-of-gold jerkin, rings, neck chains, sleeve brooches, and garters set with rubies below bony knees. His large feet, encased in spade-shaped shoes, pointed outward when he walked.

"Sandhurst! You're home! Everyone's been so worried about you! Where've you been?" he exclaimed loudly, arms outstretched.

Andrew extended his hand, avoiding the brotherly embrace Rupert sought. "Hello, Rupert. May I present Madame Micheline Tevoulère, my future wife?"

"What? What?! Did I hear correctly? *Wife?*" Letting out a rather manic laugh, he turned to Micheline. "Bun-jar! Ha-ha, as they say in France, what? Well, well, I must say, this *is* a surprise!"

Somehow Micheline managed to disguise her true reaction, smiling instead and replying, "It is a pleasure to meet you, M'sieur Topping."

"I say!" Rupert ejaculated, peering up at Sandhurst. "She speaks English! Well *done*, old boy!" He then turned to grab Micheline's hand with sweaty fingers and kissed it wetly. "None of this mon-seer folderol for us! I'm family, after all! You must call me Rupert and I'll call you Micheline."

At that point she could not resist a bit of mischief. "How sweet of you, Roo-pair!"

He stared, then laughed nervously. "Perhaps you ought to practice that a bit, Micheline. In England we say Ru*pert.*"

Andrew wanted to turn and leave right then, taking Micheline with him, but the servants were entering with platters of food. "I'm ravenous," he said. "Let's sit down."

They took their places, with Sandhurst at the head of the table and Micheline and Rupert on either side, facing each other. Wine was poured, followed by mussel and fennel stew with dumplings.

"How different the food is here!" marveled Micheline after her first bite of dumpling. "I like it!"

Sandhurst smiled fondly. Her cognac-hued hair, set a-sparkle by the sun with golden highlights, tumbled down to frame an exquisitely lovely face. At that moment, however, his favorite feature was Micheline's right cheek, which bulged out because of the dumpling she could not bear to swallow.

"You look adorable!" he chuckled. "Try to get that bite down, fondling, and then I'd advise you to try a slightly less adventurous approach to any foods you don't recognize. You mustn't expect to become English in one day!''

The affection in Sandhurst's eyes made Micheline feel giddy. She forgot all else, swallowing the dumpling with ease, then realized what had happened and joined in his gentle laughter.

"You mean to say that there are no dumplings in France?" Rupert appeared genuinely distressed by that possibility. "Lucky thing I hate traveling! Couldn't live without my dumplings!"

Remembering Rupert's nerve-racking French accent, Micheline wanted to say that his unwillingless to leave home was lucky for France as well, but she held her tongue.

Sandhurst, meanwhile, gave his half brother a sharp side-long glance. "That reminds me. Why are you *here*, Rupert? It really wasn't necessary for you to come all the way from Yorkshire just to call on me. . . ."

A salad of purslane, tarragon, and watercress was served, then fresh pink shrimp, and pike with gooseberry sauce. Rupert tasted everything before replying. "I'd travel any distance to call on you, Sandhurst! You know that! I'd go to any lengths, suffer any hardship, if it meant that—"

"I know, I know. Spare me the discourse on your familial devotion and tell me why you're in London."

"Well, *well* . . ." Rupert shifted uneasily in his chair and darted a look at Micheline. "You see, the duke—our father—sent me south to find out what's happened to you. He was rather concerned that you might have, uh—flown the coop, if you take my meaning."

"Fine. Now you can return to Aylesbury Castle and tell the duke that I only 'flew' as far as France. I wanted to meet Madame Tevoulère before sentencing her to a lifetime of my company. Fortunately for me, the lady seems to like me well enough"—at this point Micheline laughed softly and reached out to touch his cheek—"and we're both pleased that what was supposed to be an arranged betrothal is now a love match." Sandhurst paused for a bite of shrimp, then added dryly, "I'm certain that Father will be vastly relieved and pleased to learn how happy I am with the arrangement."

"Oh, yes, I'm sure he will!" Rupert nodded antically. "He's been brooding awfully about this, imagining that you were plotting some scheme to undo all his plans, but I did my very best to reassure him, as you must know! I've always taken your side, Sandhurst, since you're never there to defend yourself.''

"I've told you before that I'd rather you wouldn't.''

"God's toes, I'll be so happy when Lent is over!'' Rupert was exclaiming. "Fish, fish, fish! Not that you haven't got a fine cook, Sandhurst, but I'm sick to death of the stuff. The castle gamekeeper brought down a magnificent red deer last week, and we've all been salivating in anticipation!''

"Hmmm.'' Andrew met Micheline's eyes, his brows flicking upward almost imperceptibly.

A serving girl appeared with a covered dish of spinach fritters, one of which Micheline tasted tentatively. Under a fried batter, she discovered a mixture of spinach, bread crumbs, egg, and currants, flavored with ginger and cinnamon.

"This is very good!'' When Sandhurst gave her a look of dubious amusement, she giggled. "*Vraiment!* That is, *truly!* I like this food extremely well.''

"At least they're not fish,'' Rupert put in.

Casting about for a topic that might be bearable, Andrew inquired, "How fares my sister Cicely?''

"Her health is fine.'' Suddenly he was intent on his half-eaten pike.

"And otherwise?''

"Well, *well,* you know I don't like to carry tales, but I have to say that Cicely hasn't been particularly agreeable lately. Patience, who is unwaveringly sweet-tempered, as you will remember, has tried to interest our sister in the coming wedding, yet the girl continues to sulk about the castle. I must say that she hasn't done your case with the duke any good, Sandhurst, for Cicely continues to insist that you won't be getting married. She says that you didn't want any part of it, and that you were very angry about the whole situation.'' Flushing under the cold stare leveled at him by Andrew, he cleared his throat. "Don't suppose that was very tactful of me, what? My apologies, Micheline.''

She gave him a charming smile. Dinner had begun to take on the proportions of a comedy as far as she was concerned, and nothing could penetrate her amusement.

"Take heart!'' Rupert reassured her. "There's at least one person at Aylesbury Castle who will be kind to you, and that's my dear wife, Patience. She has already begun airing her wedding dress in case you didn't bring one from France!''

"We will *not* be needing Patience's gown," Sandhurst stated flatly.

Looking offended, Rupert tried to thrust out his nonexistent chin. "She wishes only to help." He pouted.

"Please, tell your wife that I appreciate her kind thought," Micheline said. This fellow was a twit, but it was obvious that he couldn't help it. She wished that Andrew would not make his loathing quite so apparent, at least in Rupert's company!

Candied oranges and green walnut suckets, which had been made by dipping the nuts in boiling syrup, finished the meal. After a while Sandhurst suggested they take their spiced wine outside to the garden.

"I suppose you'll want to be on your way back to Yorkshire this afternoon, Rupert," he said when they were in the sunshine. Micheline winced a little at his rudeness.

"I thought I might go to Hampton Court first. The duke would want me to pass along the news of your return to King Henry."

"Don't bother. I plan to take Micheline there myself within the next day or two, and I will speak to the king then."

Rupert glanced up at his half brother's face, about to protest, when he saw a telltale muscle flex in Andrew's jaw. "Well, all right, then. I meant only to save you the trouble."

"I have said this to you over and over, but it doesn't seem to sink in." Sandhurst stopped on the pathway and stared hard at the smaller man. "It's my life, Rupert. I'll take care of my own affairs as I see fit, whether they involve my father, the king, or my marriage, and I would appreciate it if you would turn your attention to *your* life!"

For a moment Micheline was afraid that Rupert might begin to cry. His chin trembled as he nodded in reply, then looked away toward the river. She found herself pitying him in the same way she pitied children whose high spirits were doused by hard-hearted parents. She wished she might appeal to Andrew, but he was walking away from them down the path, and the taut set of his shoulders told her that he would not soften on this issue.

In the next instant Rupert seemed to forget the unpleasantness. "Look!" he cried in a shrill voice, pointing downriver. "It's Anne Boleyn's new barge!" Excited by the fact that he knew something Sandhurst didn't, he rushed forward to provide instruction. "You see, it used to be Queen Catherine's.

Anne, I hear, grew so angry because the queen won't accept her new position as princess dowager that she had her chamberlain seize Katharine's barge on the Thames. The king knew nothing about it! Anne gave instructions that the queen's coat of arms should be erased, so the barge was then decorated in *Anne's* heraldic colors—blue and purple. King Henry granted her her own coat of arms as future queen, and I understand that it now replaces Katharine's. Oh, my, how exciting! Can you see her at all? This has all happened in just the last two days. London is *buzzing*!''

Micheline shaded her eyes against the sunshine and tried to catch a glimpse of the barge's occupant as it passed Weston House. The boat was filled with servants clad in Anne's blue and purple livery, but the one female sat in shadows—until she stood suddenly and waved to Sandhurst.

''I *say*! That was Anne Boleyn herself!'' shouted Rupert. ''I nearly forgot! You know her quite *well*, don't you, brother?''

''We're acquainted.''

Micheline felt a sharp twinge of jealousy when he raised his hand in greeting to Anne Boleyn. From a distance the Marquess of Pembroke appeared quite attractive. Jewels sparkled in her dark hair, her figure was fine, and she had a pretty smile that looked decidedly flirtatious to Micheline. When Andrew returned that smile, the twinge in her heart intensified.

''Is it true that Anne and the king were married secretly in January? I heard no confirmation in France,'' Andrew said.

''Oh, yes, it's open knowledge now,'' Rupert reported smugly. ''They say she's with child.''

''I don't doubt it,'' interjected Micheline.

Looking down at her in surprise, Sandhurst watched as color stained her cheeks. Comprehension dawned, and he wrapped an arm about her. She nestled happily against his chest, hoping that Anne Boleyn still watched them.

Inhaling the fragrance of her hair, Andrew said to his relative, ''You'd better be on your way, Rupert, if you're going to take advantage of the daylight.''

''Yes, of course. I'll go now. That reminds me—didn't I see Lady Dangerfield leaving here as I arrived at midday?'' He attempted to wink conspiratorially up at Andrew. ''I'll wager that's *one* person who didn't offer congratulations when told of your impending nuptials—though, of course, she won't be the only lady in London with a broken heart, eh what?''

Sandhurst closed his eyes for a moment and smothered an expletive. "Good-*bye*, Rupert!"

Micheline sensed that this was not the time to speak to Andrew about Rupert, and she could see that he wanted to forget that his half brother had disrupted their peace at all. She decided that it would be better to approach him after a few days had passed, when his irritation would be just a memory.

They spent the afternoon riding. Sandhurst took her into the streets of London, which were so narrow and crowded with wagons, tumbrils, barrows, and drays that at times they couldn't move at all. The Strand had been so lovely, lined with the homes of the rich, that Micheline was rather unprepared for the filth and congestion that awaited her deeper into the city, but she viewed it all as an adventure. As long as Andrew was next to her, every moment felt like an adventure.

Cheapside was one of the few wide streets in London, and also the sight of the city's largest market. In a kaleidoscope of color and noise, country folk were wedged together behind trestle tables covered with baskets of their wares. The latter included everything from butter and eggs to sturgeon and shrimp. Micheline was fascinated by the sound of so many English voices as buyers and sellers haggled over the price and quality of the goods.

Sandhurst bought her a pretty box of comfits with a painting of London on its lid, then they turned back and slowly wound their way toward Weston House. Once in the Strand, however, he asked if she would enjoy some real exercise. Micheline grinned instantly, and they rode on into the countryside below Charing Cross.

Before long they sighted a magnificent palace built along the riverfront, while new buildings had been erected covering acres and acres on the other side of the public thoroughfare.

"This is Whitehall Palace," Andrew explained. "It used to be Cardinal Wolsey's York Place, but he turned it over to the king five years ago. All of this"—he gestured to the sprawling profusion of galleries, towers, lodgings, and halls on their right—"has been built since then."

"Why would the cardinal give up such a splendid home?"

"Oh, it wasn't the first time. Hampton Court used to be Wolsey's too. This last gift, however, came at a time when the old cardinal had fallen from favor. The king expected him to efficiently arrange the divorce from Katharine of Aragon, and when that didn't come to pass, it proved Wolsey's downfall.''

"Did he go to . . . the Tower?" Micheline had heard terrifying stories about that place. It was said that a terrible fate befell anyone sent to the Tower of London. English kings could condemn men to its dungeons on a whim. The prisoners were kept in dark rat-infested cells to suffer horribly from the use of evil instruments of torture. For Micheline these spine-chilling tales had seemingly been confirmed by the sight of pirates hanging in chains from the Tower when they passed it that morning on the Thames.

"No, but I'm sure he would have if he hadn't died first.''

A shiver ran down Micheline's back. "It seems harsh punishment for something that the cardinal may not have been able to control. I mean, the pope has final say, does he not?"

"You're right, fondling, but more than just the divorce brought Wolsey low. You know the intrigues that abound at a royal court. The cardinal was a shrewd, powerful man who made many enemies—and probably earned them.'' He ran a hand through his burnished hair and smiled grimly. "Be that as it may, I have never been intimately acquainted with the machinations of King Henry's court. I stay away as much as possible, and I prefer it that way."

"Good." As they passed under one of the bridges recently built to connect the old palace with its new wings, Micheline reached out to Andrew and he grasped her hand firmly. "I never felt comfortable at Fontainebleau. I like a cozier home . . . and the company of only a few people whom I love and trust."

"We are of one mind." Sandhurst smiled, then raised his eyebrows suggestively. "Twilight approaches. Why don't we return to my conveniently *cozy* home and explore this matter in greater depth?"

CHAPTER 23

April 4–6, 1533

ANDREW AND MICHELINE ATE A LIGHT SUPPER THAT NIGHT, THEN adjourned to the second-floor library. A pile of letters and accounts due waited on Sandhurst's desk, so he sat down to catch up on business while Micheline happily perused the bookshelves.

"What a wonderful collection!" she exclaimed.

Andrew glanced up and smiled absently. "I'm glad you think so. The library at Sandhurst Manor is much more extensive, and perhaps I shouldn't allow you access to it."

She whirled around in alarm. "Why *not*?"

"There's always the possibility that you might bury yourself in books and forget about your husband."

There was a gleam in his warm brown eyes that made her blush. "You are wrong, my lord. That possibility does *not* exist, if you are to be the husband in question."

"I do believe I am, unless the prospect of becoming Rupert's relative has given you second thoughts." Andrew brought up Rupert's name only to steer the conversation out of the bedchamber. Though they had said nothing outright, the air was thick with the promise of intimacy, and Andrew had a stack of long-neglected business to attend to.

"Oh, no, I can tolerate Rupert," Micheline was replying. "I'm sure I'll deal perfectly well with your family, since my own is far from perfect. I must say, though, that it *is* difficult to comprehend that you and Rupert were sired by the same man!"

He broke the seal on a letter and smiled. "I'll take that as a compliment."

Deciding to venture forth a bit further on the subject of Rupert, Micheline said, "Actually I feel rather sorry for him. He seems to mean well, and although I understand why he irritates you, I can't help thinking that—"

"Sweeting, at any other time I would love to chat with you, but right now I really must see to all this correspondence that's accumulated over the past two months."

"Oh, of course. I'm sorry."

Sandhurst didn't seem to hear. Micheline watched him for a while, enjoying the sight of his serious, candlelit expression. Shadows played over his cheekbones and the firm line of his jaw. From time to time he would run his fingers through his ruffled hair or touch the swan's feather to his mouth before making an entry in his ledger.

The books! she reminded herself at last, and turned around to confront them. A bright fire blazed in the white stone fireplace nearby, and there were beeswax candles in sconces on every vertical beam between the library shelves, affording Micheline enough light to read the titles.

There were books on every subject: philosophy, languages, proverbs, geography, medicine, chemistry, botany, and history. In addition, Micheline discovered volumes of poetry, songs, memoirs, drama, and even romance. Many she had already read and knew that English translations had been made, yet Andrew kept the original versions.

"I'm sorry to disturb you," she exclaimed after an hour had passed, "but I am so curious! Have you read all of these?"

"Hmm? Oh, yes, of course. Most of those books are duplicates of my favorites from the library at Sandhurst Manor," he answered without looking up.

Micheline was impressed. Her thoughts skipped back to the night they'd spent at Queen Eleanor's cottage, when she had been amazed to learn that the man she believed to be lowborn had been to school. Now it turned out that Sandhurst had not only attended Oxford but was apparently self-taught as well. They both had curious minds, and that was an important trait to have in common.

Another hour passed. Micheline settled down in a chair by the fire and looked through the large pile of books she'd chosen, trying to decide which to read first. A fifteenth-century romance by Olivier de la Marche, titled *Chevalier Déliberé*, piqued her interest. Leafing through the French text, she came upon an engraving that showed the chevalier outside a castle. The ramparts were lined with women, while on the ground a sad-faced young man held the reins of the knight's horse. Beneath the miniature a caption read: "How the Actor lost his way, and arrived in front of the Palace of Love, into which Desire bade him enter, while Remembrance held him back.''

Micheline smiled. Less than a fortnight ago she had been faced with the same dilemma as the Chevalier Déliberé. Thank God she had made the right choice!

Pleasantly drowsy, she closed her eyes for a moment, only to open them a quarter hour later when Sandhurst knelt next to her chair and leaned forward to kiss the pulse at the base of her neck.

Micheline's heart leaped. ''I—I must have dozed off!''

He gave her an irresistible smile. ''You are beautiful when you sleep. Vulnerable . . . soft . . .'' His agile fingers caressed the line of her cheek, then her neck. ''Warm . . . and fragrant.''

''You must be finished with your work!'' Micheline managed to tease as his mouth strayed downward toward her breasts.

''For tonight.''

Andrew's warm, practiced lips were sending currents of fire through her body. She yearned to bury her face in his hair, to touch him, to surrender completely, but that morning she had made a decision that she was determined to carry out.

''I'm awfully tired, Andrew. It's been a long, exciting day, and—''

''You're ready for bed,'' he supplied. ''So am I. More than ready.''

He helped Micheline up, looking slightly surprised when she brought the book from her lap along with them. Holding hands, they circled the library, extinguishing the candles, then emerged into the corridor. When Sandhurst stopped in front of a door down the hall from her own, Micheline feigned surprise.

''This is not my bedchamber!''

''I thought you might like to see where Lady Sandhurst will sleep,'' he told her softly.

''With Lord Sandhurst?''

Andrew chuckled and opened the door. ''That is the general idea, fondling.''

Micheline beheld a chamber even more spacious and splendid than hers. Beautiful arched windows nearly covered the south wall, which overlooked the Thames, with a grouping of chairs in front of them. The walls were paneled in golden oak, broken only by a brick and stone fireplace. Tapestry rugs covered the floors, and there were magnificently carved dressers and chests, but the focal point of the room was a huge bed hung with dove-gray draperies hand-embroidered in blue. The covers were carefully folded back to reveal plump, inviting pillows and a down-filled tick. Micheline's eyes strayed to the table beside the bed, which held a candle, a small vase of crocuses, a decanter of wine, and two Venetian glass goblets.

"Wouldn't you be more comfortable inside? This corridor is rather drafty," Sandhurst hinted.

Micheline swallowed and summoned her resolve. "I'll be happy to go inside, and happy to spend days on end with you in that wonderful bed . . . when I *am* Lady Sandhurst." Reaching for his hand, which was warm and strong, she looked up at him. "I've been thinking about what you said to me two nights ago at the auberge, and I've decided you were right. Our next act of love will be on our wedding night."

"But when I said that, it was because you didn't know yet who I was. I felt dishonest enough as it was, without—"

"The fact remains that you were right, Andrew," she said steadfastly.

"I'm a *fool*!" He closed his eyes as if he were in pain and muttered, "One day I'll learn to keep my mouth shut."

"Don't pout!" Micheline scolded fondly. "You're a strong man; you can wait a few weeks."

Remembering the tempestuous nature of their lovemaking, Sandhurst groaned. "Yes, I am a man . . . which is precisely the problem!"

"Will you walk me to my door and kiss me good night?" she coaxed.

"Oh, I see! You plan to torture me during this enforced celibacy!"

Micheline laughed and led him down the corridor. Outside her door she turned and reached up to twine her arms around his neck. It was torture for her, too, when he caught her up against his hard body and their mouths came together. The pressure of his lips, the taste and sensation of his tongue fencing with hers, and the evidence of his arousal, plainly felt even through the layers of her gown and petticoat, combined to make her tremble in his embrace. They kissed for what seemed an eternity until Micheline's strength and reason ebbed, replaced by a throbbing hunger for Sandhurst.

Finally his lips moved to burn her throat, then her ear,

and he was whispering, "This is *ridiculous*. I promise to forgive you if you've changed your mind."

Micheline very nearly yielded, but somehow managed to cling to her position and murmur, "You'll thank me in our marriage bed."

With a heavy sigh Andrew released her and took a step backward. "Perhaps—if I *live* that long."

Two mornings later Micheline rose early to prepare for their journey to Hampton Court. She was filled with excitement and also a measure of trepidation. King Henry, Anne Boleyn, and the English court were unknown quantities. What if they disliked her because she was French, or because of something she might say amiss? Andrew might contend that he wished little contact with the royal court, but the fact remained that he was an earl and would someday be a duke— and, God willing, she would be his wife, with English titles of her own.

Little Mary, her maid, made up in enthusiasm what she lacked in skill. The girl prepared a lavishly scented bath and washed Micheline's hair so thoroughly that she had to be told, gently, that it must be clean enough. Helping her mistress dress, Mary's exuberant compliments were morale-boosting, for she rhapsodized endlessly about the utter perfection of every color, ribbon, and jewel that Micheline had chosen.

The decisions had been difficult. Finally, the night before, she had brought Sandhurst in to elicit his opinion, and had been vastly relieved when he confirmed her own first choice. The gown Micheline donned now for her first introduction to the English king was made of soft spring-green velvet, parted in front to show a petticoat of pale yellow silk. The sleeves were puffed and slashed to reveal more yellow silk, and tied at intervals with gold and yellow ribbons. The square-cut bodice accentuated the high curves of her breasts and was embroidered with golden thread and set with emeralds, while a delicate girdle of filigreed gold rode just above her hips.

Mary helped to dress Micheline's gleaming hair, parting it in the center and smoothing it into a golden crispinette sprinkled with emeralds. In contrast to the other colors were her iris-blue eyes, which seemed more vivid than ever in her state of excitement.

She had just added two thin gold necklaces and turned to

assess her reflection in the mirror, when there was a knock at the door.

"It's nearly time to leave," Micheline said nervously. "That must be Andrew."

Mary opened the door to admit Lord Sandhurst, then made a speedy exit when he silently inclined his head. Across the room Micheline stood in a ray of sunlight, looking utterly lovely and charmingly skittish all at once.

"I am terrified!" she announced.

Sandhurst went to her and lightly caressed her flushed cheeks with the back of his hand. "Don't be silly. You look dazzling, and I am convinced you'll be a huge success. My only worry is that the king will fall madly in love with you and decide he would rather wed you than Anne!"

"I fear I would have to refuse him," she replied primly, smiling at the thought of such a scenario. "And then, to keep our heads, you and I would have to run away and live secretly, as commoners. We could take the name of Selkirk!"

"You would rather be Mistress Selkirk than the queen of England?"

"Even the idea of a choice is laughable, my lord," Micheline answered, "for no queen on earth has you."

She gave him one of her radiant smiles, which seemed to outshine the sun, and his heart swelled with love. "How fortunate I am," he whispered.

"Once again, we are of one mind."

Andrew kissed her tenderly, marveling at the rich emotions that flowed between their bodies.

"I brought you a gift," he murmured at length. "Be a good girl and turn around."

Although Micheline would have preferred to go on kissing him, she obeyed. In the mirror she saw his tanned fingers clasp a beautiful necklace of diamonds and emeralds around the base of her throat.

"But it's magnificent!" she protested, thinking that she didn't deserve anything so grand and costly.

"It was my mother's. As the future Duchess of Aylesbury, all of her jewelry will be yours, Michelle."

"I shouldn't wear this until we are married!"

"These edicts of yours about what cannot happen until we are married are becoming tedious," Sandhurst said dryly. "This particular necklace was left in my care, and I am making it a betrothal gift to you."

Hesitantly Micheline raised her slim fingers and touched first the gems, which were cool against her throat, and then Andrew's hands, which were warm.

"Thank you."

He smiled. "Let's be off. The barge is waiting, and the hour advances."

When Sandhurst crossed the room to open the door for her, Micheline suddenly exclaimed, "How handsome you look! It was very selfish of me not to have noticed immediately!"

Never before, when he was pretending to be Andrew Selkirk, had she seen him so elegantly garbed, and still he looked absolutely masculine. Sandhurst wore a close-fitting doublet of rich blue velvet sparingly embroidered with golden thread and set with cut diamonds and rubies. The doublet's neck was fashionably high so that the pleats of his white fraise nearly grazed his jaw. White silk puffed through the light slashings on both sleeves and breeches, and below his left knee Sandhurst wore a gold garter set with a ruby, sapphire, and diamond.

He still disdained other jewelry except for the simple sapphire ring, and Micheline was not surprised to see that he wore no feathered cap. His hair, gilded in the sunlight, was brushed casually back from his handsome face.

"I didn't want you to think that I owned no fine clothing," Andrew replied, "but I confess that I prefer the sort of things I wore at Fontainebleau."

Reaching the doorway, Micheline ran a possessive hand over his chest. "You will be the most splendid man at Hampton Court, and I shall be the envy of every female who lays eyes on you."

"Good Lord!" He laughed fondly. "Next you'll be fighting a duel over me!"

"I would certainly do so if it were necessary," she replied, walking ahead of him into the corridor. Then Micheline glanced back and added brightly, "And I would win!"

The journey by barge up the Thames was as close to paradise as Micheline had ever come. Although accompanied by Mary and Finchley, Sandhurst's valet, and two watermen, the two lovers were in a world of their own. They lounged on cushioned seats, talking softly, drinking wine, kissing, and sharing a delicious meal packed for them by Sabine, the cook. The banks of the Thames were a light bright green now, and budding leaves covered the tree branches where larks, finches, and robins sang tributes to spring. Meanwhile, swans, mallard ducks, and dabchicks followed the barge to feed on the bits of bread Micheline scattered across the water.

Eventually Andrew broke the spell by murmuring into her ear, "There it is."

Micheline sat up straight. Ahead of them, sculpted gardens spread across the right riverbank, leading to low walls, more gardens with trees, and a sprawling mixture of towers, ramparts, and buildings of red brick and white stone. Pinnacles and chimneys topped the palace, rising skyward.

Suddenly her palms were damp. "Must we?"

"I fear so." Sandhurst nodded. "Don't worry, sweetheart. What have you to fear if I am by your side?"

"That's right!" After fending for herself for so long, it was difficult for Micheline to remember that she was not alone anymore. "You won't leave me?"

"You know full well that it is my ardent wish to remain with you constantly—day *and* night!"

His eyes crinkled at the corners, bidding her to laugh and relax. With Andrew next to her it was easy to pretend that what lay ahead was just an amusing adventure.

It wasn't Hampton Court that intimidated Micheline so much as the strangers who waited for her there. She was used to grandeur in excess, and this palace, though certainly splendid, did not outshine Fontainebleau. In fact, as she walked with Sandhurst up the pathway from the river, he told her that it was common knowledge that King Henry had begun to expand and improve his residences only to compete with François.

Richly garbed courtiers and ladies strolled about the grounds, many of them coming over to greet Lord Sandhurst and meet his future bride. Micheline saw not only curiosity but disdain in their eyes and knew the latter sprang from the fact that she was French. When the noblemen spoke to Andrew as if she were an idiot who could not understand, it delighted her to answer for herself in flawless English.

Learning that the king had just finished dinner and had not emerged from the palace, Sandhurst headed there first.

"Do you want to see your chamber? Perhaps you'd like to rest for a while." Even as he said this, he sensed her reply.

"Chamber? Are we staying overnight?"

"Michelle, we must. It would be rude to leave so abruptly,

and in any case, the journey back would take four hours at night.''

Her heart sank. Sighing, she accompanied him through two brick-paved courtyards that were surrounded by buildings. Entering a third, with a fountain in the center, Sandhurst turned into a doorway, then led Micheline up a flight of stairs. At the top they encountered a servant.

"The Earl of Sandhurst to see the king. Is he available?"

A few minutes later they were ushered into Henry VIII's audience chamber, after passing through several other presence chambers en route. All were magnificent, boasting fabulous tapestries, Eastern carpets, ornate ceilings, and damask-upholstered furniture. Micheline had been impressed, but when the king appeared, it seemed that all the palace riches paled in comparison to his person.

Huge and bejeweled, Henry held out his arms in greeting. "Sandhurst! How long it has been since you deigned to grace our court with your presence!"

Andrew smiled, hearing the note of sarcasm in the monarch's jovial voice. "My apologies, sire," he murmured in mock contrition, and bowed. "It is my honor to present to you my future bride, Madame Micheline Tevoulère."

"So, for once you have done as you were told. I might flatter myself that it was because *my* influence was added to the duke's, but obviously that was not the case." The king held out a pudgy beringed hand to Micheline, who touched it and curtsied gracefully. "How fortunate we are to have stolen such a beauty from France! I'll warrant that my friend François was loath to let you go, madame." A smile spread over his beefy face at that thought. "In any case, I bid you welcome."

"Thank you, sire. I am happy to be here."

The king raised his eyes to Sandhurst. "You have a gift for turning every obstacle into an advantage, my friend."

"In this case, I have only you and my dear father to thank, sire," he replied, his tone gently laced with irony. "You have presented me with the greatest treasure of my life."

Noting the glowing smile the Frenchwoman gave to her betrothed, King Henry cleared his throat in dismay. "I must say, it looks as if the two of you are in *love*!"

Sandhurst bit his lip to keep from laughing aloud. "Positively, sire. In fact, I can't help thinking that God must have used you as his instrument to bring us together."

The king, at odds with Pope Clement VII over his divorce,

was pleased at the notion that Sandhurst might consider him a link with God. Wine and sweetmeats were served, whereupon Henry declared that he must hear the tale behind this happy romance.

Andrew recounted his tale in an entertaining manner, interrupted from time to time by his radiant ladylove, who could not resist adding an anecdote or two of her own. As the story unfolded, however, the king found himself far more intrigued by the fact that the Earl of Sandhurst had spent two months at Fontainebleau in the company of François I. As soon as he could do so without appearing obvious, Henry exclaimed, "My dear Madame Tevoulère, you have so charmed me with your wit and beauty that I insist you meet my own Anne immediately! I know that she will be as overjoyed as I am to hear about your betrothal to Lord Sandhurst. I'll own we never thought this rogue could be tamed by true love!"

Micheline was loath to be separated from Andrew, but it seemed she had little choice. Minutes later she followed a page out of the audience chamber, reassured by Sandhurst's parting whisper: "I'll see you in a little, Michelle."

No sooner had the door closed than Henry VIII turned to his least tractable nobleman. "I would have speech with you, Lord Sandhurst. Sit down, and heed me."

Suddenly Andrew wished that he were anywhere but at Hampton Court. Biting his lower lip, he reclined against the uncomfortable carved chair back and waited with a sense of foreboding to hear what his king had to say.

CHAPTER 24

April 6, 1533

HENRY TOOK A LONG DRINK OF WINE, THEN SWALLOWED A SWEET-meat. "I must be brief." His tone was deceptively casual. "There's a tennis match at hand. Will you play?"

"If you wish it, sire," Sandhurst replied affably, wondering what was really on the shrewd monarch's mind.

"How readily you acquiesce, my friend! It gives me hope! May I be frank?"

"That would be my preference, sire."

"You know, of course, that I met with the French king this past autumn. We have been striving to help each other in dealing with the Emperor Charles V and also with the pope, who has made my divorce such a difficult business. King François claims that his sympathies lie with me, and indeed he has promised to meet with the pope to plead my case. Unfortunately this was not accomplished as swiftly as I had hoped. I could wait no longer to make the Marquess of Pembroke my wife. You understand, I'll warrant, being eager to wed Madame Tevoulère?"

"Naturally, sire." Andrew sipped his wine to hide a smile. No mention was made, of course, of Anne Boleyn's obvious pregnancy—the real reason for their sudden secret wedding in January.

"I wish that you would do a great service for your king, Sandhurst. There are not many men I would trust to execute such a plan, but I have always admired your intelligence and ingenuity. Hearing of your masquerade at the French court, I am newly convinced that you could carry off the most delicate of missions."

"You flatter me, sire."

Henry's little eyes grew penetrating. "I would like you to return to France after you and Madame Tevoulère are married. I understand that she is a great favorite of King François's, and once it becomes known that you are indeed the Earl of Sandhurst, no doubt the two of you would be the toast of that court. I would have you cultivate the king's friendship, so that you might win his confidence . . . and travel with him when he meets with Pope Clement. There is much that you could learn through your various connections in the French court, and this service would earn you my sincere gratitude. As you know, I am quite generous with those who serve me well."

A muscle clenched in Sandhurst's jaw. Setting down his goblet, he met the king's stare unflinchingly. "I appreciate the compliment that you pay me, sire, but I am afraid that I must decline your request. My first concern at the moment is Micheline, and the new life we are embarking on together. You know my family, and I am sure you will understand that they, combined with her adjustment to a new country and culture, constitute a challenge that demands all our attention for the moment. I want Micheline to grow accustomed to her new home and her role as Countess of Sandhurst as painlessly as possible. I'm afraid that right now we cannot consider returning to France, and I trust that you, newly married yourself, will appreciate my need to put Micheline's needs first." Sandhurst didn't add that, in any case, he would never spy on King François, nor did he care for whatever forms of gratitude Henry might care to show.

"What other Englishman would dare refuse his king?" Henry wondered in a voice that betrayed anger and grudging admiration. "I hardly know how to react! This time I'll let your rebelliousness pass, since you have, after all, done my bidding by agreeing to marry Madame Tevoulère. In the future, though . . ."

"Your Majesty has a benevolent spirit," Sandhurst assured the king as humbly as he was able, adding his most engaging smile for good measure. "Ascribe my foolishness to Cupid! No doubt his arrow has affected my reason! Let's away to the tennis courts, sire. Once you've beaten me soundly, your humor will improve."

Downstairs Micheline followed the page into a wing that was peopled with servants wearing blue and purple livery. Embroidered on the doublets was the legend "La Plus Heureuse." This made Micheline bristle before she ever met the future queen. How dare she proclaim herself "the most happy"—in *French*, no less!—when she was married to that pompous, corpulent man upstairs? Obviously the woman had no idea what happiness could be!

Gradually it began to occur to Micheline that she and Anne Boleyn might have different conceptions of the word. When she entered the bedchamber of the marquess, after being announced by a properly liveried page, Micheline found herself in a setting even grander than the one upstairs. All the wood was gilded, and carved with lover's knots that featured the initials *H* and *A* entwined. Golden vases filled with red and white roses reposed on every piece of valuable furniture, and the enormous, elaborately carved bed was hung with tissue of gold. In the midst of all this a young woman stood in a chemise, corset, and shakefold, surrounded by what Micheline assumed were dressmakers. Fabulous gowns that defied description were draped over chairs while Anne Boleyn chose from dozens of furs that were held up for her inspection.

When the page announced Micheline, Anne turned to greet her with a smile.

"Ah! You must be Sandhurst's little French girl! Do you speak English?"

"Yes. It is a pleasure to meet you, my lady."

"Oh, my! Andrew's good fortune has triumphed again! He's found beauty and intelligence in one package—and it was all by chance! Sit down, madame. Would you care for some wine?"

Feeling rather overwhelmed at this point, Micheline accepted. A goblet of gold embedded with diamonds was presented to her. Anne Boleyn had returned her attention to the furs, and Micheline watched her with interest.

The future queen was not beautiful. Her skin was sallow, her face was rather long, and she had almost no bosom, yet there was a compensating loveliness about her black eyes, slender neck, and finely arched brows. Micheline had heard that Katharine of Aragon was sober and pious, so it seemed likely that Henry had been drawn more to Anne's vivaciousness than to her physical beauty. This thought gave her hope for the king's character.

"All right, I've decided." Anne turned to her guest. "What do you say, Micheline? Will not this gown of white tissue look best with ermine?"

"Oh, yes!" Enthusiasm seemed proper. "It will be lovely!"

"Well, then, good! That will be all for today," Anne told the dressmakers.

A maid scurried forward to help her mistress slip into a gown of deep violet that was encrusted with sapphires and diamonds. Anne sat down near Micheline while another maid brushed out her dark silky hair.

"I'll wager that you are a happy girl," she said to Micheline, sipping her own goblet of wine. "No doubt you're in love with Sandhurst."

"Truth to tell, I am."

"Who could resist him?" She paused to appraise the young Frenchwoman and pursed her lips slightly. The chit was a beauty. Anne had been surprised to hear from Rupert Topping that Sandhurst was going along with this forced marriage, but now it did not seem so unbelievable. There had been many moments during the years since she'd won the king's favor when Anne Boleyn had felt an almost overpowering attraction to the Earl of Sandhurst. At times, lying in Henry's smothering embrace, she'd wondered what it might be like to make love with Sandhurst instead, and in her worst moments Anne had thought that if he showed even a hint of attraction to her, she would leave behind the prospect of becoming queen and go off with Andrew. Of course, that never happened. Sandhurst was rarely at court, and when he was, he was unfailingly affable and charming, but he always kept a barrier up between himself and the rest of the world. Besides, it had all been a foolish fantasy on her part, Anne thought now. All women wanted Sandhurst because he was unattainable, and her own longing had grown out of the years of frustration that preceded this final month before she would at last become queen of England. Many times it had seemed that it would never happen, but now that she was growing larger with Henry's child, they had announced their January wedding, and in just a few weeks she would wear the crown of queen!

The dreamy, faraway look in Anne Boleyn's eyes made Micheline uneasy. Casting about for another subject, she offered, "It was kind of the king to invite us to Hampton Court. I particularly enjoyed the journey up the Thames."

"We are always pleased to have Sandhurst among us," Anne said, smiling, "and, of course, everyone has been eager to meet you. But tell me, how is *your* king? I am very fond of François, and of France! You know, I lived at the French court when I was a child."

Before Micheline could reply, the door opened and a page announced, "Lady Dangerfield to see you, my lady."

"Oh, wonderful! Show her in!"

Iris swept into the chamber, her coppery curls ablaze in the sunlight. She wore a gown of blue and heliotrope satin, several necklaces of pearls, and a ring on every finger.

"Greetings, my lady, and congratulations!" she sang.

"Thank you, Iris." Anne, her hair now caught up in a gold coif, rose to embrace her guest. "Do you know Madame Tevoulère?" Her dark eyes traveled from one lady to the other, well aware of the situation.

"We have not met," Iris replied coldly.

Micheline stood up. "Good morrow, Lady Dangerfield. I have heard a great deal about you."

Like everyone else, Iris registered surprise at the sound of the girl's perfect English. Her green eyes widened, then narrowed.

"I should offer you congratulations as well, madame," she said softly, "and I wish you luck. You'll need it to succeed where so many others have failed."

Lifting her chin with its tiny cleft, Micheline replied, "I appreciate your good wishes, my lady. And now, if you'll excuse me, I must return to Andrew."

"You can't hide behind him just now, madame," Iris said with a wicked smile. "He's gone to play tennis with the king, and they will probably be occupied for *hours*."

Micheline sat in her spacious Hampton Court bedchamber, her indignation growing by the minute as she waited for Andrew to return from his afternoon of male camaraderie. It was nearly time for supper, and still he had not knocked at her door. For her own part, she had bathed again while Mary aired out her gown, and now, with her hair freshly dressed, Micheline looked even more beautiful than she had that morning, for anger stained her cheeks with color and put sparks in her eyes.

"Where can he *be*?" she demanded of Mary.

The young girl squirmed uncomfortably. "No doubt there's an explanation, ma'am. Lord Sandhurst is a very thoughtful man. Why, ever since I came to his household, he's always been frightfully kind. Most noblemen wouldn't even notice a common little kitchen maid, but Lord Sandhurst is so considerate—"

Micheline rolled her eyes. "Mary, if you are going to be my lady's maid, you ought to have the decency to at least *pretend* to take my part at times like this!"

"Yes, ma'am," she agreed meekly.

Remembering that Mary had said her sister was a pastry cook here at the palace, Micheline said, "I'm sorry if I seemed rude; certainly none of this is your fault. You're excused for the evening, Mary. I shan't need you until morning."

"Oh!" Her heart-shaped face lit up. "Thank you, ma'am!" At the door she turned, adding, "And I don't think you're one bit rude! I think you're wonderful!"

Alone in the huge chamber, Micheline murmured, "I'm glad someone does."

Then she straightened, listening. Were those voices on the

other side of the connecting door? Had Andrew returned to his rooms without even stopping to apologize to her? Fresh outrage sent her marching to the paneled door and caused her to pound on it with her fist.

"Andrew? Are you in there? I wish to see you right *now*!"

"Then by all means, enter!" he invited her, sounding infuriatingly amused.

Micheline threw open the door and boldly entered his chamber. To her consternation, she discovered Sandhurst lounging in a steaming bathtub in front of the fire.

The ever-discreet Joshua Finchley was arranging his lordship's clothing on the bed, but the sight of Micheline's shocked expression made him swallow in embarrassment.

"You may leave us, Finchley. I won't be needing you again tonight."

Gratefully the older man made a hasty exit.

Micheline stood paralyzed on the far side of the room, unsure of what to do or say until her betrothed inquired casually, "What happened to you this afternoon?"

She gasped, incredulous. "*Me?!* What happened to *me*!"

"Didn't I just say that?"

The fact that he was naked in the bathtub suddenly meant nothing to Micheline as she marched across the chamber and exclaimed, "*I* was not the one who sauntered off to play tennis for hours on end after promising never to leave the side of my betrothed!"

"Am I to assume that you are angry?" Sandhurst tried with little success to look concerned and contrite, but his mouth twitched and his eyes twinkled.

She found this expression of his particularly appealing and tried to steel herself to resist Andrew's effortless magic. "How observant you are, my lord!"

He had been soaping his chest but paused now and reached out to touch her hand with wet fingers. "Sarcasm does not become you, fondling. You must know that I had no choice but to play tennis with the king, any more than you had a choice when he decided that you must meet Anne Boleyn. Besides, I meant for you to watch our match. I bade Lady Dangerfield show you the way to the tennis court's gallery."

Helplessly Micheline felt herself soften. When he spoke to her in that low, masculine voice and gazed at her with those molten caramel eyes, anger was impossible. "Lady Danger-

field?'' she repeated rather plaintively. ''Why would you give
that woman a message for me? She hates me, Andrew!''

''The king and I passed her on the stairway, and she said
she was bound for Anne Boleyn's chamber. It seemed a
logical request at the time.''

''Well, she never told me. Your precious Iris is a witch!
How could you have loved her for so long?''

''I never loved her, sweetheart; I've told you that. In any
case, she didn't become a witch until you appeared on the
scene.''

''Do you know what she did? She *did* say that you had
gone to play tennis, but merely indicated that this pastime
would separate us for the afternoon. Then Iris and Anne
Boleyn took me out to the garden and introduced me to a lot
of strangers who stared at me as if I were very *odd*. It was
horrible! After a few minutes the two of them drifted off to
converse with their friends and left me alone with a boring
man named Cromwell. I didn't even know I was *allowed* to
watch your silly tennis match!'' She paused, thinking, and
narrowed her eyes. ''I don't suppose that *Iris* happened to
turn up in the gallery.''

Andrew began soaping his chest again, watching as if to
make certain he didn't miss a place. ''Now that you mention
it . . . I do believe I might have seen her there.''

Micheline paced angrily beside the tub. ''I knew it! That
witch! I hate her, and I hate this place, and I wish we'd never
come!''

''Fondling, come here. Sit down beside me.'' He indicated
a low stool near the fire. After a moment she grudgingly
obeyed, and Sandhurst reached out to take her hand, muscles
playing over his shoulder and arm. ''This is part of the reason
I wanted to bring you to court *before* our wedding. I'm an earl,
and you would be a countess, and we should always have to
spend some time at court, if only to keep the peace with King
Henry. I have enough trouble as it is dodging his efforts to
transform me into a faithful courtier.''

''What do you mean by *that*?''

He sighed. ''Nothing. I'll explain it all to you later, after
we've left Hampton Court.'' As much as Andrew longed to
confide in Micheline, he did not want to add to her reasons
for distress by detailing his potential problems with the king.
She had more than enough to deal with on this first day with
the English court. ''All that's important now is that you

understand that there are more burdens involved in becoming my wife than just tolerating my relatives.''

She dropped her head, pressing her cheek to his strong, damp hand. "Sometimes I wish you were just plain Andrew Selkirk after all.''

"No more than I, my love, I can assure you! However, fate dealt me a different hand. If I were a commoner, I would not only be free of royal obligations, but I could also close the door on my past. As it is, if you marry me, you shall always have to contend with women I knew before you and I met. I'm a dozen years older than you, Michelle, and I'm a man. Iris is not the only ghost from my past who will haunt us. Unfortunately the court abounds with females who once hoped to become the next Countess of Sandhurst.''

"You needn't boast!''

Andrew smiled, encouraged by her flash of humor. "I'm *trying* to be honest. I want you to be aware of the possibilities, in case you should decide that the negative aspects of marriage to me outweigh the positive. It would devastate me to see you unhappy later on.''

Now Micheline was ashamed of the harsh words she had spoken. She gazed at Sandhurst, achingly aware of his lean-muscled naked body so near to her. The firelight only accentuated his sculpted good looks, and suddenly she realized that this was the first time she had ever seen him fully unclothed in the light. Not that she was brave enough to look beyond his hard arms, tapering chest, and the handsome legs he propped on the lower rim of the bathtub. Sighing a little, Micheline thought that it would be wonderful if she could shed her costly gown and climb into bed with him, forgetting about the royal assemblage downstairs.

But Andrew was right. She had to make the best of their time at Hampton Court. Nothing would be solved if Micheline continued to alternately rage and sulk.

"I see your point, my lord,'' she told him sincerely. "I must learn to cope with Lady Dangerfield and her ilk on my own. I apologize for behaving like a spoiled child.''

"No apology is necessary, Michelle.'' Gently he drew her near until their lips touched, parted, then touched again. "Besides, I could never love a saint. You are never more ravishing than when you're angry.''

Tears stung her eyes. Reluctantly she whispered, "I suppose I should leave you to dress."

"Probably," Andrew agreed with a mock sigh. "If you stay, I shouldn't dress at all!"

CHAPTER 25

April 6–7, 1533

SUPPER PASSED PLEASANTLY ENOUGH. IN THE GREAT HALL, WHICH had been recently rebuilt to feature a towering carved hammerbeam ceiling and a fanciful minstrels' gallery, the court feasted on fish of every description, from salmon and flounder to salted eels and whiting. Micheline, as the newest guest, was seated in relative security between King Henry and Andrew. The king was kind to her, though from time to time he gazed at her bosom in a way that made her vaguely uneasy.

The king's table was reserved for the court elite. It reposed on a raised dais, while the rest of the company supped at tables that ranged down the length of the hall. There was an open hearth in the middle of the floor near the dais; the smoke found its way up into the roof and out of an elaborate louvre.

Seated near Micheline were some of the luminaries of Henry's court: Thomas Howard, Duke of Norfolk; the Earl and Countess of Oxford; the Duke of Suffolk; Thomas Wyatt, the dashing poet who was said to love Anne Boleyn; and, most prominently, Thomas Cranmer, the newly consecrated Archbishop of Canterbury, and Thomas Cromwell, the king's dour-looking new chief minister, who was assuming the position vacated by Cardinal Wolsey. Micheline watched and listened carefully and soon began to connect names with faces and form opinions about their owners.

Finally sweets were served. There were jellies of all colors and shapes, plus sugared nuts and candied nutmeg and lemons. Then two liveried pages carried in an enormous rabbit made of almond paste and marchpane mixed with isinglass and sugar. The confection had been dredged with cinnamon to resemble a real rabbit, roasted. Anne Boleyn laughed in delight when the counterfeit hare was placed before her.

"My sweet Anne has been craving rabbit for several days," Henry whispered to Micheline. "Until Easter passes, this will have to suffice."

"Very thoughtful of you, sire," she said, smiling. Meanwhile Micheline was thinking that this wasn't so difficult. All she had to do was agree, smile, and compliment to get along in the English court. It was a small price to pay for loving Andrew, and she was comforted by the knowledge that he didn't enjoy the situation any more than she did.

It was late when the boards and trestles were removed from the great hall. Micheline stifled a yawn, hoping that she and Andrew could escape after a reasonable amount of time. However, everyone seemed to be leaving the hall, amid much laughter, and she watched in growing bewilderment.

"The king has planned a masque," Sandhurst explained, reading her thoughts. "We must go, too, and conceal our identities." His voice was sardonic.

"But that's silly!" she protested. "I have no other gown but the simpler one I must wear tomorrow. Everyone will recognize me!"

Laughing softly, Andrew led her into the corridor. "We'll just don masks, sweetheart, and even those have been provided for everyone—in Anne's heraldic colors. The only person who must be entertained is the king. He imagines that he is anonymous in his costume and loves to make a game of finding his lady."

Once again Sandhurst was right. When they rejoined the rest of the court in the great hall, minstrels were playing gaily in their gallery, and blue-and-purple-masked dancers had begun to frolic. Before long another celebrant appeared in their midst. Clad entirely in green, from his jaunty feathered cap to his shoes, the man disguised as "Spring" was not only tall but barrel-chested and obese. His velvet costume was elaborately slashed and puffed, decorated with diamonds, rubies, and silken green leaves. Small eyes gleamed happily through an emerald-set mask, while their owner's ruddy cheeks contrasted with fair skin elsewhere and a reddish-gold beard.

"Hmmm," Sandhurst mused, "I wonder who *that* could be!"

Micheline giggled. "I cannot imagine!"

"Spring" stopped before every female flower in sight,

kissing hands and nuzzling necks as he inhaled various scents. When he reached Micheline, it was all she could do to smile politely and suffer his investigation. As if by design, Anne Boleyn stood at the opposite end of the crowd, now wearing an extravagant jeweled gown of cloth of gold, its bell-shaped sleeves turned up to display sable linings. Her hair was hidden under a gold gable coif, and her blue and purple mask was set with rubies. When the king finally reached her, he pretended to be unsure. He pressed kisses to her throat and ran his hands over her bodice, then caught her up in a crushing hug and let out a gusty laugh of triumph.

"How very peculiar," Micheline observed softly. The musicians had begun to play and Henry led his future queen forward to lead the first dance.

Sandhurst was about to reply, when a stocky, well-fed-looking young man appeared before them. Like King Henry, he could not conceal his identity with a simple mask, for his carrot-colored hair and flushed cheeks were clues enough.

"My lady, would you dance with me?" he inquired mysteriously.

Micheline was too surprised to play along. "M'sieur Playfair, is that *you*?"

"How ever did you guess?" Andrew teased.

"Yes, that's what I'd like to know!" Jeremy fretted. "What's the fun of these masques if everyone knows who one is? And, by the by, madame, my name is Culpepper, not Playfair!"

"My pardon, Sir Jeremy," she apologized. "I'll not forget again."

"Speaking of remaining anonymous," Sandhurst interjected, "how did you know who *we* were?"

"You're my best friend, aren't you? Besides, you two are the handsomest couple here tonight, and I've seen you wear that doublet before, Sandhurst."

This elicited a burst of laughter from Andrew. "It's good to see you here, Jeremy. When did you arrive?"

"Late this afternoon. I saw the two of you at supper, but I was seated at the other side of the hall. Not everyone is honored with a place beside the king."

"I'd have preferred your company, sir," Micheline told him sincerely. "And I'm awfully glad that you are Andrew's friend and not his manservant."

"You aren't the only one!" Jeremy harumphed. "I must say, though, that all the humiliation I suffered in France was well worth it if you two have worked things out. Word has it that you're getting married after all!" He smiled at his friend and shook his head. "Only *you* could have managed to escape successfully from that coil you were wrapped in two days ago, Sandhurst! Charm will out, eh?"

"Not charm, but love," he replied evenly.

"Well, I wouldn't know about that." Seeing the way Micheline gazed at her betrothed, he felt a twinge of envy. No wonder Sandhurst had succumbed at last to romance. "What about that dance, then?"

The floor was crowded now. All the court seemed to be dancing, laughing gaily as they pretended not to recognize one another. Micheline found Jeremy very endearing, even when he made a wrong move from time to time and stepped on her toes. Across the room she glimpsed Andrew leaning against the paneled wall under a carving of Henry VIII's royal arms impaling those of Anne Boleyn. He watched her affectionately, and it filled her with delight when she saw him shake his head after a figure she knew to be Lady Dangerfield approached him.

Micheline's dance with Jeremy was followed by two with Andrew. Thomas Wyatt begged for the next, and as he led her into the crush, she felt something slip up her sleeve. It seemed to be a piece of paper, but she promptly forgot about it as she chatted and danced with the poet.

Long past midnight Sandhurst suggested that sleep might be in order, and they went to bid the king and Anne Boleyn good night.

"When will your wedding take place?" inquired Anne.

"In a fortnight's time, my lady," Andrew replied, then looked toward King Henry. "I know that you had planned to attend, when first you and my father spoke of this marriage, but we realize that circumstances have altered in the interim. Doubtless the arrangements for the Marquess's coronation as queen will prevent you from embarking on a journey to Yorkshire." His eyes added his understanding of the fact that the king might not be kindly disposed toward him since their conversation earlier that day.

Henry nodded slowly, raising an eyebrow in silent communication with the Earl of Sandhurst. "Certainly we shouldn't come all that way on *your* account, Sandhurst!" He took care to lace his jest with an edge of steel so subtle that only the other man would perceive it. "And you are correct. There is much to keep us near London through May. However"—the king turned to beam at Micheline, lifting her hand to his small, pursed lips—"we feel that the enchanting Madame Tevoulère deserves special consideration, and there are others from our court who have expressed a wish to attend your wedding. I can make no promises, but if it is within our power, we shall make a brief journey to Aylesbury Castle to join in the nuptial celebrations."

"As always, Your Majesty demonstrates exceptional thoughtfulness and generosity," said Sandhurst. "It would give us great joy to have you present at our marriage, and I know that my father would be equally pleased." Sketching a bow before Anne Boleyn, he added, "My lady, I hope to see you in Yorkshire. Your arrival would bring new radiance to that district!"

More courtly farewells were exchanged until, at length, Andrew and Micheline escaped, climbing the stairs to their quiet wing of the palace.

"How I despise such artificial conversation!" Sandhurst muttered darkly, his bright mask dangling from his fingers.

"You seem quite adept at it, my lord," Micheline teased him, stifling a yawn. Away from the crowd, she was suddenly aware of her own fatigue. Voices, faces, music, and all the day's experiences continued to swirl in her mind; she would be glad for sleep if only to escape them.

"I need to be adept to survive, I fear. I can only hope that whatever charm I have, coupled with the king's entranced approval of you, will be enough to counteract the displeasure I've incurred when I could not bring myself to behave as an obedient subject ought." He glanced heavenward. "I've not the temperament for a lord of the realm, I fear. Obedience is not in my nature."

"Will you rebel against the bonds of matrimony too?"

They had reached Micheline's door, and he slid his arms around her slender waist. "This is the first time in my life I've faced a commitment to which it will be a pleasure to submit. Besides, you don't want to rule me."

"That's true." She opened her mouth as they exchanged a sleepy, sensual kiss. "And neither will you rule *me*!"

"If I imagined it were possible, I couldn't love you as I do," Sandhurst told her honestly. "We think and feel alike, Michelle, and we understand and respect each other. Aside from that"—he paused to kiss her peacefully drooping eyelids—

"there are other extremely pleasurable considerations. No doubt you'll be relieved to learn that I'm too tired to press that issue now. My own fatigue is such that tonight I shall not lie awake, in tormented solitude, for very long."

"*Je t'adore* . . ." Micheline whispered, gazing at him in wonder.

"Go to bed." Sandhurst laughed gently. "Sleep will allow you to think more clearly! Not that I object—"

They shared another sweet, drowsy kiss, then parted. Alone in her bedchamber, Micheline managed to unlace the back of her gown unaided. When she drew off the velvet sleeves, a small piece of parchment dropped to the floor, reminding her of that moment in the great hall when she had felt it slide against her wrist. Puzzled, Micheline removed her gown, petticoat, and shakefold, then picked up the paper and sat down on the bed in her chemise to open it.

Printed in tiny, barely legible characters were the words: *"Leave England alone, or die."*

She blinked in confusion. As the message sank in, Micheline's heart began to pound and her hands perspired. Still, it didn't seem real. Mechanically she walked about the huge, chilly bedchamber, removing her crispinette, brushing out her hair, washing her face, and even cleaning her teeth, all the while trying to block the ominous note from her thoughts. Perhaps it was someone's idea of a joke. Perhaps it had fallen into her sleeve by accident and had not been intended for her at all.

Finally she blew out the candles and crawled into the enormous bed, but sleep would not come. Over and over again Micheline considered waking Andrew, but there seemed no purpose. Her door was latched. Who would be foolish enough to harm her with Sandhurst in the next room? Moreover, who would want to harm her at all? Could Iris Dangerfield be that wicked? Perhaps, if she had written the note, the threat was empty—simply an attempt to frighten Micheline into running home to France . . . unmarried.

An hour passed, and still her heart drummed against her breastbone. Occasionally there were footsteps and voices in the corridor. Each new sound made her start—and then, suddenly, when all was quiet, there came a soft scratching noise at Micheline's door. No sooner did she sit up straight in bed, wide-eyed and terrified in the darkness, than the scratching stopped. A full minute passed during which Micheline neither

moved nor breathed, then . . . *scratch-scratch*. The sound
was all the more sinister because it was barely audible, but
then it grew to alarming proportions.

Somehow, she made herself act. Scrambling off the other
side of the bed, Micheline ran through the darkness, bumping
into furniture. There was barely enough firelight remaining
for her to make out the shape of the connecting door to
Sandhurst's room. Praying that no one had locked it, she
found the latch, lifted it, pushed on the door, and it swung
open.

"Andrew!" Micheline gasped. There was more light from
his fireplace, allowing her to see the shadowed bed, and then a
silhouette as he sat up.

"Michelle?" Sandhurst wondered. Was this a dream? Wish-
ful thinking?

In the next instant she was upon him, clinging to him,
trembling violently.

"Sweetheart, what is it? Did you have a nightmare?" He
held her tightly, stroking her lustrous curls, rubbing her back
through the thin fabric of her chemise. "I can feel your heart
beating against my chest! Tell me what's wrong. You're safe
now."

"*C'est vrai*, I know." It was true; she felt a hundred times
better in the shelter of Sandhurst's strong embrace. She buried her face in the taut curve between his shoulder and neck,
shivering in reaction. He continued to soothe her, kissing her
brow and temple, speaking to her tenderly until Micheline
relaxed enough to tell him what had happened.

"Someone put a tiny piece of paper in my sleeve while I
was dancing with Thomas Wyatt. I barely noticed at the time;
I'd forgotten all about it until I removed my gown and the
note fell out. It said—it said—"

"You're all right, Michelle," he reminded her. "You're
with me now."

"It said that I must leave England, alone—or die!" Her
voice dropped to a whisper on the last word.

"What?!" Sandhurst was incredulous. "Why didn't you
bring it to me right then?"

"I don't know. I knew you were probably already asleep,
and it seemed so ludicrous and impossible. At first, I told
myself that it was some sort of mistake . . . or bizarre joke
. . . but I couldn't sleep, and then—just now, someone was
scratching at my door!"

"Scratching!"

"To scare me, I suppose. It was a very tiny sound at first, but then it grew louder and louder till I was nearly terrified!"

"No doubt," Sandhurst said grimly. "Loose me a moment, sweetheart; I'll light a candle and have a look around."

Micheline nodded bravely and even managed a smile as he tucked the covers snugly around her. Her eyes followed him as he donned hose and a white shirt, then took a candle and went into her chamber. Barely a minute passed before Andrew reappeared. After bolting the connecting door, he sat down beside her on the bed.

"Naturally whoever it was has gone." He held up a small square of parchment. "This is the note, I take it." He stared at it broodingly. "I can't make sense of this. Who would want to threaten *you*? And *why*?"

"I don't know!" Her voice broke on a sob. "There's only one person I can think of."

Andrew glanced over at her. "Iris? No, she's simply not capable of such a thing. Underneath her feline façade, she's really rather sweet and loving."

"I don't mean to cast aspersions on your former mistress," Micheline heard herself reply tartly, "but you don't know how it feels to be in love with you!"

His brows went up slightly. "Pardon?"

"I can appreciate Lady Dangerfield's agony, because I can imagine my own devastation if you were to suddenly tell me that you loved another woman and wanted to marry her instead. I might contemplate murder myself!"

"There's a tremendous difference between thought and deed, Michelle."

"Perhaps Iris hopes only to frighten me off."

"So you think *she* was scratching at your door tonight?" he countered in disbelief.

"Who *else* could it be?"

Sandhurst bit his lip and sighed. "I don't know."

Softly Micheline asked, "Will you let me stay here tonight? With you?"

"Of course you'll stay here. Tomorrow morning we leave for London, and until then I promise not to let you out of my sight—and this time I mean it! You can even hold my hand while I shave if you like."

He gave her a reassuring smile, but his eyes were on the menacing piece of paper he'd set on the table. Absently he drew his shirt over his gilded head, then reached down to pull off his hose, unaware of the blush that was spreading across Micheline's cheeks.

Her gaze wandered helplessly down his long, tapering back and lingered on the hard curves of his buttocks. When Andrew stood to blow out the candle and place it on a chest, she caught a fleeting glimpse of his manhood in its nest of dark gold curls. At that instant he felt the heat of her gaze and forgot about the mysterious note.

When Sandhurst drew back the covers and climbed into bed beside her, Micheline was eager to put that frightening message out of her mind too. She snuggled against him, shivering, as if she couldn't get close enough.

"You're freezing, sweetheart!" he exclaimed softly as her bare foot found its way between his calves.

"Andrew, I love you. I love you!"

"And I love you, Micheline."

Glorying in the warm strength of his embrace, Micheline sought his mouth with her own and kissed him passionately. She wrapped her arms tight about Sandhurst's neck and held fast, as if she were drowning and he was the shore. As they kissed, with Micheline's tongue the aggressor, she felt him harden fully against her thigh.

"Christ!" he gasped at last when she turned her hungry lips to his jaw, neck, ear, and eyes. "What are you *doing*?"

She giggled wickedly. "Don't you know?"

"What happened to your vow of chastity?" Sandhurst knew, of course. She was trying to blot out the terror, and would regret it tomorrow if they made love now.

"Must we talk?" Micheline was kissing her way down his corded neck.

"I can't believe I'm saying this, but yes, we must." He groaned and glanced heavenward while prying her arms from his shoulders. "Remember this next time you wonder how much I really love you. I'm astonishing *myself* here!"

"What's wrong? I thought you wanted to—"

"I did. I do! But not like this, Michelle." Turning onto his back, he held her cradled against his chest. The throbbing heat in his loins was torture. "You're just upset right now, and it would be selfish for me to press my advantage."

Embarrassed by her brazen behavior and the fact that she, too, was fully aroused and aching for release, Micheline grew suddenly motionless. Tears stung her eyes.

Sensing her humiliation, Sandhurst reached up to stroke the soft hair back from Micheline's face. "Cheer up, fondling," he coaxed, kissing her brow with smiling lips. "You'll thank me, you know . . . in our marriage bed!"

CHAPTER 26

April 18, 1533
Yorkshire, England

THE DAY THAT BROUGHT ANDREW AND MICHELINE TO AYLESBURY Castle began leisurely, for they had spent the previous night at the Starre Inn in York and were little more than an hour's ride from their destination.

Not only were they accompanied on their journey by Mary, Finchley, and squires for their coach and horses, but Sir Jeremy Culpepper had joined them as well. Micheline hadn't been particularly surprised to discover that Jeremy had grown up on the estate bordering Aylesbury Castle. Since childhood, he had been as close as a brother to Andrew, and now he was eager to combine a visit with his family in Yorkshire with the opportunity to attend Sandhurst's wedding.

With Jeremy along, the journey northward had been fraught with amusement, yet crowded as well. The two men shared a chamber at every inn, while Mary slept with Micheline, and the remaining three servants had a third room to themselves. Sandhurst and Micheline were rarely alone. Because of intermittent rain, he insisted that she ride in the coach with Mary. Mealtime conversation, which Culpepper cheerfully monopolized, was generally the only opportunity Micheline had to share Andrew's company.

On this last morning they both rose early by previous arrangement and met in the common room of the inn. When Sandhurst put an arm around her waist and bent to graze her lips, Micheline flushed with excitement. It seemed that their moments of intimacy belonged to another lifetime, for now each casual touch sent currents of fire over her nerves.

He took her on a brief walking tour of York, and both of

them were heady with mischief, like adolescents who had escaped the watchful eyes of parents. First, they walked up Stonegate, Andrew explaining that the oft-used suffix of "gate" in the city of York was derived from the Scandinavian word for street. It seemed that the Vikings had captured York in the mid-800s, and their influence was still felt.

"You're probably descended from a Viking yourself!" Micheline exclaimed, drawing back to stare at his golden hair.

"That's the rumor," he said, smiling. "In fact, Aylesbury Castle stands on the site of a Viking fort. Unlike most of England, which was overrun with Danes, Yorkshire was conquered by Norsemen." Laughing softly, Sandhurst added, "My mother used to tell a story about a beautiful Saxon maiden from York who was taken prisoner by a handsome, flaxen-haired Viking and brought to the fort—now our castle— where he surprised everyone by making her his wife. According to Mother, the Westons sprang from that tempestuous union."

"That must account for your wild streak," she mused.

"If so, I take after my ancestor. Even he, celebrated as a heathen, was susceptible to the mellowing power of love."

Micheline tucked her hand through his arm and leaned against his velvet-clad shoulder. Clad in a doublet of slashed buff-colored velvet set with only a handful of round emeralds, Andrew seemed to grow more handsome with each passing day. His hair, brushed casually back from his sculpted face, shone in the soft rosy light of dawn, and his elegantly restrained clothing served to set him apart from not only the poor who thronged the streets but also the more ostentatiously clad rich.

Content just to be together, touching, they strolled north to Petergate, where Micheline viewed the great minster for the first time. Sandhurst took her inside the cathedral for a proper look at the spectacular ninety-foot-high vaulted nave and the stained-glass windows that were justly celebrated. In the nave was the great west window, with tracery in the form of a heart, while the south transcept boasted the rose window, which commemorated the end of the War of the Roses nearly fifty years earlier. Andrew and Micheline knelt together, praying silently but with one heart, then lit a candle before leaving the cathedral.

On Low Petergate, Sandhurst stopped to buy warm sugared

buns for them to eat, and then a nosegay of violets from an old flower woman. Micheline was wearing a gown of rose and lavender silk, and the violets made a charming accessory.

Petergate wound into the Shambles, an especially narrow street lined with butcher shops whose overhanging eaves nearly touched at some points. The sun was fully visible over the River Foss when Andrew and Micheline began to circle back to the Starre Inn. He chose a meandering route along the streets of Highousegate, Spurriergate, and Davygate, which eventually brought them back to their lodgings in Stonegate.

"I like York," Micheline told him. "I like all of England, so far . . . except, perhaps, for Hampton Court, and that is no fault of Middlesex or the palace itself." Feeling Sandhurst's eyes on her, she hurried on. "I enjoy the differences between England and France, and it is pleasurable in another way to note the similarities."

"I'm glad you like England, Michelle," he said, pausing outside the Starre's doorway to hold her against him. "That was one of my chief concerns before we left France. There is so much for you to become accustomed to, and I feared that I would not be adequate compensation for those aspects of your new life that you might dislike." Andrew sighed, breathing in the fragrance of her hair. "A new country, new customs, a new family, friends, potential responsibilities dealing with a new king—it's a great load."

"I'm up to the challenge, my lord," Micheline told him, amusement infecting her voice. "Why, I'm even learning to like *dumplings*!"

Laughing, Sandhurst led her into the inn, where they found Jeremy and the servants waiting for them and eager to compete the journey. So within the hour the band of travelers passed through the towered Walmgate Bar, the eastern gate to the city, bound for Aylesbury Castle.

Micheline looked back out of the coach window at the banks of daffodils that rose up to touch the magnificent white walls encircling York, and wondered what sort of surprises the rest of the day held in store.

The sky grew darker as morning progressed. Still, Micheline found Yorkshire beautiful in a haunting sort of way. Gray clouds scudded over bright green vales dotted with trees and sheep and brightened with liberal sprinklings of buttercups. Especially interesting to Micheline were the intersecting lime-

stone walls that seemed to snake endlessly over the wind-
swept landscape. She chatted with Mary, enjoying the scenery,
until her heart caught in her throat at the sight of a castle
silhouetted against the swirling gray sky.

Sandhurst rode up alongside the coach, pointing, to con-
firm the fact that Aylesbury Castle was at hand. Unlike the
charming, peaceful-looking châteaus of France, which were
set amid parkland and gardens, this castle had a stark, wild
look about it. The closer they drew to the cluster of bastions,
crenellations, and towers, the more nervous Micheline felt.
The place did not look welcoming, nor could she imagine it
as her home.

Noticing her mistress's apprehensive expression, Mary
soothed, "It's not so bad, ma'am, and his lordship hardly
ever comes here. You'll like Sandhurst Manor much better,
I'll warrant."

Micheline nodded bravely, but she was thinking that the
austere appearance of the castle merely seemed to forebode
the atmosphere within.

A chilling wind penetrated the coach as it climbed a twisting lane to the castle. Andrew led the way as they crossed a
drawbridge that led them into the barbican with its surrounding curtain wall. Servants had already begun to appear, rushing to welcome the Earl of Sandhurst as he rode over a
second drawbridge, through the gatehouse, and into the enormous inner courtyard of Aylesbury Castle.

Andrew swung down from his horse and handed the reins
over to his squire, then made his way through the group of
familiar happy faces, greeting each servant by name. Reaching the coach, he opened the door and helped Micheline
down, holding her against him as he announced, "I want all
of you to meet Madame Micheline Tevoulère, who will become my wife and the Countess of Sandhurst just as soon as
we can arrange the wedding!" Laughing in response to their
cries of excitement, he added, "There may be some extra
work involved for many of you, but I'm confident that you'll
understand my plight and take pity on me. Each day of
waiting is torment!"

Sandhurst's exaggerated expression of agony drew laughter
from the servants, followed by a rush to bow or curtsy before
the beautiful Frenchwoman. His lordship introduced each of
them by name, and Micheline realized that his visits must
always be a cause for celebration. If the duke was as sour as

she'd been led to believe, then this retinue was surely starved for the affection and respect shown them by the Earl of Sandhurst.

At length they were free to enter the castle. Micheline knew a measure of apprehension as Andrew led her toward the arched doorway, then suddenly distraction appeared in the form of a lovely dark-haired girl who burst through the portal and ran forward to throw her arms around Sandhurst.

"Andrew! Oh, Andrew! You've come!" She was actually weeping with joy, her face buried against his shoulder.

He had to let go of Micheline to return the girl's fervent embrace, a fond smile warming his brown eyes.

"Of course I've come, child. Did you doubt it?"

"Don't leave me again, Andrew. I couldn't bear it! Please, you must *promise*!"

"I've asked you before not to demand that I make promises I cannot keep, and in any case, this is certainly not the time for arguments. Loose me, Cicely, and meet your new sister, Micheline."

The girl pressed her lips together and reluctantly withdrew her arms from Andrew's neck. Micheline, who had been somewhat taken aback by the emotional scene she'd just witnessed, mustered a warm smile. Although Cicely kept her eyes averted, it was readily apparent that she was a beauty. Lustrous black curls tumbled over her shoulders and the gently curving bodice of her pink satin gown, and her face was delicately enchanting.

"Greetings, Cicely. I'm so happy to meet you at last, for I know how dear you are to Andrew."

Cicely raised wet sable-brown eyes and replied in a monotone, "Welcome to Aylesbury Castle, mademoiselle."

"I'm sure you two will be great friends!" declared Andrew with forced cheerfulness. Silently he remembered the words his sister had spoken that night in London: "I hope that Mademoiselle Tevoulère is a toad!" Cicely was by far the most endearing member of his family. If she would not open her heart to Micheline, it appeared that there was little chance for a happy relationship between his wife and her new family.

For Andrew's sake, Micheline decided to try again. "You know, Cicely, I have always wished for a sister. Much like you, I had only an older brother who had left home by the time I was your age. Perhaps we will be able to be the sisters that neither of us had before."

The younger girl shrugged and looked away. "Pretending's not the same, is it? Besides, I've been through this sort of thing before, inheriting fully grown family members. Rupert and Patience aren't exactly my idea of—"

Sandhurst gripped her arm tightly and interjected, "Micheline is not Rupert or Patience, child—I can assure you of that! Let's go inside now. I can hardly wait to see the rest of my *wonderful* family!" His voice was acid with sarcasm.

Although Cicely had always lived in dread of making her brother angry, this time her resentment of Micheline was stronger than her need for Andrew's approval. She allowed herself to be dragged along into the castle, and when he gave her a dangerous glare, Cicely returned it defiantly.

The trio climbed a spiraling newel staircase in single file, emerging in a broad stone corridor that passed the family apartments. Micheline looked about as she walked, noting the fine tapestries displayed on the white walls and the woven rush mats that took the place of loose rushes. She'd expected the place to be gloomy, but in fact the castle's interior was remarkably clean and bright.

They came into the solar, which served as a private living room. Its southern exposure and high arched windows filled the airy chamber with April sunlight, while the hall, in the adjoining east wing of the castle, was too large and shadowy for the comfort of a small gathering.

Seated in a velvet-upholstered chair was a bony old man who narrowed his eyes at Micheline. A fur-lined satin coverlet was draped over his shrunken frame, and his feet were propped on an oaken stool. Behind him stood Rupert Topping, while a pale, long-faced young lady occupied a settle near the windows. She put down an elaborate piece of embroidery and watched the proceedings with tiny, alert eyes.

"You're looking well, Father," Andrew said in greeting. Holding Micheline's hand, he drew her across the room until the two of them stood before the craggy-faced Duke of Aylesbury.

"Bah! I'm dying and you know it!" The old man briefly took the hand proffered by his son.

Sandhurst wanted to throw up his hands and stalk out of the solar, but instead he clenched his teeth in a smile. "Let us hope, then, that your health may be restored by some happy news. Father, I would like you to meet Madame Micheline Tevoulère, who will be my wife and your daughter. We've come to Aylesbury Castle, just as you requested, for the wedding." This last was particularly difficult for him to say in a neutral tone of voice since the duke had never been kind enough to make a "request" in Andrew's memory. His father's propensity for issuing ultimatums had resulted invariably in his refusal to comply. Now, however, he thought that peace might be served by his pretending that Micheline was here because the duke had wished it. Sandhurst would have done anything to make her new life more pleasant. It was one thing for him to turn away from his family when he was independent, but there were other considerations now—not only for Micheline but for their children.

Micheline stepped forward and dropped into a brief curtsy. The lavender of her gown and the nosegay of violets tucked into its bodice served to emphasize the vivid color of her eyes. Sunbeams burnished her hair and lent an aura to her lovely face.

"I am so pleased to meet you at last, Your Grace."

"You speak English! Well, well. And you're a beauty. My son is very fortunate."

"Not so fortunate as I, Your Grace," she replied firmly.

"Hmmph!" The old man arched his white brows. "That's a matter of opinion, but then, Andrew always has been skilled at charming the ladies." He turned his attention back to his son. "I suppose you're expecting me to lavish praise on you for doing as you were bidden!"

Sandhurst's entire body was taut. "Far from it, Father. I am marrying Micheline because we love each other, and I had hoped that you and I might declare a truce for her sake."

"I thought so. You couldn't resist telling me that you are doing this because *you* want to, and not because *I* wished it! As usual, you go your own way without any respect for other people—least of all your own father!"

"Are you saying that you'd be *happy* if there were no love between Micheline and me, if I were marrying her only because I'd been *told* to?" His eyes were dark with rage.

"Don't prattle on to me about love, boy! It's beside the point. What I can't forgive is the way you disappeared for two full months! No one knew where you were; it was impossible to make wedding plans in view of your record of rebelliousness. Now you turn up unannounced and declare that you've been a good boy and expect me to smile and pat you on the head! April's nearly gone. It's too late to send

invitations for your wedding to London. I wanted every nobleman in England to come to Aylesbury Castle for this
occasion, but—''

"In the first place," Sandhurst ground out, "the last thing
I yearn for in this life is to be patted on the head by anyone,
least of all *you*! Secondly, this is Micheline's and my wedding—
not yours. If I'd had my way, we'd have been married a
fortnight ago in London, but because you had expressed a
desire to have the ceremony here, I thought to comply in the
hope that it would please you. I'd hoped that this might be an
opportunity for all of us to make peace and a fresh beginning.
As for your desire to draw every nobleman in England to
Aylesbury Castle, I don't give a damn who attends this
wedding so long as Micheline and I and the priest are there. It
would be agreeable to have family and friends present as
well, but even that isn't necessary as far as I'm concerned.
Now, if you want us to leave and be married elsewhere, just
say so. Otherwise, I would appreciate it if you could endeavor
to soften your tongue, at least in Micheline's presence."

The duke's face had gradually turned a shade of mauve. "I
knew you hadn't changed. I heard that you were going to
marry the girl, but I knew that you'd never admit defeat."

Micheline wanted to speak up and ask why a father would
want to defeat his own son, but the air was so heavy with
tension that she lost her nerve.

"I'm not broken, if that's what you mean," Sandhurst
said, an edge of steel in his voice. "And as you know, I have
no desire to continue these perverse little games of yours, the
object of which seems to *be* the breaking of my spirit. I have
more important, productive ways to spend my time."

"Oh, I'm well aware of that. You've always had something better to do than obey your father." The duke heaved a
mournful sigh and dropped his head back against the chair,
then glanced over to Rupert, smiling wanly. "Fortunately, not
all my offspring are so arrogantly selfish." Now the old man
turned his attention back to Micheline, who was looking
bewildered and stricken all at once. Silkily he murmured, "I
must apologize on behalf of Andrew, my dear. This has no
doubt been a rather unpleasant scene for you to witness. Let
me assure you that you *shall* have your wedding here, and I
will see to it that it is as fine an occasion as possible. I had
hoped to make it a day that all of England would remember,
but . . .''

"I assure you, Your Grace, that the ceremony itself is all that matters to me," Micheline replied as politely as she was able. "Whether or not all England remembers isn't important. The day I become Andrew's wife will be the most meaningful of my entire life, and my only other desire is that his family share in our joy."

The duke shrugged and looked away from her again as if she were a child spouting nonsense. "The king himself expressed a desire to attend."

"Father, I spoke to King Henry myself," Sandhurst said flatly. "Micheline and I went to see him at Hampton Court. He was pleased about our betrothal and sends you his best regards. I had assumed that the preparations for Anne Boleyn's coronation next month would prevent them from attending this wedding, but you should be pleased to learn that he hopes to make the journey after all, bringing the Marquess of Pembroke and other members of the court with him. He couldn't promise, but—"

The old man merely turned his craggy face toward the windows as if he hadn't heard.

In the silence that followed, Rupert cleared his throat.

"I haven't had a chance to say hello to you two!" he exclaimed loudly. Rushing forward, he shook his half brother's hand, then turned to Micheline. "Madame, you are looking more beautiful than ever! *Tress* bell, what?"

A bubble of amusement rose through her tension. "Hello again, Roo-pair! But no, that is wrong! Hello, Roo-*poort*!"

Even Sandhurst forgot his consuming rage for a moment and smiled. Thank God for Micheline. What had he ever done without her? Slipping a hand around her tiny waist, he drew her near and kissed her shining hair.

"You must meet my dear wife!" Rupert was declaring. "She's been looking forward to it so much!" He turned his head without taking his eyes off Micheline. "Patience, darling, do come and join us!"

Smiling shyly, Patience complied. As Rupert's wife drew near, it became painfully apparent to Micheline that the woman was singularly unattractive. Much taller than Rupert, and nearly on a level with Andrew, Patience Topping had no breasts or hips to speak of, and her face was long and pasty, with thin lips, a sharp nose, round little eyes, and a receding chin not unlike her husband's. Lank hair of no definable color was parted in the middle and tucked into an unflattering gable-hooded headdress, completing the picture of plainness. Micheline's heart went out to her.

"This is Micheline, dearest!" Rupert enthused. "Isn't she everything I told you? Aren't we fortunate to have her as our *sister*?"

Sandhurst winced slightly at that, but Patience was smiling at Micheline with awe. "We are indeed, dear husband. Hello, Sister, and welcome to our family."

"Thank you, Patience." Bemusedly she looked around the room, her eyes falling on a petulant Cecily; the shrunken, sour-faced Duke of Aylesbury; gawky, overeager Rupert; and Patience, who possessed the face of a horse but none of its elegance. Finally Micheline turned her gaze up to Andrew. There was wry humor in the set of his mouth and the way he lifted his brows as if to say, I *told* you they were different!

The warmth of his gaze melted her despair. As long as they were together, they could surmount any obstacle and bear any hardship.

This resolve was put to the test minutes later when Patience kindly volunteered to show Micheline to her bedchamber so that she might wash and rest.

"You'll be safe from Andrew until the wedding, just in case he should become impatient!" Patience announced proudly. "His chamber is at the opposite end of the corridor!"

"Oh." Micheline nodded, feeling slightly ill. "How thoughtful of you."

CHAPTER 27

April 18–19, 1533

SANDHURST WAS STANDING IN HIS BEDCHAMBER, PUTTING FOLDED doublets into a carved chest, when Cicely appeared at the door.

"I've brought you some wine," she said hesitantly, holding out the pewter goblet. "And . . . I came to say I am sorry for the way I behaved."

He was still tense with anger, but the sight of her looking so small and repentant in the doorway softened his heart. Cicely was still a child, after all, and deserved a second chance.

Stretching out an arm, Andrew smiled slightly when she put down the wine and rushed into his embrace.

"Say you've forgiven me!" she begged, her face pressed against his velvet doublet. "You're the only person I love in all the world!"

"Of course I forgive you, child. That goes without saying. But"—he tipped her chin up and stared hard into her tear-filled eyes—"you must never behave that way toward Micheline again. She needs your help to feel comfortable here, and, of course, you will be her sister and should treat her accordingly."

Cicely's lips tightened. "I don't see how you can talk that way, Andrew. I heard what you said that night in London; you and Jeremy made fun of her! You didn't want to marry her! How do you think it makes me feel to hear everyone talking about you, about the way you went along with the king's and Father's wishes to marry a stranger—"

"Who is *everyone*?" he interrupted coldly.

She dropped her eyes. "I went for a visit to our aunt Margaret's in Oxfordshire late in February. I was going mad here, and Rupert had to journey to London, so he took me to Oxfordshire on his way. I stayed until last week. We went to Hampton Court to watch a day of jousting in the tilting field. That was just after you and—your *betrothed* were there, and the court could talk of nothing else. Of course, I'd heard already that you had decided to marry that woman after all, but I didn't really believe it until Hampton Court."

"Why didn't you come to visit us in London?" he demanded. "And how did you return to Yorkshire? You could have come with Micheline and me!"

"Rupert brought me back. As much as I despise him, it was better than watching you moon over that Frenchwoman."

"I thought Rupert returned here on the fourth of April."

"What difference does it make? I met him by arrangement at Hampton Court, and I must say that at least he remembered my existence, which is more than I can say for you!"

Sandhurst put other thoughts from his mind and concentrated on the problem of his sister. "Cecily, sit down." He went to fetch the goblet of wine and took a long drink. "I confess that I am at a loss to understand your animosity toward Micheline. I know what I said two months ago in London, but that was before I had met the lady. In France everything was different. I fell in love almost against my will, and *she* fell in love as well, not with the Earl of Sandhurst but with a painter named Andrew Selkirk. Don't you see? Micheline turned aside the marriage King François had arranged for her in favor of the man she loved. Doesn't that convince you that she is a good, sincere person?''

Fussing with the folds of her satin skirt, Cecily would not meet his eyes. ''You're besot. It's as if someone's put a spell on you, but it will wear off! As for Madame Tevoulère, she doesn't deserve you. It wouldn't surprise me if she knew all along who you really were.''

He sat down beside her and gripped her arm. ''Are you in league with our father to make me miserable? Cicely, you have always been my most loving, delightful relative, and you know how dearly I love you. We can deal just as happily together in the future as we have in the past, but first you will have to surrender all these nonsensical ideas you have about Micheline! I know her as surely as I know myself, and I can tell you that she is a fine, intelligent, tender person. She *wants* to be your friend!''

''She can never be my sister,'' Cicely replied stubbornly. ''You will always be my only sibling. I could never love anyone else as much.''

Sandhurst felt as if he were beating his head against the wall. ''You try my patience, child. I cannot understand why you are so set against Micheline. You complain about our family—with justification, I might add—and now someone has come into our world who would happily brighten your life as well as mine. Once I am married, you can visit us at Sandhurst Manor and in London, for Micheline will be there to look after you when I cannot. She is the most wonderful, enchanting female I have ever known. Why do you turn away from her?''

Cicely was thinking, I don't want her, I want *you*, but she couldn't say that to him. Instead, she whispered brokenly, ''All my life I've loved you best, Andrew. After Mother died, you were so good to me, and lately, since I was getting older, I almost believed you might let me come to live with you.'' Tears spilled onto her cheeks. ''It's not the same with that woman here. You act as if you've forgotten there's anyone else alive in the world!''

"Sweet child, you must have realized that I had to marry one day. I'm an adult, and the love between Micheline and me is not the same as the love I feel for you. I'm your brother; I shall always love you. Nothing can change that."

Any response she might make was too mean-spirited to verbalize. Instead, Cicely turned and buried her face against him, weeping. Andrew had been the center of her existence, and now she felt that he was lost to her.

"If you love me," he continued gently, "you must want me to be happy. In Micheline I've found a treasure; she enriches every aspect of my life. I implore you to share my joy and extend a hand of friendship to the woman I love."

There was nothing Cicely could say. If she had spoken, it would have been to tell her brother that her greatest wish was that Micheline Tevoulère had never been born—or at least that she had never met Andrew. When he was near that French-woman, it seemed to her that he was cursed, for he gazed at her in a way that was completely unknown to Cicely. Every other person was superfluous to him now, including his once-beloved sister. Even now, when he gave her his time and attention, all he could speak of was *Micheline*!

"Will you be kind to Micheline?" Sandhurst was asking again. "As a favor to me?"

Cicely lifted her chin. "I cannot change my feelings, Andrew, any more than you wish to change yours. I will try to be polite to her, but I can't promise more than that."

A muscle twitched in his jaw. "I begin to think that Father is wearing off on you."

"I may as well go, since we seem to have exhausted the only subject you are conversant with these days." Giving her brother what she hoped was a frosty glance, Cicely stood and swept out the door. Rounding the corner, however, she nearly collided with Micheline, who was standing there as if frozen, her eyes swimming with tears and one hand covering her mouth.

"Eavesdropper!" Cicely accused.

"I didn't mean—" Micheline tried to explain, but Andrew's sister had already turned away and started down the corridor.

Suddenly Sandhurst was behind her, enfolding her in his arms and drawing her into his bedchamber. He closed the door, then led her over to the velvet-curtained bed.

"I am so sorry," he whispered against her hair. Micheline's

arms were wrapped tightly around his neck as she wept quietly. "I hope that you didn't hear very much. My sister seems to have been transformed into a little witch in my absence."

She managed to control the urge to make the same declaration she had at Hampton Court, that she hated this place and wished they'd never come. However, Micheline hadn't forgotten the conversation that had followed that particular outburst. Somehow, she must find a way to cope with Aylesbury Castle and everyone in it. This was even more important than the challenge of dealing with the English royal court, for this was Andrew's ancestral home and these people were his family.

"Cicely despises me," she said with a ragged sob. "What have I done to earn her ill will?"

"Nothing. You have done nothing. My sister is too possessive; it's time she learned that I do not belong to her."

Micheline raised her tear-stained face to his, and Andrew bent to kiss her. "Perhaps the problem is your mother's death," she mused. "It must have left a tremendous void in Cicely's life, and she's looked to you to fill it. When I put myself in her place and imagine living here with your father, Rupert, and Patience, it's easier to understand how she must feel."

"Believe me, I've agonized over this for the past five years, and my guilt has only increased as she's gotten older."

"I heard what she said about hoping that she might come to live with you. Andrew, couldn't she do that now? Is there any reason why Cicely couldn't make her home with us?"

He was stunned. "You can't be serious! As a new bride you would actually welcome the presence of that rude little vixen?"

"We could try it. It might make all the difference for Cicely. She would be part of a normal, loving home and have the opportunity to associate with young people her own age. Certainly her attitude toward me would have to change, but I wouldn't expect miracles overnight. On the other hand, if I began to fear for my life, she would obviously have to leave!"

Micheline smiled a little at what she had meant as an exaggeration, but Sandhurst gazed absently out the window, his face grim. "I'll think about it, sweetheart. In the meantime, I love you for making such an open-hearted suggestion.'' To prove his point, he bent and kissed her long and slowly, groaning a bit when her lips clung to his as he raised his head. "This is torture. Did you come here solely for that purpose?"

Her smile faded. "No, I came because I found myself growing rather panicky at the thought of having a room so far from yours. Silly, I know, but after Hampton Court—"

"No, it's not silly at all. We'll arrange for Mary to share your chamber again, and I'll see that there's a proper lock on the door.''

"I know that there's nothing to be afraid of here—except, perhaps, carrying on a conversation with your father!—but I can't seem to quell these unreasonable fears. I'm sure that they'll pass with time, and once we're married, I'll be *much* better! What could I fear with you in my bed?"

"Mmm.'' Sandhurst pressed warm, smiling lips to her throat. "Your only worry then will be the possibility of never sleeping again. . . .''

"Andrew,'' she continued tentatively, "since I've mentioned the duke, I may as well ask you—is there anything I should do differently to win his favor? I tried to be tactful this afternoon, but he didn't seem to appreciate any of the things I had to say.''

His body tensed against her; Micheline sensed him withdrawing. "For God's sake, don't even consider saying what you think he wants to hear! Go on just as you have, speaking the truth and being yourself. It's a game! If he senses your weakness, he'll pounce and try to control you just as he controls that sniveling half brother of mine.''

Micheline sighed. "I wish we were already married—and alone at Sandhurst Manor.''

"As always, fondling, we are of one mind.'' He paused, mentally reviewing all that had happened that day and all that had been said. "In fact, I see no reason to linger in Yorkshire any longer than necessary. We shall be married as soon as it is humanly possible. I told the king a fortnight, so if he decides to come, he'll arrive in time. Why should we delay?''

Micheline gave him one of her blinding smiles. Suddenly filled with joy, she teased, "Patience warned me that you might grow overeager to exercise your rights as a husband!''

Sandhurst grinned. His right hand slid slowly down to the

base of her spine before drawing Micheline's body firmly against his. "For once in her life, Patience is absolutely correct."

An interminable, tension-laden supper that night in the drafty hall only strengthened Sandhurst's resolve. He waited until everyone else had retired before approaching his father.

The duke was back in his favorite chair in the solar, peering at a book under the light of a brace of candles. When Andrew walked over and sat down opposite him, the old man pretended not to notice.

"Father, there is something I wish to discuss with you."

A long minute passed before the duke glanced up. "A rare occurrence! How fortunate that you happen to be here at the castle rather than in London or Gloucestershire or France! One of life's happy coincidences, hmm?"

"Quite," Sandhurst agreed laconically. "Would you be terribly disappointed if I got to the point?"

"Not at all." These conversations with his son reminded him of the fencing matches he'd engaged in when he was younger. Certainly the rules were the same. "I am eager to get back to my book."

"This won't take long. I only wanted to say that Micheline and I would like to be married as soon as possible. There has been so much in her life that's new lately that I think it would be beneficial to get on with the wedding so that I can take her to Sandhurst Manor, where she can enjoy a bit of peace and continuity. I said a fortnight to King Henry, which would be tomorrow, and time is precious to him as well. Why not have the wedding two days hence?"

The duke smiled wolfishly, watching his strong, handsome son. Andrew was better-looking than he had ever been. More than once he'd wondered what upward turns his own life might have taken if he'd been blessed with such physical gifts.

"Next you'll tell me that this urgency on your part has nothing to do with your desire to bed that saucy French minx!" the old man snorted. "I'd have thought you were man enough to spread her legs back in France!"

Sandhurst went white. It took every ounce of his control to refrain from hitting his own father. "I'll ignore that vulgar speech—this time," he replied in a tone quietly laced with danger. "Will you agree to the wedding taking place in two days' time? The servants assure me that it is possible. I'll ride tomorrow to inform the priest and any friends that might like to attend. Sir Jeremy Culpepper traveled north with us so that he might be present, and no doubt his parents will come too. If there are others you care to notify, kindly inform me by tomorrow morning.''

The Duke of Aylesbury pursed his lips. ''As usual, you have taken matters into your own hands. Far be it from me to interfere!''

Micheline slept fitfully in her comfortable feather bed. She would doze and dream, then wake to change positions, staring up at the two narrow windows that overlooked the York-shire countryside. Bright shafts of moonlight streamed into the room, annoying Micheline to the extent that she finally scrambled up to close the bedcurtains on that side.

Mary occupied a little truckle bed nearby. It was good to have her there; since Hampton Court, Micheline dreaded the idea of being alone in the darkness. However, the little maid slept soundly in the extreme, breathing deeply and making soft dream noises from time to time.

Midnight came and went. Micheline dreamed that she lay in Andrew's arms, soaking up his warmth, nestling against his lean-muscled chest and listening to his heartbeat as he slept. In reality she felt lost in this huge bed, and was unaccountably chilled in spite of an abundance of covers. Half-conscious, she turned onto her stomach and burrowed into the pillows, trying to pretend that they were Andrew.

A distant sound, a rattling, disturbed her further. Gradually Micheline came fully awake, wondering fuzzily what could be making that irritating noise. It seemed to be coming from the door.

Her eyes opened and her heart began to pound. The rattling had stopped, and she reminded herself that she was safe, for Andrew had attached a heavy iron lock to the bedchamber door, not unlike the one that Henry VIII took with him from castle to castle to ensure his privacy and security.

Had someone been trying to open the door in spite of the lock? Memories of that terrifying night at Hampton Court returned in a flood.

''Mary? Mary, are you awake?''

''Hmmm?'' the girl mumbled.

Micheline threw back her covers and rushed over to the

maid's little bed. "Did you hear that noise just now? That rattling at the door?"

Mary propped herself on an elbow and blinked in the moonlight. Her mistress was positively wild-eyed. "No, ma'am, I heard nothing! Was it like that scratching sound at the king's palace?" She'd been told that story the next day and ever since had felt rather uneasy about sharing Micheline's rooms. Now, however, Mary began to wonder if the Frenchwoman might have an overactive imagination. The only other people here who had also been at Hampton Court were Lord Sandhurst and Joshua Finchley, and certainly neither one of them would prowl around in the middle of the night scratching on doors!

"No—no, it was different, as though someone were trying to open the lock."

"Pardon me for saying so, ma'am, but I wonder if you might have dreamed this. You're still nervous after that other night, and this is an exciting time, what with your wedding coming. Perhaps the sound you heard was part of your dream and it only *seemed* real. I've had lots of dreams like that!"

"You're absolutely certain that you heard nothing at all?" Micheline persisted anxiously.

"Nothing." Mary's voice was firm.

"Well," she sighed, "perhaps you're right, then. I'm sorry for disturbing you, Mary."

"That's all right, ma'am. I've had nightmares myself. You know we're safe with that lock Lord Sandhurst put on the door. Why don't you go back to sleep and order up a happy dream about your wedding?" The girl beamed in the shadows. "Just think, ma'am, you'll soon be the wife of the man every other English girl only *can* know in her dreams! You ought to be far too happy to let a little rattle at the door disturb you!"

Micheline smiled. "You're right, of course. Thank you, Mary."

"Good night, ma'am."

Micheline crawled back into her bed and closed her eyes. Silently she repeated, "It was only a dream," over and over again until sleep came at last.

CHAPTER 28

April 19–20, 1533

THE NEW DAY DAWNED SO REPLETE WITH BUTTERY SUNSHINE THAT Micheline was able to laugh with Mary about the noise she had heard during the night. Now she ascribed the entire incident to an understandable case of nerves.

After a refreshing scented bath, Micheline dressed in a favorite gown of yellow silk that flattered her spicy-bright hair and iris-blue eyes. Mary was just brushing out her curls when a knock sounded at the door.

The maid opened it to admit Lord Sandhurst, who further enhanced the cheerful atmosphere. His hair agleam in the morning light, he was carrying a large orange and a bouquet of daffodils and bluebells.

"Good morrow, ladies! Have you ever beheld a finer day?" White teeth flashed against Andrew's tanned face as he presented Micheline with her gifts. When his hands were free, he cupped her face and kissed her warmly. "One thing's certain. No man has ever beheld a more beautiful woman. Any day would be fine with you in it."

"You're biased, my lord."

"But truthful. Honesty is but one of my sterling qualities."

Micheline was radiant with love as she gazed up into his warm brown eyes. " 'Twould seem you lack only modesty," she teased.

Shrugging lightly, Sandhurst gave a mock serious sigh. "In my case, it's difficult to be honest and modest at the same time."

She laughed as he bent to brand her throat with his mouth. "What accounts for this lighthearted mood?"

"Haven't you heard? I'm in love!" Stepping back, he reclaimed the orange and began to peel it, smiling at Micheline as she buried her tip-tilted nose in the blooms, which still glistened with dew.

"I've already heard that rumor, my lord."

"Oh." He feigned perplexity. "Well, let me try another. Have you also heard that I'm to be married . . . tomorrow?"

She nearly dropped the flowers. "What? Is this a jest? How can such a thing be possible?"

He took the daffodils and bluebells from her and stuck them into a nearby pitcher of water, then laughingly put a segment of orange into her mouth, which was open with shock. "It's possible because I made it so, fondling," Sandhurst explained blithely.

Because her mouth was full, she couldn't speak, and then he was kissing her, sharing the juicy orange. A wave of passion broke over Micheline's body as his large hands slid around her hips and drew her hard against him. There were moments, like this one, when the combination of emotional and physical sensation seemed almost impossibly explosive. She half expected her heart to simply burst one day.

"Christ," Andrew muttered harshly while kissing her ear with burning lips, "even one more day seems an eternity. I don't know if I can survive until tomorrow."

"You'd better!" she warned shakily. Her skin was so sensitive that each brush of his mouth touched off lightning currents of arousal. "Tomorrow. Tomorrow!" She repeated the word in wonder, caressing the hair that curled behind his ears.

"It may as well be next year for all the good it does me now!" The ache in his loins was beginning to annoy him.

"Andrew, what shall I wear?! Will I be reduced to borrowing Patience's wedding gown after all?"

He drew back and stared at her with raised brows. "Now we're getting *serious,* I see!" Remembering Mary, Sandhurst looked over a shoulder to discover her pressed against the far wall, staring at them. "Mary, you're blushing! Try to compose yourself and show your mistress what she will wear for her wedding."

The girl could only manage to bob her head nervously in response, then darted out of the room. Sandhurst, meanwhile, released Micheline and perched on the edge of the bed. In the interest of his health, it seemed wise to avoid prolonged contact between his hips and Micheline's.

"Eat your orange, sweetheart," he advised. "You need to keep up your strength for the marriage bed."

She offered him a segment of fruit and watched as he ate it, the picture of nonchalance in his fitted burgundy velvet doublet, breeches, and boots of black leather. Longing to sit beside him and suck the juice from his tanned fingers, Micheline tried to content herself instead with the orange.

"You're wearing boots," she remarked. "Have you been out riding already?"

"I had a few calls to pay"—Sandhurst nodded—"most notably to our parish priest. He'll be here tomorrow, which was naturally my only real concern. I also stopped at Greenwood, the Culpeppers' home, to alert Jeremy and his family, and I'll ride farther afield this afternoon."

"What does your father have to say about all this?"

"Why do you ask questions like that when you know you won't like the answer?" He sighed when she merely lifted her brows at him in imitation of his own favorite wordless response. "You can probably guess what the duke said. He would have complained and accused me of selfish arrogance no matter what date I named. My father is an incurable curmudgeon, and since it's impossible to please him, I've finally learned to do what I think is best." Sandhurst's expression softened as he watched Micheline bite into the last piece of orange, her lips and fingers wet with juice. "Now, of course, I have your interests to consider, and they far outweigh any opinions Father might have."

"Well, you certainly know him better than I. All we can do, I suppose, is hope that one day he'll thaw. Does the duke like babies?"

Sandhurst shrugged. "I do seem to recall seeing him smile on occasion when Cicely was tiny, but he was different then. My mother wouldn't have tolerated this unstinting irascibility."

"Did he love your mother?"

"I never gave it much thought, but I suppose he did. She was one person he never found fault with; that much is certain. He thought Mother was the epitome of womanhood."

Micheline went to sit beside him on the bed. "Well, then, perhaps there's hope for him. We'll just have to be patient."

"Patient? Hmmm." Sandhurst lifted her slim, orange-scented hand and kissed each finger. "If you don't mind, I'll leave that to you."

"Have you given any more thought to Cicely?"

"Now I know why you slithered over here next to me! It's a plot to weaken my defenses!" Still, he was smiling, exploring her fingers and palm with his mouth as if this were the most intimate part of Micheline's body. "Frankly I thought you would change your mind about Cicely, but if you're determined that she live with us, I'll agree to a compromise."

His lips were scorching the tender inside of her wrist and Micheline shivered in reaction. "Why do I feel naked even though I am fully clothed?" she moaned half-heartedly. "Must I wear gloves as well?"

Ignoring her, Sandhurst went on. "I want a few weeks alone with you at Sandhurst Manor, but Cicely may join us in London in time for Anne Boleyn's coronation the end of May. She can return to Gloucestershire with us in June—on a trial basis. As long as she behaves and the two of you get along, she can stay, but I won't have Cicely making life miserable for you in your own home. As far as I'm concerned, your happiness is of greatest importance, fondling."

Finished with that serious speech, Andrew returned to her hand, kissing it warmly once more as he raised his eyes to meet her own. Micheline sighed, thinking that his compelling gaze had the power in itself to arouse her.

From the doorway Mary cleared her throat loudly.

"I have the gown, your lordship!" Her arms were laden with masses of white satin.

"Thank you, Mary." Sandhurst went to relieve her of her burden, returning to spread the gown out over the dark green counterpane.

Micheline came to stand beside him. She stared, speechless, for a long minute while Andrew watched her, waiting for her reaction.

"I realize it's not the current fashion," he said, beginning to worry that she didn't like it, "but I thought—"

"Oh, Andrew!" she breathed. "It's perfectly lovely! This is the kind of wedding dress I used to dream of as a child!"

It was true. The gown was of an older style that Micheline adored. Fashioned of rich white satin, it had a very low round neckline edged with delicate embroidered flowers of gold and rose. A collar of lacy golden net, called a neck whisk, stood up in back. The sleeves were puffed down to the elbows, then tight-fitting at the forearm, and a trail of embroidered flowers and tiny green leaves meandered down their length. The gown had a narrow, pointed waistline over a skirt that was pleated at first before belling out and ending in a long train. Unlike the fashion of the day, this skirt was closed in front; no underskirt would be displayed.

Micheline leaned forward reverently to touch the dainty rose and gold flowers that outlined the gown's pointed waist, then brushed her fingers over the romantic neck whisk. "It's absolutely exquisite."

"You wouldn't prefer a gown covered with jewels?"

"Oh, no!" She looked up at Andrew in alarm and found him smiling at her. "I love these little flowers. I love everything about this gown! Where did you find it?"

"It was my mother's. I think Father may have forgotten it exists, but I never did. One day, when I was a child, I was helping Mother look for something in a storage room in the keep. She opened a chest and took this out to show me, almost as if she'd forgotten where it was stored herself. She told me that the rose-colored flowers were supposed to be bird's-eye primroses, which only grow in Yorkshire meadows, and the golden ones represented buttercups, for those were her favorites. Then Mother stood up and held the gown against herself . . . I can still see her in my mind's eye. Odd, isn't it, that you should say you always dreamed of a wedding dress like this, because for years I assumed that this must be what all brides wore."

Tears pricked her eyes. " 'Twould seem we've been of one mind all our lives."

He gathered Micheline near and kissed her shining hair. "Well said, my love."

"I'm so pleased that you remembered this gown, Andrew, and I'll be honored to wear it, but are you certain the duke won't mind?"

"Stop fretting about Father. I'll be surprised if he even recognizes it. It's not as if you look at all like my mother, so I doubt he'll think he's seen a ghost. At any rate, I know that it would please her above all things."

"It will feel a little as if she's with us after all," Micheline agreed.

"Well, now that that's settled, there's a great deal more to be done today, and I'd better be off."

"I'll go with you to the courtyard. I think I may walk on the hills for a while."

Arm in arm they emerged into the corridor. Micheline glanced toward the solar and caught her breath at the sight of a tall slim woman with coppery hair.

It can't be! she thought wildly.

Slowly the woman turned, and Micheline found herself staring into the icy green eyes of Lady Iris Dangerfield.

Feeling Micheline stiffen, Sandhurst looked down, then followed her stricken gaze to the solar.

"Iris! What are *you* doing here?"

"Shame on you, Andrew." She pouted. "Is that any way to welcome one of your oldest and dearest friends?"

Since everyone in the room was watching them, he had no choice but to force a smile and guide Micheline forward to greet Iris Dangerfield.

"My apologies, madame," Sandhurst said evenly. He sketched a bow, then lifted her hand to brush cool lips across it. "I was merely surprised to see you."

Another voice spoke from the settle near the window. "We weren't following you, Sandhurst." Timothy Dangerfield walked over to stand beside his wife. Very tall and thin, with dark hair and pale skin, he had a pointed nose and chin, and rather rabbitlike teeth. "A party of us traveled up from London at the king's behest, arriving last night after you had retired."

"So I heard," Andrew replied. "I had to leave this morning before any of you had risen, so I wasn't aware that you and your wife were among the party. Your journey was pleasant?"

Dangerfield shrugged. "Overlong. We were all quite fatigued. Everyone's been looking for you. The others finally went off to wander around the castle. Doubtless you'll be pleased to learn that His Majesty and the Marquess of Pembroke will also arrive later today."

"Micheline and I are happy to have all our friends here for this joyous occasion." Andrew's keen eyes met those of the younger man, remembering that Dangerfield had known of his wife's infidelity. There was only one possible reason for him to wish to attend this wedding, and that was to punish Iris and drive home the point that Lord Sandhurst was no longer available. "I'm sure that my father is especially pleased that King Henry and London nobility will be represented at the wedding after all," Andrew commented obliquely. "Dangerfield, I don't believe you met my betrothed when we were at Hampton Court." Introductions were performed, in which Micheline participated warily, then Sandhurst consulted his watch and drew on soft doeskin gloves. "I trust you both will understand if Micheline and I leave your entertainment to the other members of my family. It's a busy time for us.''

"Don't worry, Sandhurst!" Rupert piped up eagerly, rushing over to gain his half brother's attention. "Patience and I have a game of chance planned for the afternoon. I'm going to teach our guests to play passe-dix and lansquenet! Of course, it won't be as amusing as those card tricks you do, but I'll try to be a proper substitute.''

Micheline wrinkled her nose slightly at Rupert's horrendous pronunciation of the French game, while Sandhurst glanced at him in mild surprise.

"Where did you learn passe-dix and lansquenet?"

"Oh, a Frenchman taught me one night in a tavern in London.'' Rupert turned excitedly to the Dangerfields, gesturing with both spindly arms. "You can teach these games to the royal court when you go back! They'll make you terribly popular, I'll wager!''

"We'll leave you to it, then," Andrew said dryly as he wondered how much resemblance Rupert's interpretation of the games would bear to the authentic versions.

As they left the solar, Micheline could feel Iris's eyes burning the place where Sandhurst's hand rode at the small of her back. She couldn't help thinking about the noise she'd heard during the night, now that she knew Iris had been in the castle, but told herself that it was silly to imagine anything so farfetched. At any rate, Timothy Dangerfield was here to keep an eye on his wife, and Micheline herself was too happy to waste time brooding about Iris's ill feelings.

When they emerged into the sunlight, Micheline looked up at Sandhurst's thoughtful countenance. "Why didn't you tell me about these important visitors?''

He laughed and wrapped an arm around her. "Truth to tell, I forgot! Your nearness, and the prospect of our wedding, drove all else from my mind. I find that I can scarcely spare a thought for anyone else.''

Micheline felt drenched in bliss, but a shadow lingered. When Andrew led his horse out of the stable into the sunsplashed courtyard and asked if she might prefer to accompany him on his errands, Micheline was tempted.

"I suppose you think I'm quaking with fear because your Iris Dangerfield is in the castle!''

He smiled fondly at the sight of her, shielding her eyes

against the sun with a small hand, her delicately clefted chin raised in mock challenge.

"She's not *my* Iris Dangerfield!" he rejoined in protest.

"Well, she used to be." Micheline pretended to pout. "And she'd still like to be."

Sandhurst left his horse and went forward to slide both hands around Micheline's slender waist, drawing her firmly against his hard body. "She *never* was *my* Iris Dangerfield," he corrected in a low, mesmerizing voice. "I was only passing time, waiting to find you." His mouth grazed hers. "My best friend." Another tantalizing kiss. "My love . . . and, on the morrow, my wife." When her lips parted helplessly under his, he allowed their tongues to touch for an instant. Then Andrew's hand came up to frame her piquantly lovely face, his fingers laced through glossy hair as he stared down at her.

"My Micheline."

No sooner had Andrew ridden off than Micheline encountered the rest of the party from London as they entered the courtyard after inspecting the keep. Among them were the Dukes of Suffolk and Norfolk, Thomas Wyatt, and Robert Cheseman, the king's falconer. Richly garbed ladies of the court accompanied them, and Micheline went forward to offer greetings as charmingly as she was able. Though she continued to feel that these members of the English nobility were inspecting and even looking down on her, it mattered little. The memory of Andrew's voice and touch lingered, infusing her with a dreamy glow.

The others went inside after hearing that French games were the order of the afternoon, but Micheline decided impetuously to remain outdoors and ride over the Yorkshire hillsides. A groom provided a sweet-tempered mare who cantered past limestone walls, fat sheep, black-stockinged lambs, and groves of trees where tiny long-tailed tits sang *ze-ze* as they searched for insects.

At length Micheline dismounted, deciding to pick a bouquet of exquisite bird's-eye primroses and tender buttercups to make a wedding garland for her hair. However, it was impossible to resist the other spring flowers that abounded on the hillsides. Soon her arms were filled with bright scented blooms: globeflowers, dainty yellow cowslips, wild pansies, daisies, and pale pink lady smocks. In shaded hedges she discovered a profusion of violets and the star of Bethlehem, which had braved the late-winter cold to open its white petals amid fern and ivy.

The afternoon was waning when Micheline remounted the patient mare and they started back toward the castle. Suddenly it occurred to her that the king and Anne Boleyn might be arriving shortly, and since Andrew was absent, she ought to be present to greet them. A certain amount of tidying up would be in order, first, though. Urging the mare into a reluctant gallop, Micheline tipped her head back, enjoying the sensation of the cool air, scented sweetly with vernal grass, against her face. Pipits, wheatears, and twites chirped and hopped along the winding limestone walls.

Her feeling of contentment was such that she barely noticed the odd flash of light from the trees on a hill above, but the mare was not so preoccupied. It caught the horse by surprise, blinding her so that she reared back abruptly, sending the unsuspecting Micheline flying into the air. A lesser horsewoman would have been gravely injured, or even killed, but Micheline had taken so many spills in her time she instinctively curled up and relaxed all at once before striking the ground. When she sat up and tested her bones, she saw that she'd come inches from hitting one of the stone walls. Micheline's heart began to pound as she considered the flash of light. What else could have caused it except a mirror?

For a long moment she closed her eyes against the terror that washed over her, then made up her mind to put it aside. It seemed that whoever it was that wanted to harm her hadn't the courage to approach her directly, and it was still possible that all that had happened so far at Aylesbury Castle was not a direct threat but merely the product of her imagination. In any case, Micheline resolved that nothing and no one would interfere with her happiness on the eve of her wedding.

Still trembling, she regathered her scattered bouquet, then went over to the mare, stroking her neck and whispering words of reassurance to herself as much as to the horse. Eventually, when both of them were calm, they rode slowly back to Aylesbury Castle and crossed the two drawbridges that led to the inner courtyard. She'd been hoping that Andrew might return before she had to go back inside, but now she told herself that everyone would still be engaged in game-playing and would pay no attention to her if she slipped into her chambers. With Rupert as the instructor, the games seemed likely to go on until supper.

Climbing the spiral staircase to the family apartments, Micheline felt her fears dissolving. Perhaps it *had* all been a simple accident. Certainly it was better to believe that than to allow herself to be terrorized on the eve of her wedding!

She expected to find the living quarters of the castle filled with activity, and wondered at the absolute silence in the corridor. A need for distraction mixed with curiosity, and Micheline tiptoed down to peek around the corner of the solar.

"Hmmph!" grunted the Duke of Aylesbury. "What are you doing skulking about? Thinking to spy on someone?"

Micheline started at the sight of him, all alone in the sun-washed chamber. The old man sat in his favorite chair, wearing a nightgown faced with rabbit and overlaid with a worn gray silk coverlet.

She stepped into the open. "Of course not, Your Grace! I would never spy on anyone! I only wondered if the others weren't still playing games. I confess that I tried to remain undetected because I feared they would ask me to join them, and I didn't want to appear rude by refusing."

His eyes twinkled almost imperceptibly in reaction to her frankness. It was difficult to resist this fresh young beauty, with her spicy windblown curls, sun-pinkened cheeks, and arms filled with a haphazard assortment of wild flowers.

"In that case, I don't blame you for hiding, but it's safe. They've all gone to their rooms to prepare for the king's arrival," the duke replied gruffly. "That's quite a bouquet you've amassed. I hope you left a few on the hillsides."

"Oh, yes, of course, Your Grace! One would never know I'd picked these! Aren't they lovely? You have many sorts of flowers here in England that I don't believe grow in France." Her eyes were vividly blue as she selected some of the loveliest and crossed the solar to hold them out to him. "Won't you take these for your chambers? They smell wonderful! You know, I set out to pick just a few, to make a garland to wear for the wedding, but I confess I was carried away."

The duke clasped the flowers in his bony hand, feeling foolish, yet unable to resist the girl's enchantment. "So, madame, I suppose you consider yourself worthy to become Countess of Sandhurst, and one day, Duchess of Aylesbury."

Conscious of his scrutiny, Micheline replied carefully, "To be perfectly honest, Your Grace, I haven't given much thought

to my title. All I know is that I love your son better than my
own life, and I shall do everything in my power to make our
marriage happy and prosperous. It will be a joy, because I
know that Andrew will be beside me, sharing this commitment. Our home and family will be important for both of us,
but I certainly will be proud to be Countess of Sandhurst."
She took a breath and impulsively reached out to touch the
old man's arm. "Your wise son has helped me learn to feel
and live in the present, yet I can assure you that if and when
he inherits your title, I shall try to live up to the example your
wife set as Duchess of Aylesbury."

For a moment the duke's throat closed up. He blinked, then
looked away from Micheline. "Well, good," he muttered,
coughing. "Go on, then, child. I want to rest."

She walked away, but glanced back once before turning
down the corridor. Andrew's father sat hunched over, staring
at the wild flowers clutched in his gnarled hand.

Micheline's conversation with the Duke of Aylesbury
drove all the dark thoughts from her mind. Perhaps there
could be peace between Andrew and his father after all!
Walking to and fro in her chamber, which was now crowded
with vases of fragrant blooms, she waited impatiently for
Sandhurst to return.

A soft, lavender-rose veil of twilight covered the sky when
Micheline heard the sound of hoofbeats on the cobbled courtyard. Looking out her deeply recessed window, she saw
grooms wearing the king's livery.

Without a second thought Micheline went to greet King
Henry and his entourage. The castle was no longer quiet.
The sound of voices and footsteps followed her as she
closed her paneled door and set off for the circular newel
staircase. Her only wish was that Andrew might be by her
side.

She was used to these spiral stairways, for in France there
was no other kind, but this one was especially precipitous and
Micheline had learned to take care with her footing on the
treacherously narrow wedge-shaped steps. Today, however,
her thoughts were elsewhere—on the arrival of the royal party
and her impending wedding.

She'd descended just a few steps when she vaguely noticed
a shadow spill down from behind her, then felt a pressure

against her back before losing her foothold. Micheline raked her nails wildly over the smooth stone walls, searching in vain for something to save her as she pitched forward, screaming, down the steep staircase.

CHAPTER 29

April 19–20, 1533

MICHELINE HAD TUMBLED HEADLONG DOWN THE STAIRWAY, BUT an instant before her face crashed into the sharp edge of a step, Sandhurst caught her. The impact of her falling body sent him reeling against the curving wall, and he very nearly lost his own footing, but through sheer force of will he remained erect.

A long moment passed before Micheline even realized what had happened, that the abrupt horror of her fall into what seemed certain death had ended in Andrew's embrace. It was the harsh sound of his breathing and the thunder of his heart against her cheek that brought her out of her daze.

"Andrew—how—where—?"

"I had just started up the stairs when I heard you scream! Micheline, for God's sake, what *happened*?" Sandhurst's voice was as hoarse as if he'd just brushed death himself.

He was holding her so tightly she could scarcely breathe, and the muscles in his arms and chest were like steel against her face. "I don't know. I must have just lost my balance. I was thinking about you, about the wedding, and I wasn't paying proper attention to the steps."

"You aren't hurt?"

"No. No, I'm fine." Micheline tried to pry her head loose enough to look up at him. "Because of you, Andrew, you saved my life!"

Suddenly she was free of his iron embrace, only to be grasped bruisingly by each shoulder and confronted with the sight of his furious expression. Golden sparks blazed in

Sandhurst's eyes, his nostrils flared, muscles clenched in his jaw.

"Don't you *ever* be so thoughtless again! Do you understand me? By not 'paying proper attention,' you'd be bloody well *dead* right now if I hadn't happened to be in exactly the perfect spot to save you! What do you suppose the odds are of my being right there again? Nil! *Christ,* Michelle, if anything happened to you—" Tears glinted in his eyes before he crushed her against him once more. "Just be careful. *Please!*"

Micheline's reply went unheard as castle guests pushed past them on the staircase, hurrying to greet the king and Anne Boleyn. They had little choice but to join the assemblage in the courtyard, and, for the moment, Micheline's brush with disaster was forgotten.

For once, King Henry had traveled light. Only a dozen grooms and another two dozen assorted servants accompanied them, along with a large wagon packed with the necessary amenities.

Henry and Anne had ridden in a magnificent coach, and the sight of them emerging into the twilit courtyard was dazzling. The Marquess of Pembroke was resplendent in crimson velvet trimmed with emeralds and ermine, while the king wore plum satin and cloth of gold. His fingers were a mass of jeweled rings, and around his neck was a gold collar from which hung a diamond as big as a walnut.

"Your Majesty," Sandhurst said, leading Micheline forward, "you honor us."

"Welcome, sire," Micheline added with sincerity. She dropped into a low, graceful curtsy before the huge monarch, rising only when he reached for her hand.

"It was worth the journey to gaze once more upon your lovely countenance, madame," Henry told her.

Greetings were exchanged with Anne Boleyn, then the castle guests came forward one by one to pay their respects. Finally Henry boomed, "I am ravenous! I hope your cooks have been busy!"

Andrew smiled. "My father awaits us in the great hall, where you may sup immediately if you like, sire. Shall we join him?"

Sandhurst wouldn't let Micheline out of his sight that evening, which pleased her tremendously. After supper the tired king and his lady retired to their chambers, so Andrew and Micheline were able to steal away early. He went with her to her room, where they played chess and piquet until midnight. When she began to nod over the cards, Andrew bade her go to bed, averting his eyes as she undressed and slid between the covers. Although it was the eve of their wedding and he'd been randy as a stallion for weeks, tonight his mood was tense rather than amorous. It was as if he feared that fate might be conspiring to remove Micheline from him before they could be married, and he was determined not to allow that to happen. Irrationally Sandhurst thought that once she was his wife, no harm could come to her.

Lying in bed, Micheline opened her eyes just enough to gaze at Andrew's chiseled profile. Meanwhile, in the truckle bed across the room, Mary was making her usual variety of sleep noises.

Many times that evening Micheline had thought of telling Andrew about the riding accident and the brief impression she'd had of a shadow and of something touching her back before she fell down the stairs, but it seemed that those revelations would cause more trouble than good, especially on the eve of their marriage. She had been so preoccupied on the stairs that it was impossible to be certain now if there really *had* been a shadow, let alone identify it, and the pressure against her back might have been the wall. Unless Micheline could point to the person who had pushed her, what was there to gain by upsetting Andrew, especially since he was watching over her anyway.

Once they were married, Iris Dangerfield would have to adjust to reality, Micheline thought drowsily as she closed her eyes. The woman would seek out another lover and leave them in peace.

At daybreak Micheline awoke to find Andrew sleeping in a chair next to her bed, fully dressed, his feet propped on a footstool. Blond lashes brushed his cheekbones, and the stubble of his beard gleamed golden in the new sunlight. Birdsong filled the air.

Languorously Micheline stretched out a hand to lightly caress his cheek. Slowly Sandhurst's brown eyes opened as his brows went up. Catching her fingers, he kissed them.

"Good morning, my lord," she murmured.

"Go back to sleep, fondling. You'll need the extra rest to stay awake"—he grinned wickedly—"*later*."

She smiled at that thought and dozed again, dreaming that she was falling from a horse, sailing through the air, only to land safely in drifts of meadow flowers. Andrew waited for her there and both of them were naked. He smiled down at her, brushing aside violets, scarlet pimpernels, and primroses from her breasts and belly, then bending to replace the flowers with kisses.

"Time to wake up!" Mary was calling. "It's your wedding day, ma'am!"

Rolling over, Micheline opened her eyes. The chair beside the bed was empty. "Where's Lord Sandhurst?"

"Why, in his own rooms, I expect. Be patient, ma'am; you'll have him next to you when day breaks again!" The girl sighed a little. "Just think, you'll be the wife of the Earl of Sandhurst, the most handsome, charming man in Britain, and you'll become a countess in the bargain. A more fortunate lady never breathed."

Micheline had no desire to argue that point, nor had she time to wonder what had become of Andrew, for Mary soon had her out of bed and into a steaming, scented bath. It was nearly ten o'clock, and there was much to be done before the wedding that afternoon.

Midday found Micheline in her lacy silk chemise, petticoats, and shakefold, eating a plum while Mary finished weaving the coral-pink bird's-eye primroses and rich yellow buttercups into an extravagant garland for her hair. When that was done, the little maid helped her mistress into her wedding gown. Mary had expected the earl to order a sumptuous, jewel-encrusted creation from the best dressmakers in London, but as long as Micheline liked this gown so well, nothing else mattered.

Micheline was standing in her stocking feet before the mirror, the white satin train flowing out behind her, when Cicely came into the chamber.

Andrew's sister looked lovelier than ever, the soft curves of her figure accentuated by a gown of dark rose silk and gold brocade. Sapphires edged the square neckline and sparkled on the golden caul that tamed Cicely's abundant black curls.

"Hello, Micheline," she said. Her restrained tone was belied by the color that stained her cheeks. "I suppose I should wish you well."

Trying to ignore the rather backhanded nature of her blessing, Micheline crossed the room and gave Cicely the warmest
smile she could muster.

"Thank you. I promise to take good care of your brother."

"No doubt," the girl muttered.

"Cicely, I have some news for you that I think you'll
like." She took a chair near the window and motioned for
Cicely to sit beside her. "I know how unhappy you have been
here at Aylesbury Castle, and also how much it means to you
to spend time with Andrew. My situation was not so very
different from yours when I was young, and I can understand
what you are feeling. I've asked Andrew if you might come
to live with us at Sandhurst Manor."

Part of Cicely wanted to throw her arms around Micheline,
but resentment and wariness prevailed. "And?"

"He has agreed, but there are a few conditions attached.
Andrew says that you may join us in London next month, in
time for Anne Boleyn's coronation. After that we will all
return to Gloucestershire, where you will remain . . . provid-
ing you and I can live happily together. Andrew says that he
will not tolerate ongoing hard feelings in our household, and I
am inclined to agree with him. However, if you and I can
learn to be friends—"

At that moment Iris Dangerfield swept into the room.

"Well, if it isn't the almost bride and her almost sister!
What a cozy family scene."

Micheline stood up, meeting the other woman's acrimoni-
ous eyes with a level gaze. She was certain that Iris was
behind all the menacing events that had lately colored her
life, but she was equally certain that this day's wedding
would mark an end to those troubles. It still seemed to
Micheline that Iris's main purpose had been to frighten her
into backing out of the betrothal; failing that, she had tried to
harm her in a moment of desperation. If Andrew had cared
for Iris Dangerfield, Micheline couldn't quite believe that she
was evil at heart. She was a human being, with an obsessive
weakness for the Earl of Sandhurst. Micheline could understand that.

"Good morrow, Lady Dangerfield," she greeted her calmly.

"So, the bride is garbed in her finery. I must compliment
you on your gown, madame. That's a very subtle approach—
using flowers instead of gems." Iris herself wore a magnifi-

cent creation of cream satin and green velvet, studded with pearls and emeralds.

"I'm glad you like it," Micheline returned with a touch of irony. "This gown has special meaning, since Andrew's mother wore it when she married the duke."

"That's very sweet, but should you really be wearing *white*? Everyone knows you aren't a virgin, after all."

Micheline lifted her lightly clefted chin. "It was Andrew's wish that I wear this gown, my lady. His opinion is the only one that matters to me." She turned away. "Now, if you will excuse me . . ."

No sooner had Iris Dangerfield taken her leave, complete with a venomous glance that went unseen by her hostess, than Cicely was on her feet.

"How dare you wear my mother's dress?" she cried. "This is outrageous!"

"I only dare because your brother bade me do so," Micheline replied as quietly as she could.

"You'll never take her place!"

"Cicely, my only intent is to be Andrew's wife. I would have married him, happily, if he had been a penniless commoner. It is love that guides me, not greed or desire to acquire lofty titles. As for your mother, I revere her memory. I've no intention of trying to replace her—even if I should one day become Duchess of Aylesbury. I can only be myself and do my best."

The girl seemed not to hear. Sable-brown eyes blazing, she vowed, "You may think you love Andrew, but you barely know him! I've known him for thirteen years! You'll never understand him the way I do!"

Micheline was saved from losing her temper, or answering at all, by the timely appearance of Patience Topping. She seemed to assess the situation immediately, and gave Micheline a sympathetic smile.

"The guests are arriving," she announced. "Cicely, dear, you'll have to leave our new sister so that she can complete her preparations."

The girl stamped across the chamber, pausing in the doorway to declare, "I have no *sisters*!"

The nuptial mass was held in the chapel, located in the castle keep, which boasted a barrel-vaulted nave, stained-glass windows, and wall paintings. Despite the fact that the bride and groom cared little whether anyone else was present besides themselves and the priest, the wedding guests were the finest England could offer. King Henry and Anne Boleyn, glittering with jewels, were seated next to the Duke of Aylesbury and his family, and behind them were ranged the cream of British nobility. Every seat in the chapel was occupied, for friends and villagers had flocked from the countryside of York at Andrew's invitation.

As Micheline walked down the aisle, however, she saw none of the sumptuously garbed guests. All her attention was focused on the man she loved.

Even from a distance she basked in the loving warmth of Sandhurst's gaze, and thought that he had never looked so dazzlingly handsome, not even the night they met, when she had thought him more attractive in his plain fawn garb than any other man at the French court. For his wedding Andrew wore a doublet and haut-de-chausses of dove gray and blue velvet sewn with silver thread. White silk showed through the slashed sleeves and made a snowy fraise against Sandhurst's tanned jaw. His ruffled hair shone golden in the shafts of sunlight that poured into the chapel. He wore a smile, too, which grew more irresistible as Micheline neared.

As the bride drew closer to the groom, the guests beheld Micheline's beautiful face and her gleaming cognac-hued locks, pinned up in a fashion that corresponded with her wedding gown, freeing soft, curling wisps to frame her face and brush her bare shoulders. The garland of bird's-eye primroses and buttercups encircled her hair like a crown. Most lovely of all, however, in Sandhurst's opinion, was the joyous smile that lit the face of the woman he loved. It called up all manner of fierce emotions within him, ranging from intense love in its purest form to the burning ache of desire.

Currents of warmth flowed between their bodies when Micheline put her small hand in Sandhurst's large, bronzed one. They were both oblivious to the crowd that filled the chapel, and Micheline was only dimly aware of the priest's voice. She knelt beside Andrew, trying to pray, but all she could think of was the nearness of his hard body.

At length they rose, and Sandhurst's melting brown eyes captured her own.

"I, Andrew, take thee, Micheline, to my wedded wife," he said, his whole heart exposed in the tone of his voice.

"I, Micheline, take thee, Andrew, to my wedded husband," she vowed softly, drowning in his gaze.

Sir Jeremy Culpepper, grinning from ear to ear, stepped forward to present a band of solid gold to his friend. Sandhurst held it deftly between two fingertips. In a voice so intimate that it seemed they were alone together, he told Micheline, "With this ring I thee wed. This gold and silver I thee give. With my body I thee worship." He paused to smile almost imperceptibly. "And with all my worldly goods I thee endow. In the name of the Father"—he slid the ring partway down her thumb, then withdrew it—"and the Son"—now Micheline was staring at his masculine fingers as they tantalized each of her fingertips in turn with the golden band—"and the Holy Ghost." Reaching her wedding finger, Andrew gently slid the ring down to its proper place and concluded, "Amen."

Moments later, after a benediction from the priest, Micheline gloried in the sensation of being gathered into Sandhurst's embrace. One of his hands came up to hold the back of her head, while the other completely rounded her waist, and then their smiling lips touched. It was a gentle, loving, sensuous kiss, filled with promise. Micheline felt weak with elation.

They stayed in the church to drink from a loving cup with wine sops, then accepted the first flurry of congratulations from Henry, Anne, and the other guests. Only Cicely, Iris, and the Duke of Aylesbury held back. The two females watched the bride and groom with resentment, but the sharp-boned old man was staring at his new daughter-in-law with tears in his eyes. Finally, when Andrew glanced over questioningly, the duke came forward. First, he extended a hand to his son, then turned to Micheline.

"You look every bit as beautiful as my Jessica when she wore that gown thirty-five years ago. Buttercups and bird's-eye primroses . . ." His voice was thick with emotion. "I'll wager she's watching right now and is as proud as I am to welcome you to our family, Countess. My son is a fortunate man."

Sandhurst felt a long-forgotten stirring of emotion as he watched his father. When Micheline replied by kissing the old duke's parchmentlike cheek, it seemed a symbolic gesture of peace. Somehow, Andrew managed to speak.

"I have you to thank, Father," he said softly. "You brought us together."

PART IV

Now welcome, night, thou night so long expected,
That long day's labour dost at last defray,
And all my cares, which cruel love collected,
Hast summed in one, and cancelled for aye:
Spread thy broad wing over my love and me,
That no man may us see,
And in thy sable mantle us enwrap,
From fear of peril and foul horror free.
Let no false treason seek us to entrap,
Nor any dread disquiet once annoy
The safety of our joy.

—EDMUND SPENSER 1552?–1599

CHAPTER 30

April 20, 1533

THE WEDDING PARTY ADJOURNED TO THE GREAT HALL, A LONG, magnificent room with an oak-beamed ceiling, a huge fireplace with an elaborately carved overmantel, and white stone walls hung with priceless tapestries.

The marriage ceremony now seemed but a prelude to the real purpose of the day: serious gluttony and merrymaking. The next few hours passed in a blur for Micheline. She could scarcely hear the conversation at her table over the shouts of laughter. Meanwhile, dish after dish was offered, and it seemed that most of those present partook of them all. There was oyster pie; lettuce stuffed with forcemeat; spinach froise; an omelet filled with bacon and herbs; venison stewed in beer; salad of watercress, herbs, and cabbage; capon stuffed with apple, raisins, almonds, and bread crumbs, then glazed with butter and honey; and fried artichokes flavored with orange. More dishes were passed that Micheline declined, plus bowls of juicy new strawberries, an assortment of cheeses, and loaves of warm white bread. Throughout the feast wine and ale flowed freely. Micheline sipped fragrant Burgundy wine from a jeweled goblet which intensified the warmth that suffused her loins when Andrew's lean-muscled thigh pressed through her skirts under the table. Every time their hands brushed, color stained Micheline's cheeks. Even during their first supper together at Fontainebleau, she had not been so undone by his nearness. Shyness mingled with excitement in her breast when she thought fleetingly, constantly, of what lay ahead for them that evening.

Dozens of toasts were proposed, including several by Rupert Topping, who appeared to have imbibed too freely. At one point he staggered to his feet and shouted, ''I propose a toast to the most splendid brother any Englishman has ever known!'' He took a hearty swig, spilling on his doublet of apple-green satin, while the similarly overfestive guests drank along with him. ''And a toast to the Countess of Sandhurst, whose beauty and charm make her the only woman in the world worthy to become my brother's wife!''

''Hear, hear!'' exclaimed the king, drinking heartily. He and Anne Boleyn were seated across the table from the bride and groom. There had been little chance for conversation, but now, as the toasts subsided, Henry leaned forward, his beefy face ruddy with wine, and addressed Micheline. ''I can scarce find words to tell you how pleased we are that you are now an English countess, Lady Sandhurst!''

Micheline made a demure reply, then looked at her husband with radiant eyes.

''In fact,'' Henry went on determinedly, ''I wish that the two of you would consider traveling to France in the near future! What attractive ambassadors you would make! What do you say, my lady?''

Sandhurst intervened at this point. ''We mean no disrespect, sire, but as I have already explained to you, Micheline and I would like to remain in England for the time being.''

The king's hands tightened into fat, powerful fists, betraying his displeasure, but his smile barely faltered. ''Will you not allow your wife to answer for herself?''

''I fear I must agree with Andrew, Your Majesty,'' Micheline said clearly. ''I am eager to settle into our new life together and to enjoy England. One day I might like to return to France, but only to visit dear friends. I've no desire whatever to linger at the French court again. That was part of another lifetime for me.''

Henry's lips thinned. ''I can only hope that the two of you will reconsider.'' He gave Sandhurst a hard stare.

Anne Boleyn had been watching this exchange with increasing disquiet. ''Can we not speak about something more cheerful? Pardon me for saying so, sire, but I do not think you should press Lord Sandhurst on this matter. Leave him to enjoy his wedding day!''

The king glared at her, outraged that she should take Andrew's side against him, but further conversation was interrupted by another toast from Rupert.

Watching his half brother weave and ramble incoherently, Andrew looked at Micheline askance, a smile playing over his mouth. ''Have you had enough?'' he whispered.

"Easily!" The mischief in his expression nearly made her giggle.

Sandhurst leaned over to speak to his father, who nodded approval, then waved away the servants who approached with curd and cheese tarts and orange pudding. Rising lithely, he addressed the assembled guests.

"My wife and I would like to thank you all for coming today to share in our happiness." He nodded toward King Henry, hoping to allay any ill feelings. "We'll stay for one dance, after the boards are removed, then I trust you'll understand if we take our leave." He paused, smiling. "I have a great deal of respect for tradition, but today I hope you won't be disappointed if we dispense with the bedding of the bride . . . and attendant customs. I've waited a long time for this day, and I'd like to undress Lady Sandhurst *myself*."

The sun had just set when Sandhurst closed the paneled door to what had been Micheline's chamber but now would be occupied by both of them. The white stone fireplace danced with a freshly lit blaze, sending shadows capering happily over the walls while the sounds of music and dancing drifted in from the hall.

The first thing Micheline noticed was a delicate gold casket that reposed in the middle of the bed. "What's this?" she wondered, picking it up.

"I don't know! Someone must have left it as a wedding gift."

Pleased, Micheline lifted the carved lid, but her expression changed to one of horror when she saw what lay inside the casket. Nestled in folds of white satin was a gold wedding ring, broken in half. "Andrew! What can it mean?"

Immediately he took the box from her and closed the lid with a snap. "A cruel joke, no doubt perpetrated by someone who desired to taint the joy of this night." Gathering her into his embrace, he whispered, "You must forget about it. Forget about everything save the two of us."

Oddly enough, Micheline was able to obey with ease. Her bliss was such that nothing else could intrude.

"Let me dispose of this, sweetheart," Andrew said. "I'll be only a moment."

In the corridor he had the good fortune to encounter Jeremy Culpepper.

"Take this thing and destroy it," Sandhurst said flatly, showing his friend the contents of the casket.

Culpepper's eyes widened and a cold chill ran down his spine. "Who would do such a thing? Iris Dangerfield?"

"I know not, and for tonight I do not care." Sandhurst's sculpted profile was hard with anger. "Later, though, I intend to find out. Too many sinister events have been taking place lately, and I mean to discover who is responsible."

With that he turned away and reentered the chamber, giving his wife a warm smile as he closed the door. "Now, where were we?"

Curiously nervous, Micheline perched on the edge of the bed, conscious of the hot blood that stained her cheeks. She watched apprehensively as Andrew lit a candle and placed it on the table next to the bed. The lean lines of his body in profile as he bent over filled her with a skittish passion.

"I want to see you," Sandhurst said huskily, "the first time we make love as husband and wife."

"Oh." Her lips formed the word, but no sound came out.

"What's amiss, sweetheart?" Sitting down beside her, Andrew raised one slender hand to his mouth and kissed the ring on Micheline's wedding finger. "Surely you're not afraid of *me*?" This last word was emphasized fondly, as if he found her shyness rather amusing.

"No . . ." She gasped involuntarily when he began to suck on her fingertip, slowly and sensual, looking up at her all the while from under tawny lashes. "No, of course I'm not afraid of you." A tremor of arousal traveled downward to the place between her legs.

"I know." Understanding and playfulness mingled in Andrew's smile. Now he merely held her hand and looked into her eyes. "The other times, our lovemaking was unexpected. You're feeling uneasy because it's inevitable . . . and you're my wife."

She nodded mutely.

"Fondling, don't you imagine I would be just as worried about pleasing you—if I didn't know that our love is all that really matters. This"—Sandhurst drew her against him and kissed her with frank desire, then whispered to her open mouth—"this is just a physical expression of that love. As long as our feelings are genuine, we cannot disappoint each other."

Micheline warmed to his tender, eloquent words, yet a part

of her remained afraid. It was as if the past were trying to pull her back, back into the safety of solitary existence. The responsibility of loving Andrew suddenly seemed overwhelming. Could she possibly make him happy? Already she feared that he might be disappointed on this first night of their marriage; how could she be enough for him year after year, for the rest of their lives? The future stretched out ahead of them in her mind, fraught with risks and possibilities for failure.

Inevitably Micheline found herself thinking back to the day she had married Bernard Tevoulère. It had become apparent to her lately that she hadn't known then the true possibilities love held, yet she had been more confident on that first wedding day than she was now. Micheline realized that she had been far more naive at sixteen; that fact alone gave her pause. If she hadn't been able to fulfill Bernard, how could she possibly be enough for someone as wonderful and richly textured as Andrew?

As usual, Sandhurst gazed into her troubled eyes and guessed her thoughts.

"Michelle," he said quietly, "put aside the past and future. Let us deal with the present, moment by moment, day by day."

She sighed heavily. "But—"

Putting a forefinger under her chin, he tilted her face up so that she could not avoid his penetrating eyes. "I love you, sweetheart." He touched his mouth to hers and their lips clung. "I want you."

Those poignant words were her undoing. Micheline's doubts fell away as she gave in to the magic of Sandhurst's nearness. He affected all her senses: touch, sight, taste, smell, and even hearing. There were moments when just the sound of his low masculine laughter could set the embers of desire aflame inside her. Perhaps that was the real problem. Sometimes, Micheline felt as if she were obsessed with this man. It was hard to keep the fear of losing him perpetually at bay, but for now those worries were lost under a rising tide of arousal.

"I want you, too, Andrew," she said shakily. Reaching out, Micheline caressed the contours of his side; the lateral muscles that tapered down to his narrow waist. Even through the velvet doublet she could feel the warmth of his skin. "I love you."

"Then there's nothing to worry about, is there," Sandhurst said gently, yet with a note of finality.

Micheline watched as his fingers, strong and graceful all at once, unlaced her gown. She could feel the heat and moisture between her legs, and then she was reaching to unfasten his doublet. Andrew lowered the bodice of her gown with tantalizing slowness, bringing her chemise with it, until her breasts were bared, round and glowing in the firelight. Dark rose nipples stood out and Sandhurst bent his golden head to kiss each one in turn lingeringly, until Micheline moaned with pleasure.

After a time they both were naked and Andrew rose to draw back the green velvet counterpane. Her eyes were drawn helplessly to his erect manhood. How beautifully he is made! she thought, aching to touch him. When he smiled at her and gestured toward the waiting bed, Micheline looked over to discover that the silken sheets were strewn with colorful flowers: yellow primroses, violets, pink lady-smocks, apple blossoms, and tiny bells of white hyacinth. Her eyes swam with tears.

Sandhurst drew her into his embrace and they knelt pressed together for long minutes, exploring and tasting each other's mouths. Yearning broke in long, exquisite waves over Micheline's body as she melted against him, her fingers traveling over each taut muscle in his back and shoulders, then down to the hard curves of his buttocks.

Soon they were lying amid the fragrant spring flowers. Micheline loved this extra gift of sight, for in the past they had made love in total darkness. She basked in the warmth of Andrew's caramel-colored eyes and gazed euphorically on his candlelit face, the corded muscles that joined his neck and shoulders, the strength of his arms, and the lean beauty of his chest. Even as Micheline gloried in the scorching kisses he trailed over her body, she also gloried in watching him move. Never had she imagined such a combination of strength and elegant grace.

Sandhurst knew exactly where and how to touch her. His mouth found the sensitive nape of her neck, the bend of her arm, her inner wrist, then lingered over her breasts before blazing a trail down her belly to the insides of her thighs. Micheline writhed against him, unable to bear further stimulation. Sheer passion had burned away all intruding thoughts. As much as she wanted to touch and kiss Andrew's body, at that moment the need to feel him inside of her overrode all else.

"Please!" she whispered.

When Sandhurst finally came up to kiss her mouth deeply, Micheline reached out to brush her fingertips over his manhood. It was hard as steel, yet warm, pulsating slightly against her palm.

"Oh, Andrew," she whispered, her voice breaking on a sob, "I love you."

He drew back to stare at her. "Michelle, you are more than my wife. You are my mate. For all our lives."

At that moment he plunged into her, filling her, moaning aloud at the sensation of her sweet, moist warmth tightening around him. They arched together, moving fervently, the sound of their gasps filling the room, until a wild surging climax shook Micheline's very soul. Sandhurst found his own shuddering release in the next instant. When his breathing slowed a bit, he lifted his face from the cloud of her hair and ran the backs of his fingertips over her damp brow. Their bodies were still united, and a slow smile spread over Andrew's face that said more than words ever could. Micheline felt as if she were floating on a cloud of utter bliss.

Later, after they had shared quiet caresses, Andrew poured one goblet of wine for them both and they lay against the pillows, sipping. Micheline arranged flowers over his chest, then he went a step further and put primroses in the tangle of curls between her legs.

The sight of his flickering grin ignited a fresh fire of love inside of her.

"I am so happy, Andrew. That's what frightens me. Does anyone deserve to be so happy?"

"Only you, fondling," Sandhurst assured her. He reached over to set the goblet of wine on the table by the bed, then returned to find Micheline's lips parted sensual in anticipation of his kiss. Unable to help himself, he obliged, then flashed an irresistible smile, adding, "And *me*, of course!"

CHAPTER 31

April 25–26, 1533
Gloucestershire, England

To reach Sandhurst Manor, traveling as they were from the northeast, Andrew and Micheline had to pass through Stratford-upon-Avon, a quaint town of fewer than two hundred half-timbered houses. Accompanied, as usual, by Finchley, Mary, and two squires, they spent the night at a cozy inn on Chapel Lane.

Micheline slept little that night. Snuggled in the circle of Andrew's embrace, she thought about the first happy days of her marriage and wondered what life in her new home would be like. Three times she heard the watchman pass, calling out eventually, "Give ear to the clock, beware your lock, your fire, and your light, and God give you good night: three o'clock."

In the morning Micheline was radiant with energy and anticipation.

"Every day is an adventure," she told Andrew as they broke their fast, "because I am seeing places and things for the first time!"

He paused in the midst of chewing a bite of plum to give her an affectionate smile. The enthusiasm of his wife was contagious; Sandhurst felt as if he were exploring England anew because he was seeing it through her eyes.

After Andrew paid their bill—twenty-four pence for lodging, meals, fodder for the horses, and a fire in their rooms—the group of six rode leisurely out of Stratford-upon-Avon. They kept to the river, which led them straight into the beautiful Cotswold hills, one of the loveliest areas in all of Britain.

Above them the sky was vividly azure, dotted with snowy puffs of clouds, while the air was spring-sweet and warm. There were water meadows all along the River Avon, drenched in violets, wild thyme, and yellow oxlips. The Cotswolds themselves were green hillsides that were shaped, as Sandhurst said, "like whales' backs." The light was slightly hazy, almost iridescent, reminding Micheline of the Loire Valley in France.

"I've never seen so many *sheep*!" she exclaimed at one point, which elicited a chuckle from her husband.

"This is sheep country, sweetheart. The wool merchants are getting rich from them. You see, Cotswold sheep are unique, or so we claim hereabouts. They are long-necked and big-boned, with lustrous soft wool that's really quite special."

Before long they turned south from the River Avon. Micheline delighted in the rolling hills fringed with beech trees, and the secluded valleys lined with pollard willows and threaded with silvery brooks. The Cotswolds exuded charm and a kind of magic that made Micheline feel happy in a different way than she felt with Andrew. This emotion emanated from her surroundings. The softly undulating hills seemed to embrace her, welcoming her home at last.

When they rode into the village of Chipping Campden, Micheline was surprised to find all the buildings and houses composed of honey-colored stone. High Street curved ahead of them, tinted golden in the midday light.

"It's Cotswold limestone," Sandhurst explained, anticipating her question. "Like our sheep, it is unique in that, with time, it mellows from bleached gray to the warm honey color you see here."

They wound their way through the market-day crowds of people, carts, and livestock. Andrew kept silent, letting Micheline observe on her own, until they drew alongside the church with its tall, elegant tower.

"That's a 'wool' church," he said with more than a touch of humor. "There's one in nearly every town, built by the wool staplers, who are eager to put at least part of their wealth into works of piety and charity. No doubt they hope to live as well in heaven as they have on earth."

Down one of the quieter lanes of town they paused at the Crooked Billet inn for a meal of pigeon pie, asparagus with oil and vinegar, brown bread and honey, and stewed apples. To Micheline's surprise the innkeeper recognized Sandhurst and called his wife and children out to welcome "his lordship" home. When Andrew informed them that the lady at his side was the new Countess of Sandhurst, they behaved as if she were royalty.

Later, outside the inn, he told her wryly, "We're still two hours from the village of Sandhurst. If you think these people treated you with reverence, you'd be wise to prepare yourself for even more enthusiasm, Michelle. For years the villagers there have been pestering me to marry. 'Twould seem it's become an epidemic, spreading north to Chipping Campden and God knows where else!"

Fortunately they came upon Sandhurst, a hamlet caught in a fold of hills, late in the afternoon, when most people were off the streets having a rest from the labors of the day. To the others who rushed forth to greet Lord Sandhurst, he merely said that he was eager to get home and would return soon for a proper visit. Micheline felt the curious gazes of the towns-people and smiled in return. Some of them wore looks of comprehension, as if they sensed the bond of love that existed between her and Andrew.

Micheline barely had a chance to look at the village, though it seemed much like the others they had passed through that day. The buildings predictably blushed a tawny hue, and there was a magnificent church that struck Micheline as both dignified and primitive.

"It's Norman," Andrew told her succinctly. "No wonder you like it!"

South of the village were more sheep-covered hills as well as fields being plowed by oxen. Occasionally one of the farm laborers caught sight of Sandhurst's golden head and grace-ful, erect form on horseback and called a greeting to him. Micheline's surprise grew when she heard him reply, invaria-bly calling each man by name.

"These people work for me," he explained.

"But how can you recognize each one from such a distance?"

Andrew shrugged lightly. "Instinct, I suppose. I've known most of those men all my life."

Finally they reached the curving brow of a hill and Sandhurst reined in his horse. "There it is," he said warmly. "That's your new home."

Below them, in a deep, rounded valley, lay Sandhurst Manor. Micheline could see only that it was rose-colored, rather than golden, and sprawling, with lots of chimneys. Smooth, well-tended gardens spread out to the edges of the hillsides, and there were beechwoods to the north.

"Some people call it Sandhurst-in-the-Hole," he said with an ironic smile. "You can see why."

Micheline was already mesmerized. "It's perfectly lovely."

As they rode down into the vale, Andrew explained, "the manor house was rebuilt during my youth. Due to the boldness of my mother, brick was chosen instead of limestone. As for the rest . . . I've never been certain who was responsible. If it *was* Mother, then she was more imaginative than I ever realized. At any rate, this house is exactly my own taste. It could have been created with me in mind."

Their horses slowed to a walk as they passed a lily pond and clipped yew trees. Ahead, an eccentrically splendid manor house of salmon-pink brick rose up, charming in its irregularity. The house was tall, turreted, and gabled, with exotically decorated chimneys rising haphazardly above the battlemented parapet. The half-timbered gables were of different sizes, as were the turrets crowding to the east of the front. The porch was not in the center of the façade, and even the spacious, square-headed windows seemed scattered at random.

Micheline stared, speechless, for a long minute, then turned toward Sandhurst, beaming. "I feel as if I am having a dream! Can this really be your home?"

"*Our* home," he amended. Andrew followed her gaze and the corners of his mouth turned up slightly. "Rather odd, isn't it!"

"Rather *wonderful*!" Micheline corrected him adamantly. "I love it."

"Then we're of one mind again."

"It's a happy-looking house," she decided.

"Happy in its oddity," Sandhurst agreed. In spite of his offhand manner, he was immensely relieved by Micheline's reactions, not just now, but all day long. With some women, he might have suspected pretense, but never with Micheline. Since the moment she'd owned up to her ill-concealed feelings for him, he'd never had reason to doubt her word.

"It's *beautiful* in its oddity." She was rising up to defend the house as if it had always been her own and Sandhurst were the newcomer.

"Pardon me." Laughing, he reached out to catch her hand. "Don't take me to task! I'm on your side."

As they drew nearer the manor, Micheline finally noticed the long-legged horses silhouetted against one hillside, while sheep covered the rest of the valley. Dry stone walls separated the two kinds of animals. There were extensive stables to the west, and a long-suppressed thrill leaped inside Micheline at the thought of so many magnificent steeds. Surely paradise itself could not be better suited to her tastes!

Andrew himself was becoming distracted by the various elements of homecoming. He could sense the house coming to life, and, meanwhile, he was wondering if the horses had been tended properly, if the gardens had thrived in his absence, and if anything had changed within the manor.

Stableboys were rushing forward to take the horses as they neared the entrance to the house and dismounted. Sandhurst had no sooner lifted Micheline lightly to the ground than a plump, middle-aged lady with light brown hair drawn back tightly into a hood came flying out of the manor, arms outstretched.

"My lord, my lord!" she cried, tears dripping onto her pink cheeks. "Is it really you?"

"Of course it's me, Betsy," he assured her, holding her close. When the woman drew back to gaze at him, Sandhurst reached out a hand to Micheline. "I've a surprise for you. This is my wife, Lady Sandhurst. Micheline, I want you to meet Betsy, otherwise known as Mistress Trymme. She's kept this place running smoothly for years. I couldn't leave in good conscience if Betsy weren't here."

"A wife!" Mistress Trymme ejaculated. "Our Lord has answered my prayers."

Micheline extended her hand, instantly drawn to the older woman. "It's a pleasure to meet you, Mistress Trymme."

"Oh, no, your ladyship, the pleasure is *mine*!" Looking up at Sandhurst, she nodded approval in a way that indicated a long-standing closeness between the two. "You've picked a marvelously lovely countess, Lord Andrew! Now you *know* none of us will rest until there's a babe on the way!"

He feigned exasperation. "I'm doing my best! Nan Goodwyn had already begun bothering me on this very subject in London, a fortnight before Micheline and I were even married!"

To Micheline's astonishment Betsy laughed and replied, "I hope you don't expect me to believe that you let a few simple words spoken in church hold you off!" She waggled a finger at him. "I know you better than that, my boy!"

Sandhurst blinked, then chuckled. "Would you make me out a lecher before my blushing bride?"

"Your lady looks as if she has her wits about her, Lord Andrew, and I wouldn't expect you to marry less. Surely I haven't said more than she already knows!" Betsy beamed at

Micheline and pinched her cheek, then declared, "You all must be tired, and no doubt our countess is eager to see more of her new home."

The manor's buildings were grouped around a square courtyard that contained charming flower beds and carved benches. Inside, there were a bewildering number of rooms: twenty bedchambers, a private dining room plus summer and winter parlors, a high-arched, two-story great hall with its connecting chapel, and not only a pantry and buttery but also pastry, laundry, and linen rooms. There was also a magnificent library and a long gallery lined with windows on one side and exquisite Flemish tapestries on the other. One of the reasons the house was so warm and inviting, in Micheline's opinion, was the generous use of artfully refined linenfold paneling, its edges decorated with carvings to counterfeit embroidery.

The great hall was bathed in sunlight and strewn with fresh herbs and fragrant hyacinths. Paintings lined the walls and Micheline was on her way to look at them when a spaniel came bounding into the room. The dog ran straight for Sandhurst, who knelt to welcome him, laughing.

"Meet Wimbledon," he said to Micheline.

"That's rather an unusual name!" She came over to pet the spaniel's sleek head, smiling. Wimbledon was mainly white, with a few dark brown patches on his body and long, silky sable-colored ears.

"I made the mistake of letting Cicely name him when he was a puppy. She was only five or so at the time and decided that he looked like a friend of mine called Sir Percy Wimbledon. As a result, I've had to hide the dog the few times Percy's visited. I don't imagine he'd be flattered to meet his namesake."

Wimbledon let out a short woof of appreciation and licked his master's cheek. When Sandhurst stood up and walked over to the paintings with Micheline, the spaniel trotted along at his side, attempting to assume a position between the two people.

"Oh, dear," Micheline whispered in pretended anxiety. "I'm afraid your friend is jealous. I hope he's not used to sleeping on your bed!"

Andrew's teeth flashed white against his golden-brown face as he laughed in response. "Rest easy, my lady. In fact, you'll discover a dog gate on the stairs to keep Wimbledon in his place." Bending down, he gently but firmly dragged the reluctant spaniel over to his right side. "Speaking of places, *this* is yours, Wimbledon. Don't look at me like that! The lady is my wife, and I won't share her with you."

Wimbledon hung his head. "There, you see!" Sandhurst declared to Micheline. "It's not you he's jealous of; it's me! Obviously the beast was hoping to steal you away from me. Edging in between us, indeed. If Wimbledon aspires to become a true rogue, he'll have to adopt a more subtle approach."

Although Micheline laughed softly, she felt a twinge of sympathy for the dog. No doubt he was used to having his master's undivided attention, for it seemed unlikely that Sandhurst had brought many ladies all the way to Gloucestershire. Instinct told her that he had kept his more socially oriented life in London apart from the quieter existence at Sandhurst Manor. Already, that very day, Micheline had begun to detect aspects of his personality that she had not seen before. It was exciting to realize that he wanted her to share in every phase of his life.

Gesturing toward a wonderfully executed painting of a dark-haired lady, Micheline queried, "Is this your mother?"

"How did you know?"

"Well, it did seem logical, and there's a family resemblance. On the surface she looks like Cicely, but her eyes are yours exactly. Extraordinarily warm and compelling."

Sandhurst's forefinger drew circles on his thumb. It was a casual mannerism, but one Micheline had come to realize signified intense thoughts or feelings on his part. "Odd that you should mention Mother's eyes. She was a very proper lady, quite restrained, yet one learned to gauge her mood by looking at her eyes. When I painted this, they were the most difficult aspect to capture." He gave Micheline a sidelong smile. "The same was true when I painted you. Even more so, I'd say."

"That's because all my feelings were penned up inside— and when I was in the same room with you, there was a veritable storm brewing inside of me!" She laughed softly, remembering. "I didn't realize at first that you did this painting, Andrew. Don't tell me that you're responsible for *all* of these!"

"I confess, if you'll promise not to hold them against me," he replied a trifle ruefully. "In the past I tended to spend nearly every minute here either out with the horses or painting in the gallery. After Mother died, it seemed a good idea to hang this portrait, along with the one of my father. Betsy began complaining, quite shrewdly, that the wall needed 'balancing,' and soon she started bringing out all the other paintings I'd hidden away. I fear that the room's beginning to look like a shrine to my rather average abilities.''

"Average?'' echoed Micheline, "*Pas du tout!* You are very talented!''

He shrugged lightly. "I paint only because I enjoy it. It's a challenge, and it relaxes me. The results are incidental.''

Micheline had moved down to stare at the portrait of the Duke of Aylesbury. In it, he was younger and more contented-looking. His hair was sandy, threaded with white strands, and the angles of his face were softer.

"I did that a dozen years ago, just after returning from my studies in Florence. Mother 'commissioned' it for Father's birthday, hoping, I suppose, that the project would improve our relationship, but it all turned out badly, as usual. He was so critical of the finished product that I brought the painting back here and stored it in a cupboard. Years went by before I even looked at it again.''

"Don't you think the duke has changed somewhat lately?''

Sandhurst made a sound that was half-sigh, half-laughter. "Perhaps. And perhaps you're responsible. Look what you've done to *my* well-ordered existence!'' Putting an arm around her waist, he kissed her hair. "In any event, I won't be crushed if Father returns to his usual curmudgeonly ways. I'm accustomed to them by now. If he *has* changed, I'll be happy for his sake, not mine. I outgrew the need for parental approval before I ever left home. At this stage in my life, all I need is you, Michelle.''

He spoke in a matter-of-fact way that warmed her heart long after they'd finished looking at the rest of the paintings. There were two village scenes, one of the Cotswold hills at sunset, one of Cicely standing next to a beautiful horse, one of Betsy ("The thrill of her life,'' he said wryly), and lastly, a whimsical portrait of Wimbledon the spaniel.

"Let's go upstairs and have a bath,'' Sandhurst said when they'd finished touring the hall. "Together.''

Micheline pretended to be scandalized, then twined her arms about his neck and pressed her body against Andrew's. "I'd love it . . . if Wimbledon isn't included in that invitation.''

The spaniel stood on the other side of the carved dog gate, looking forlorn as they climbed the wide staircase and disappeared from sight.

CHAPTER 32

April 26–May 29, 1533

AT DAWN, MICHELINE AWOKE TO FIND HERSELF WARM IN THE circle of Andrew's arm, her face against his lean-muscled chest. The bedhangings of forest-green velvet were drawn back at the posts to allow the entrance of sunlight, and Sandhurst's body was golden brown in its glow. Wonderingly Micheline gazed at his sculpted face, the lips parted slightly, vulnerably, as he slept. Tawny brows, so mobile when Andrew was awake, were still, and long lashes closed his eyes.

He slept with her, and made love to her, with confidence these days. Micheline gloried in the knowlege that he trusted her now, and acknowledged his need of her with equal ease. There was no reason to speak the words aloud in constant reassurance; both of them could comprehend each other's feelings with barely a touch or a glance.

Micheline's eyes roamed over Sandhurst's body, for the warm spring nights invariably caused him to toss off the covers in his sleep. In all her years with Bernard, she had never been acquainted with him as intimately as she already was with Andrew. She knew every contour of his face, the tendons of his neck and shoulders, the tapering lines of his chest, with its small mole on the far right side, the muscled ridges that progressed down his flat belly, and the sleek, hard contours of his rider's legs. She knew the texture of the soft blond hair on his arms and legs—and elsewhere. In the past, her first husband's maleness had been a source of slight embarrassment. Neither it nor what was done with it was ever really acknowledged by either Micheline or Bernard. With Andrew, all was new and different. They shared everything, every feeling and delight. In the bath the day before, Micheline had found herself teasing him outrageously, until Sandhurst called her bluff and lifted her through the water, impaling her on the length of his hardness. To her surprise, she'd felt no embarrassment, only overwhelming pleasure and satisfaction as they moved rhythmically in the water, her hands in his damp hair, his mouth at her breasts.

Now she stared down past Andrew's trim waist, thinking that his manhood was as beautifully made as his hands. When she touched it lightly, it awoke, and seemed more than ever like his fingers: long, rather thick, yet somehow graceful.

"Good morrow," Sandhurst whispered huskily into her ear, then nibbled on the lobe. "My lady wife. What sweet words."

Although they'd loved thrice the night before, Micheline found that her hunger for him could not be appeased. She turned on her side just as he did, her breasts and hips pressing against the lean lines of his body.

"I'm so pleased to be here," she whispered, smiling. "So pleased to be your wife."

Sandhurst's kisses scorched the curve of her throat while his agile fingers wandered down her spine to explore the satiny curves of her derriere.

"Mmm" was the only verbal response he could manage.

Later that morning Andrew took Micheline out to the stables. Already it was a glorious day. The sun shone brightly, wildflowers lent their fragrance to the breeze, and even Wimbledon pranced hither and yon in high spirits.

The stables were built of honey-colored stone and handsomely maintained. Grooms busied themselves exercising or grooming the horses outside, while a tall, raw-boned man with wind-blown white hair walked forward to greet the Earl and Countess of Sandhurst.

"Welcome home, my lord," he said soberly, though his tone was belied by warm gray eyes. " 'Tis good to have you back."

"It's good to be back." Andrew extended his hand, smiling. "I'd like you to meet Lady Sandhurst. Sweetheart, this is Trymme, the marshal here at Sandhurst Manor—and also Betsy's husband. Trymme is in charge of the stables, the grooms, and all the horses."

"I'm happy to know you, sir," Micheline said sincerely.

"Likewise, my lady. I hope you are pleased with your new home."

Her iris-blue eyes shone with pleasure. "I love it!"

"My wife has a fondness for horses, Trymme," Andrew

confided. "I thought I'd let her choose one for her own—and I ought to say hello to Hampstead. He's well, I trust?"

"Quite! He serviced Willow, that young mare you approved of, and that went very well. He's just been groomed and is waiting to see you, your lordship. I thought you might be along to exercise him."

"Thanks, Trymme. How fares little Stroller? Has she foaled yet?"

"No, my lord. Any day now."

Micheline listened with only half an ear as the two men continued to talk. They all walked along the stable boxes, where Andrew petted each muzzle and smiled into each pair of large, hopeful eyes.

"I've never *seen* such beautiful horses!" Micheline finally exclaimed. "Is this a breed you've developed yourself?"

Sandhurst couldn't repress a chuckle. "On the contrary, fondling. These are all Arabian horses. There's no finer horse on earth, in my opinion, and for the most part, I'm keeping the bloodlines pure. We have done a small amount of experimenting—crossbreeding between the Arabs and some Welsh Mountain ponies, which, though similar in looks and temperament, are naturally smaller. The king keeps threatening to decree that all stock under fourteen hands high must be eliminated, so we've been working to make these pretty ponies larger. We've also bred a few of the Arabians with Chapman horses from Yorkshire, to see what improvements might be made on some of the native breeds." He smiled ironically. "Make no mistake; I'm very fond of British and European horses, but once one becomes used to Arabians . . ."

"One is spoiled?" Micheline supplied, beginning to understand. Each of these horses possessed a lovely head, with large eyes and a small muzzle, carried on an elegant neck. Their bodies were compact, their legs long, slender, and strong. Although colors varied, the silky texture of each horse's coat, mane, and high-set tail was constant.

Sandhurst nodded. "There's much more than beauty involved, though, as you'll discover. Arabs are intelligent, gay-spirited, and gentle. They're also extraordinarily fast, with great stamina and an ability to carry weight. Most endearing to me, however, is the love of these horses for human companionship. That's the real reason I breed them. I love them in return."

He'd stopped in front of an open box, where a young

groom was putting a bridle on an elegant sable-brown stallion. When the horse saw Sandhurst, it neighed softly and nodded its head.

"This is Hampstead." He walked forward to greet his favorite steed and Micheline was touched by the scene. Andrew, with his own lithe strength, seemed to belong among such beautiful horses. "Come and say hello, sweetheart."

When Micheline reached the stallion, Sandhurst slipped a wedge of apple into her hand and she offered it with a few gentle words of greeting. Hampstead munched the fruit slowly, as if scrutinizing her, then he seemed to smile, showing strong white teeth.

Happiness welled up inside of Micheline as she stroked his sleek mane and coat. In the past there had been few people she'd liked as well as horses, particularly her Gustave, who must be languishing without her at Angoulême.

Andrew took Hampstead's reins and led him out of the box. "Have you seen a horse yet that strikes your fancy?" he inquired of Micheline.

"Oh, Andrew, each is more splendid than the last! I couldn't begin—" At that moment her eyes fell on an exquisite long-legged filly being groomed in the sunlight. The horse was a warm shade of chestnut, with white stockings and a long white blaze accentuating the beauty of her face. As if sensing Micheline's admiration, the filly tilted her head slightly, returning her gaze.

"Aha." Sandhurst's murmur was scarcely audible. He smiled in Trymme's direction. "I'd say we've just made a match."

During the next month Micheline settled into life at Sandhurst Manor as if she had lived there always. Indeed, she had never been nearly so happy in the home where she had grown up.

Each morning Sandhurst and his bride rose early, usually sharing a piece or two of fresh fruit en route to the stables. Micheline was fascinated by the various aspects of horse-breeding and was never bored by the sometimes long conversations between Andrew and Trymme. Often she was there early enough to feed Primrose, her white-stockinged filly, a light breakfast of oats, timothy and clover hay, peas, sliced carrots, and apple peelings. Then she and Andrew would exercise Primrose and Hampstead, riding either south over the hills or north to the village. Usually they would stop at some point, leaving the horses to graze and drink at a stream, while they lay down in the meadows.

Drifts of flowers blanketed the hillsides. Micheline was enchanted by the snakeshead fritallery, a flower mottled with light and dark purple which hung its head in the spring sunshine. One day she and Sandhurst lay kissing in a sea of cowslip, scarlet pimpernels, and forget-me-nots while Wimbledon chased elusive green-veined white butterflies and wobbly little lambs over the sloping hill. They were far from the manor, seemingly alone in a world of their own. When Andrew loosened her bodice to free her breasts, warm and pale in the sunshine, Micheline could only stretch sensuously and bask in the shivery sensations his mouth and hands evoked. Her own hands caressed him through his buff doublet and breeches, curving around the ridge of his arousal until her skirts somehow were hitched up and Micheline felt soft hay and wildflowers under her thighs. She unfastened Andrew's codpiece and their bodies joined in a torrent of sweet desire. Above her was a sky that Andrew called "heaven's own blue," and as they mated there in the sun-drenched meadow, it seemed to Micheline that heaven itself could not possibly surpass the life they'd fashioned together on earth.

Even when they were apart, she was happy. Some afternoons Sandhurst painted or looked after business while she rode Primrose alone or became acquainted with the workings of her new household. The servants adored Micheline, since she refused to put on airs, and even the cook, a sturdy old woman called Lettice, welcomed her into the kitchen, where they worked at inventing dishes that combined the elements Micheline liked best in French cooking with the usual English preparations.

May Day came, and the manor house wore garlands of flowers and hawthorn branches on its windows and doors. That afternoon Micheline put on a gown of white muslin trimmed with thin yellow silk ribbons, and Mary helped her secure a wreath of colorful flowers in her loose fire-gold curls. She and Andrew rode into the village to preside over the crowning of the Queen of the May, an honor bestowed upon a comely milkmaid called Isabel. The townspeople danced and sang all day long, many of them cavorting in circles around a flower-decked maypole near the parish church. Everyone was delighted by the new Countess of Sandhurst, who was prettier and gayer than any of the rosy-cheeked village girls.

As May progressed, Micheline's contentment grew apace. The absence of her monthly flow confirmed her happy suspicion that she and Andrew had created new life that spring along with the rest of nature's creatures. Sandhurst was delighted, but far from surprised. Laughing, he told her that he'd have been frankly astonished if she *hadn't been* with child by now.

The kind of reality Micheline had been forced to deal with in Yorkshire couldn't be held at bay indefinitely, however. The third week of the month brought several days of rain, which refreshed the landscape but kept Micheline and Andrew indoors. One afternoon they sat side by side in a library window seat, sharing a volume of *The Book of Merlin*.

Sandhurst stretched out lean-muscled legs and propped them on a placet. Unused to prolonged inactivity, he was finding it harder by the minute to resist the distracting charms of his bride. As raindrops splashed the mullioned window behind them, Andrew's gaze wandered from the printed page to the generous display of Micheline's bosom above a low square neckline.

"What are you looking at, my lord?" she inquired primly.

"I find you far more absorbing than Merlin, my lady." His golden head dipped to kiss the tempting curve of her flesh.

"An interesting choice of words," Micheline observed, shifting against the window seat in a way that told Andrew she was already aroused.

He looked up and smiled boyishly. "Very apt." His eyes softened at the sight of her face, the picture of radiant beauty framed by a spill of brandy-colored curls. He couldn't remember the last time she'd pinned up her hair since arriving at Sandhurst Manor. "You know, you positively glow."

"Marriage . . . and your baby would seem to agree with me." She ran her fingers through Andrew's luxuriant hair, gilded almost completely blond now by long days spent in the sun, while his face had been bronzed in contrast.

Tenderly he kissed her mouth. "I'm glad you're happy here." Sitting back next to her, Sandhurst distractedly drew a pattern with his forefinger on the slim back of Micheline's hand. "I rather hate to bring this up, but you probably realize that we must begin preparations to travel to London. If it were anything except the coronation, I'd say devil take it and remain here, but it's just not that easy. If we don't make the effort, King Henry will remember.''

"It's even more than that, Andrew. We're to meet Cicely in London. You hadn't forgotten, had you?''

He sighed. "I've been trying to. Sweetheart, are you certain you want to carry through with those plans, in light of the baby? I don't want Cicely upsetting you. I worry that you'll feel unwell and never mention it.''

"You must *not* worry,'' she insisted, aware that his anxiety was rooted in the knowledge that Micheline had lost a baby during her first marriage. "The other time, I felt completely different right from the first day. It was as if that baby was not meant to be born.''

"Swear that you'll tell me if you have any pain.''

"Honestly, I've never felt better in my life! You've seen how I've been eating! I'm thriving, Andrew.''

"You must swear,'' he persisted, squeezing her hand.

"Very well, then, I swear.''

The twenty-ninth of May fell on a Thursday. Dawn had scarcely begun to lighten the London sky when a knock sounded on the door of Andrew and Micheline's spacious bedchamber at Weston House.

Sandhurst slowly opened one eye to find his wife looking at him in bewilderment. "If that's Rupert, I'll kill him for certain this time,'' he muttered, his voice husky with sleep.

"Please, don't. I so deplore violence.'' Micheline playfully pulled the covers over her head to escape his withering glance.

The knock was repeated and Andrew called, "Who is it?''

Cicely replied, "Andrew, you haven't forgotten that you promised to take me downriver to watch the queen's entry into the city, have you?''

"I am not awake enough to even think yet, let alone forget our plans for the day!'' He fell back on the pillows and closed his eyes. "Come back in two hours and I'll let you know then if I forgot.''

"Stop teasing me!'' Her voice rose childishly.

"I assure you, I am quite serious. The procession of boats won't be leaving London for Greenwich Palace until midday. I'm not so old and doddering that I require a half-dozen hours to dress and walk outside to the barge.''

"But the river is already thronged with boats!''

"There will always be space for one more. I hereby close

the subject, advising you to make yourself scarce until eight o'clock.''

''But *Andrew*—''

''Leave us! If you want to depart for Greenwich now, get Rupert to take you! I want to *sleep*!''

When there was no further argument from the hallway, Sandhurst burrowed under the covers and enfolded Micheline in his arms. ''Actually that's not *quite* true. Mmm, you're warm.'' Kissing her throat, he caressed a breast, hip, and slim thigh. ''And soft.'' His hand lightly traveled back up the inside of her leg until Micheline flinched slightly.

''Your sister still doesn't like me.''

''I thought she'd been behaving rather well,'' he murmured absently. ''Better, certainly, than in Yorkshire.''

''Didn't you notice the way she purposely failed to include me when speaking about the plans for today? It's as if she's trying to pretend I don't really exist.''

''Oh, you exist, my love. I can certainly vouch for that.''

His fingers were exploring intimately, expertly, and Micheline's thighs opened in surrender. Cicely was forgotten as Sandhurst's mouth covered hers; the love storm that dominated their lives was swelling to another crescendo.

That afternoon, while boats blanketed the river itself, the banks of the Thames were thronged with people. Everyone wanted to watch the magnificent procession for Queen Anne, though most subjects still judged Katharine the real queen. For despite the Archbishop of Canterbury's recent decree that King Henry's first marriage was invalid, no such decision had been handed down by the pope!

Micheline could not imagine a more sumptuous pageant than the one taking place around her on the Thames. Perhaps the procession had been made so overwhelmingly lavish in order to impress and thereby win over the skeptical citizens. The incurably stubborn were said to crowd the dungeons of the Tower of London.

Music, cannon fire, and trumpet calls filled the warm air. Numerous barges had sailed down to Greenwich Palace more than an hour ago. Now they were returning. Cicely, clad in a pretty new gown of ruby silk, clapped her hands in excitement while Rupert shouted ''I *say*!'' over and over again.

The first barge held Queen Anne herself, dressed in cloth of gold, attended by the colorfully decorated vessels of bishops and lords. The mayor even had a dragon on board, which thrashed about and spat fire into the river. More than two hundred other boats followed, embellished with tinkling bells and Anne's coat of arms paired with the king's. Streamers fluttered and danced in the breeze while musicians played with gusto from every craft.

When the queen's barge reached the water gate of the Tower of London, the mighty guns above her boomed in welcome. The constable and lieutenant came out of the crowd to greet Anne and take her to join the king, who waited at the postern gate.

"She'll spend the next two nights in the queen's apartments in the Tower," Andrew explained to his wife. "It's a tradition. On Saturday there will be another procession—this time through the streets of London, bearing her to Westminster, where she'll be crowned on Sunday."

Nibbling at a sweetmeat, Cicely proclaimed, "I intend to be queen one day, but I suppose I shall have to be patient, for I would not marry King Hal!"

Micheline smiled wanly. For the first time in her pregnancy, she felt the heat and was conscious of an enervating malaise, compounded by all the commotion and ceaseless music. "It's all very exciting." She gave Sandhurst a hopeful look. "Are we going home now?"

"No!" cried Cicely. "Please, Andrew, take us to join the celebrations! I don't want to return to that boring house!"

He had already given a signal that sent the oars dipping into the glittering water. As the barge glided upriver, he said, "Spare a thought for Micheline. She's with child, as I have told you, and deserves an extra measure of consideration."

The girl wore a petulant frown. "This is the most exciting day of my life! I don't see why—"

"No need for all this!" Rupert exclaimed, moving forward to clap Sandhurst on the back. "Patience and I would be happy to take Cicely out to enjoy the festivities, wouldn't we, my darling?"

Patience surveyed them all with calm, tiny eyes. Her face was colorless in the sunlight. "Naturally," she said, smiling.

CHAPTER 33

May 31–June 5, 1533

SATURDAY FOUND MICHELINE STANDING WITH CICELY, RUPERT, and Patience behind one of the rails that lined the route of Queen Anne's procession through the streets of London. Although she felt better today, Micheline nonetheless missed Andrew's company, especially since she was surrounded by her new and less than ideal relatives.

The roads were hung with tapestry, velvets, and silks, through which traveled twelve Frenchmen, in blue velvet coats with sleeves of yellow, on horseback. Most of them Micheline recognized from Fontainebleau, but this was not the time for greetings.

Following the Frenchmen came all manner of officials in ceremonial robes, Knights of the Bath in their purple gowns, and finally noblemen in crimson velvet. There was Andrew, Earl of Sandhurst, his hair agleam in the sunlight, standing out from the crowd as usual.

"Isn't he handsome!" cried Cicely, waving.

Micheline merely smiled. Sandhurst saw the hand in the air and winked, but it was his wife who caught the flash of warmth from his eyes.

"That crimson velvet would flatter any man, it seems to me," Patience observed quietly.

Rupert took up his half brother's defense. "Sandhurst is always the best-looking man in any gathering! Surely you realize that, my love!"

More richly garbed officials appeared, including the lord chancellor of England, the mayor of London, and an assortment of archbishops and ambassadors. In their midst came Anne, perched in an open litter covered with cloth of gold which was borne by two white damask-comparisoned palfreys. Dark hair flowed down her back so that she seemed to be sitting on it, and on her head was a coif whose circlet was set with jewels. She wore a surcoat and mantle of silver tissue, the latter lined with ermine. From under a cloth-of-gold canopy held over her by four knights, Queen Anne scanned the crowds, searching for signs of admiration.

The citizens might admire her beauty, but they withheld the approval she sought. Micheline noticed that few men removed their caps, and the sound of cheering was muted and unenthusiastic. The people seemed more curious than worshipful.

In an effort to rectify the situation, Anne's fool, capering at the edge of the parade, shouted, "I think you all have scurvy heads and dare not uncover!"

Stubbornly the crowd refused to laugh . . . or take the hint.

"Why is it that you were not asked to ride in one of the chariots?" Cicely inquired of Micheline, referring to the crimson-clad ladies who followed Anne in decorated chariots.

"I'm not certain," Micheline replied honestly. "Perhaps it's because I'm French, and so new a countess. Or perhaps it's because they weren't certain we'd be here. As you know, Andrew was told only last night that he would be required to join in the procession. In any case, my feelings are not bruised. I've had my fill of pageantry these past few months."

Cicely exchanged a look of disbelief with Patience but said only, "You are more forbearing than I, madame. I should feel quite insulted if I were you."

"I am too content with the important aspects of my life to take offense over trivialities."

After the procession passed, the crowd returned to its daylong celebrations. Rhenish wine flowed freely from London's fountains and music filled the air. Even the conduits of Cheapside ran with white wine at one end and claret at the other. Micheline watched as Rupert filled cups for himself, Cicely, and Patience. Now that the queen was gone, the mood turned festive, but Micheline had no taste for it. She could feel men's hands on her in the crowd, and her head had begun to ache.

"Have some wine, dear sister!" Rupert urged. " 'Twill lighten your mood!"

"Thank you, but I must refuse. It's past seven o'clock, I'll wager, and the day has been a tiring one. I would like to go home and wait for Andrew to return from Westminster."

"My brother's wife seems intent on spoiling our fun,"

Cicely said to Patience as if Micheline were not there. "Next she'll insist that we accompany her back to Weston House."

"That's not necessary, my lady." Finchley stepped forward from his place behind them in the crowd. "I'll be happy to escort the countess home."

Micheline gave the manservant a radiantly grateful smile, which melted his usual reserve and caused him to beam in response. "How very kind you are, Finchley!"

Farewells were made and Micheline set off with Finchley while her relatives watched her go over the rims of their wine cups.

"Are you certain you feel up to this?" Sandhurst asked again. Seated in a chair by the window, he was watching Mary dress Micheline's hair with diamonds and sapphires.

"Stop repeating that tiresome question! I've only been a bit fatigued lately. It's normal, considering my condition. Do you imagine that I'm the sort of female who takes to her bed at the least excuse?" She took a deep breath, hoping to ease the vague feeling of nausea that plagued her. "Besides, I wouldn't miss this coronation for anything."

Andrew threw up his hands and sighed. "What am I to do with you?"

"That's easy." She gave him an enchanting smile, but he only narrowed his eyes in return. "You'll take me to Westminster, Lord Sandhurst, and allow me to enjoy the pleasure of being presented as your wife."

"You'll tell me if you feel the slightest discomfort?"

"Did I not swear?" Micheline glanced back at Mary, who was taking in the scene with wide eyes. "Don't you think that my husband looks magnificent today, Mary?"

"Oh—oh, yes, but of course, your ladyship!" This was a major understatement, for the girl had been casting surreptitious glances of awed admiration his way all morning. Lord Sandhurst was clad in a slashed, tailored doublet and breeches of rich amber velvet sewn with gold thread and set with diamonds. The colors served to emphasize his tanned skin, warm brown eyes, and burnished hair.

"Do you imagine that you can change the subject by appealing to my vanity?" Sandhurst was asking his wife, half amused by such an obvious ploy. Rising, he crossed over to look down into her eyes.

"A valiant effort, you must admit." She laughed.

He shook his head, smiling. Mary had finished with her mistress's hair and now stood back to admire the effect.

"You look glorious," Andrew murmured, softening in spite of himself.

Micheline glanced in the mirror. Her gown, of soft violet satin set with sapphires and diamonds, parted in front to reveal a petticoat of sapphire silk lavishly embroidered with gold thread. The neckline was low and flattering, and the sleeves were puffed, divided by golden ribbons, and slashed to reveal more sapphire silk. Micheline wore a girdle of gold filigree set with diamonds that grazed her hips, from which hung a cordelière with a small mirror attached. Her only other jewelry consisted of necklaces of delicate gold and pearls, small sapphire earrings, and her wedding band.

Sandhurst's warm gaze traveled over his wife's tiny waist, the curves of her breasts and throat, then lingered on her face. He adored the little cleft in her chin, her sensuous mouth, the tilt of her nose, and the eloquent beauty of her iris-blue eyes with their thick lashes. Reaching out, he brushed the backs of his fingers over Micheline's cheekbone and smiled when he saw a blush spread under his touch.

"It is I who will be afflicted with vanity if you continue to stare at me so," she whispered.

"The diamonds and sapphires in your hair dim in comparison to your eyes, my love. You're the loveliest woman in England."

"My nose is too short," Micheline protested weakly.

This statement, combined with the sight of little Mary bumping into furniture as she attempted to back out the door, drew a chuckle from Andrew. "Your nose is perfect." He bent to kiss it, then grazed her parted lips. "Perfect because it is part of you."

The day passed in a blur for Micheline. She stood beside her husband in Westminster Abbey, watching as the new queen advanced up the aisle. Anne wore a robe and surcoat of purple velvet trimmed with ermine. Her train was carried by the Dowager Duchess of Norfolk, and the laps of her robe were held by four bishops. Micheline recognized the man who walked in front, bearing the crown of St. Edward, as the Duke of Suffolk, high constable of England, who had tried with all his might since Cardinal Wolsey's fall to keep this event from happening. Anne's lips curved triumphantly as she stared at the duke's back.

No pains had been taken to disguise the queen's five-month pregnancy. Micheline had remarked on this to Andrew the night before, and he had explained that Henry VIII felt his subjects might approve the marriage because Anne would give England a prince. Apparently the king would not consider the possibility that he might have sired another daughter like Mary, Katharine's offspring.

At the high altar, Thomas Cranmer, Archbishop of Canterbury, spoke in Latin, then anointed Anne on her head and breast. Slowly the heavy, jeweled crown was placed over her hair. She was given a scepter to hold in her right hand, a rod of ivory with the dove for her left. Victoriously the newly crowned queen of England turned to face the assembled guests.

"Well," Micheline whispered doubtfully, "I hope she'll be happy. She's certainly waited long enough for this day."

"Six years." Sandhurst nodded. "Unfortunately, I have a feeling her troubles will worsen rather than cease. Our king is not the sort of man who finds contentment in the blessings of the present. He tends to want what he does not have."

The Earl and Countess of Sandhurst were privileged guests at the banquet that followed the coronation. Cicely, the only other family member who had been invited that day, sat next to Lord and Lady Dangerfield at one of the four long tables that ranged down Westminster Hall, while Micheline had a place at the queen's table on the dais with other chosen ladies.

Although the king was not present, he watched the feast through a hole in the wall of a closet he'd had specially made in the adjoining church of St. Stephen. Lord Sandhurst was one of the earls designated to serve the new queen. He was the carver, while others executed the tasks of cup bearer, officer, and chief butler. Lords of the realm performed lesser serving duties.

Queen Anne, under her cloth of estate, with Cranmer seated to her right, was in her glory. She allowed her old favorite Thomas Wyatt to pour scented water from a ewer over her hands, and then the first course, consisting of twenty-seven separate dishes, was brought in. During the banquet the Duke of Suffolk and Lord William Howard rode up and down the hall on horseback, accompanied by the sounds of trumpets and hautbois to herald each new course.

Not for the first time that week, Micheline wished she and Andrew were back at Sandhurst Manor. She would have gladly traded all the rich food and titled company for a hard gallop on Primrose over the sunlit Cotswold hills followed by an afternoon in Andrew's arms on a bed of meadow grass and wildflowers.

"Good morrow, my lady!" Betsy Trymme entered the spacious bedchamber carrying a tray of warm gingered bread and rosy peaches. "How are you feeling?"

"Sleepy, but so happy to be back." Micheline sat up in bed and smiled. "I've missed this house and all of you."

"And we've missed you, your ladyship." Betsy set the tray on a chest beside the bed and beamed down at her mistress. "It's as if you've lived here always. Even my husband agrees that it's hard to imagine those days when Lord Andrew was unmarried."

"Speaking of Lord Andrew—"

"He's gone to the stables. Didn't want to wake you. He's quite concerned about you, you know, and bade me bring you this food when you woke."

Micheline moved to get out of bed. "What time is it?"

"Half past nine, my lady." Firmly, Mistress Trymme pressed her back into the pillows. "There's no hurry. Lord Andrew and your Primrose will wait. You've a baby to think about, you know. I've even brought you a mug of fresh milk. His lordship tells me you've not been eating properly this past week, and I mean to rectify that! Just have yourself a nice quiet breakfast and I'll have a bath sent up for you."

Micheline sighed in surrender. "It would seem I have no choice."

"None whatever!" Betsy declared with a grin.

Before the housekeeper disappeared out the door, Micheline called, "How fares Lady Cicely—and Mistress Topping?"

"Lady Cicely went riding with her brother, and Mistress Patience is doing needlework in the gallery, your ladyship."

"Oh. Well, thank you again."

Alone, Micheline sipped the rich milk, then set it down and stared up at the green velvet tester. It was a great relief to be back at Sandhurst Manor, but her contentment was marred by several worries that she hoped were minor. Before they left

London, Rupert had informed Sandhurst that their father wanted them to take care of some business of his there, then suggested that the women go on to Gloucestershire without them. Andrew had refused, saying that his wife was his chief concern, but Micheline sensed that part of him regretted cutting short their stay in the city, for she knew that he must have business of his own to look after. She felt so bad about the effect her "condition" was having on his activities that she insisted that he go about his affairs without her the last two days in London, even to the extent of pressing him to take Cicely to a masque at Whitehall Palace that she felt too fatigued to attend herself.

Somehow, Patience inserted herself into the group traveling to Sandhurst Manor. It seemed the least they could do, inviting her there, since Rupert would be occupied in London. In spite of Patience's quietly gracious manner, Micheline felt doubly uneasy when left alone with both her "sisters." Instinct told her that Patience sympathized with Cicely.

Meanwhile, Lady Cicely Weston was on her best behavior. She was unfailingly polite to Micheline, especially when Andrew was nearby, but there was no real affection in her voice or manner. Cicely seemed to truly wish her sister-in-law did not exist. One day, when they'd found themselves alone in the summer parlor at Weston House, Micheline had decided not to strike up a conversation, just to see how her sister-in-law would react. A full five minutes had passed during which Cicely refused to look up from her book, pretending that she hadn't noticed Micheline's unremarkable presence.

Micheline sighed now, staring at the tray of food. She felt drained of energy these days, though she continued to hope that the combination of rest and the Cotswold hills would reinvigorate her. After all, they'd just arrived the night before, and it was a rather long trip, but tears came unbidden to her eyes as she thought of Cicely out riding with Andrew in her place. Was she even riding Primrose?

Betsy reappeared to direct the serving girls who brought in the copper bathtub and buckets of steaming water. After scolding Micheline for not eating, she stood over her mistress and watched as she managed to swallow a few bites of gingered bread. Mary came to wash her hair, then Micheline asked to be left alone for a soak in the tub.

Resting her head against the copper rim, she closed her

eyes, helpless to resist the strong pull of fatigue. This longing to sleep was entirely new to her, and extremely frustrating. She longed to rush about, dressing, then hurry out to join Andrew at the stables when he returned from his ride, but even the thought of so much activity made her wait to attempt it. Just a few more minutes of rest . . . Micheline sighed, and a tear slid down her cheek, but she did not stir.

"You look altogether too sad for one so lovely," Sandhurst's voice remarked from the doorway.

Her eyes flew open. "Andrew!"

"None other." He was leaning against a carved dresser, the picture of casual strength in the fawn doublet, breeches, and boots he'd worn the first night at Fontalnebleau. His brown eyes watched her intently. "What ails you, sweetheart?"

Micheline searched for her soap in an effort to avoid her husband's gaze. "You know well enough what ails me—and how much I wish I felt otherwise . . . but after all, it *is* for a good cause!"

"I wasn't speaking of your recent passion for sleep," Andrew said, walking over to sit back on his heels beside the bathtub. Gently he traced the course of her tear with one fingertip. "What's all this?"

Laying her cheek against his warm hand, Micheline sighed. She had no intention of burdening him with her insignificant worries. "I don't know what's wrong with me. I'm just not myself, and I don't like it any better than you do."

"Michelle, I *always* like you." Sandhurst flashed a grin then and her heart melted. "I'm in need of a bath. Do you suppose there's room for me?"

Copying his tone, Micheline smiled radiantly and assured him, "My lord, there's *always* room for you!"

CHAPTER 34

June 9–11, 1533

EACH MORNING, MICHELINE WOULD WAKE WHEN ANDREW ROSE at dawn, but then a tide of sleep would pull her under for more long, dream-filled hours. As if drugged, she would drift upward toward consciousness every so often, then sink back into oblivion. Her greatest challenge during early June was summoning the resolve to stay awake at some point, and then getting out of bed to bathe and dress.

So when Micheline found herself outdoors in the garden before eleven o'clock one morning, her mood was self-congratulatory. Clad in a pretty summer gown of white and azure silk, she wound her way through the formal walks and shady alleys, past knotbeds and borders of damask roses, columbine, purple bugles, snapdragons, pinks, and red campion, cutting flowers and dropping them into the basket looped over her arm.

"My, don't you look the country gentlewoman!"

Micheline glanced up to see Cicely approaching from one of the clipped expanses of lawn.

"I love it here," she replied simply, ignoring the hint of derisiveness in the younger girl's voice. "It's especially enjoyable this first year, since I am never certain what nature will unveil next."

Cicely selected a fragrant damask rose from the basket and held it to her nose. "You'll be happy to know that your filly, Primrose, is well. I've been exercising her in your absence and just came from the stables; they're going to see about mating Zachariah, the white stallion, with a mare who's in season. I don't imagine Andrew will be back for hours."

In spite of a twinge in the area of her heart, Micheline managed to smile. "I appreciate your help with Primrose. I'm sure this is only a phase of my pregnancy that will soon pass.

Everyone tells me that the first three months are the hardest. I yearn to take up my usual routine here again.''

"But then your body will be changing," Cicely remarked as they walked toward a herb plot. "I mean, you may not be shaped for outdoor activity.''

In the shadow of the charmingly mismatched manor house, Micheline bent to cut rosemary and flowering lavender, barely noticing the butterflies on the wing that flitted among a nearby shrub of honeysuckle. She couldn't decide what Cicely was getting at, or how to reply.

"I do not intend to become an invalid for the next seven months," she said at last.

Examining the folds of her soft pink skirt, Cicely murmured, "I hope, for your sake, that you will not. I mean, we both know how active my brother is. Already he's begun to show signs of restlessness, what with your new habit of retiring early and rising late. I'm not suggesting that he doesn't care for you," she suddenly assured a stricken-looking Micheline, "but Andrew's always been a selfish man in that he's used to having his needs met.''

A cold chill ran down Micheline's spine and her heart began to pound. "What are you saying?''

"I only meant to caution you. You weren't here in England prior to your marriage, and you may not realize how many ladies would happily supply my brother with female companionship.''

"I'm not a fool, Cicely. I am fully cognizant of the fact that Andrew is immensely attractive to women, but I also know that he *loves* me. He would not stray just because—''

"Not without encouragement, perhaps, but he *is* human.'' Cicely started toward the manor, then turned on the path to stare at Micheline. "I'm not saying these things just to hear myself talk. You were not at Whitehall Palace the other night; I was. I may not have proved myself a very affectionate sister to you in the past, but I assure you that I would rather see Andrew with you than with Lady Dangerfield!''

Waves of nausea swept over Micheline as she stood next to the herb plot, watching Cicely disappear from sight. No! she thought wildly. No, it's not true! Not *Andrew!*

Staring down at the basket of flowers in her arms, she was reminded of the day in the gardens at Fontainebleau when she'd learned of Bernard's infidelities. Until that moment it had been impossible for her to imagine him capable of betrayal, but he certainly had been. Were all men alike?

Her imagination burned with possible scenes that might have taken place at Whitehall that night. She saw Andrew in her mind's eye, bored and lonely, succumbing to Iris Dangerfield's entreaties that he dance with her. She saw him responding to Iris's open desire, imagined him putting her from his mind as Iris pressed her hips against his.

No. No, she must not condemn Andrew on the basis of Cicely's words. It wasn't fair. Cicely was a resentful thirteen-year-old girl. In the past the possibility had even occurred to Micheline that Cicely might have been responsible for the threats on her life, though she'd been quick to dismiss such thoughts. Still, in this case, it was easier to believe that Cicely might tell stories out of spite than accept the fact that Andrew had been unfaithful since their marriage. The mere thought seemed to reach down and stab Micheline through the heart.

She found a bench in the shelter of blooming apple trees and tried to calm herself. Finally it came to her that Patience and Rupert had also gone out to Whitehall Palace that night. Perhaps Patience could throw cold water on Cicely's horrible tale.

Bolstered with hope, Micheline went into the manor house through the kitchen door and discovered Patience herself working at one of the long, bleached tables.

"Hello!" she managed to exclaim.

"Oh, good morrow, Micheline. You've been out in the garden, I see."

"It's just glorious, and a beautiful day too. There's no need to stay indoors, Patience. There are plenty of servants to see to the meals."

Lettice, who was chopping parsnips next to Patience, spoke up. "Mistress Topping's showing me her recipe for stewing venison in ale. Nothing like this in France, I'll warrant, eh, your ladyship?"

"No. No, I suppose not." Micheline was beset by a sinking feeling. Why was she beginning to feel like a stranger in her own home? "Lettice, I saw some lovely ripe cherries on the trees outside. Why don't you go out and pick them and we'll have tarts tonight?"

"Oh. Of course. As you wish, my lady." The cook cast a

curious glance in her direction but wiped her hands and took a basket out into the garden.

Micheline drifted over to stand beside Patience, who was much taller and somehow intimidating in her horse-faced inscrutability.

"I'm nearly done trimming the venison, then it must marinate in ale for an hour."

"I see." The dish sounded particularly unappetizing to Micheline. She sighed. "Patience, can I be frank with you?"

"By all means, Sister. I hope that I've made it clear that I am your friend."

"Yes, certainly . . . you've been very kind. Now I wish that you will be honest as well." The eyes she turned up to Patience were liquid with emotion. "Forgive me for being blunt, but Lettice or one of the other kitchen servants might come in at any moment."

"What is it you want to know?"

"Will you tell me what occurred during the masque at Whitehall Palace . . . the night when I was too fatigued to attend? I am referring specifically to my husband's actions."

Patience dropped her eyes and returned her attention to the venison. "I don't know what you mean," she muttered in a way that froze Micheline's heart.

"I think you do," she replied huskily.

"There's really no point in going over it; you'll only be hurt. What Lord Sandhurst did at Whitehall was nothing personal against you. Men are just like that. Somehow they manage to keep the pleasure they take from women in a little compartment separate from their consciences." Patience looked at her sympathetically and touched her arm. "It doesn't mean he doesn't care for you. He was just passing the time."

Micheline shook her head in disbelief, tears stinging her eyes. "But—but Andrew is *different*!" The last word came out on a sob.

"Every woman thinks that at first, and I certainly don't blame you for being beguiled by Lord Sandhurst. There's something about his eyes that compels one's trust. Still, he's human, Micheline, just like the rest, and it's probably better you found out now and learned to live with it rather than continuing in a dream world."

Tears spilled onto the table and Micheline wiped them away with the back of her hand. "Please—tell me—what *did* he do that night?"

Patience sniffed as if that were of no real consequence and turned back to trimming the venison. "How should I know? We all saw them together in the ballroom, cuddling in a corner. Mind you, he didn't behave as if he were besot by any means, but he certainly wasn't discouraging Lady Dangerfield. Her husband was absent for some reason. Everyone had had quite a lot to drink. I saw them kissing at one point." Micheline flinched at that and Patience touched her arm again. "And later they left together. Rupert and I brought Cicely back to Weston House before your Andrew reappeared. I've no idea what time he came home."

Numbly Micheline nodded. "Thank you. I appreciate your frankness."

"You'd have had to face the truth sometime, my dear."

"Yes, I suppose so. Excuse me, won't you?"

In a daze she brushed past Betsy Trymme in the gallery and climbed the stairs to the bedchamber, where she and Andrew had been so happy. Lying far over on her side of the bed, Micheline shivered, dry-eyed, for a long while. Her mind seemed to wait, considerately, before allowing thoughts to filter into her consciousness. When they did, her imagination was activated, and tears began to flow. All of Micheline's misery was compounded by memories of the heartache she'd suffered at Fontainebleau. Lately all of that had seemed part of another life. With Andrew she'd felt reborn, but now she knew such miracles were impossible. Faces and circumstances might change, but the pattern of life remained the same. Love was a cruel illusion.

When her tears were spent at last, Micheline allowed hostility to form a seal over her wound. Remembering every word of love and devotion Sandhurst had ever spoken, her outrage grew. Had it all been a joke to him after all? Had he been laughing to himself in Paris when she came chasing after him? She thought of his skill at chess and felt as if he'd played her like a pawn. She felt like the most ridiculous of fools for succumbing to Andrew's charm. Even Iris Dangerfield was wiser than she, for she dealt with the truth of the situation.

Micheline pressed a hand to her belly, which had begun to harden, and her eyes swam with fresh, harsh tears. This baby, whom she'd thought of as a child of love, now seemed fathered by a stranger.

*   *   *

Dusk was enveloping the valley when Andrew burst through the front door, laughing. Wimbledon the spaniel, caught up in his master's festive mood, let out a long howl.

"Look who's come to visit!" Sandhurst shouted to Betsy as she rushed into the entryway.

"Why, Sir Jeremy! How good it is to see you! Are you here for long?"

Jeremy Culpepper shook his head of red curls. "Afraid not, Mistress Trymme. Off to London tomorrow morning. Just passing through."

"Then this is a celebration. You men will doubtless want some ale or wine."

"Your good husband has anticipated our needs already!" Sandhurst laughed. "We've been toasting Jeremy's arrival at the stables for the past two hours, but I don't think it's possible to be too excessive at times like these." Leaning rather heavily against his friend, he sought Culpepper's advice. "Is it?"

Jeremy pursed his lips in a fair imitation of sobriety and shook his head. "Not t'my knowledge."

"What we *need*, though, is the company of my beautiful wife! Betsy, where's Lady Sandhurst?"

"Upstairs, your lordship, but—"

"Ahhh!" He raised tawny brows in Culpepper's direction. "Her afternoon nap! Such a pleasure to wake her from those! Jeremy, find yourself something to drink and a comfortable chair. We'll join you directly."

Watching Sandhurst run lithely up the stairway, Betsy Trymme was relieved to see that he was less intoxicated than he pretended. Although she couldn't pinpoint the problem, Betsy was certain that something was amiss with Lady Sandhurst.

Entering the rose-shadowed bedchamber, Andrew made out the figure of Micheline, lying on her side at the far edge of the bed. He'd missed her that day, and would have returned long before if Jeremy hadn't appeared. Now, although he was dusty and in need of a bath, Sandhurst joined his wife on the bed, boots and all.

"Michelle," he whispered gently, caressing the curve of her hip with one large hand, "are you awake?"

"Don't touch me."

He blinked at the sound of her voice. It told him that she

was not only wide awake but angry. More than angry, in fact. "Sweetheart, you're trembling! What's wrong? Are you ill?"

Sandhurst's concerned tone and warm gaze made her feel as if an invisible knife were twisting inside of her. Scrambling off the bed, Micheline cried, "Yes, I'm sick. *Parbleu!* I've never been sicker! Sick of men and their lies, sick of disappointment, sick of——"

"Me? Is that what you're saying?" Andrew sat on the bed, staring at his wife in disbelief.

"Yes. *C'est vrai*. I'm sick of you! Your charm and your eyes and your promises of love! You've played me for a fool, Lord Sandhurst, and I certainly was a willing victim. I, of all women, should have known better, but I succumbed to your spell just as you must have known I would. Has it failed you yet?"

This conversation was beginning to remind him of countless others in the past, when his father had fervently listed character traits that Andrew didn't recognize as his own. Instinctively he erected a familiar barrier. "Micheline, I don't know what you are talking about."

"I'm talking about your power over women! Your ability to make one believe and trust you implicitly with just a few words spoken in that intoxicating voice accompanied by one of your famous heart-melting gazes! Is it possible that you will now have the audacity to claim that you are unaware of these spellbinding abilities you possess?"

Sandhurst was dumbfounded by this unexpected attack. He wished he knew what had set Micheline off—and further wished he hadn't drunk so much ale with Jeremy. Anger welled up inside him, but he tried to keep it at bay. Micheline was pregnant, after all, and her moods had been mercurial of late. Perhaps there was a rational explanation for this outburst. Sliding off the bed, he came around to look down at her through the lavender shadows.

"I won't lie to you, fondling," Andrew said quietly. "Of course I'm aware that women tend to find me attractive, just as you must know that you possess a beauty that makes men weak. But what does any of that mean now? We're married. The only lady whose approval I seek is standing here before me."

"Your tongue is as seductive as the rest of you," she answered stubbornly, and looked away from him.

He gripped her arms. "Don't talk nonsense! What is all

this about? If I have committed some crime, name it and allow me to defend myself!''

''Your crime, sir, is that you are a man like all the rest.'' Micheline's eyes flashed with pain and rage in the darkening room. ''No wonder you are so happy these days! You have everything you needed and wanted. Your title and inheritance are safely intact, there's an adoring woman in your bed at night, and you've even managed to sire an offspring during the first weeks of your marriage! If I give birth to a son, all your problems will be solved and you won't have to continue this farce any longer!''

''What the devil are you raving about?'' Andrew's voice was a mixture of outrage and bafflement.

''You needn't pretend any longer. Your seed's been planted, hasn't it? I can't undo the marriage. Why not admit the truth?''

''*What* truth?''

''That nothing's changed. That you have no more intention of devoting yourself to me than you do to Iris Dangerfield! After all, it would be a crime to deprive womankind of your virtuosic gifts when you can satisfy a wife and still manage to spread your talents around!''

A muscle clenched in his jaw. ''I think you've gone quite mad, my lady.''

''On the contrary! I've seen the light! I'll own that it's not very pretty, but it's better than languishing in the darkness of ignorant contentment!''

Sandhurst's frustration was such that he felt an urge to shake some rational explanation from her, but his love for Micheline ran too deep. Again and again it rose up to push aside his rage, arguing for understanding.

''Micheline, won't you tell me what's brought this on? If I knew—''

''If you knew, you would weave some tale to pull over my eyes!'' In the shadows, through her tears, there were moments when it seemed that Bernard stood there before her instead of Andrew. Remembering him made it easier to resist the urge to forgive and forget. ''You know what you've done, my lord. There's no point in pretending innocence; I'm aware of the facts.''

''*What* facts?'' Sandhurst felt as if he were in the midst of a bizarre nightmare. Even this conversation reminded him of some awful garden maze. Each promising turn became a dead end.

Micheline presented her back and walked to the window. "I don't wish to discuss this further. Please go."

His entire body taut, Andrew raked a hand through his hair. Closing his eyes, he swallowed further words of appeal. "This is insane . . . and the time will come, Michelle, when you will beg my pardon for each word you've spoken here tonight."

A moment later the door slammed, and Micheline was alone in the darkened bedchamber. A tremor shook her body, and she buried her face in her hands, sobbing.

PART V

Western wind, when will thou blow,
The small rain down can rain?
Christ, if my love were in my arms
And I in my bed again!

ANONYMOUS

CHAPTER 35

June 10–11, 1533

LARKS, FINCHES, ROBINS, AND CUCKOOS BEGAN TO SING BEFORE dawn, but Micheline could not be consoled as she lay alone in the bed that had been a cozy haven during the first weeks of her marriage to Andrew. It seemed that she hadn't slept all night. Where was he? His parting words, "This is insane," echoed in her mind, and she wondered if they'd been truer than he guessed. Micheline's world, which had been so happy just a day ago, was now turned upside down, and she felt as if she were falling down a dark, bottomless tunnel.

"Lady Sandhurst?" Betsy's voice came from the other side of the door, sounding unusually apprehensive. "Are you awake?"

Micheline almost smiled at the housekeeper's intuition. On a normal morning Betsy wouldn't have dreamed of asking such a question, for it couldn't have been more than six o'clock, and the sun had scarcely begun to rise over the rounded Cotswold hills.

"Come in, Betsy."

The older woman entered slowly. She tried not to react to the sight of her mistress, though Micheline's pale face and the shadows under her beautiful eyes gave her cause for instant worry. "My lady, whatever it is that's bothering you must be resolved—for the sake of your baby."

Tears stung Micheline's eyes. "I don't know if that's even possible, Betsy."

Sighing, the housekeeper held out a folded sheet of parchment closed with Sandhurst's seal. "Lord Andrew asked me to give you this."

She took it, trembling slightly, and whispered, "Where is he?"

"Gone to London, my lady. He left with Sir Jeremy Culpepper late last night."

"Oh." No matter how many times she told herself that she hated Andrew and didn't care what he did, her heart would not be convinced. "Please, stay for a few minutes, Betsy."

Haltingly Micheline broke the seal and opened the paper, reading:

> Michelle,
>
> I have business in London, as you know, and this seemed a proper time to take care of it.
>
> My hope is that you will resolve whatever it is that's troubling you while I'm away. Since you don't seem to want my help (just the opposite), I've taken you at your word and am leaving you alone.
>
> Do, please, remember that I love you.
>
> > By your husband,
> > Sandhurst.

It was very terse and to the point, right down to his signature. Micheline tried to dismiss the austere declaration of love, but a rush of emotion in her breast would not be denied.

"Did he say anything to you, Betsy?"

"Very little, your ladyship. He asked me if I knew what might be upsetting you, and I said no. I can't recall the last time I saw Lord Andrew in so black a mood. At first I thought the ale he and Sir Jeremy drank at the stables might be the cause, but I soon realized that whatever passed between the two of you had rendered him utterly sober." She gave Micheline a searching look. "Do you want to hear the rest?"

"Yes. Please."

"He asked me if anyone had been here talking to you during the day. He seemed to think that someone had been putting ideas into your head, and quite frankly I had the feeling he was rather upset that you might accept someone else's lies over the truth from his own lips."

"I see you've taken his side, and I'm not surprised. You'd be wise, though, to think twice before accepting the word of so charming a man. I trusted him, too, until I learned of his infidelity from two different sources."

Betsy studied the younger woman's stubborn profile. "I don't know what you heard, my lady, but I've known Lord Andrew nearly all my life. Charming he may be, but he's never used it as a weapon—and he's *never* lied to me or anyone else here at Sandhurst Manor!'' She stood up, then paused to look back at the bed, trying to keep the anger from her voice. "There's one thing I do know, and you should too! Lord Andrew *loves* you better than his life! When he left, he asked me to look after you, and I'll do so, but I must say I'm not very happy right now to claim you as my mistress!''

That evening Micheline dined with Patience and Cicely in the summer parlor. There was venison left over from the day before, plus mushroom and orange salad, an herb pudding, and almond soup that Patience had made that afternoon and now served with her own hands.

Micheline had come downstairs only because Patience had urged her to do so. She needed to get out of that bedchamber and eat a wholesome meal, Patience insisted, if only for the sake of her baby.

During supper Cicely stared at her new sister-in-law as if seeing her for the first time. Although she'd made up her mind before they ever met that she detested the Frenchwoman, she now found her heart softening as she regarded Micheline's poignantly sad expression. There were lilac-hued smudges under her luminous eyes, and her mouth turned down at the corners in a way that constantly threatened tears.

"I hope you're not worried about Andrew," Cicely ventured at one point. "He'll be fine on his own . . . and I know he'll be back here soon."

Micheline nibbled at a wedge of orange, then pushed the food around her dish with a new pearl-handled fork. "I suppose . . ."

"It's probably a good thing that he's away for a bit," Patience said, leaning over to put a bowl of soup in front of Micheline. "You've had a shock, my dear, and can use this time to adjust."

Cicely's expression was troubled as she looked from one woman to the other. "Andrew's not a monster, Micheline! I mean, there's no reason for you to stop—uh—caring about him."

Arching a warning brow at the younger girl, Patience agreed, "That will come in time, of course."

At that moment Betsy Trymme appeared in the doorway. "Pardon the interruption, your ladyship, but I don't seem to

be feeling very well. The soup may have been a bit rich for
me. If you don't mind, I'll go on to bed now.''

"Certainly, Betsy. I hope you're feeling better in the morning.'' When the housekeeper had departed, Micheline sighed.
''I don't have much of an appetite myself. Will you both
excuse me?''

"But you haven't touched your soup!'' Patience exclaimed,
wounded. "I ground the almonds and picked the herbs myself! Please, at least try it! Whatever ails Mistress Trymme
has nothing to do with my soup!''

Prepared to do anything to stop Patience's whining, which
sounded remarkably similar to Rupert's customary tone,
Micheline obediently swallowed several spoonfuls of soup.
Thick with ham, cream, sherry, and almonds, it was far too
rich for her taste that evening. "It's delicious, Patience, and I
appreciate your efforts, but I fear that I simply haven't much
of an appetite.''

"What do you think, Cicely?'' Patience pointed her long
chin in the younger girl's direction.

"I can't say, I'm afraid. I despise almonds. Sorry, but I
won't taste it even for you, Patience.''

They were still arguing about whether Cicely should try the
soup as Micheline rose and slipped from the room. Upstairs,
she shed her gown and petticoat, then walked over to the
dresser and picked up her looking glass.

"Mon Dieu," she whispered, "I look ghastly.''

Still wearing her chemise, Micheline crossed the chamber
and crawled into the bed that now seemed cold and uncomfortable without Andrew. His face swam before her, even
after she closed her eyes, but at least tonight sleep stepped in
to provide an escape. In fact, Micheline found that once again
she was unable to resist its seductive force.

In her own bedchamber Lady Cicely Weston lay wide
awake, though the manor house was dark and she guessed it
must be nearly midnight. Aside from the guilt she felt for
causing her brother and his new wife so much distress, she
also had the uneasy feeling that something else was wrong.
Patience had been acting awfully odd lately. Of course, she'd
always been odd, but there was a twist to this new mood that
disturbed Cicely.

Why should Patience want to conspire to drive away Andrew's wife? When she'd suggested that they tell Micheline

he'd been unfaithful, her explanation about sympathizing with Cicely and knowing that Micheline was wrong for Andrew seemed to make sense, but now Cicely had second thoughts. It had seemed rather a joke yesterday—until she saw her brother's face late that night when he was preparing to leave for London. She'd understood then just how deeply he loved Micheline. It was a love too real to be killed by an unkind prank. The thought of him in pain, because of her, had haunted Cicely ever since.

Complicating the situation further was the fact that Cicely was beginning to like Micheline. She realized now that sparks of affection had been struck many times, beginning the day in Yorkshire when Micheline had invited her to live with them, but all along Cicely had obstinately refused to open her heart. Tonight at supper, however, the sight of Micheline's stricken pale face had struck a chord within Cicely. She was starting to understand that this French girl Andrew loved so completely might become a lifelong friend rather than the enemy she'd imagined.

Sighing, Cicely turned on her side and closed her eyes, trying to relax enough to sleep. Tomorrow she resolved to treat Micheline with kindness. Perhaps overtures of friendship might be made . . . if it wasn't too late.

An odd, soft sound outside her door caused Cicely to lift her head from the pillow. Someone was out in the corridor! Who could it be—and why? She sat up, listening. It seemed to her that the person was moving down the hall, toward Andrew and Micheline's bedchamber. Moments later all was silent, but Cicely continued to feel uneasy.

Finally she climbed out of bed, donned a robe over her nightgown, and instinctively picked up a candlestick. Strangely fearful, she stood next to her own door for a full minute before summoning the courage to open it and step into the corridor. At first, the only sound Cicely heard was the pounding of blood in her temples, and she was surrounded by darkness. Then she saw Patience emerge from Micheline and Andrew's room in a blaze of light. When the bony woman closed the door behind her, the hallway went black once again.

Cicely sniffed the air, terror-stricken. Could there be a fire? If so, why wasn't Patience screaming for help, sounding an alarm? A horrible thought occurred to Cicely . . . almost too horrible to entertain.

She had no idea where Patience was, but she had no choice. It was imperative that she enter Micheline's bedchamber. The increasingly strong smell of smoke told her that all their lives depended on her actions now.

Cicely ran as lightly as she could down the corridor, hoping that Patience had gone downstairs—or outside, in search of safety. Her palm was wet clutching the candlestick, and it seemed that her heart would burst with terror, but she found the latch. No sooner had Cicely's fingers touched it than she was savagely thrown to the floor. Sharp fingernails clawed at her face and closed around her throat, squeezing, but Cicely was younger and stronger than her attacker. She brought up the candlestick, aiming for the shadow above her, and struck repeatedly with all her might. Finally she felt the fingers go slack against her neck as a body slumped over her own. Cicely recognized Patience's cloying scent and shoved her aside with revulsion.

An instant later Cicely was scrambling to her feet and feeling for the latch. She pushed it upward, opened the door, and felt as if she had stepped into the sun. The entire room was on fire, it seemed. Blinking, Cicely discovered that the flames were centered on the bed. The velvet tester and curtains were ablaze, but incredibly Micheline lay sound asleep and untouched in the middle of the feather tick.

"Micheline!" she screamed, shaking her brother's wife. "Get up!" When the girl merely moaned in response, Cicely grabbed her arms and dragged her off the bed. Sparks dropped onto Micheline's chemise and caught fire, but Cicely rubbed them out with her own hands. "Help!" she screamed. "Someone—help!"

No one came. Cicely's heart seemed to be throbbing over every inch of her body as she ripped the fiery bedhangings down piece by piece and covered them with the Turkey carpet. She didn't feel the burns on her hands or notice the scorched smell of her own hair. When at last there was no more fire, Cicely collapsed beside the unconscious Micheline and sobbed hysterically.

"It must have been that horrid almond soup," Micheline murmured weakly. Propped against a carved chest, she surveyed the wreckage of her bed, then looked at Cicely. "Even the servants were drugged."

The younger girl nodded, glancing out into the corridor where Patience's body lay. "She's dead, you know."

"I'd say she deserved her fate, and that you have demonstrated incredible courage, *ma soeur*. We have to get you to a physician, though. Your face—and hands—" Micheline struggled to rise. She still felt as if she could sleep for days, and her limbs were like water, but whatever it was that Patience had put into the soup would have to be overcome. Staggering slightly, she reached out to Cicely, who warmly accepted her embrace. "I owe you my life," she whispered thickly.

They hugged tightly, tears mingling on their cheeks. "I'm only sorry for—"

"No. The present begins now," Micheline said firmly.

"It wasn't true, you know, what we told you about Andrew." Cicely began to weep, in reaction to the night's events as well as the confession she was making. "Lady Dangerfield tried to seduce him that night at Whitehall, but he was positively rude to her. I couldn't really understand it at the time."

Micheline stiffened as her mind began to return to normal. "Andrew!" she breathed as if terrified. "He's in London— with Rupert! Patience must have been in league with him. Oh, *mon Dieu!* I must go to him at once!"

Cicely looked equally stricken. "Micheline, you don't actually think—"

"I'll tell you what I think. I think those two plotted all of this very carefully. They tried to dispatch me before the wedding, and when that didn't work, they worked out an elaborate plan whereby they could kill each of us separately. An accidental fire for me—"

"But if you're right," Cicely interrupted, breaking into tears, "Andrew could already be dead!"

CHAPTER 36

June 11–12, 1533

MICHELINE ARRIVED IN LONDON THE NEXT EVENING AFTER A LONG hard ride on Primrose. Although it was pleasantly warm, summer also meant an intensification of some of the worst smells Micheline had ever endured. She rode behind a groom through the city's impossibly cramped, twisting streets, following him to the home of Sir Jeremy Culpepper. Micheline feared that Rupert might be at Weston House, and she had no intention of alerting him to the fact that she was still alive.

They drew to a halt in front of a tall, narrow, half-timbered house in Drury Lane. Micheline dismounted quickly and handed Primrose's reins to the groom, then rushed over to pound on the door.

Jeremy himself opened it. Never had Micheline seen him looking so drawn and worried. Her heart, which had been pounding madly, seemed to stop for a long moment.

"Andrew—" she gasped, fearing the worst. "Is he all right?"

If Culpepper was surprised to see her, he didn't show it. Waving her into the entryway, he said, "Come in and sit down. Are you alone?"

"I came with a groom. We just arrived from Gloucestershire."

Jeremy spoke to a servant, ordering food and water for the groom and horses, then he took Micheline into a small parlor and poured goblets of wine for both of them.

"You've heard the news?"

A cold, sickening chill swept over her. "No. That is—I have news of my own, but you go first. I want to hear about my husband. Where is he?"

Culpepper ran a pudgy hand through his red curls. "Sandhurst was arrested last night. He's imprisoned in the Tower."

"The—Tower?" She drew a harsh breath, remembering

314

the pirates hanging in chains from the Tower walls, not to mention the countless stories she'd heard about the rat-infested dungeons with their instruments of torture. "Andrew—arrested?! On what charge?"

"It's not entirely clear to me. I went to Weston House this morning and Rupert told me the news. Apparently Sandhurst's been accused of attempted adultery with the queen, and there was something about treason as well. I gather someone overheard him making derogatory comments about King Henry."

"Adultery? Treason?" Micheline was livid. "This is insane! You probably think that I would believe the first charge, but—"

"Why do you say that?"

"Didn't Andrew tell you what passed between us the night he left Sandhurst Manor with you?"

"Your husband does not discuss such things with other people, not even me. I nearly went mad at Fontainebleau trying to get him to tell me what was going on between you two!" Jeremy flushed. "I wasn't prying, you understand, but my own life was affected."

"I must go to him at once," Micheline said suddenly, oblivious to what Jeremy had been saying. He'd opened his mouth to reply when she pounded her fist on the chair arm and exclaimed, "*Rupert* is behind all of this! I could kill that weasel! When I think of the times I tried to persuade Andrew to be more generous in his treatment of Rupert, I could kick myself! He's been absolutely right all along, and it's I who've been wrong!"

Baffled, Jeremy gulped his wine and said, "I beg your pardon?"

Micheline spilled out the story of all that had transpired the night before at Sandhurst Manor, digressing briefly to add details about the threats she'd received since coming to England and the "accidents" while out riding and on the steps at Aylesbury Castle.

"I was such a *fool*! I thought Iris Dangerfield was behind it all! I took Rupert and Patience at face value, believing that awkwardly sincere act of theirs! Now I realize that those two would do *anything* to achieve their goal—and the first step involves killing Andrew, me, and our unborn child."

"And you believe that Rupert set up Sandhurst's arrest?"

"Of course! He probably paid someone—or better yet, two or three people—to go to the king and denounce Andrew. He wouldn't make the accusations himself, but I've no doubt that he's somehow taken credit for all of this.''

"It's not hard to imagine Rupert standing before King Henry and mourning what he had to do for the good of the country,'' agreed Jeremy.

"The charges are awfully serious, aren't they?'' Micheline mused rhetorically.

"Life-threatening, I should think.''

"Rupert made certain that Andrew would have no chance of reprieve. He's very smart! Rather than killing us both outright, he and Patience decided to take a more difficult route in dispatching Andrew. People might have been suspicious if we'd both died 'accidentally.' I'm sure, too, that he felt Andrew's disgrace would make *him* look better when he usurped his place as Earl of Sandhurst!''

Jeremy poured another goblet of wine, noticing that Micheline had not touched hers. "I confess, my lady, that all this has set my head spinning.''

"We haven't time to discuss it any further, either. I must go to Andrew immediately, and then we have to concentrate on finding a way to free him.''

"I don't know if they'll allow him a visitor at this hour,'' Culpepper said doubtfully.

"You'll let me stay here, won't you? You understand that I cannot let Rupert see me? Good. Then show me where I can freshen up. I'll see if I can repair my appearance sufficiently to ensure the guards' cooperation at the Tower.''

Jeremy had to smile at that. The Countess of Sandhurst might be a bit dusty, and her curls were tangled, but her eyes sparkled with a new kind of passion. She looked simply dazzling.

The Tower of London was far more than just one building. The name referred to an entire fortress, with the turreted, whitewashed palace keep built by William the Conqueror at its center. This was known as the White Tower, but there were many other buildings within the ramparted walls, as well as many other towers, which were used for everything from housing the king's menagerie of lions and other exotic beasts to sheltering prisoners of the crown.

Exactly what sort of existence a prisoner suffered in the Tower depended largely on who he was. If a man had rank and privilege in life, he usually was given fairly comfortable quarters. In Sandhurst's case, these consisted of a large stone room in the Garden Tower, with windows that overlooked the Thames, the moat, and the Traitor's Gate on one side and the Tower Green, where condemned prisoners were beheaded, on the other. He had a bed, table, and chairs, and a chest for storage. Best of all, if Sandhurst had been disposed to look on the bright side, his guard was unusually amiable and brought him adequate amounts of food. He'd barely touched it this first day, but realized that in time he would be grateful for the fact that he wouldn't suffer from starvation before meeting the headsman.

There was even a seemingly endless supply of candles. Andrew had too much on his mind to sleep, in spite of the fact that he'd lain awake the night before. Sitting in one chair, his booted legs propped on the other, he stared at the guttering candle flame and tried for the hundredth time to unravel the coil in which he found himself tangled.

" 'Ey there, yer lordship!'' It was Carson, the guard, his key clattering in the lock before he threw open the door to Sandhurst's tower room. ''Look what I found wandering about on the Water Lane! Such a pretty thing, none of the guards've been able to resist her pleas to see you. Almost makes me wish *I* were a prisoner!''

''What are you driveling about, Carson?'' Sandhurst straightened, but his voice broke off at the sight of Micheline, haloed in the torchlight. ''Good Lord.''

''Against the rules, you know, havin' visitors this late, but you aren't the first. The lieutenant'd have my head if he knew—'' Carson paused here to guffaw at his own joke. ''But this seems a special case. I'll allow you a quarter hour with your wife.''

The burly flaxen-haired man took his leave then, eyes a-twinkle, and Sandhurst stood slowly, scarcely able to believe that Micheline was real.

''Can it be you?'' he wondered hoarsely.

Clad in a summer gown of apricot silk, her cognac-colored hair shining as it spilled over her shoulders, Micheline looked beautiful—and totally out of place in what were supposed to be surroundings of utter deprivation.

Meanwhile, her eyes were feasting on the sight of him. In view of all the trouble Rupert and Patience had caused within twenty-four hours, it seemed a miracle that Sandhurst was standing here, whole and strong, before her. He wore boots, buff breeches, and a white linen shirt without a doublet in the balmy June night. Micheline searched his face for clues to his mood. Might Andrew still be angry with her?

"I'm very real, but do you want me?" she asked softly in reply to his first words. Crossing the floor, Micheline knelt suddenly on the damp stones a few feet away from her husband. "My lord, I beg your pardon and your forgiveness for every wrong word I spoke night before last. I was cruelly in error."

Sandhurst lifted her up into his arms, burying his face in her fragrant hair. "Forget it, fondling. I have." Their mouths came together and both of them were jolted by a powerful current of feeling. "Good God, Michelle, how can you be here?"

Tears glistened in her iris-blue eyes. "How could I be anywhere else? Oh, Andrew, I wish we could spend this time mending the trouble I caused the other night, but there are more urgent matters to deal with. We'd better sit down. I have so much to tell you!"

Holding fast to his hand, she quickly related what had transpired at Sandhurst Manor, from the almond soup to the fire and the death of Patience Topping. "Your sister saved my life, and the manor as well, Andrew. She was extremely brave."

"It sounds as if you two are truly sisters now as well," he said softly while his mind sorted out all that Micheline had told him. "How is Cicely?"

"I saw to her burns as best I could and sent a page to the village to bring a physician. I also left instructions that Patience's body should be buried in the village churchyard. It was uncharitable of me, perhaps, but I didn't want her grave at Sandhurst Manor—reminding us . . ."

Rather distractedly Andrew pressed a kiss to her hand and answered, "No, you were quite right. Too bad Yorkshire is so far away and it's so hot. I'd have preferred that she was returned to her family's village of Bubwith."

Micheline hurried on to more pertinent conversation. "You see how it was, though, don't you? I mean, the connection—"

"With Rupert? Oh, yes, I see," said Sandhurst thoughtfully. "It's perfectly clear now. I only wonder I didn't suspect him before. Remembering his unexplained absences from Aylesbury Castle these past months, a great deal becomes plain. Not just the incidents at Hampton Court and Aylesbury

Castle, but also your riding accident and strange illness while
we were still in France.''

Micheline was rather taken aback by these deductions.
Tiny hairs stood up on the back of her neck as the true extent
of Rupert's villainy became apparent. ''I was so obtuse! I
completely misjudged him!''

''Not completely.'' Sandhurst gave her a grim smile. ''He
really is a bumbling fool, lucky for us, or he'd have succeeded in doing away with both of us long ago.''

''He must be behind your arrest, though! How can we ever
convince the king of your innocence, Andrew?''

''Rupert certainly aimed straight for Henry's weak spot—
his jealous possessiveness of Anne. No doubt the king's rage
has blinded him to other considerations.'' Sandhurst stared in
the distance for a long minute, his eyes hard. Micheline could
feel him thinking. Nearly overcome with anxiety, she reached
out to caress his sleeve and felt the tensile strength of Andrew's shoulder and arm, betraying his own state of mind.
Still, when he spoke again, his tone was almost jaunty.
''There's only one thing for it, I suppose. We shall have to
maneuver Rupert into giving himself away in front of King
Henry.''

''We?'' she echoed.

''I ought to be present, I think. I've a few questions of my
own for that reptile who calls himself my brother.''

A smile flickered over his well-shaped mouth, setting off a
wave of elation inside of Micheline. ''But how?''

He pulled her onto his lap and kissed her deeply. ''Are you
up to participating in an escape from the Tower of London?''

Micheline blinked in the face of his amused nonchalance,
then slowly a radiant smile lit her countenance. ''I shall
cancel my other social engagements on your behalf, my
lord.''

Sandhurst's brown eyes were warm as he chuckled, ''I
rather thought you might.''

''I do *not* believe I am *doing* this!'' Sir Jeremy Culpepper
muttered under his breath, glaring at Micheline as they approached the Tower of London's barbican.

She nearly giggled, as much from nerves as amusement. ''I
know you don't mean that, Jeremy!''

''You do?'' Pausing in the moonlight, he scratched the
false white beard wrapped around his double chin. ''Sandhurst

has coerced me into taking part in some bizarre adventures in the past—one of which involved *you*, my lady—but this is unquestionably the topper!''

''It was I who coerced you,'' Micheline corrected him. ''Stop complaining! Past experience should have convinced you to trust Andrew's plans.''

''You're as mad as he is. Two of a kind!''

''Such lavish flattery!'' She laughed, then whispered soberly, ''You're certain the message was sent to Rupert?''

''Finchley took care of it this afternoon. He bribed a royal page to deliver the note personally.''

''Good.'' They were outside the barbican. ''Here we are. Behave yourself now.''

At the sound of their voices a guard appeared. ''Who comes there?''

''Oh, good evening, Sergeant!'' Micheline greeted the man as if they were old friends. ''It's nice to see you again!''

''Lady Sandhurst?'' he wondered doubtfully. The woman really was too beautiful; Sergeant Pease ached just looking at her. Her hair flowed loose, like liquid silk, and there were rosebuds pinned in it that matched her low-necked gown. The sight of the upper portion of the countess's delicious-looking breasts made him salivate.

''You remember me! How sweet!''

''I hope you haven't come to see your husband. It's past nine o'clock. Too late. We lock the gates at ten, you know.''

Her face fell tragically and tears welled in her eyes. ''Say that you will overlook the rules this time, Sergeant, please! I'm late only because I've brought my husband's father, the Duke of Aylesbury. He's quite old and wasn't feeling well enough to go out earlier today. Won't you grant him a few minutes with his son? I promise that we shall take our leave well before ten o'clock!''

Lady Sandhurst's appealing tone wore away at Pease. ''Well . . .'' He glanced over at the bent old man who stood wavering in the arched doorway. ''I can hardly say no, Your Grace. I have a son myself and can appreciate how you feel. All of us here like Lord Sandhurst and hope he'll find a way out of this predicament.'' This last was spoken in a strained tone, for the sergeant knew there would be no reprieve for a man accused of trying to seduce the queen.

Micheline had taken Jeremy's arm and was already turning

away when Pease said, "Pardon me, my lady, but you'll have to show me what's in your basket."

Her heart skipped a beat. "Just a few things we brought for my husband. Clean clothes, you understand." She lifted the cover and pulled out a shirt-sleeve. "Now that you mention it, though, there is something here that I'd like you to have—in return for your kindness." Reaching down, Micheline withdrew a bottle of wine. "It's one of my own, from France. I do hope you'll enjoy it."

The sergeant blushed in the light of her smile. "Very kind of you, my lady. I appreciate it."

"If you'll excuse us, then—time is short!"

As they walked hurriedly toward the Middle Tower, Jeremy pulled his soft velvet bonnet lower on his brow. "You're a little minx, Lady Sandhurst!" he muttered, amused in spite of himself.

"Call me Micheline." She smiled.

At the Middle Tower Micheline told the guard, "Sergeant Pease has given us permission, but we must be brief!" barely pausing to hear his reply.

They walked under the Byward Tower with equal ease, and then arrived at the Garden Tower itself. The flaxen-haired guard met them with a look of astonishment. Briefly Micheline gave her explanation, punctuated with charming smiles and melting glances, and moments later the guard was letting them into Sandhurst's chamber.

"Dear Father!" exclaimed Andrew. Crossing the stone floor, he clasped Jeremy against him. "How good it is to see you!"

Culpepper's response was muffled. In the doorway Micheline stood beside Carson, the guard, and sighed. "You've all been very kind to allow this reunion."

"Rather touching, isn't it?" Carson allowed generously.

"Father, I would like you to meet my guard," Sandhurst declared, gesturing for Carson to come forward and join them.

Jeremy pasted on a feeble smile. "Eh?"

"Quite an honor, Your Grace!" The guard took two steps before Micheline walked up behind him and struck the back of his head with a brick she'd taken out of the basket.

Andrew caught the man in his arms and glanced up at Micheline. "Well done," he praised her.

"No time for chitchat!" Jeremy exclaimed hysterically. "We'll all go to the block if we're caught!"

"Nonsense," Sandhurst soothed his friend. "Help me out, won't you?"

The two men dragged Carson to the bed, undressed him, and then covered him so that only the back of his blond head showed.

"Poor Carson. He was so nice to us," Micheline reflected while Andrew donned the guard's uniform. "I think he deserves a reward."

"Depends on what you have in mind!" Sandhurst laughed, lacing the guard's ill-fitting breeches.

Micheline took five gold crowns from the basket and held them up. "Perhaps these will ease his headache tomorrow." Reaching under the blanket, she put the coins in Carson's hand.

"Please!" Jeremy was beside himself. "Let's get *out* of here!"

"How do I look?" Andrew inquired, pulling on Carson's Tudor bonnet.

"Ridiculous," his wife decided, "but not ridiculous enough. You'll need some padding."

While Micheline stuffed wads of clothing up the doublet of his uniform, Sandhurst stared at her so intensely that hot blood rushed to her cheeks. When she had finished, she wrapped her arms around his expanded waistline and pressed her face to the hard breadth of his chest. The even beat of Andrew's heart nourished her spirit.

"God's bones! Are you two *ready*?" demanded Jeremy.

"Quite, but I don't think this is the proper time or place." Seeing his friend's eyes bug out with exasperation, Andrew walked over and patted him on the back. "Don't look so worried, old man. This is just one more escapade to recount to your children!"

"I'd like to live to produce them!" Jeremy shot back hotly.

"I think he wants to go," Micheline informed her husband.

"Lord knows *I've* been ready ever since I arrived!" Andrew laughed again.

The comical-looking trio emerged onto the twisting staircase that spiraled down through the Garden Tower. Outside in the night air, Sandhurst inhaled the breeze off the Thames and gave Micheline a brief, meaningful grin. Then he put his arm around Jeremy, who sagged against his old friend as if he were ill.

Micheline was looking on with convincing anxiety as they came under the Byward Tower.

"The duke collapsed from the shock of seeing his son," Andrew muttered to the guard. "I thought it best to help him out before the ceremony of the keys."

The story worked until they came to Sergeant Pease. He heard Andrew out, then peered doubtfully at him in the darkness. Warm fog had rolled in off the river, making it difficult to see.

"Is that you, Carson?"

Fearing the worst, Jeremy let out a tortured groan. "I'm dying!" he gasped.

"Please, take my father-in-law to our carriage!" Micheline said to Sandhurst in an urgent tone. Turning back to the sergeant, she could see by the way his eyes followed the two men that he would wait only a minute or two for "Carson" to reappear. His distraction was such that Pease didn't notice her step back behind him and reach for the bottle of wine she'd given him earlier. An instant later he lay slumped against the stone wall of the barbican.

Lifting her skirts, Micheline ran to catch up with Andrew and Jeremy. "We've only a few minutes!" she cried. "They'll find him when they lock the gates!"

Sandhurst clasped her hand as the three of them sprinted to reach the horses tethered at the top of Tower Hill. He lifted Micheline onto Primrose, then swung up on Hampstead, patting the stallion's neck.

"God's teeth!" Jeremy ejaculated. "Let's be away!"

Tossing his guard's bonnet into the street, Andrew laughed with relief. "My thanks to you, old friend. Go home to the safety of your bed. My wife and I are bound for Whitehall Palace, where we shall effect act two of this drama!"

As the horses broke into a trot on Byward Street, Micheline looked over to meet Sandhurst's gaze. In spite of the danger that infused the very air they breathed, she had the sensation that he was kissing her with his eyes.

CHAPTER 37

June 12, 1533

MOONLIGHT SILVERED THE KING'S STREET GATE, WHICH BRIDGED the thoroughfare, allowing access from the river wings of the Whitehall Palace to the newer collection of buildings, gardens, tennis courts, a cockpit, tiltyard, and bowling alley that sprawled west of the street.

Sandhurst tethered their horses in a darkened court, then stripped off Carson's uniform and the added padding, revealing his sage-green doublet, buff breeches, and boots. To Micheline's astonishment he then caught her in his arms, and she found herself pressed up against the side of a building. Sandhurst's hands curved over her buttocks, aligning their hips as his mouth captured Micheline's. They shared a long passionate kiss, hearts pounding in unison.

"You don't know how long I've been waiting to do this," Andrew murmured finally, tasting the sweetness of her parted lips with his tongue.

He'd been hard the instant their bodies met. Micheline arched her hips suggestively against him. "My *goodness*!" she sighed.

"I don't suppose you'd consider lifting your skirts . . . . "

"Shame on you!" She couldn't resist one more intoxicating kiss, though, and her tone was less assured when she added, "I should think you'd have more important matters on your mind tonight."

"*Nothing* is more important than you, Michelle!" His smile flashed in the darkness before he gave an exaggerated sigh. "However, I suppose we ought bring this adventure to a close so that I can take you home to bed."

"To sleep?"

Sandhurst's brows flew up. "Sleep! What's *that*? Oh, no, my love, I had in mind a new adventure. The earlier events of the night will seem mundane in comparison!"

Micheline giggled softly as he took her hand and pulled her off toward the turreted Palace Gate.

The watchmen were crying "Ten o'clock!" when Andrew and Micheline parted company in the gardens outside the royal apartments. To the east the River Thames glittered in the starlight.

"You have half an hour before Rupert arrives," he told her softly. "I'll see you soon."

"But how will you—"

Mischief infected his tone. "It's a surprise. Now, go!"

She was pushed firmly toward the imposing palace steps, and then Sandhurst disappeared into the shadows.

It took nearly a quarter hour for Micheline to talk her way into an audience with King Henry. By the time she was admitted to his presence chamber, after passing through endless windowed, tapestry-hung galleries with ceilings wrought in stone and gold, her nerve was beginning to fail her.

In the cavernous presence chamber, Henry VIII sat on his throne of red and gold brocade. It was on a raised dais, with a canopy above, serving to make Micheline feel very small and insignificant.

Garbed in rich blue velvet and cloth of silver that was slashed, padded, and encrusted with all manner of gems, the king narrowed his tiny eyes at Micheline. Next to him sat Queen Anne, her rounded belly draped with violet silk. Her gaze was fixed not on their visitor but on Henry, and it appeared exceedingly anxious.

"Good evening, Countess," he said in tone that made her heart sink. "I do not remember inviting you to Whitehall for this late interview."

Micheline sank into a curtsy before the dais. "It was very gracious of Your Majesty to see me. I would not trouble you, but I am here concerning a matter of life and death."

"I thought as much." Henry sighed as if bored, and reached for his wine goblet. "If you've come to beg for Lord Sandhurst's life, you are doomed to diappointment. Any man foolish enough to make advances to my queen deserves to lose his head."

Anne spoke up imploringly. "I have told you, sire, that these accusations are lies! It is true that Lord Sandhurst smiled on me from time to time, but that was long before our marriage, and it went no further. He never touched me!"

Anger reddened the king's face. "Silence! When you take his part, it makes me think that you encouraged him!"

"The queen speaks the truth, Your Majesty! This plot against my husband was concocted by Rupert and Patience Topping! They meant to see both of us dead and Andrew disgraced, hoping that our titles would pass to them!"

"What nonsense! Why, Topping could scarcely bring himself to disclose Sandhurst's behavior to me. His loyalty to his brother was nearly greater than his loyalty to me, but fortunately he saw that, morally, he had no other choice."

"I don't mean to contradict you, sire, but I think that when you hear what I have to tell you, you'll see things differently."

"This is a waste of my time," the king grumbled. Still, it was hard to be completely indifferent to Lady Sandhurst's anguished beauty. "Go on, then. Tell your story, but be brief!"

A shortage of time left her no alternative. Quickly Micheline related the various accidents and threats of the past few months and ended with an account of the events related to the fire at Sandhurst Manor.

"Rupert thinks that I am dead, Your Majesty, that Patience succeeded in her part of their plan. He can be tricked into revealing his true colors—if you will help."

Henry cocked a skeptical brow. "How do I know that *you* are telling the truth? And what part do you propose that I play in this scheme? After all, Sandhurst has refused to lift a finger to help his king of late! I really can't see why I should bother."

"I think you are wise enough to recognize the truth in my eyes, sire. In France I heard that you were both wise and just. Please help me now to right a terrible wrong, not only for the sake of me and my husband but for our unborn child and the Duke of Aylesbury. He would want his title to go to the proper person, a good man who will uphold the proud tradition of his family."

Henry shifted on his throne. The girl had appealed to his vanity. If he turned away from her, it would look as if he *weren't* fair and just! Also, her mention of France had given him pause. Henry had heard that King François was quite fond of the former Madame Tevoulère. Perhaps it would be better all around to humor her, just to be on the safe side.

"Very well, then, I'll go along with your plan. I've ever

been one for digging out the truth. What do you want me to do?"

Micheline gave him an incandescent smile. "Thank you, sire! I must explain rapidly, for Rupert will be arriving at any moment."

"I beg your pardon!" King Henry exploded.

"It's part of the plan, Your Majesty! Please, hear me out!"

"Colossal nerve," he muttered under his breath while Micheline launched into detailed instructions of all that the king must say to Rupert Topping. When she was finished, Henry's mouth, which was quite small in his heavily fleshed face, curved upward slightly. "An interesting scheme, my lady. This may be more amusing than I anticipated."

At that moment a footman appeared to announce that Rupert Topping was waiting to see His Majesty. The king instructed him to show him up.

"Where may I hide?" Micheline asked anxiously.

"It's a warm night. Why don't you wait on the balcony," Anne suggested.

Quickly she curtsied and exited through the tall French doors. Micheline was backing onto the balcony, closing the doors in front of her, her heart pounding madly, when she bumped into a shadowy figure. Before she could scream involuntarily, a hand came around to cover her mouth. It smelled wonderfully familiar.

"Romantic, isn't it?" Sandhurst's breath was warm against her ear. "A moonlit June night, the Thames shimmering in the distance, the two of us alone on a palace balcony . . ." His lips grazed her temple. "The possibilities are intriguing."

Micheline heaved a gusty sigh of relief, turning in his arms. "Andrew!" She nearly laughed aloud in reaction. "How did you get up here?" The king's apartments were on the third floor of Whitehall Palace.

"I climbed."

Glancing down the sheer side of the building, Micheline ruefully shook her head. "I'm glad, then, that you didn't tell me beforehand. I'd have been worried sick!"

Andrew smiled down at her as she put up a shaky hand and smoothed his ruffled blond hair. Then, out of the corner of his eye, he glimpsed Rupert Topping entering the presence chamber. Sandhurst laid an agile finger over Micheline's mouth and slowly turned her around. He kept an arm curved around her midriff and she leaned back against him as they listened through the slightly parted doors.

Rupert was wearing an ill-fitting doublet of orange silk topped by a bright green jerkin trimmed with fox. He looked very hot and very nervous as he bowed before the king and queen. Every so often the right side of his face twitched as though it had a life of its own.

"I have come, just as you commanded, Your Majesty!" Rupert declared grandly, his voice cracking. "How may I serve you?"

"I appreciate your efforts, Topping. I know what a strain you've been under—what with Sandhurst's imprisonment and all."

"Such a tragedy," the spindly young man agreed. "I've scarcely had a wink of sleep, trying to deal with the misgivings I have about my role in his arrest."

"You were only doing your duty, weren't you? You were honor-bound to tell what you knew. I shouldn't feel guilty if I were you, Topping. After all, the crime was not *yours* but *his*. Correct?"

The twitch was spreading downward to Rupert's arm. Sandhurst listened to him blubber a reply, smiling to himself as he realized that the king was enjoying this little charade. He had the manner of a cat toying with a panic-stricken mouse.

"I hesitate to add to your trials, Topping," Henry was continuing smoothly, "but I received some news this evening that I thought you should hear."

"Oh! I say! That was very considerate of you, sire!"

"Sad stuff, I fear." The king leaned forward slightly in his throne, watching Rupert's face. "It seems that there was a fire at Sandhurst Manor—in the countess's bedchamber. Tragically she did not survive."

"What? Oh, my *God*! It can't be true! This is unthinkable!" Rupert staggered backward, clutching his heart and gaping at the king and queen. "She was so *young*, so *beautiful*!"

"Deplorable acting," Andrew whispered laconically out on the balcony. Micheline turned her face up and grinned in reply.

"It certainly is a tragedy." Henry was nodding soberly. "I was thinking that it might be best if *you* broke the news to your brother."

Rupert flinched in surprise. "Me? Tell Sandhurst? Oh, well, I don't know—that is to say—well, it's just that—"

"Good. You know, my sympathies are aroused by this calamity. I'd made up my mind that Sandhurst should go to the block by week's end, but now I'm having second thoughts. Perhaps the suffering he'll endure over his bride's untimely death will be punishment enough."

Perspiration rolled down Rupert's pasty face. "Very—uh—kind of you, sire, but—I just—that is, do you really think it would be *wise*?"

"It's not as if your brother is a dangerous man, is it, Topping? We needn't fear for our lives if he's set free!" The king chuckled at this, but there was a wicked glint in his eyes. "After all, there is quite a difference between a man who becomes rather awed by the queen's rare beauty and a *murderer*. Don't you agree?"

Rupert mopped his brow with a large handkerchief. "It's only that, well, others might misunderstand your mercifulness. Your Majesty!"

"I have a moral obligation to justice, though. I must say, Topping, you surprise me! I expected you to rejoice at the prospect of your brother's freedom!"

"Oh, yes! Of course, of course!" Rupert's entire right side twitched convulsively. "It's just that, well, I didn't want to have to reveal this—family honor and all that—but the fact is, Sandhurst is not the man we believed him to be!"

"Is he not?" The king made a show of innocent surprise.

"No! There have been other crimes. The—the treason I hinted at earlie. It's been worse that you know! He mocks your stand against the pope all the time! And—and—I've come to think that Sandhurst is quite *evil* beneath that golden, charming façde of his!"

"Really! Do go on!"

"This is very hard for me, you understand, but in the interest of justice—"

Out on the balcony Micheline pressed Andrew's hand to her mouth to smother the laughter that would barely be surpressed. Glancing up, she saw her husband bite his lip and cast his eyes heavenward.

"Courage, man!" King Henry was urging. "What is it you have to tell me?"

"This is the hardest speech I've ever had to make!" Rupert

cried plaintively. "You see, the fact is—I already heard about Lady Sandhurst's death in the fire."

Henry started in astonishment and glanced quickly at the queen. "You *did*!"

"Yes, yes, I received word from my dear wife, Patience, who had been staying at Sandhurst Manor with the countess and Lady Cicely Weston. It seems that Sandhurst himself left abruptly for London following a terrible row with his wife." He paused here to sigh dramatically and wipe his brow again. The handkerchief was drenched. "In fact . . . Patience wrote me that Lady Sandhurst's death may not have been an accident after all. There appears to be conclusive evidence that the fire was arranged by—by *her husband*!"

"God's bones, that *is* a shock!" The king agreed. "So it's your opinion that the earl should not be released from the Tower? That I should speed his execution?"

"It breaks my heart to say it, Your Majesty, but . . . yes! I think my brother deserves to die! As quickly as possible!"

When Sandhurst himself emerged soundlessly from the balcony, King Henry barely blinked, though inwardly he was astounded. He cleared his throat to avoid an immediate reply to Rupert, watching with one eye as Andrew drew his sword and walked up behind his sniveling half-brother.

Rupert literally jumped into the air when he felt the sword tip at his back.

"Rupert, I am desolated to learn your true opinion of me!" Sandhurst said with deft sarcasm. "All these years I have basked in your devotion, only to discover that you really don't *like* me!" His tone was laced with laughter. "I'm crushed!"

"Your Majesty! The guards!" screamed Rupert. "Call the guards! Have this man arrested before he kills *me* too!"

The king merely reclined in his throne, enjoying the show.

"I have some good news for you, Rupert!" Sandhurst was saying. "My wife isn't dead after all. Aren't you relieved?"

On cue Micheline walked in from the balcony and made a wide circle around the two men, staring at Rupert with frosty blue eyes. Rupert himself was too upset to speak; his entire body quaked against Andrew's sword point.

"The bad news is that Patience was caught in the act of setting fire to Micheline's bed. When Cicely intervened, she tried to dispatch my sister as well, but luckily Cicely had thought to bring a candlestick with her. Let us say that justice was done." He paused strategically. "What? No tears for your *dear* wife? Don't tell me that you're concerned only about your own survival!"

"Don't listen to him!" Drops of sweat fell from the point of Rupert's nose. "He's lying, Your Majesty! He's always hated me!"

"That's rather a strong word," Sandhurst protested. "*Detest* might better describe my feelings. Why is that, do you suppose? I've often thought it odd that I never felt even the smallest twinge of familial affection for you. It's occurred to me, from time to time, that perhaps you're not really a relative at all!" His sword cut through Rupert's jerkin and doublet, finding his bony back.

"Your Majesty!" he begged, trying to summon tears.

"You're going to die anyway, Topping," Henry said dispassionately. "Tell the truth or I'll allow Sandhurst to save the headsman the trouble."

"All right!" Rupert shouted and sobbed at once, cracking open like a walnut. "It's true! I'm not the duke's son! My father was the farrier in Giggleswick! He was a drunkard, though, and wouldn't marry my mother, and so she began looking to see if the Duke of Aylesbury wouldn't like to have her back as a mistress. She hung about the castle to no avail, and one day the frustration became too much. Mother decided to take control of fate. She pushed the duchess down the stairs one day, and after that it wasn't long before the duke weakened enough to take us in."

Micheline was stunned by these revelations but saw that Andrew wasn't. His chiseled face showed no reaction except for a gradual whitening of the scar above his mouth.

"Sandhurst wasn't much of a son, and though I hated the duke myself, I knew that my only chance for success would be to court his favor. Everything was progressing according to plan until Sandhurst actually obeyed the old man for once and married this French chit!"

"You followed me to Fontainebleau, didn't you?" Andrew demanded coldly.

"Of course I did! Not that I thought there was a chance in hell you'd fall in love—but it did seem wise to try to nip the thing in the bud. Unfortunately, Madame was frustratingly resilient."

"It was you who pushed me down the steps at Aylesbury

Castle, wasn't it!'' Micheline accused him. ''The same steps where the duchess met her death!''

Rupert merely shrugged in reply.

''I think we've heard enough,'' the king said. ''It's late, and I am growing fatigued.'' He called for the guards, who took Rupert Topping off to the Tower of London. Henry gave instructions that he should have one of the rat-infested cells in the Bell Tower rather than accommodations befitting a gentleman.

Micheline ran to her husband, clinging to his neck as he slipped his sword back into its scabbard.

''Quite an exciting entertainment, eh, my sweetheart?'' Henry was saying to Anne as he heaved himself to a standing position.

''I'm glad it all turned out so happily,'' agreed the queen.

Wrapping a strong arm around the shivering form of his wife, Sandhurst said, ''My heartfelt thanks for your help, sire. And I hope you'll overlook my premature departure from the Tower.''

''Considering the circumstances, yes. And I won't even ask how you came to be out on that balcony! Now, if you'll excuse us—''

''Perhaps Lord and Lady Sandhurst would prefer to sleep here at Whitehall after their ordeal,'' Anne wondered.

''Oh, no!'' Andrew replied, laughing softly. ''I mean to spend this night in our own bed!''

Sandhurst was suffering from the kind of extreme exhaustion that kept him wide awake. He lay on his back in the great bed at Weston House, bathed in the moonbeams that come just before the dawn. The night was balmy, and all he needed to keep warm was Micheline. She curled against him, soft and trusting as a kitten, her rich cognac hair spilling over his bare chest.

Andrew's left arm was bent behind his head, while his right encircled his wife's back so that his fingers rested on the curve of her hip. From time to time he opened his eyes, thinking about the events of the last few days, about his marriage, about Micheline, and what lay ahead for them.

It was difficult for Sandhurst to realize that they had known each other only a few months; life before Micheline seemed hazy to him. She was the center of his existence, yet the time they'd shared so far had been mostly fraught with turmoil.

The one oasis of peace had been the few weeks they'd spent alone in Gloucestershire following their marriage, and he looked forward to returning there to share a lifetime of contented tranquility with Micheline, and soon, with their child. Smiling ironically, Andrew thought of the years he'd spent trying to elude the specter of boredom. He'd believed then that tranquility and boredom were synonymous somehow.

Caressing Micheline's silky hair, Sandhurst considered the tumultuousness that always seemed to color their lovemaking. Tonight had been no exception. Passion had crackled in the air as they came together, expressing physically all the emotions that had no words. There was never time to linger. It seemed that whenever they touched, mutual arousal flared almost instantly into a storm of wild proportions.

Andrew wondered if the future would bring calmer times. He longed to explore each inch of Micheline's body with tantalizing slowness. He wanted to savor her. Given both their passionate natures, it seemed unlikely that the storms generated by their love would ever repose for long, but the prospect of variety was definitely appealing.

Micheline made a soft purring sound in her sleep. Glancing down at her parted lips, and then to the creamy curves of her naked body, Andrew smiled to himself. Slowly he turned on his side, brushing his mouth over the satiny line of her neck and caressing her breast with exquisite gentleness.

"Mmm . . ." she murmured happily.

"My sentiments exactly, Michelle," Sandhurst whispered. "There's no time to begin like the present."

EPILOGUE

Thou walkest with me when I walk;
When to my bed for rest I go,
I find thee there
And everywhere;
Not youngest thought in me doth grow,
No, not one word I cast to talk,
But, unuttered, thou dost know.

—MARY HERBERT, COUNTESS OF PEMBROKE
1561–1621

Gloucestershire, England
October 10, 1533

MICHELINE, ACCOMPANIED BY WIMBLEDON THE SPANIEL, CAME over the brow of the hill and gazed down over the curving slope. The meadow grasses were still covered with daisies, wild marjoram, pink clover, nodding blue harebells, and a scattering of scarlet pimpernels. There had been a frost just three nights before, though, and the trees were turning yellow, crimson, and russet.

Winter would soon be upon the Cotswolds. It was a time to savor each fine day, like this one. The sky was a clear, vivid blue, the air was crisp, and in the vale below, Andrew and Hampstead were one as they galloped and then sailed over a wall of golden limestone. Cicely, who was riding Primrose, appeared to challenge her brother to a contest, though there was never any real question as to which horse would win. They raced across the valley, jumping four successive walls, then retraced the course.

Smiling, Micheline settled down amid the wildflowers to watch. For an instant she was reminded of herself and Bernard, in the days when they galloped in unspoken competition through the woods of Angoulême. Her present was so full that she spared little time for thoughts of the past, but now Micheline remembered Aimée telling her that one day she would remember Bernard with fondness. At last she was able to separate the good memories from the bad. Bernard had not been a villain—only immature and misguided. And for a time he had loved her, and she had loved him. Who could say what would have become of Micheline if Bernard had not helped her bridge the gulf from adolescence to womanhood?

With a bittersweet sigh she looked down at the letter in her hands, rereading it. Micheline was engrossed in the ending, when Sandhurst called her name.

Looking up, she saw him leading Hampstead up the hill. Her heart contracted in a familiar way at the sight of Andrew's elegantly lithe rider's body, clad today in dove-gray velvet, and his golden hair ruffling back from his handsome face in the breeze. Reaching his wife, Sandhurst gave Hampstead a light slap to send him back to the stables, Wimbledon frolicking behind, then dropped down into the fragrant grass.

"My God, you're beautiful," he told her softly.

Micheline wore a simple low-necked gown of yellow velvet, cut high at the waist to drape over her ripening belly. The sun brushed her loose brandy-hued curls with fire, and her eyes shone as she smiled.

"So are you, my lord."

"Beautiful?" He frowned in mock consternation. "Hmm. That's an opinion best kept in the family. Speaking of which— how fares my offspring?"

"Very well!" Micheline lay back in Andrew's embrace, watching as his hands curved expectantly over her belly, waiting. When the baby kicked, he flashed a grin.

"Three more months! It seems a lifetime!"

"Anticipation is half the fun," she replied, kissing the hard line of his jaw, then held up the parchment. "We've had a letter from Thomas and Aimée. She gave birth to their son last month!"

"So they had a boy. He's healthy?"

"Yes. And you know they lost a son before, their first child, so this baby is especially precious. They named him Étienne."

"Stephen," Andrew translated absently. "That's nice."

Gazing up at his profile, she sighed a little. "Will you be disappointed if this child is a girl?"

"I'd adore a daughter! As long as it's either a girl or a boy, I'll be content." When Micheline didn't laugh at that, Sandhurst watched her for a moment. "You're not married to Henry the Eighth, you know. Just because he thinks that Anne failed him by presenting him with a baby girl last month—"

"Odious man. I could almost smell the queen's despair when we saw her at Greenwich after Elizabeth was born. The way the king was behaving, as if the birth of a lovely, healthy child could be cause for *disappointment*!"

Andrew continued to watch Micheline as she gazed out over the hills. "What of you? Has this letter from France made you homesick?"

"My home is here," she returned quietly.

"Perhaps we might visit the St. Briacs next year. Would you like that?"

A dazzling smile lit her face. "That's a wonderful idea! Could we take the baby? And Cicely?"

"I don't see why not."

Micheline buried her face against his warm neck. "Oh, Andrew, how I love you!"

He took her back with him to lie in a bed of daisies. "And I love you, Michelle." He smiled into her iris-blue eyes. "As always . . ."

". . . we're of one mind!" She laughed.

"And one heart."

ABOUT THE AUTHOR

Cynthia Wright lives in Sacramento, California in a sunny house across from the river. She and her twelve-year-old daughter, Jenna, enjoy bicycling and cooking for friends.

When she isn't working on her new book, set in America and Regency England, Cynthia escapes for frequent visits with writer friends in the Bay Area.

Ms. Wright loves to correspond with her faithful fans and invites all interested readers to write to her in care of her publisher.

One of the most beloved historical romance writers...

CYNTHIA WRIGHT

...casts her magic spell.